The Son Of Durnin

By Jaden Moss

This work is ultimately dedicated to
the Lord, who is our Sovereign.

Lord, this is the first fruit of my labor.
I pray you receive it from me with the faith of Abel.
Even though my harvest is only produce like Cain's.

Dedicated To:

My mother. Because you were the constant listener, reader, enthusiast, and voice who assured me, "It is good." Even after I cried over the same thing for the fourth time in the same week (arguably day).

My father. Who happily kept his part-time employed, eccentric, kid-daughter alive while she wrote a book in his home.

My sister and editor, Jessica. Thank heavens the Lord gave you a mind for grammar and a willingness to edit my book knowing how I can be.

This story would have never been attempted, possible, and bound between two ends without each of you.

TABLE OF CONTENTS

Ever Shifting

Some rule by fire. Others rule by sword. Many rule by ropes hung and chains heavy. History proves that all rule by the demand of strength. Strength forged or won, stolen or given, cursed or blessed.

Deeper still, strength is set. It can only shift from hand to hand, people to tribe, one to many. Strength's pinnacle remains constant whether held by one over all or by many over most. Gathered, dispersed, lost but never gone, strength remains.

The man who holds the most strength in the world will die to gain more. In return, he loses all. This begs for one stronger. One outside of the shift. One who yields all and holds more.

Something Like a Mainger Tree

Prologue
Old History

Acklina had gathered strength to herself, more than any other had even attempted to obtain before her. Her lands were broad and full. Her walls were high and sturdy. Fleshly was her heart, desiring many things that were less than the realities she had seen. Namely the Reality. However, her strength was cursed before it was ever won.

At one time, Acklina had laid stoned and scarred, desperate for life at all. She had been redeemed by one who, at that time, walked in the likeness of a man and held that same appearance, but was no man at all. He, in fact, was the Greater. Outside of the shift, Forger of the Bountiful Lands, the Sovereign. He mended her being with a whisper alone and opened her eyes to see the world as he did. Acklina came to live with the Greater along with the others who he'd saved in the Bountiful Lands. They spoke together daily. He explained to her his ways. She looked out onto the land as if she was looking at it with his eyes.

"Acklina, I came to you in your weakness and made you strong. I have given you my strength that remains my own.

Because of this I must warn you: there is an Opposer. The one who was first to fall. He will want to allure you as he has allured the depths of the land. You will have the freedom to move towards him; but if you do, the closer you become, the more you will not merely die in body but also in mind. You will continue to die daily, your soul will wither, but it can not be lost," the Greater said gently to Acklina as they walked. "A day will come with judgment. All will receive what is truly just. Only some will receive mercy. This mercy will be given as mercy can only be: a gift, not a reward. On that day, your flesh will die and you will be restored to a greater glory than you ever were. I have given you eyes to see. I have given you my voice to hear. I have given you shelter from the darkness. But if you want the darkness, you will find it." She went to him first, always. But this would not be so forever. Acklina, though plucked out by the Greater, was still vengeful towards man. By man's hand she was not even given the mercy of death, only misery itself.

In time, while walking along the shore of the Bountiful Lands, she discovered a cave. Dark and hollow laid the grave under the mountains. She recognized the darkness and found her heart lusting after it. She heard the call of her Greater but chose to listen to the darkness that turned his call into a faded sound, easily drowned by the waves of the ocean. Instead of the Greater's voice meeting her ears, an unfamiliar voice met them. Sweet and persuasive. It called her by her name. Looking back she found only darkness all around. Nothing more.

"You are not lost, Acklina," the voice said, comforting her. It was the first to break the ominous silence. The voice seemed to encircle her.

"I do not know where I am. This means I am lost," she answered the beingless one.

"You do not know where you are? Did the one you call 'Greater' not warn you of me and tell you of my domain?" The voice sounded offended by her apparent ignorance. Her heart did not beat faster. She still did not understand the severity of her being lost, or far worse, somewhere she knew.

Acklina said, "You must be the Opposer, and I must be in your depths."

"Opposer?" the voice said slyly and confidently though it hid from the sun like a coward. "Is that the name he gave to me? I can attest these depths are my domain. They are the stomach of the snake that rubs the ground. The darkness hidden from the sun. Acklina, I have called you because the one you claim to be Greater has wronged you." At these words, Acklina felt the darkness thicken, as if it was beginning to rob her of her air. Still, she did not fear for herself. Her heart felt no guilt conversing in the darkness.

She argued saying, "The Greater has done no wrong by me. He redeemed me from the fallen." She closed her eyes to get relief from her surroundings, only to realize the darkness her eyes provided was no different from the darkness of reality when they had been open.

"Acklina, you are not redeemed," the Opposer said, contradicting her. "The one you call Greater has done nothing but lie to you. He called you redeemed yet has done nothing to avenge the ones who hurt you. The ones who took from you everything. Don't you know you will not be restored until they suffer and return to you what they stole? He gave you strength that he still calls his own; but I can give you your own strength. Bound not to the Greater. Strength to crush the heads of the ones who made you lick dirt and drink your own blood." As he spoke, she listened. Every word she recounted in her mind. She was surprised, for he spoke with *truth*. This "Opposer" knew what the Greater had told her. He understood the place from which she came. Perhaps he saw what she could not see. Perhaps, the promise of the Greater was a lie to keep her down.

"How can I gain this strength?" she asked, in total comfort with the darkness around her.

"You must allow me to rule beside you as the voice in your head, the reason in your mind. Do as I say. All that I say. I will remain unseen unless you command me otherwise," he said in a near whisper. He slithered simple reason into each sentence. Acklina became completely still for a moment. Her stillness was not caused by thinking of the Opposer's proposal, instead it was a stillness of reluctance. She felt as though there was something she had forgotten. But her mind could find nothing. All she could remember was the wrong that had been done to her. All the misery she'd known. The strength that she did not possess, but could.

She relented, saying, "If that is the price, then give me all so that I may rule justly and avenge myself."

Darkness whistled around her bones. Mixing with the stormy wind, the voice of one of the men who'd fragmenter her laughed then shouted then raged. He was not in that place, but the Opposer had mimicked his voice so that the memory of him would be. This made vengeance flood her reasoning. The bodiless voice smiled, put his shadowed hand on her shoulder, satisfied with himself. Returning to the shore, Acklina's eyes were pierced by the light from above. She shouted in pain feeling like her mind had been set on fire. She had a new sensitivity to the sun's rays. Falling to the ground, she crawled to any shadows that could be found. Tearing her cloak, she covered her eyes with a veil to make the sun bearable. A chill she had not felt before crawled up her spine. Nothing was touching her, yet a presence was felt. It was the Greater's presence. He stood by the sea gazing over the waters. He was still, like he knew all that had happened.

"Hide," the voice from the cave whispered. There was nowhere for her to hide. The darkness was too far and the Greater too close.

"Acklina, why do you cover your eyes as if I did not give them to you to be used to see?" the Greater asked. He walked closer, sure of every step.

"The sun scorched them," she replied. She had tried to run but her feet had been set to stone on the ground.

"How did it scorch them? Only when one visits company in deep darkness can the sun scorch their eyes." His stature was gentle but there was an unquestionable power to him.

"I've found my own strength," Acklina began. She did not have the same confidence she did when speaking to the being in the cave. "By it I will rule and redeem myself."

He questioned her, asking, "Did I not redeem you already?" His eyes refused to look away from her while she ever desperately wished to vanish.

"I will not be redeemed until I regain what was stolen from me."

"Your desire is aimless. Seek and you will not find. The blood of the guilty does not restore. You have chosen a false reality. You will suffer until your final days, but because I called you, you will return to me and mercy will be only what mercy is: a gift, not a reward. To the Opposer I now speak." His voice boomed across the shoreline. From the shadow's behind Acklina, where she had tried to escape to, a being came. Had her eyes not been covered, Acklina would've been able to see the one called the Opposer. He looked like he'd been born of shadow and was different from them. His color was a pure black that was nearly mesmerizing to the eyes. He was tall, slender, and carried a sword of black rock on his hip. Although he was full of pride, there was a clear fear and hatred of the Greater, even though, at this time, he was smaller than the Opposer being in his likeness of a man. The Greater, whoever, had no fear of this Opposer. No, fearful breathing or even a stamered step backwards. Instead, he spoke thus, "Because you have deceived my own, I will curse you. Because you have chosen to make an embodied-being your means, I will curse you to confinement. Never will you receive a fleshly body of your own or be one in the domain of man. If your hand wishes to strike a man, with another's hand you will have to do it. Forever you will not be wholly your own one way or another. In chains, walls, or hosts whose skin rubs and imprisons you. In this time, you will rise high as the heart of man lust after you and your lies of fulfillment. So, I will give them over to you in this time. You will have your way with man, aside from the ones

I keep from you. Because you have chosen to doom man, by a man will you be doomed. Be warned, Fallen, as high as you rise your fall will be all the greater. As I have said it, so it will be." The Greater had declared therefore it would be so. He then took Acklina's face between his hands and kissed her forehead. The vengeance she had gathered in the cave melted, but something new was quick to overtake it. Shame. What had she done? She pulled herself away from the Greater and fled to the waters, but could only go as far as the Severed Shores. The Opposer followed her there, where she then turned to bones and skin in an attempt to end herself out of sorrow knowing that she had forsaken the Greater, the one she first loved. However, the darkness beside her was coming. What he could do with vengeance was good and well, but what he could do with shame, all the more destructive. He was slow with her, allowing her to nearly kill her ownself. He told her that her fear was true, "You have forsaken him. Now you have fled from him. Never can you return to him." The greatest lie she was ever deceived by was that. After a while, she could do no more than lay with subtle breathing. Having lost all of her own strength, the Opposer reminded her of another thing. "Look at you. Broken. Weak. Hollow. You can not go back to the Greater and I have promised you strength. You can be whole again. I will help you." He lied. Being apart from the Greater for so long, Acklina had nearly forgotten all of their days together, as man is forgetful. She was filled with rage thinking, "Had they never wronged me, I would not be like this now." That night, the Opposer took her to the nearest village. There, she nurtured herself to strength for several weeks with the Opposer whispering in her ear. The longer she was in the presence of darkness, the more the sun seemed to burn her eyes. Even the moon's glow pained her now. Soon, the Opposer decided it was the day to use Acklina for what he had intended.

"It is time," the Opposer whispered in her ear.

"Time for what?" she asked, hollowed in emotions aside from regret and anger.

"Time for your rule and reign. Time for justice. Time for strength."

***

And the Opposer was right. That night Acklina murdered her first. The Severed Shores is where the Greater had found her years ago. The ones who wronged her still dwelled there. She went to the home where the cruelest of them lived.

"Woman? I knew you as dead!" the man cried out as Acklina neared him. "This must be your spirit! I cannot fathom this!" He was the man who had harmed her within the walls of this home in the past. It was his voice the Opposer mimicked in the cave. Now her strength was far greater than his, using the strong arm of the Opposer. Putting her power heavy hand over his mortal mouth, bounding his arms and legs, she brought him to a high place.

"You took advantage of my weakness, but now I am strong, and your hands cannot touch me. I am greater than spirit and I am greater than bone. I will crush you in your weakness, as you crushed me in mine." She lifted his feet off the ground by his throat and threw him off the cliff into the ocean. The Opposer had given her strength beyond reason, and she used it powerfully. Within the year, her following was stronger than any other and the Severed Shore was under her rule. Man hardly struggled against the Opposer, and he had his way with them as the Greater had said. Acklina ruled them by black water and the torture of darkness. "It is time," she said to her armies as the Opposer had said to her. Her dark eyes seemed to almost glow beneath the shadow of her metal helmet which now adorned her always. She had gathered a great fleet of ships to sail across the Luminous Sea and take the Bountiful Lands as the Greater was the last that had wronged her and the last she was to conquer. For in her years of pain, vengeance, and shame, she had deceived herself into believing the Greater was against her, as the patient Opposer had said.

Upon arriving at the Bountiful Lands, Acklina found the Greater had gone back to his unseen kingdom, high above the place of Orina. The anger of the Opposer mounted as he realized his defeat. "Do you see! He has left you!" The Opposer screeched. Her eyes had still never seen his frame, but she knew his voice well. Not understanding why she felt lost by this, she struck the Bountiful Lands until the graves beneath it became the ground on which they walked. And she walked the land alone.

Centuries more had passed and Acklina's hands had almost conquered all the lands within the boundaries of the cliff falls of the Severed Shores, for the Opposer's strength extended her life. She was unrecognizable. Whether this change came about by time or by the Opposer no one was certain nor tried to discern. For each generation had lost sight of who she was before what she'd become. Now, at the end, she had laid to rest her mind and body as the Opposer finished with her.

"You have done me well," the Opposer said to Acklina in her last moments.

"And by me you have done much wrong. By him, I have done much wrong," she said with her old reason, which she hadn't used for many centuries. "I now understand, as I lay emptier than when I was scarred and bruised before you first called to me. I have trampled every man only to gain what? I have done wrong against the Greater who redeemed me. I relinquish the strength you've given to me. I do not want it. Make me weak again, then perhaps he will be strong. Take my lands. Take my power. Take my throne. But give me my soul." The Opposer exhaled in disappointment more than anything.

He whispered, "It was never mine." He departed from her as quickly as he came. What had she done? How could she do all that she'd done? She had become the terror that destroyed her. She had become like him. She had become like the Opposer. What was to be done now? With all the might Acklina had left, she cried out to the Greater. Even if she was certain he would not have her. Her shame ultimately brought her back to him. And he answered. She did not know if she was dead or alive but she knew the Greater was with her, as he smiled and granted her mercy that was only given out of love.

As for the Opposer, his spirit-like being had chains draped around him as a necklace. Layers of weighted cuffs were around his ankles. He loathed the new kind of confinement the Greater had put him in. He released a terrible sound and infiltrated every being who stood close to him with ash-filled minds, hollowing their bodies. The few he did spare, he spared by giving them death. His rise was not over. But he did not forget the Greater's promise that he'd one day be defeated. Word of his spreading plague came to a small village on the downward side of the Severed Shores. Their village was once in the mountains of the Bountiful Lands. But the Greater, before ascending to his hidden kingdom, warned them to flee and told them of a hidden way. So, they listened to the warning given and the way shown, remaining hidden in the time of Acklina's power as none aside from them knew the hidden way behind the falls. The town that was once full of splendor was now rugged. The dwellers were men. The far descendants of the ones who'd known the Greater. Knowing the unhindered hand of darkness would swallow them before a sword could be raised, they fled by boat leaving everything behind. The Bountiful Lands that they had dwelled in before the reign of Acklina had been named Pravity. Their home had been destroyed, and their next home would soon follow. The ones left behind became beasts, slaves to the Opposer and his darkness, and most of them died. The ones who fled braved the water with nothing more than a fear of what they left behind would follow. For seasons they wandered upon the water, and many were lost to hunger and depletion of hope. Others were swallowed up by the sea. But they never dared try and go back to their homeland. Knowing that death by sea was mercy compared to a mind turned to ash.

After much time had passed, they saw a shadow of a land. Not knowing if it was an illusion their minds had created or a reality, they risked everything and used the rest of their strength to land upon its sands. They had found a deserted wasteland. It looked as if it would continue on until the end of time. For many days, they searched the land for any sources of water or life. Instead, they were met with dunes, beasts of the sun, and death which left only four men. When the four men had almost given up, they were met by a being. One greater than any they'd ever seen. They fell before it in fear and begged for mercy from the sun and the evil they knew was coming to devour them. The being, shining brighter than the sun's reflection on a mirror, lifted his hand and the land was covered with dark clouds and water began to fall from the sky. The men had been saved from the elements. Yet they were still afraid and knew they'd meet death if the Opposer found them. They cried out again for mercy. So the being, now known to be the Greater, decided to give them each a gift. To the first wisdom, to the second nobility, and to the third physical strength. They were all grateful and praised the Greater for their newly received abilities. When he came to the fourth man, the man spoke brazenly, "If you're so powerful, why have you let us wander the wilderness until you can see every one of our bones and the blistered and burnt state of our skin? Why did you allow us to witness the Opposer and watch him destroy everything we know? Why did you allow all of those things, and still expect us to praise you as Greater?" The others did not interject but waited patiently to hear the beings' response.

"You question with your idea of reason. But your understanding of reason is limited as a child's is to his father. If you understood my strength, you'd praise my name in fear of what I could do. If you understood my ways, you'd rejoice over me. Yet, in spite of your ignorance, I had mercy on you and saved you from the wilderness, saved your bones from piercing through your wounded skin. It was I who told your ancestors to flee the Bountiful Lands and showed them a safe place with good escape on the Severed Shore. Neither did I allow the sea to swallow you up or the dunes to sweep you away. I plucked you from the darkness after letting you see its destruction in an effort for you to grasp the magnitude of this grace. I chose you from the masses to be redeemed. You do not and will not understand all of my ways for they are far beyond you. Because you have remained blind to my mercy and rebuked my goodness, I will withhold any gift from you. And because the rest of you did not rebuke your brother's ignorant tongue, I will establish you a kingdom that will prosper for some time, but will finally fall to the evil you fear most. But from you, the ones I have saved, I will take one of your own to destroy the Opposer by my strength. I am the Greater and you are the man. As I have said, it will be done." The Greater lifted his hands and from the ground arose a formation, strong and stable. He struck his foot to the ground and the ground opened letting water arise in the desert and a stream began to flow over the formation allowing green earth to grow. He established a wall around it and clouds above it. The men looked to the creation and praised it instead of the creator. The Greater said to them, "Because you praise the lesser thing, you will be confined to this land alone. If you venture beyond these walls, you will surely die, until the day the snake is slain, the waters rise, and the unfaithful is found. As I have said, so it will be done." The Greater placed an immortal to guard the walls. These walls were now both a protection and a prison. He called livestock and wild animals to roam the land, and brought others who ventured the way of the sea to find shelter inside the walls he established. The Greater left them and alone they began to establish themselves. But they were a forgetful people. After their toil they looked at the kingdom they'd built and said to one another, "Look what we have done. We were the weakest and now we are the strong. We have built our own domain. Because of this, we will call it Strength."

For three centuries the kingdom would grow in number and power. The four Founders together established a throne at the highest peak of the mountain. They would divide Strength into three rings, four areas and twelve sections. Each ring being a different class, every area having one judge, and a section mark to keep well filed. When the founder's bodies were close to death and their minds were beginning to fade, the four men came together once more to establish a way to determine kingship. They wrestled among themselves, each arguing his own way.

The man who had been gifted strength claimed the people had to have a mighty hand to lead them. Someone strong and mighty to prepare for the day the walls would be opened. For him only blood would satisfy. The noble man knew strength alone would corrupt the people. He fought for a king of morals above all. The man who received no gift became a common man, blending in with all the peoples instead of the lords. He argued that the kingship must be placed within reach of the common man, believing it couldn't just trickle down a line of men who thought themselves better than the people they were built upon. The man who had been gifted wisdom listened to them all. He seldom spoke which caused his lips to tear and bleed whenever he did venture to speak. He remembered the Greater and how it was by His hands that Strength was established. He remembered that Strength would eventually fade away as the one called the Greater had decreed. He understood the reason for the desires all the others had proclaimed. He also saw how, if left to one alone, everything would perish.

Only through fists being pounded on the table and voices being raised above others, together they deemed a tournament, one that would satisfy them all. The man of wisdom warned the rest that tests are good and well, but snakes fit through cracks you cannot see. Yet, they proceed with their ideas.

The tournament would begin with five men who would establish a union. One to be king and the other four would be set as lords, one to each area. Five men from any section could establish a union, this was to satisfy the man with no gifts desired for the common man. Second, at a ceremony each area would vote on one union to represent them. Furthering the power of the common man. Third, the noble man spent the rest of his life compiling letters. Each letter contained a challenge of nobility, as you cannot teach one to be truly noble, you can only test to see what nobility he already possessed. He made many letters so none would ever know when or how they were supposed to be noble. Every tournament, one would be randomly selected by one of the Children of Nobility. They would perform the task secretly and expose the unions as being either noble or not. Fourth, the man of wisdom established a test. A judgment. The one to be king would be put in the place of judge. Brought before him would be one accused. He would have to question and then decide on the fate of the one accused. If he judged correctly, he would continue on. If he judged incorrectly, he'd be sentenced to the same fate as the one he accused. Unless he pardoned, then he would be condemned to the punishment the accused had ought to have received. Fifth, to satisfy the one strong, the tournament would end by the remaining unions fighting by sword and hand until all others surrendered or died. For one to surrender he was to be shamed as weak and forgotten. If one was to die, the desire for blood would be satisfied. Because of this each union would be given their own choice of two amalgamates, ones who would act as a substitute, if one of the five were to be killed in the final task. Only two were given because if three from the chosen union remained, it would still be predominately the people's choice. If three members of a union die leaving only two, then they must forfeit. All of this to crown a king.

They named their tournament the Sovereign Days. It would be set to take place every eighteen years. Every task and challenge to thin those who desired the throne. Furthermore, during these times, there would be feasting and celebrations, days of reflection and mystery. Those celebrations would be called the Last Days Feast, for it would be the last days of their old king, for those who died trying to get there, and the last common days for the men who won the throne.

Everything built upon a place that was destined to fall. A patient people waiting for evil to consume her. Waiting for one to rise, one to destroy the darkness that ruled their freedom and consumed their pride. This was now the way and waiting of Strength.

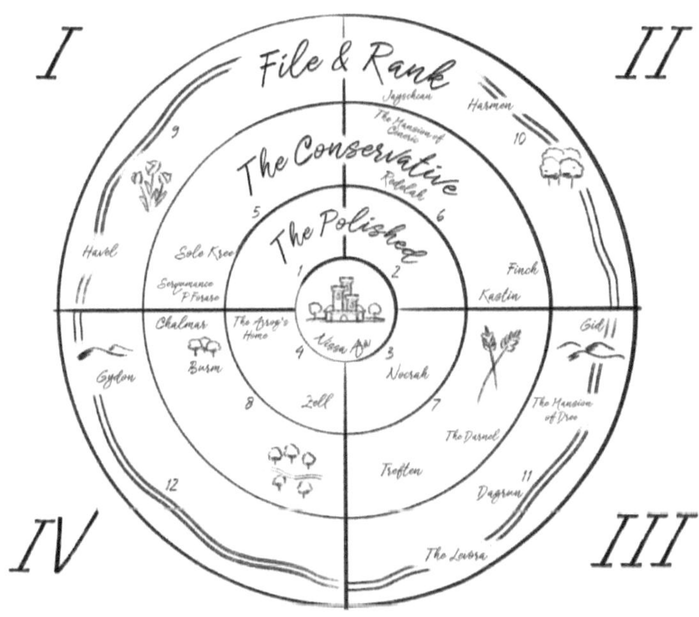

Strength From A Tall Glance
Rings: Polished, Conservative, File & Rank
Areas: I, II, III, IV
Sections: 1, 2, 3, 4, 5, 6, 7, 8, 9, 10, 11, 12
****

Prominent Places: The Palace Of Nissa Ara, The Mansion Of Ceneric,
The Mansion Of Dree
Seasons In The Mountain: Spruse, Brumal, Cordial
Ruled By: 1 King & 4 Lords
Crowned By The Sovereign Days

Chapter 1
Gravestones, Eyes, and A Fox

"Gravestones are a tragic thing. We seal the death of one by name deep in stone. To remember we say. Believing that death done cannot be undone. That once gone, gone for good. Good as in forever." The low toned voice of the man speaking would convince you to believe almost everything he said. As for gravestones, I think I did.

"You're the one to speak, Shervan. Being that you are forced to never forget." I was referring to the job given to him. At least, I assume it was given to him and not taken by him. All in Strength bring their dead to him. It is his task to honor them well and burn their forsaken body. "I don't want to speak of death. He has the power to take too much from me. Always threatening to make reality and me sworn enemies. I'm sure if any would know the kind of hatred I speak of, it'd be you."

"I have seen many pass away. For most, it is the worst tragedy as they do not know what is to come. But as the one who has remained, I've been cursed to see the ones who are still alive suffer great tragedy. Death isn't natural, so we shrivel and squirm when it comes near us. Some build illusions, some have hope. The ones who build an illusion I pity most. For they, just like the ones who died in darkness, can't grasp the destruction ahead and save themselves while they still remain." Shervan spoke above my understanding. He did that more often than not. I enjoyed his talk, nonetheless. He satisfied something in me. A desire for greater things, I think.

"We should speak more, Shervan. Perhaps one day you'll come to my home for dinner? That is if you eat. Do you eat? I don't think I've ever seen you with a crumb of food. Kind of hard to imagine it truthfully," I smiled. I stood to go.

"Yes, boy, I eat. I need food to sustain, same as you," he replied, grinning.

"I'll visit you with more haste next time," I said as I embraced him.

"Please do. I find your company good." I felt sorry for Shervan in many ways. Our walls limited the range of our land thus making peoples' only option to bring their dead to him. He would make gravestones by carving directly into the walls of our kingdom. Making him live among the names of all the dead. He tells me it is good to be on this side of the wall as if he really understands what is actually on the other side. I first think of it as a sandy waste land. I know there are lands beyond, but beyond is a very far place. There are those who believe in the stories of the prowling evil and a great savior. They'd argue there is much more. That our wall wasn't built by the hands of men over many, many generations. Instead, it was crafted by a great being who raised the mountain and the wall from the sands of the deserts by his word alone. I don't know if I could imagine such a thing. I agree that it is safer on this side, but I find the walls to be equally a prison. In other ways I envied Shervan. It is quiet around him because he was the only one who lived on the side closest to the wall. A gully-like stream no more than three feet wide lapped the entirety of the mountain. Being as File and Rank was the outermost ring, some people from the ring would allow their cattle to graze on the vacant side but none would ever build their home. It is a full mile to the stream providing plenty of distance and time for me to think. I wasn't from the Ring of File and Rank. I lived in the Conservative Ring. The middle ring of the mountain. I was simply a visitor passing through here. Rather, I was descending only to ascend back from where I'd come. I have the freedom to do so because I have a smith's paper. I am one who works with metal. More specifically, I work with iron. Each area was given a metal: Area One, silver; Area Two, copper; Area Three, bronze; and iron to Area Four. Being a smith is an honorable trade and it's been in my family for generations. It allows us to travel through our section as tradesmen by setting up wagons and tents to exchange or sell our work. That freedom is a rarity because of the 'Laws Upon the Mountain'. The laws make it extremely difficult to travel outside of your own section. The throne will teach you its laws are in place to maintain peace and order. However, my father would argue wherever order is, control is slithering close behind with its power thirsty tongue to claim it. By this day in our history, we have been claimed by that control. None move without being watched. None speak without a listening ear. None work without looking over his shoulder or trembling hands. None live before their tax is paid.

"Son, come. We must be preparing to leave," my father

said. He had met me at the bridge that went just over the narrow and plunging stream. The water that splashed onto rocks had begun to freeze mid-day. We're in the brumal season. A time where the sun is still present but its warmth is farther from us. Our days are cold and our nights are arctic. Coming from the season of cordial when the air is always fresh and new and the sun is warm but not burning, the season of brumal is a hard adjustment regardless of how prepared one thinks he is.

"Yes, Father. I was visiting with Shervan," I replied. He knew it was a rare thing for me to do. I'm accompanying my father through the outskirts of the poor town to the square where our wagon is waiting to be prepared for our departure.

"Ah, my dear old friend. I think it'd be good if I visited him soon. Not because his time is limited, but because my own time is." My father had the frame of a strong man that years had not been kind to. Like me, he equally has been a smith for most of life making his body strong after being put through harsh labor. He looks rugged but well kept. Gray is slowly starting to overtake his black hair. A young man's rebellious years marked by a scarred face were hidden by a full beard. My father was what my mind defined as a man. "Your brother took the first wagon ahead to stop in a small square before heading home." The brother he speaks of belongs to the name Magnar. My hatred. He would claim equal contempt for me.

File and Rank's villages weren't crowded. How could they be? It was known that all in File and Rank were slowly dying under the rule of our king. They can't harvest enough food to sustain themselves after they gave to the throne what had been deemed its possession. If they were crafty enough to hide food or goods, they had better hide it perfectly. If found out, they'd be killed anyway or sold to the Polished as slaves. In their towns, each establishment had much space between itself and the next. Their roofs were covered in moss and stones built their walls; unlike the Conservative Ring where our homes are built of trees taken from the mountain side and our roofs of beams and wood. Beautiful to behold. While walking a hand grabbed the back of my shirt.

"Can you help an old woman whose back is crooked lift a trunk into her wagon?" I turned to see the old, raspy voice belonged to a woman of her own description. Her spine was hunched as if it'd been bent in the middle. Her hair appeared matted down from lack of washing. I knew she wasn't ashamed of her several missing teeth because of the smile she tried to give me. Like her hair, her skin had begun to gray whether by the cold or age, I didn't know.

"Yes! Just point and I'll assist," I replied. Her looks didn't deter me from helping her. If anything they encouraged me to. The king has not been kind to the people of File and Rank. Here you're born, you grow up fast, you tend to the ground, make the most of what little has been given to you, then, you either die having been turned thankful by grace or cynical by reality. My father has taught me to help when asked and my mother taught me to help even if I wasn't. My father accompanied me in following the old lady who led me just to the side of the grassy road which was only made visible by years of wagons rolling over it. Just beside the way was an open wagon being pulled by one mule, a few odds and ends in the back, and a trunk that appeared to have fallen as some of the goods were scattered on the ground.

"Just there! In the back will do. I didn't see that bump just there and it hopped right off the back!"

"A shame. You should write a letter to the lord requesting your roads be mended," my father suggested. I picked up the rest of the things and placed them in the trunk. It was full of what I assumed to be this woman's most valuable things: a child's blanket, two books ripping at the seams, a fine linen dress, some other clothes, a small journal, and a picture of a handsome man. I smiled at her things and my father assisted me in lifting the trunk into the wagon.

"Kind suggestion, sir, but I'm afraid the lord hasn't heard a request from my people in some years. Even if he did, it wouldn't be worth your name being put on record." She fidgeted, rolling one hand over the knuckles of the other. "Thank you much for the help and kindness you've already shown to me. I am venturing to reach my daughter in the Conservative Ring, Area Three. Being as we're in this blessed year of the Sovereign Days! Oh! Forgiveness! Forgiveness! Forgive my joyous proclamation. Long rule the king!" she retracted. She had, in fact, shamed the throne by her celebratory words. How dare she desire the reign of Thann Arrogs, king of Strength, to end? How dare she imply that this year be blessed if it would come to mean Thann's end. And yet, I'd celebrate his end with her all the same. I've never known of another to be the head. I've never known of a good king.

"You're welcome," my father said with the slightest nod. The woman bowed back to him with a large grin. A nod is what one does to show respect. An acknowledgment of one as a peer or even friend.

"Please, allow me to gift you something!" She turned quickly and reached in the trunk which had just been placed in the wagon. Being too short to see inside, she blindly moved her hand about until finding what she was after. She pulled out her arm to reveal the journal I had seen only moments before. She flipped open its pages to reveal beautiful paintings of scenery. I was trying to recall if I had ever seen more brilliant ones. Frantically finding a certain page, she ripped it out. The seemingly careless way in which she tore the page pained me even though I knew she was only trying to be gracious.

"Here. Here. Please, accept this." Her hands quivered, gifting it to me with much joy. "My husband created it by mixing spices and water. He said it is of the Bountiful Lands," she explained.

My father asked, "The Bountiful Lands? Did he have the Eyes of a Gazer?" I understood very little of the things he spoke of.

"Yes, yes, he was magnificent! His eyes themselves were the brightest green! The pictures he made me and my children were the light of our lives!" She spoke swooningly about him which I admired greatly.

"Thank you for this gift. I shall treasure it always." I smiled sincerely through closed lips and nodded to the old woman. We departed shortly after and continued our walk to the square and our wagon.

"The lords of this kingdom are vines to this land. They've slowly grown over all and now, reigning, choke out whatever is still alive," my father said angrily in regard to the old woman's previous comment about the roads, the letter, and her lord.

"Their time is ending," I said, looking from the land to my father's tired eyes.

"I pray that happens sooner than it seems it will," he replied. This roused my mind. I believe the dissatisfaction with what I know will drive me to do many things most wouldn't. His embittered words were wood upon that fire. My father was a civil man. He hated the Sovereign Days and chose to speak little in regard to our king. However, in the past months I had heard whispers and seen shadows. We are now in the year of the Sovereign Days, the tournament which will call up the next king. This proposes something new. It proposes last days. For thirty-six years, Thann has sat high on his throne. Too much has been surrendered. Thann has been a wicked king and his lords along with him. He's diminished our kingdom and made the walls feel more like a curse than a blessing for many. After only his first reign he was hated; even still Area Four would present his union for the tournament yet again. Many believe Thann gained the throne through deception. However, no one has been able to gain knowledge and evidence enough to condemn him. Seekers from every Ring who sought to expose this treachery lost heart after years of finding nothing to bring to light. This is where my father asserts himself. For the past few months, he's been slipping in the shadows to meet with others yet speaks nothing of it. I've only gathered whispers of names and things greater than I am allowed to know. I believe it all has to do with Thann and the Sovereign Days and the throne. Why else be so secretive? Only this alone would require such silence.

Further it is known that Thann's grandson, the son of Lord Arres, is preparing a union to compete in the Sovereign Days. This means Thann's own blood would continue on if his grandson was to win the tournament.

"I've only once seen a picture made by one with the Eyes of a Gazer," my father said, referring back to our conversation with the old woman. He had broken my wandering mind's concentration.

"Yes, this is the first that I myself have held. I've seen some in books and heard of what others made of them. A gift far greater than I gave to her," I said now looking at the painting again. What I could make of the picture was only the edge of a great beauty. Down the middle of the page a shore with ground white and clean, to the left water more abundant and bluer than all rivers I'd seen, to the right a cliff with stone silver. Many features I didn't even know by which words they were named. They were each wonders from the outside of our wall that I had never seen. I knew little of the gifted ones they spoke of. I had learned of it in some books and my parents' occasional conversation of it but didn't know much for myself. I knew when one possesses the gift of Eyes of a Gazer, it is said that they are granted a unique vision of the land in which the Greater dwelled. Tragically, I don't understand it. Detailed in the Old History of Strength, the Bountiful Lands were burned and turned to graves. Some say the Gazers see what once was. Others say they see what is to come. I don't know what I think.

"Help your own old man. I must finish some business in a house down the road. I will need you to pack the wagon speedily. I will meet you by the old crow house."

"What sort of business?" I questioned. He looked at me with a face of surprise.

"None you need to meddle with for now," he replied uneasily. He cupped his hands and blew his breath in between them in an attempt to warm them.

"Is it greater than me?" I persisted. A wagon passed on the faded path and my father delayed any response until the driver's listening ears were too far to hear.

He answered with a deep tone and even deeper seriousness, "You must understand, my son. There are things above us all. The Greater choses to give to some and to others something else for their own. You mustn't think of all things as greater than yourself. Rather, all things are not your own. And not the load given to you to carry. As for me and my own, it may become yours in time. Lands, I can only beg it doesn't! It is the burden given to me that I'd be grieved to give to you on my own account." Rarely did my father speak in such ways. When he did, it sank in my mind as something that can't be forgotten. As for his answer, it didn't satisfy me. Unfortunately, the circumstances forced his answer to suffice for now. My mother and father believed the Greater was real. They believed the Old History. The history containing the prophecies and evil beings and great ones too. I suppose I hadn't rejected it like many in my generation, but still I paid little mind to it. I had not seen any of these things and found little need or reason to believe them to be true.

The square where we'd set our wagon up for trade was pitiful by all standards. Many would pass through not realizing it to be a square at all. In the middle was a stack of stones four high. A monument of unity. Both the Old History and current History say it was the first thing the Founders established together. A silly reflection of the kingdom they would build. Anyone belonging to the Polished Ring would be proud to knock it down themselves. I suppose they only haven't done so because they will never bother to descend to the scum of File and Rank. The pillar of unity split the path. Seven stone buildings were positioned in various spots around the two paths. These buildings held the essentials: medical and liquid remedies, fabrics for clothing, tools to work the land, and other such things. We often bring our wagon and sell various iron pieces. Mainly things like nails and spoons. Some of the men would buy small knives or axes from us. I began to cover all of our goods and my father continued to pass through the town onto his own business. I was not ignorant in seeing that we did poorly in business. We sold little and it proved to be a worthless trip after accounting for the time spent and iron used. This has been the common thing for the past years. The people don't have money or goods to be able to buy or trade anything. They are becoming less while the throne demands more. Claiming to be building us up all the while we are beginning to cave in at the bottom. We only make real profit from the people in the Polished Ring. I've never ascended to the Polished Ring, but Father and Magnar have gone for trades. I continued to gather our things in an orderly fashion with efficiency having done this task many times. When I had completed my labor, I looked around the small town to observe the people who dwelt in such places. The square wasn't crowded with men because their men didn't have the time to be in the square. Instead, they were hard laborers who stayed in the mines or worked their own fields. When they did come into the square, it was only to get provisions for several weeks at a time. Women would come through with their children only to buy or trade things needed for their homes. They wore clothes made by their own hands. The women of File and Rank were excellent seamstresses. Many of the Polished women and some Conservative women would even send fabric to File and Rank, hiring the women to make dresses and other fancy pieces of clothing for them. The children played around the stone pillar with happiness rooted in knowing nothing better was possible. At least, I imagined that's what they knew. But perhaps they did know and just didn't care. Maybe they only saw what was before them and chose to make stone shacks into castles and the birds of the sky into dragons. I decided I'd go into the small medical building and pick up a gift for my dearest friend, Amos. He is studying medicine and speaks frequently of the odd remedies found throughout the mountain.

"Your eyes overlook many things. What is it you want, Conservative?" asked an old man who had glanced over his spectacles. I assumed he was the shopkeeper. He sat comfortably nestled in a wooden chair. He seemed as if he was trying to mask how closely he was paying attention to me by reaching up and smoothing the cloud of white hair on top of his head in an impetuous way.

I answered, "I don't look over everything because it is invaluable. I simply don't know what any of it is." Inside the stone building was simple enough. A rough square on the outside and no different on the inside. I noticed the shelves of varying height, each appearing to be holding hundreds of things. One shelf held lots of small bottles filled with liquids colored from clear to black while another held jars of different looking herbs and leaves. One had rocks and powders, another held books and flowers.

"Well then, you'll look over everything. If you do not know what you are looking for, then why search?" he asked.

"You don't seem fond of Conservatives, sir?" I stopped my browsing and turned to him.

"Not Conservatives, just everyone. I'm fond of none and none are fond of me. Now please leave until you know what you desire and then return and make yourself hasty in here." I found him to be a most unpleasant man. I could understand why no one cared for him. My mother would remind me that surely there was a reason for his unhappiness and cruelty. And that reason was probably hard and breaking.

"I'm looking for something to bring home to my friend. He is practicing medicine and I wish to give him something he'll find intriguing. He is always telling me of things he reads about in regard to File and Rank but he is unable to travel here himself until he is granted permission by our lord. I don't search aimlessly just ignorantly. Please, suggest something. I'm sure you have a better idea than I do," I requested in a respectful yet persuasive manner even though he'd just asked me to leave. He mumbled something I couldn't make out under his breath while shaking his head disapprovingly. He either wasn't aware I was still watching him, or he didn't mind publicly displaying his distaste for me. I assumed the latter was probably true. Eventually, at an irritatingly slow pace, he got out of his chair and fetched some herbs from a low shelf. The thorn covered herb looked as if it would prick me and draw my blood if I was foolish enough to grab hold of the dark purple root.

Almost insultingly he said, "This will suit his fancy if he has any head for medicine."

"Then I'm sure he will adore it," I replied wisely, not allowing his rude tongue to be left as if it went over my head. He wrapped the herb in thick parchment and handed it to me. "The cost?"

"You're a smith?" he asked, sitting back down into his chair.

"I am." I could see his shoes from under the table. They were clean and appeared to be of Polished design. I then began to notice many rare things among his person: he wore a ring of fine silver, thin but genuine; on his desk stood a frame of wood inlaid with a fine stone at the bottom; and near the papers stacked on that same desk, a wax stamp with an iron head laid. I gathered that he was a tradesman. Tradesmen were more hated for a sly hand than they were for a rude mouth.

"I've seen your wagon across the lane." He crossed his arms to sit over his stomach. "You owe me nothing in currency. Instead, I want an iron quill tip from you."

"I see. You're a man of trade. What is your name?" He was wearing the slightest grin as I said this. I was now in *his* domain.

"Yes, I am. If one cannot travel about then one learns to trade within. That is how valuable things are gained. My name is Fox Tramp," he replied. He put out his hand for me to shake. While I didn't have a particular fancy for his ways, I understood them. They were unarguably clever.

"Pleasure, Mr. Tramp." I took his hand and shook it. "You are in the Greater's good graces today. I have a single pen head in my wagon. It is made of pure iron though. I will have to ask that you give me something in addition to this purple plant." He scowled but was, in fact, a man of business. He scavenged around until he found an extremely thin book. It couldn't have had any more than thirty or forty pages. It was worn and busted. The book seemed worthless.

"I am an old man. I haven't mixed anything in years, nor have I mended a body since..." he paused. "Well, never mind that. You speak highly of your young friend. To make the exchange worth more than an ignorant medicine man, such as yourself, could realize, I offer you this book. Ask me no questions and take your chance," Fox offered. As he slid the light blue book across the table, one of the frayed edges caught on a crack of the wood surface.

"Do you take me as a fool?" I questioned him. After all, he had only recently confessed he enjoyed no one and traded for value alone.

"Actually, I'm testing you to determine that. You are different from those who've previously visited me from other rings and areas and sections. Perhaps it is your tone or posture. It's more of a sense to me," he said in a genuine tone. A fool to him would likely be the one who accepted his offer. I weighed his words. He didn't seem to say them as one seeking his way by flattery. After all, he could have easily denied my offer and given me nothing more than the herbs. We had a common trouble of the throne; I was aware of that. I decided to take him as a man of honest business. I left before replying and fetched the quill head from the wagon. The iron quill head was in a small box along with other little valuables. I brought the box back inside and opened it before him to prove an honest trade.

"I fashioned this on my own. You'll find it's pure iron and sharp for precision." I handed the head to him and he scrutinized the tiny object. "You stopped your practices after your wife passed away?" I asked him. He looked past the quill head and met my eyes. "The picture of the woman," I continued, pointing to the painted portrait in the frame I had noticed earlier. "She is lovely," I finished.

"She is not my wife, nor is she dead," he said fiercely. He shifted the picture slightly towards himself.

"Forgive my curiosity."

"Do not apologize for your curiosity, apologize for your assumptions."

"You were a doctor?" This time I asked, instead of assuming.

"Much more than that," he replied, finally breaking away from the picture to look back at the quill head.

"Why'd you stop?"

"Again, with your assumptions!" he shouted. I believed he would prefer to have no trade at all than for me to go on any longer.

"I'm not assuming, sir. You said you are fond of no thing and have made it perfectly clear that you wouldn't do a thing you were not fond of doing. One would not have to assume anything about your healing of others," I said. I was unintimidated. He exhaled deeply which sounded more like a growl than a deep breath.

"I stopped healing because I stopped caring. Another dead is another freed from this prison of a land." The way his eyes saw the world burdened me. I suddenly found compassion for him.

"I will take the herbs, the book, and the wisdom you've given to me. I only now wish I could restore your hope. It was a pleasure to meet you, Mr. Tramp. You can no longer say that none like you, as I, myself, do." I picked up the book, smiled sincerely, and left. I now had to hurry to reach the crow house before my father reached it. I placed my new belongings under the bench of the wagon and started on towards my father.

Chapter 2
Father and Son

When I was in visible distance of the crow house, I could see my
father walking alone. He nearly beat me there. It looked as if he
was smoking a pipe judging by the puffs of air floating skyward
from his mouth. He looked over his shoulder and at the sight of
me stopped his walking and waited for me to pull beside him.
He was silent as he climbed in and sat beside me which I took as
a sign to ride on towards home. The silence continued for a
while before my father eventually said, "You should have already
been at the house. What kept you?"

"I went into the medicine building to find something to
bring for Amos." I looked to the sky and found only heavy
clouds. It was always an odd display to see the contrast of
Strength to the desert. Outside of the walls, the desert held its
dominion. Inside of Strength, our sky was our own. We had the
same sun and stars as the desert, but within our walls we had
our own winds and seasons. It was most visible when the clouds
would circle the mountain alone in a terrifying display of
beauty. It reminded me of the world we were forbidden to

enter. The place beyond that we cannot know, and it cannot know us.

"I happen to know the old man who owns that establishment. At one time he was a healer. Rumor says he was gifted. Some even suspected he possessed the Hands of Plenty. Now, he's a cynic with twisted ideals." my father said. I thought of the book he gave to me. How he offered it as his chance. Perhaps it held as much knowledge as his gifted hands has held healing. My father reached out his hands for me to give him the reins. Contrary to his gesture, I am able to steer and lead on my own. However, no matter my age or ability, I believe my father will always ask to take the reins from me.

"Yes, Mr. Fox Tramp. An interesting man. I pity him. He retains much wisdom even though a cynic. I found his company to be good for learning," I said, defending my new friend even though I doubted he would have done the same for me.

"Don't let his morals and beaten heart corrupt your own. The greatest wisdom he can give is that knowledge alone is as good as a well with no water." My father was gifted in finding a blemish in anything, even ideas. I don't know if he ever rested from such a task. Always on guard. Always listening. Always questioning.

We continued on the same path for many hours until we reached the Conservative Ring's gate. Along the way, we were able to see much of the File and Rank land. I always thought I enjoyed traveling. Watching the land go by. Simply seeing more. But all it ever did was remind me of the place we were in. The best places in File and Rank were the ones left untouched by any hand. Seeing a glimpse of a town in the distance reminded me of File and Rank's lack. Seeing a home was even worse. We hardly passed a home without seeing a dilapidated barn rotted to its foundations or a black patch of ground where something had been destroyed by fire. The closer we got to the Conservative Ring the more trees there were and the steeper the roads became. Arriving at the gate, we could now see the metal fence which was joined to the gate on either side weaving in and out of the trees. Some trees were even woven through the fence. I have ridden through this particular gate more than I have any other. Mainly because my father lets me come to shows with him in File and Rank most often. I had been through other gates on the mountain before also. Between every ring is a gate of sorts: the wall acts as the gate for File and Rank; an actual black metal gate shared by trees made up the Conservative gate; and, more than a fence or a gate, a stoned wall kept the Polished safe from the rest of us. Naturally, the wall we share with the Polished is covered by vines and bushes on our side, but on their side, it is perfectly clean, not a single vine nor weed grew from it. At least, that is what I've been told. The Conservative gate was my favorite. Not because I'm biased, I have genuine reason for liking it more than the other two. First, File and Rank's gate, though grand, reminds me of the situation we are in: namely, how we are confined within and how a supposed prowling evil dwells outside. The Polished gate is merely too clean. It doesn't feel alive but stiff and angry. The Conservative feels as though it came into existence when the mountain herself did.

"Mr. Durnin." The man standing by the gate nodded.

He was the gatekeeper for this crossing. He seemed not much younger than my father and quite average looking. Mando Mahglin had been the gatekeeper for Conservative Ring, Area Four or, in short, Section Eight for as long as I have been going to shows. It was convenient to have a gatekeeper who knew us and didn't have to see proof of our marks or license every time we ventured through its doors. Especially at a time such as now while the Sovereign Days approach and everyone is seeking to travel across borders.

"Mando Mahglin," my father replied with a nod. Mando opened the gates for us to pass through. The Conservative Ring was truly another world compared to that of File and Rank. Trees stood tall and their branches consumed the sky. Only through windows placed strategically far above the foliage could the circling clouds be spotted. I inhaled the familiar air which my lungs loved. Our roads were more defined and clearer. In the warm season of spruse, the roads are lined with bushes full of berries and flowers. However, we are not in the spruse season. And, just as the season had begun to shift, the roads too began to shift into a more dull, barren land. Nonetheless, the Conservative Ring still managed to look full and alive despite the cold weather and the lack of green things.

"How was the business?" Mando asked. He was always concerning himself with the business of others. Not in a way for gossip, rather, in a way of caring for troubles and joys besides his own.

"Slow. The people have nothing to offer since the king began to require a higher charge. I'm not far from just giving them what I have," answered my father. It was a more resent happening for my father to speak illy of our king. Before, he never would have said such things besides the rare comments within our own home. However, as the time of our king is coming to an end, he, King Thann, has become more overbearing than all his previous years of reigning by raising what we owe to the throne, making trade and travel even more strict, and favoring those higher up the mountain.

"A terrible day it is for our kingdom. I pray to the Greater hoping *he* raises one strong enough to take the throne," Mando replied leaning upon his gate.

My father was cautioning him, "You should whisper such things, Mando. The king has increased command and has his men listening in the trees."

"That seems to be suspicious behavior for one who has a clean conscience," I said. My father didn't correct me. This was a surprise. I have a bad habit of speaking out of turn and my parents have been striving to correct that habit for years. Mando nodded at me with a grin.

"I agree, boy. Good on you for having the wits and courage to say such things," he said. I couldn't help but grin back at the compliment.

"Has my elder son been through here yet?" Father asked Mando. He was talking about Magnar.

"Your elder son? Yes, Magnar by name?" Mando looked for my father to confirm. My father nodded and Mando proceeded, "Yes, a few hours before you did. Wagon and horse, same as you. He was a bit angry if I may add. I blamed his frustration on long days of travel and bad business."

"To that you'd be right. Easy to become discouraged in

such times," Father answered. "We best be off, friend. Dara is expecting us home for dinner." The name Dara belongs to my mother. She is one of the greatest people I know. Kind to all, lover of many, and dedicated to some.

Mando agreed, "Yes! Do bid her I said hello."

"Of course. To you, I know she'd say the same. Be safe," my father finished and began to pull away.

"And to you be steady," replied Mando. This was the traditional farewell in the Conservative way of life. A sending off with our priorities in mind. I waved as we passed onward. Mando closed the gate behind us. Though we had made it into Conservative Ring, living at the top of the ring meant we still had much time before arriving home. I settled in for the rest of the ride. My thoughts strayed to what Mando had said about Magnar. As Mando had commented, Magnar is oftentimes coarse and angry. It's one of the many reasons I have such distaste for him. I certainly would not have blamed his anger on bad business. That's simply who Magnar is. The way my father had answered Mando made me curious. He told me Magnar went ahead to another square, meaning he shouldn't have come through the gate yet. Especially hours before. Yet, my father didn't seem to question that action. This led me to believe it was intentional. Magnar has been deeply invested in my father's dealings as of late. I don't think I'm supposed to know that but Magnar hints too freely. He is haughty and proud. In an effort to taunt me with his greatness, he gifts me instead with specks of knowledge. My obsession with such things angers some of my friends, Amos and Phoebus. Amos still allows me to reason aloud with him though. Phoebus rebukes me often. Adalric, on the other hand, becomes passionate with me. That is his nature though.

My father spoke shortly after our departure from Mando's gate, "I know you wonder why I told you Magnar was going to another square, and why I was not surprised when he miraculously beat us to the gate. It's a game of faces, son. If I appeared shocked before Mando he'd gain suspicion. As I said to him, the king has ears to listen everywhere. Even recruiting common men not of his fold. We must be careful where we place our steps and to whom we speak our words." I was surprised he'd accused Mando.

"If it is a game of faces then I will always fail. Clearly, you have read my entire mind while I've been sitting here," I replied. I was being mostly honest. My father is a cunning man. Thankfully, I inherited the same trait. He did read most of my mind and had answered most of my questions. He hadn't, however, explained the reasoning for Magnar not going to another square. Why had he not done this? That was the deeper question. To prevent my father from knowing my deeper question, I agreed with his own statement. I knew my father was playing this same game with me. He didn't answer the deeper question. Instead, he shifted to another subject to avert my suspicions. A dangerous game to play. We didn't play it often, at least I think that's what we both tried to convince ourselves. I often was too transparent for such a business. I'd call to question the things unspoken. On some matters, though, I did wear the face my father spoke of and wear it convincingly I did. Today, he chose to shift the subject entirely.

"It will all come with time," he concluded and then

moved on. "What did Shervan have to speak of?" We didn't have much more time to converse as we were approaching Chalmar. My home.

"Gravestones, death, and the ones still living. All fitting topics for a man of his trade."

"Agreed. Did he speak of anything new?" he asked me. "New?"

"Yes, shifting of the winds, clouds ceasing to drift, things of that matter." He explained his definition of the word "new".

I furrowed my brow and said, "No." I didn't know why he would be asking about the sky. It seemed as though he was asking if it were going to rain. In fact, that *is* what he was asking. Why would Shervan know about such things? He wasn't a cloud watcher and never seemed to take interest in the winds. This question alluded to deeper subject matters. The Old History. The Prophecy. The one that says no one can leave Strength until the day the snake is slain, the waters rise, and the unfaithful is found. Rain would mean rising waters. Surely my father wasn't asking if the time of the prophecy was nearing? He wouldn't be. Rather, why would he be?

"Evening, Durnin!" a man named Aris called to my father as we passed by his home.

My father called back, "Evening, Aris!" We were riding deeper into my hometown. This meant more familiar faces. My people, as others say. Aris Hawthorn was my friend Amos' father. A man kind enough to his friend's faces, but evil behind closed doors and shut blinds. Amos has come to my home many nights after his father had become enraged and was in a fit. A short, round man whose hair was good as gone on the top. He keeps and sells chicken for a living, being taxed for coin and not possessions. He was tending his garden when we passed, which was a good thing. He only gardens when he's in good spirits. I detest the man. I've never smiled at him nor greeted him with "good" no matter the time of day. A little way past I spoke of my distaste for him. My father nodded and exhaled.

"I can't fault you. Men like him I would describe as snakes."

"And snakes belong in the ground," I replied coarsely. I stole those words from my father. He was the first to say, "Snakes belong in the ground." I remember it so clearly. A snake had slithered into the forge and, without hesitation, my father chopped off its head. He had proceeded the execution with those five words. I don't know if he meant for the idea to apply to his fellow man, but what's the difference? If one is said to be a snake, then the statement "snakes belong in the ground" ought not change. My father said nothing to my bold words. I took this to mean he agreed with me. Passing through the square, most of the places for business had closed. Chalmar was a wealthier, more established town than some other towns in the Conservative Ring. Mainly because Chalmar was so close to the Polished wall and our tradesmen are more easily able to go to shows inside their ring. However, our people were slowly falling into the same pit as File and Rank. At this time, few had extra goods. We had enough to live and not wither away in body like File and Rank, but anything considered a mere want or desire was hardly found. For my people, our heaviest burdens were the taxes placed upon us. No one spoke much of this reality: none of us knew of rest. We all had to labor constantly to meet the demand and provide enough for ourselves. That is why the first of our taxes is called the bondage tax. The only ones who sat with raised feet and fine clothes were the ones who'd found good fortune with the Polished, married from the Polished Ring to the Conservative, or was a higher-ranked soldier for the King's Host.

The sky had deepened to a dark blue hue by the time our home was in sight. I liked my home in this lighting. A small home built of wood and slanting a bit. A slow stream of gray came from the chimney top. A light breeze pushed outward the curtains hanging from the top of the cracked windows. My mother came to the front door and began to wave at my father and me. My father left the horses for me and ran to the door to meet his love.

"Dara, dear. The stars over my head!" my father cheered, holding my mother by the shoulders to look at her face. He always greeted her like this. My mother smiled warmly, overjoyed by her husband's delight in her. I rode on behind the house and put up the horses and the wagon. I pulled Amos' things out from the back and carried them with me. Inside, our home was neat and warm. The walls were wooden planks, decorated with dried flowers, greenery, candles my mother makes, and other attractive ornaments. Our home was small and modest. Two bedrooms. One shared by my brother and I, now my own. The second was for my parents. The kitchen and dining room were divided by a wall on the same side of the house. The room with the fire, a place to lounge, and the front door was its own. I cherished my home and the woods surrounding it. It was a place I felt I could be completely vulnerable and exposed and I'd be okay afterwards, perhaps even more loved than when I had been previously covered. At one time, that was even truer than it is now. Because of my father's secretiveness, I feel as though I must be secret. This was not the case before a few months ago. But much had changed.

The remaining night was quiet. Nothing eventful. We ate, conversed, and I found my bed shortly thereafter. Drifting to sleep by meditating on ideas. Ideas of treason while looking through eyes that see things the rest of us can only imagine. Ideas of how long a day can be. Of the kinds of secrets we could keep.

Chapter 3
Off Again

"Why do you try to leave my house unnoticed?" my mother asked me, noticing I was nearly half vanished through the front door.

"I am not trying to leave unnoticed. Rather, I try to leave not as a bother," I said though I knew my mother had spoken what was true: trying not to bother was trying to leave unnoticed.

"Good morning to you as well, my son," she said from the kitchen, ignoring my reply. "Come, eat," she demanded. I obeyed. I loved our kitchen, especially in the morning and especially at breakfast. It held windows that welcomed the sun rays in the early hours. My mother always kept the window behind the sink cracked for fresh air and the smell of the pines. The cabinets were a fair green color, and the dishes were cream. Naturally, our utensils were iron and had been handed down by my father's father. A few lonesome pieces were carved from wood though. At the table in the dining room, my mother placed in front of me toasted bread and a variety of flavored honeys.

After first eating and thanking my mother for the meal, I asked her, "Where is Father?"

"He left early to take the wagon to the forge and reload." She was plucking the dead leaves from her plants in the window seal.

"Reload it? We just got back from a trade. We don't have time before the next tax of work is due." I was on the edge of offense by the matter. I quickly stood to leave and meet my father.

"Son, I know you don't understand. Your father knows you don't understand. As unreasonable as it feels, I'm going to have to ask that you allow it to seem normal," she said. I paused and paid attention to my breathing. I needed to speak to Amos. He was the only one who allowed me anger and passion, when all others demanded a discipline I didn't possess. I strive to serve my family well, but all of these things-all of these unknowns. Each of them taunted me with the knowledge they possessed by emphasizing that I did not also possess it. I nodded, wearing discontentment on my face. I grabbed my bag containing the gifts I gathered for Amos and left. From my last show, I brought home an old book of poems for Adalric that I found in an old leather shop. Before that, a candle made of black wax for Phoebus. My mother wasn't very glad I traded for a candle when she could have made him one, but thankfully she understood the uniqueness of the one I'd found. Now I was eager to bring Amos something he could take much joy in.

"Son!" my mother called from the front door. I turned and acknowledged her. "Be safe."

"And to you be steady." I turned and left her there.

***

I enjoyed my walks to the forge greatly. A moment of peace alone in a place I love. It was becoming harder and harder to come by moments such as these. Strength was a most beautiful place. Unfortunately, her beauty has already begun to wither compared to tales of a distant time before. A time when, before one would find black towns and barren fields, he would find only meadows and forest streams. A meeting was already in place for me this morning before going to the forge. Decided before I left, Amos was going to meet me at the Fordwin. It's a particular part in the stream outside of town that we've claimed as our own. I looked around myself to admire the trees on the mountain that are broad and deep rooted. So full at the top that if I was to climb high enough, I could get lost in the clouds above. Few leaves were still managing to hold on before they were swept away by their fragile holds and the heavy winds of the cordial season that we came from. The roots of the trees intertwined, spreading across the ground and over paths. They held many memories belonging each to their own. At the bridge over the stream to town, I turned just before and trotted into the woods until I came to an opening with rocks for land.

Amos was grinning as he yelled, "Adinorium!" He embraced me. He was only a few inches shorter than I was. His hair was brown but in the sun, many would claim it to be red. He was slender and quiet with a sense of reticence about him.

"How have your days been?" I asked him eagerly. I had missed him and genuinely wanted to know how he'd been.

"Monotonous. How about your time? How were trades?" He was quick to ask his own questions. Always selfless and wanting to know more about whomever he was talking to then going on endlessly about himself. Together we sat on the rocks with our boots hanging down into the chasm. It was cold, but not enough for us to give up our meetings at the Fordwin.

"Not good." I was fidgeting with a tall piece of grass that was stuck between the stones. "It is proving fruitless to even go. Though I think my father pities the people there. They have nothing left." It was easy to sink into slowness when beside the Fordwin. It had the ability to make the rush of life seem pointless. I also knew it would take my father longer to reload the wagon then it'd take me to pack it all up. Meaning, I had time to sit for a while.

"So, we have come to hopeless times," Amos said. His eyes were calm, giving the look of being satisfied with what they saw before them. But really, they were just pale green. I imagine mine to be much different. The dim blue they were. More of the eager sort that would make one think I was quickly bored with what they had been saying. That was true most of the time.

"Hopeless, yes. But, hopefully, ending soon. Actually, they will be ending soon! We are in fact in the year of The Sovereign Days! Don't be quick to forget, Amos." I was halfway playing but the sentiment was more than true.

He laughed, "I'm glad that's your perspective. I believe most people know Haben Arrogs will be king next, and Strength will be all the closer to destruction."

"I'm glad I have my perspective then too! This is no time to lose hope. This is the one opportunity we, as a people, have to redeem our home. Save what we've already lost. We will hear of unions being established any day now. You will see hope." I was envisioning what could be. I believed it, I think. I had hope for Strength. Surely someone will rise up to fight for king and demand this tragedy to stop.

"Keep your hope, Nori. I will keep my wits," he said to me. We looked out into the woods. Occasionally, you'd see a deer or a fox or a squirrel most likely. I was amazed by the freedom the woods gave. An illusion without question. Remembering Amos' things, I grabbed the herbs and the book from my leather bag.

"I did have one profitable trade. This is from a man named Fox Tramp. He owns a medicine shop in the square we were doing trades in yesterday. He said you'd love those if you had any head for medicine. The book was an addition to seal the trade. I haven't looked in it, but apparently, it's good for medicine." I gave Amos the parcels and a grin crossed his face.

"This is fantastic! This is a Prulah Vine. Only found at the outskirts of File and Rank if one is lucky. A gem certainly. Thank you, friend." He examined the purple plant in the sun. He opened the book next and looked at a few of the first pages with a furrowed brow. "What dialect is this? I cannot read it. It appears to be more of a journal belonging to one who discovered more than he taught. I'll take it with me to the practice today and see if Dr. Yooldee can make anything out of it." He closed the book and slid it into his coat pocket. I tilted my head to the opposite side and thought back to the idea of Mr. Tramp having Hands of Plenty. Perhaps, with time, Amos could too. If that really was something that could be taught. I decided I wanted him to discover it. I wanted it to be nothing of my own accord nor even did I want to get his hopes up when it was nothing more than a cruel play by my friend, Mr. Fox Tramp. "Were you able to see your friend?" he asked.

"Yes! Shervan is well. I have no doubt that you will meet him one day. You'll both have the grandest conversations. We spoke of many things." I then shared with him the wisdom and admiration I had for my friend. "And look! I can't believe I almost forgot." I wrestled in my pocket to pull out the journal paper the woman had given me. "This was gifted to me by an old woman. Her husband created it. Apparently, he had the Eyes of a Gazer." Amos took and observed every inch of the page. I felt as if I was seeing it for the first time as I watched him examine the piece of art.

"It's beautiful. I've never seen such things," he said, handing it back to me.

I agreed, "Greater things. All beyond these walls, past the sands, for however far away."

"I wish I could see as they do. I really believe there is one Greater, beyond us. I simply wish I could see the current workings of his hands." Amos said, laying down and closing his eyes. I didn't know what to think of the Greater. It was a venture I hadn't chosen to make. Probably to my own destruction. I did know if he was anything he was beautiful. The things he created were of my obsessions. But like Amos said, I do not see him. I have not heard of things he's done. Aside from what the Old History says. Even then, that would only be the creation of it all. But what about now? What about these present moments? Was the Greater creator of the present too?

"I need to get to the forge. My father is already reloading to go on another trade," I paused as if the idea didn't bother me, but that was short lived as I couldn't contain my thoughts. I continued, "I'm curious, Amos. While in File and Rank he left me to pack the wagon for him to go to a home for a meeting. That's the third show in the past two months that I've accompanied him, and he's had to go away for things not spoken." Amos looked down at the stream not wanting to look at my eyes. He knew of my suspicions. He knew the game I was trying to play.

"I don't know. I don't know what to make of any of it," Amos said. His hands were moving about in an unconvincingly carefree way. "I suppose we can only wait." Amos was calm but could become ardent in his movements. His hands always waved about when he was speaking.

"Wait? Wait for what? Magnar knows, my mother knows, why can't I know. What knowledge is too great for me to bear if Magnar can bear it? Waiting is the excuse of a coward!" I was upset. Amos inhaled and lowered his hand as a sign I needed to quiet down. We knew there was always a chance we were being listened to. I was beginning not to care.

"Patience is a virtue of the men of wisdom. You need to trust your father's patience." His short, disheveled hair bounced as he nodded his head in agreement with himself. I looked out among the trees. I actually paused and tamed my tongue so as to hear the water flowing steadily on its way.

"Perhaps, he needs to trust me," I said. Amos didn't even bother to bring up all the other reasons which I'm sure he had thought of. Like how I couldn't use the same idea in regard to myself. I was thankful he didn't. We sat for a moment and Amos was the first to stand to his feet. He offered his hand to help me up.

"I know you feel the unknown laughing at you in your head. I know you desperately desire greater things, beyond what has been given to you. But I ask you to listen to me as a brother, you must wait. Time will grant you knowledge," Amos said. Now he wouldn't break my stare. I nodded and I truly agreed. Amos has for many years been my voice of reason, as Phoebus has been too, but in a more unemotional way.

"I'm just afraid, Amos. This world of ours does not do well with secrets. I'm afraid the punishment will be harsher than justice calls for. And yes, I know there are greater things at work here and that's burning me! I want to know them, be a part of them."

"Even if knowing these things and potentially fighting for these things will bring you greater punishment than justice calls for?" he asked with all sincerity in his voice.

"If the punishment isn't just, then I'd be willing to fight for anything." I meant what I said. Amos knows I meant it fully. He inhaled slowly and started walking back towards the bridge. I followed behind him.

"With notions like that swimming in your head, you're going to get yourself killed." The thing that separated Amos and I most was what we desired from life. If he was to stay here for the rest of his days, finish his studies, build a home and a family, and mend people until he was dead, he would be satisfied. I would not be. Deep in my soul, I'm restless. This can't be all there is. I cannot be satisfied with the world in which I find myself. This causes a tear in me. I have too much fire in me to quench and Amos is stable and is as rooted as the broad trees.

"Don't be angry with me, Amos. If I have you then

clearly I won't do anything terribly foolish." I smiled trying to lift his heavy spirit.

"That I will try my best to make true," he pledged looking back at my grinning face. "I can't stay angry, and it makes me angry!" he yelled, shoving me away even further from him. I laughed and pushed forwards coming to the bridge.

"Lost?" asked a voice belonging to Captain Allester of the Bolg. I disliked the man but I was confident he hated me ten times more. He clearly lived a life only as a mind and not as a body. He had light grayed hair that he kept slicked back. He wore a white uniform which only belonged to captains of the King's Host who were here to keep "peace and order." Kind words which actually meant "tax and control."

"No, sir," I replied sternly. "Enjoying the land, that's all." He was riding on a horse that seemed as anxious and giddy as I've ever seen. I believe it was that way for my sake as it annoyed the captain so much he cut his interrogation short.

"That's good and well. If you'll excuse me, I have the responsibilities of a man that beckon me," he sneered at us and rode onward.

"I swear he'd be happy to find me dead in the stream," I said after the captain was out of hearing.

"It would take much more than that to make him happy," Amos replied, causing us both to laugh at his absurdity. We crossed the bridge and continued into the town square. Ours was far more full of life than that of File and Rank's town square. Businesses of many trades, bustling all together. Aside from being Section Eight or Conservative Ring Four, our town was called Chalmar. It was one of the first towns to be established when the Founders began to build their kingdom. The plot had good trees and a more even land. The man who had been granted wisdom gave this place the name Chalmar and chose to live here in his final days. The Founders were all buried at the top of the mountain in the palace gardens, even the man given no gift. There is a headstone for the man granted wisdom there, but his body lies in our meadow.

"Nori! My brother!" Adalric yelled from a distance. He was standing on a wooden barrel with an angry looking Phoebus on the ground below him. I think it was just the sun in his eyes.

"Adalric! Phoebus! The two of you behaved yourselves, didn't you?" I asked, embracing each of them.

"Be hard not to behave with stiff old Amos," Phoebus joked. The statement was entirely true actually.

Adalric smirked and said, "I think we may have put a little bend in the board when we convinced a drunk man at the Hummer that all three of us were brigadiers."

"You did what?" I asked, envying the time they had had together without me. The Hummer was the place we'd all go together. A place for food and good company. The one luxury given to all of us because of the good fortune of its owner.

"Yes, of course we told him I was the most skilled," Adalric added quickly. He was referring to being a brigadier. The brigadiers are members of a rebel group who call themselves the Ebony Winds. They've become bolder as of late by killing soldiers and setting things on fire. Apparently, they are impossible to capture and even more difficult to find.

"Naturally," I agreed. Adalric was always quick to find trouble and Phoebus was quick to follow.

"I simply didn't interrupt. I would hardly say I helped persuade the man," Amos said, removing himself from their immature fun. I put my hand on Amos' shoulder and grinned at his stiffness. Adalric and Phoebus were the rest of our brotherhood. We've been together for years. No one hardly knew us apart. Adalric was charming, handsome, and well aware of both of those things. His hair was straight compared to mine and ashy blonde. He boasts often of his gladness in being half Polished. It was his Polished mother who married his Conservative father and everyone who knows of his family is completely aware of it, as it is now his mother's demise. Phoebus is stocky, but also tall. Appearing to be more frightening than he really is. He's far less impressive looking than Adalric. Really we all were less impressive than Adalric. Phoebus has a wide nose and dirty looking blonde hair, unlike Adalric's blonde that is nearly glimmering. His family are all miners. He joined them young at the age of sixteen. Though Phoebus can be cautious, when joined with Adalric, he can be a fool in the best way possible.

"Well done then, men! That alone deserves celebration!" I cheered. Even though we were young, we liked to think of ourselves as proper gentlemen. "Say Phoebus, why aren't you within the mountain today?"

Phoebus answered, "I'm supposed to be. My father heard word that you and your father returned home last night and allowed me to wait to visit you before joining them. He had some business with your father and iron." Our group was hated by most mothers in Chalmar because of the fact that four of age men with good trades and smart heads remained happily without a partner. All of us with the exception of Adalric. Not that he had a girl, but that he wasn't happy about that as the rest of us were.

"And what of you, Adalric? Shouldn't you be practicing the harp or picking roses?" I joked. Adalric was fortunate with his mother's wealth to be freer with his time than the rest of us were. An aspiring poet or painter, we all believe he is emotional and walks with enough air under his feet to do either. It is only natural for him to love the Polished or at least their way of life. I find it impractical but can see its allurement.

"No, Nori. I have a book reading this afternoon with Mrs. Growse. Unfortunately, she finds my voice most amazing and it pleases my mother that I entertain her in her old age." Adalric spoke of lighthearted troubles. Thankfully, the only reason I think I love him is because he's entirely aware of himself. He'll be the first to tell you of his pathetically easy life. It makes him a comedian in many ways. We began walking to the room and board that also held Dr. Yooldee's practice.

"Busier than normal," Amos remarked as we passed multiple wagons, men mounted on horses, and women busy with business.

"It's the nearing of the Sovereign Days," I said. "Preparing for whatever could come." Prepare they should. Thann is a despicable man but a smart one. One who knew the balance of being hated and being despised, as slender as that is. His grandson, who is the unspoken heir, seems to possess many similar qualities. They aren't mindless men. Foolish, perhaps, but not lacking knowledge. Smooth tongues that slither out of their mouths. I've never seen his grandson, but I've heard things about him. His name is Haben. Haben Arrogs. He's older than I am. Closer to Magnar's age. He's unmarried which is intentional many say. Handfuls of rich men would be glad if their daughters married him, even more so if he were king, making them more willing to fight for it to be so. Naturally, I understand Haben's lack of interest in that world. As for Thann, I've seen his face, I've heard his voice, I've watched the way he persuades with his tongue. More than that, I have seen what he has made with his hands. I see how by his command File and Rank is close to collapsing. I see how many are getting restless and angry in the Conservative Ring. He has planted anger in all towards that of the Polished who he's offered ignorant eyes and separating them as greater.

Amos asked me, "Do you think they're sure Haben is going to take the throne?"

"Maybe? Perhaps that would explain their business. If Haben does become king that means eighteen more grueling years. So many unknowns. We've seen Thann, but perhaps we can't even imagine Haben." Necessities were beginning to be gathered. I saw many faces I'd never seen before in town. Men who appeared to be hard laborers, who never chose to venture to any establishments. Women who looked frightened by every passing soul.

Phoebus frowned and said, "That means they are hopeless. They don't find joy in what is to come, only fear." He was right, like Amos in many ways. Thann being king meant an upper hand in the tournament. If he could win twice, surely, he has the power to make Haben win once.

"My, my, you sound like Amos now," I said.

"Maybe we are misreading the downcast looks on everyone's faces. Perhaps they are just beginning to prepare for the Sovereign Days. As, might I add, they should." Adalric's witty self gave perspective to the debate.

"Yes, they should! And we need to as well. We will not waste this moment of history that is taking place before our very eyes. We will watch a union rise above the others strong, wise, and noble. Then they will take back the throne and we will live in an eighteen-year celebration." I joined the ridiculous ranting. I had hope for Strength, but I was not ignorant about her. This entire year has felt different. A continual holding of our breath. Wanting to believe everything is going to be better, but close to sure that it won't be. Believing that Haben will rise and rule and reign and we'll do our best to simply live. I remember my father's new venture and feel an urgent shift to get to the forge.

"I must be going now," I stated, turning to my friends, and breaking the truthfully pitiful watch of the people.

Phoebus agreed, "Yes, I need to be getting to my father as well."

"And I must be getting back to dear old Mrs. Growse," Adalric said as he mockingly clasped his hands together and put them to his face.

"I'll come by later," Amos said, before going to the practice.

The Bored Daisy was the name of the inn that took residence on the top and majority of the bottom of the building next to that of the Hummer. Fashioned of logs and beams, it truly was a fine establishment. The most popular resting places in our area. Bringing many interesting folks to Chalmar. The

Practice of Dr. Yooldee was a small room and office that lay to a door on the left of the building down a side road. Not the best of locations but a central one.

I turned to leave the others saying, "Be safe, friends."

"And to you be steady," Adalric and Amos said together. Phoebus walked with me to the forge where our fathers would be together. Inconveniently, the forge was on the other side of town. We'd have to go through Chalmar, past the Bolg, and the small school house on the road leading out of Chalmar towards the town of Burm. The forge wasn't connected or directly beside any other buildings. A two-part structure. One area being closed in and the other just being covered. There was no smoke rising from the open vent, nor could I smell fire. It was running cold, and I hated seeing it that way. I loved my forge. A place in which control was mine. I can take something as strong as iron and demand it to bend to my desire. My father was loading the wagon. Only a single wagon, combined with that of my brother's. This meant they would go on together and I would stay. Phoebus' father was also there waiting on his own wagon for his son.

"Be safe, friend," Phoebus said, climbing the wagon to be beside his father.

"And to you be steady." I nodded to the pair of them and waited for my father first to speak.

My father apologized, "Adinorium, I'm sorry to leave again so quickly. It is important as I know you'll understand." I didn't reply now. I just began assisting them in loading the wagon. They took many things: swords with iron blades and wooden handles; quills with fine tips and full feathers; hand carved boxes with iron embellishments and locks. Wealthy things that must go on to the Polished Ring. Magnar stood in the wagon to receive and organize the goods. I imagined he could have finished loading the wagon by himself while Father was talking to Berg Alder, Phoebus' father. Nonetheless, I helped them now. I looked up at Magnar as I handed him another box. He was always more handsome than I was, and I noticed that again. Many complimented him as tall, strong, fierce. I just saw anger and cowardice, combined with ignorance and hatred. A being with too much strength for his own good. Or the good of others.

"I'm staying?" I asked knowing I was.

"Yes. I need you to finish the swords required for the bondage tax."

"They have to be well done," Magnar said, trying to belittle my labors.

"Then let's be glad it's me doing them and not you," I said, not looking at him, just continuing to pack as needed. "Another meeting, I presume," I asked Father. My father stopped his work and looked at me.

"Yes. It is just that," he answered softer than I expected him to.

I asked next, "Polished?"

"Yes." The answer he chose to give was blunt.

"Good and well. I'll keep in order all that is here," I said, making my tongue speak what is right instead of what is desired. My knowledge even got Magnar's attention as he stepped down from the wagon.

"Keep your ignorant thoughts in your head," he spat.

He was coming too close to my face. I chose to say nothing in hopes that it would make me more of a man in the situation. My father stared at my refraining face and dropped his head. He wasn't going to speak against Magnar. He never seemed to find the words to do so. They finished their tasks, and I began to prepare the forge by kindling fires and gathering my tools. I would be able to complete the tax, but I would have no time for eased labor. Everyone's taxes had to be completed by the beginning of the Sovereign Days unless they were given an extended allowance. For my forge, our date required was much sooner, but this was because we always delivered our taxes early. I worked with hands very familiar with the things they held. Not hesitating to move or guessing what needed to be done next. We did most of the forging on the side with open walls and a roof. I picked up the papers and read over all that needed to be done to fulfill the demand.

"Adinorium, is Magnar here?" a gentle voice asked. I looked up to see a lovely woman before me. A bit shorter than average, small in size, but truly lovely. Her hair was light and had been put up neatly, although by this time in the day many smaller pieces had fallen out framing her face. She wore a cream colored dress that fit her comfortably and a closed lip smile that suited her even better. All of these things belonged to that of my sister-in-law, Amaryllis. She was Magnar's wife, and it only made me hate him more. It wasn't that I was in love with Amaryllis, I just thought of her as too good for him. She is so kind and pure, unlike my brother. Magnar spoke to her harshly, like she was beneath him. Every time he did this, I burned within. Their marriage was highly praised. Her father is a carpenter and carpenters have been known to be the best of friends to a smith. It was almost a business union more than a marriage. At least, that's how I saw it. I think Magnar was better to her before they wed, but not good enough. Now, Amaryllis was faithful and Magnar content.

"Yes, he's inside with father. How are you this morning?" She smiled but before she answered my father and Magnar came outside.

"Amaryllis, why are you here?" Magnar asked with a tone of annoyance more than joy.

"I went to visit your mother this morning and she told me you were leaving. I came here to see you before you left," she said. He didn't even care to tell her where he was going or for how long he might be away. And he dared to be angry with her? Amaryllis was hardly older than me. Sometimes it feels a bit strange how different our lives are when we have lived close to the same amount of time. She feels ten years older than I am. I think it's a certain grace she has towards life.

"How good of you. You two can go on and say your goodbyes," my father said. Amaryllis smiled at my father, but it quickly left when she looked at Magnar. My father turned to me.

"Adinorium, I need you for a moment." I followed him inside the forge where there were many things: my father's table and chair for all of his books and records; massive cabinets of tools and materials; tables, baskets, and shelves of the goods we had. "Come and look." My father motioned with his hand for me to look at the paper on his desk. It was a sketch of a dagger. The most delicate I'd seen. It was to be fashioned of pure iron, blade, and handle. The handle itself was to be five inches tall and the blade another nine. No stone embellishments. Crafted from the foot to the head with a snake wrapping around mixed with a vine.

"Who is this for?" I asked, picking up the parchment to see it closer.

"That much cannot be said at this present time," he replied, walking around the table to the other side. "Son," he began, and I looked at him. "For some time now, it has been proven that your abilities surpass even mine. Magnar never was or is going to be as good at this trade as you. You have a gift. I'm asking you to forge this blade. My eyes aren't as keen, and my hands are not as steady as they were when I was a younger man. I could not make this as beautifully as you could. Will you do this for me, son?" my father said to me sincerely. In the same voice that would remain in one's mind forever. I had never heard my father admit that I am more skilled at this than Magnar and, even greater, himself.

"When must it be done?"

"In your own time."

"This will take me some days. The other swords will take me many days more. Weeks, likely." I spoke with concern. I was making sure my father was aware of what was being requested and the time it could take.

"I know. I will be gone for days even more. I truly am sorry, son, to leave you with so much." He put his hand to my face. "You resemble your mother more; but that look there, that is all mine," he said after examining my face.

"Will you be home before the Sovereign Days begins?" I

asked him. He sighed deeply. He must be home before then. It was weeks away. He answered concisely, "Yes." A man of simple answers. More useful than that of the poets in many ways. Together we walked to the wagon where Magnar was already seated. Amaryllis was standing beside the wagon speaking up to him. My father hoisted himself up and requested the reins from Magnar.

"Be safe," my father said as he smiled and nodded to me.

"And to you be steady," I replied. I didn't share his smile. I was afraid as I had told Amos. So much is unknown. Playing with those who rule by fire. I stood beside Amaryllis and together we watched until they were gone. I would consider Amaryllis one of my dearest friends outside of my brotherhood. She has spent many days and hours with my family, and being the delight she is, we've shared many laughs and late nights with all of us together. Once they were out of sight she sighed deeply.

"Do you regret marrying my brother?" I asked her out of nothing. I suppose I thought of such things because of this morning's renewed hatred of him: the way she sighed, the sorry looks he gave her. She looked down and walked out of the sun under the covering, even though it did nothing to warm her.

"I have chosen not to dwell on what could have been done. To dwell is a dangerous deal which can drive any man into a chasm he carved himself," she spoke with clever words, crafted well.

"So you do?" I asked, pushing her ideas. This time she looked at me sharply.

"No. I do not. To say so would break loyalty. He has been good to me. Given me a home, clothing, food, I cannot and will not speak against that," she answered with a tinge of anger in her voice. "Magnar loves me." It sounded like she was trying to convince herself of such things even still. I chose to press on the matter no more. She sat down and fixed her boots that she wore beneath her dress.

"When will you marry?" she asked me. I rolled my eyes and huffed at her absurdity. This was in the realm of the most frequent things she asked of me. I always answer it about the same.

"Truthfully, I don't think of it much. I have too many other things to keep my mind full," I answered her distractedly, getting back to my work.

"That's not very far thinking," she said, standing and readying herself to continue wherever she must go.

"I'm young, Amaryllis. Let me live," I answered, meeting her at the edge of the forge before she left.

"As if you've found life?" she questioned in a way that made one believe they were entirely wrong even if they didn't know why. I looked down at her and she grinned back at me. I shook my head and wouldn't allow such ideas to get in my view as I had terribly pressing things at hand.

"Be safe, Amaryllis."

"Be steady, Nori," she said, being sure I acknowledged what was really being said. She departed after that, leaving me to my labor. The day's hours had already been lost, more so than I desired. I worked by the sweat of my brow with hard labor, until those passing strangers were few and far between and the moon replaced the sun. I was tempted to stay the night at the forge, but my stomach convinced me to return home.

Chapter 4
The Forge, The Bolg, The Hummer, and Home

"Are you going to work until your body breaks?" Captain Allester hissed, dismounting his horse. He brought my mind back to reality. While my hands had been at work, my head had been elsewhere. It had been days since my father had left for the Polished Ring and I had spent every day from sunrise to sundown at the forge. Amos and I would meet at the Fordwin some mornings and he'd tell me of all the preparations taking place for the Sovereign Days. I was impressed that there remained such a rhythm and way of doing things considering there's eighteen years between each tournament. Adalric would come by in the little spare time he had to read me his poems of love and conquest. He'd tell me of all the gossip going around our highest Conservatives, never anything interesting. Most helpful, however, he would also tell me of the king's business, the judgements taking place, and any new decrees or speeches he had made that were published for the public. He'd also tell me of anything the Ebony Winds did, but these matters were always talked about vaguely and quietly.

"And the first union aside from Haben has broken their

silence," he told me. "Some small band from Section Eleven. A town called Gid." I had been waiting to hear if any were going to challenge Haben's assumed victory. My heart strengthened because of their strength. I felt them to be my brothers, because of our shared foe. I only saw Phoebus when he was delivering coal wherever it needed to go. He understood my long hours more than all the others. We shared the burden of having our families depended upon our success. We were best able to give mercy to one another. In the late evening, my mother happily waited at home for me. She has yet to be at peace since my father has increased his travels and meetings. She is able to fill her time with her candle making. She learned the craft from her mother alongside her sister, my aunt, Kaya. In addition to the works of iron Father takes to the Polished shows, he also takes Mother's candles. There have been times when her candles and their scents are more profitable than our iron work. It turned out to be a good business for my family.

"If that is what is required." My work never faltered even with the unrelenting pretentiousness of Captain Allester hanging over my head and even when my mind was preoccupied.

"I admire that." He helped himself to a seat on a log close by. He snorted and coughed as if he'd caught a cold in this brumal season that was now settled in. Our seasons come quickly here. They come as if they themselves were the primary beings of a home rather than a guest. As for Allester's words, they were more disturbing than that of his threats and insults. Never does Captain Allester compliment. Never. I don't think he'd even compliment King Thann if he stood in front of him.

"Shame. This old forge is holding you back. You could've made a name for yourself being in the King's Host." He took off his hat and wiped his face with it. I couldn't help but cringe at his uncivil manners. There was an open barrel of drinking water by the fire where the captain soon came and, cupping his hands to hold the water, refreshed himself. Before his hands froze over he wrapped them in cloth and folded them together. All I could think of was how I'd now have to dump out my water before using it again myself.

"To what do I owe the pleasure of this visit?" I asked, setting my things to the side to listen. He postured himself before choosing to speak.

"This labor you do so faithfully. However, our records show that there are three able smiths that this forge is in possession of. This requirement of swords should have been easy, aside from gathering materials, to complete. It simply concerned me to see all of the weight falling upon your back. Makes me wonder why your father would pay such a price to leave again. So soon too." The captain possessed terrible amounts of sarcastic pity.

"These are trying times, even you cannot deny. As you said, gathering materials is a challenge. Our last show was to File and Rank and because of their own hardships it was terribly unsuccessful. My father had no choice but to leave again in hopes of selling more," I replied as if this was true. Which in a way it was. However, our forge was completely satisfied with iron. In all logic, my father and Magnar could have and should have assisted me with this before leaving. But Allester didn't know that.

He continued on, "I asked the miners and by their records and your own, you should have a sufficient amount of iron to complete such things." I began my work again trying to get him to leave.

"Never enough, Captain. A man who believes he is set is a foolish one," I answered. I could feel my heart begin to beat faster. I was being questioned about my father's business. But why? What did the captain think he knew? What *did* he know?

"Unless he is set. Then he would be a fool all the more," Allester replied smoothly. I felt as though I was saying exactly what he wanted me to and that terrified me. I knew I had to keep composure and convenience him I was no more than the stupid boy he assumed I was.

"I suppose hard times provide many foolish men. All of them do their best to justify their own choices," I said, trying to explain the reason for both ways. Allester wasn't wrong. If anything, I completely agreed with him. If my father was truly in this for business, he would've stayed until this tax was completed. If anyone was paying attention it should cause suspicion.

"Defending your old man. Makes me wonder how far you would go for his name's sake." The captain wanted me to flip a table and scream at his face to prove his point. However, I was my father's son: I do not slip easily.

"I suppose you will have to continue to question, captain. That may be the foolish thing you will have to continue striving to justify," I said, keeping my posture steady as if I hadn't just called a captain of the King's Host a fool. Captain Allester made a face looking like something between a smile and a grimace. He nodded his head a little, taking time to look up at the sun.

"I extend my advice to you, Durnin. Learn to speak with a little less pride and perhaps a little more respect before you get your tongue cut out of your mouth." His words were quick and very well pronounced. I stood silently after hearing his choice of words and watched him leave quickly after. I exhaled, not realizing that I'd been holding my breath. I had made the captain into a potential fool and that did not settle well with him. He was confident that my father had sly dealings and I mocked that very confidence. I continued on with my work allowing myself to think of all the possible things the captain could do to me. Even though there was no profit to it, it helped pass the time which was all the value I needed these days.

Tonight was long awaited. Adalric, Phoebus, Amos, and I would be accompanying one another to the Hummer. Not only that, but it was the first day since I arrived home that I ended a day while sunlight was still visible. Arranging the forge back to its unused, sleepful self, I began towards the Hummer. It wasn't a terribly strenuous walk, but my tired legs made it feel that way. Chalmar was level on the mountain side. There weren't many hills, mostly sudden cliffs. The most unfortunate part of my travel between the town and the forge was passing by the Bolg. The Bolg was the quarters that held the King's Host. Those establishments are usually called the Capital Doors of the King's Host, but everyone here calls it the Bolg. I don't think there's any reason for that. Maybe it was just muttered out one day and stuck around. The Bolg is made up of two stories of wood and stone to match the same look of our section. The ground floor was open with three blazing fireplaces. Tables took up most of the room. To the right was a bar under the stairs that was for any conversations that needed to have a direction to be moved in when they began to get out of hand. I'd never seen the second floor, but it's been described to me as being split in half. On one half there are no walls and multiple beds stacked two tall. The other side consists of closed off rooms for planning, business, and the captains' sleeping quarters. They seemed rather lively on this particular evening making me laugh to myself of how much joy that must bring to Captain Allester. Curiosity beckoned me to peek through the doors to see what was conspiring. It seemed harmless since I had some time to spare before meeting the others. I peered through the wooden frame and saw a large cluster of men. Even from outside I could smell the cold sweat and wet dirt coming from the crowd. They were all cheering and clashing their hands together over the main event happening in front of them. On top of the center table stood two soldiers with swords drawn. They were in the middle of a duel. They cheered as if this was exciting and lively. It was not. It was just sloppy and stupid. However, regardless of the lack of wisdom, it was entertaining. My father was in the King's Host for ten years before leaving and choosing to join his father at the forge. Those were his years of rebellion. Being both a smith and a soldier, he became a ferocious swordsman. Unmatched in all of his time. He forged Magnar and I dulled swords and had trained us since we were boys. Only recently have we stopped practicing together. Magnar became too dominant over me, and cruelty followed suit. Now I only practice with my father or alone. Before long I found my own hand slamming on the table and heard my own voice yelling demands at the soldier I had favored to win. This was the third fight of the evening, and so far, the most brutal. They fought until surrender because there was no higher man to establish any order or boundaries.

"Watch his feet! He's telling you how he's going to attack!" I yelled trying to make my voice louder than the chaos of the crowd.

"Quiet!" Captain Allester said. His heavy and strong voice filled the room. I would've smiled if I wasn't terrified to be seen by him. Captain Allester had finally returned from whatever business he was on and didn't seem pleased with what he found. "Anyone here has three seconds to tell me exactly what is happening!" he growled. I needed to get to the door. I needed to get exactly where Allester was standing with his arms crossed confidently. For every step he took into the swarm of men, I took a step towards the door.

"A bit of live practice, sir. Some real experience. It's been going around you know. We all just thought it'd be smart to practice in case we found ourselves in the middle of a real one with a commoner or a brigadier," some low class transfer said timidly. He was on the opposite side of the room making it perfect for me to pass Allester while his head was turned.

"Oh, you thought that'd be smart? Getting a little real experience. Soldier, I'd be more than happy to give you some real experience. All of you will hike down to the File and Rank Ring tonight and all of you had better be back here by the time I wake up in the morning! I'll be checking in with the gatekeeper to make sure each one of you met him! For those who do not make it back, there will be consequences! You will then feel the real experience of pain and punishment!" Captain Allester yelled. It seemed as if that cold I thought I had noticed earlier had completely left him. I found freedom through the front doors unnoticed as the men began to shuffle around to leave for their evening stroll. The captain had asked an impossible task of the soldiers. The light of the day was already fading and while the trip down to the ring would not be as challenging the way back up would be either extremely long or terribly difficult. Most of them wouldn't be making it back up and the punishment they received in the journey would be punished by whatever other "real experience" the captain could conjure. I almost felt as if I needed to go with them since I'd joined in the excitement. However, I wasn't moved enough to do so. I would enjoy my freedom from the clutches of Captain Allester for at least tonight.

"Nori!" Phoebus called me from across the way. They all sat waiting for me in the square. I hadn't realized how much time I'd spent at the Bolg. Our friend, Mr. Doolby, is the one who runs the Hummer. We are well acquainted as we've pledged our loyalty to his place in an unnecessarily dramatic way. He's kind to us. He's always allowing us to have our own table whenever we visit. Also, he gave us many things for no cost. Somehow we'd found favor with him and somehow we've kept it. The atmosphere of the Hummer changed with the time of day and day of the week. Tonight was slower. Being midweek, most people didn't feel the need to get out. The town didn't appear much different to me having heard everything Amos had described to be going on. I suppose everything looked as if it was getting cleaned up. Some of the signs on the buildings had new paint and the stoned streets appeared cleaner, maybe? I couldn't really see a difference.

"What took you so long? We told you to close the forge early tonight," Phoebus complained as we found our table.

"And why do you smell so badly?" Adalric asked. I smiled and sat down happy to be here over anywhere else.

"Four spritz!" I yelled to Mr. Doolby from across the room. "I did close the forge early. I got a little caught up when passing the Bolg."

"Your spritz!" Doolby smiled, placing the four glasses on the table. He had already begun to bring them over when I had requested them. Spritz was water that appeared to be boiling when poured into a cup even though it was cold. It slightly burns your throat as you swallow. It comes in a few different tastes; but if not specified, it comes as gumberry, a sweet, pink fruit with yellow insides and green seeds.

"I'm awfully glad to see all of you! You in particular, Mr. Durnin. I was beginning to think I'd lost your good favor!" Mr. Doolby said. He was a short, round man with a full head of dark auburn hair. He was always wearing his shirt tucked into his pants. Doolby was very proper in the way he addresses people of all kinds. Even his wife who occasionally made an appearance was only known to him as "Mrs. Doolby".

"Never, Doolby. My neglect is from business alone I assure you," I said, placing my hand over my heart in a display of loyalty.

"In that case, the spritz are on me! Wonderful to have you all back together!" We all raised our glasses to him as he hobbled back over to his bar.

Adalric asked, "Get into a grapple with our beloved Captain Allester?" He sat on the far side across from me, Amos sat directly across from me, and Phoebus beside me.

"Nearly. Some of the soldiers were dueling and doing poorly if I may add. Naturally, I felt the arrogant need to assist them." Amos shook his head at me and Adalric laughed.

"Dueling? Like fighting?" Phoebus asked with a fearfulness in his tone.

Amos said, "Apparently duels have begun as a bit of campaigning for future unions. Swords, daggers, pure fist blows. I'm sure you will all be hearing them and seeing them soon."

"How did you hear about fights?" I asked with a furrowed brow. Amos typically was never in the circle of gossip and news. We left that to Adalric.

"Because wounded men must go somewhere to heal those wounds. So, they come to a doctor," Amos said smartly.

"I was wondering what they were for. One of the soldiers said they'd been going around," I added. "Afraid of brigadiers too."

Adalric joked, puffing up his chest, "They better not challenge me or they'll have another thing coming!"

"Yes, your mother can be quite terrifying," Phoebus mocked. We did enjoy making fun of one another. It was too easy to do.

"I heard of a union being gathered in Area Seven. But I only heard of them because one of my aunts was talking about it. It seems the union is small and unimpressive," Adalric said, trying to bring something positive but it ended in nearly the same place as it had started.

"I don't think any union will form that could contest Haben Arrogs," Phoebus said.

"Perhaps. I suppose we shall be patient and see," Amos balanced the thoughts.

"I did have a direct interaction with the captain today," I said grimly. I thought back to how afraid I felt while he questioned me. My father had begun to pique the interest of dangerous men.

"You know, Nori, if I didn't know the captain hated you, I'd think he liked your company." Amos snickered making fun of Captain Allester more than anyone. "What did he have to say?"

"Less of stating anything, more questioning everything. He was giving his condolences for my father's absence. Leaving me to finish the tax alone," I explained, taking a sip of my spritz and letting it burn my throat on the way down to my stomach.

"Again, if I didn't know he hated you," said Amos.

"That's actually kind of nice of him to acknowledge," said Adalric.

"Except Allester is never nice. So, his acknowledgement is not pity but plot. He had done research too. Went to the miners and asked about our iron supply. He said he wondered how far I would go to defend my father," I said in a hush and kept my eyes mostly down.

"How'd you get out of that?" Phoebus questioned.

"How do you know I got out of it?"

"You're here, not in a full robe of shackles, and you

always get out of everything." He didn't hesitate with his reasons. It actually made me crack a smile. I don't think any of them were really compliments, but he knew me well.

"Fair enough," I said. "I called him a fool," I added confidently as if that was the obvious thing for me to have done.

"I'm sorry, come again?" Adalric looked far more confused than I had.

"Yes, a fool trying to justify his foolishness," I said with a stone expression. Adalric's jaw dropped and he ruptured into a laugh. Phoebus was petrified by the idea and Amos smiled shaking his head. Adalric started ranting about the absurdity of it all, making Phoebus laugh along with him. Amos, however, looked at me with a dropped chin and his dim green eyes steady. He knew I was being audacious like my father. Although we all wanted to laugh and make fun of the captain and go back to the day's when it was a victory that I made it out alive, those days were long gone. I was acting too recklessly. Being too bold for the position I was in.

"What did he say to that?" Adalric asked. He was eager for whatever drama he could squeeze out of this. I exhaled and returned the smile to my face that had been lost in the reality of life. I took a fork from the table and pointed it directly at Adalric.

"I'm going to give you my advice. You better learn to speak with a little less pride and a little more respect before someone cuts out your tongue," I said in my best Captain Allester impression. Being that I was alive, not in shackles and still had my tongue, Adalric took full liberty in making it a laughing matter.

"He isn't wrong," Phoebus muttered as if angry with me. I went to press, but found I preferred hearing Adalric laugh and Amos chuckle in disbelief much better.

***

"I know you're curious, suspicious, terrified perhaps. Although it's always hard for me to imagine you can actually be terrified," Amos said while we walked to my home. The evening had been pure delight. Mr. Doolby entertained us with his stories of embarrassment over the years while we dined. He carried on for hours and we enjoyed every moment of it. Now the cold took over us and the idea of warmth felt like a distant memory. "Maybe Allester is just bored and, in a twisted way, he's just looking for anyone to capture." Amos tried to find another perspective that would satisfy the problem.

"Perhaps. Or perhaps he knows when something is amiss. Like a deer who hears and sees nothing but knows they're being watched." We walked allowing the quiet to be quiet, but our heads were both raging with thoughts and conversation. Before either of us had an arranged enough idea, I saw my home in the distance. A sense of comfort greets me even though I'm still freezing and embodied by the darkness of night. Just knowing that soon I will be home. Soon I will be safe and at ease.

"I didn't like that, Nori!" Mother exclaimed as I came through the door.

"I'm sorry, Mother. Doolby was telling his tales and I forgot there was such a thing as time and mothers who keep track of it."

"Well, do well and remember," she said with a stern

look that I knew was in love. "I was worried about you too, Amos," she continued standing from my father's chair where it appeared she'd been reading to pass the slow ticking time that fled our understanding so quickly.

"Sincerest apologies, Mrs. Durnin." Amos always meant what he said. Good to his word. He could have omitted the "sincere" and we would have believed him still. For land's sake, he could have said nothing, and we would have believed he was sincerely sorry.

"I take it you are off to bed?" She gathered her things to follow suit.

I replied, "I'm afraid so. I'll be leaving early tomorrow. The tax is due in a few days, and it will look much better if it's done even before that. That's how Father likes it." There was no need to explain Allester's visit to the forge today. It would simply make her fret and worry about all of it. I kissed her forehead allowing her to rest well. Once she disappeared into her room, I added wood to the fire to make sure all of the home's needs were met. In my room, Amos was already asleep in Magnar's old bed. I found my bed shortly after. My body relaxed and I was lost to sleep.

Chapter 5
A Great Honor

"Norium. Adinorium, wake up."

"I can't. I must sleep until I can move without aching," I moaned, not wanting to leave the cover's embrace.

"You will have to be dead for that to happen. Come on. There will soon be days for sleeping." I clutched my eyes shut knowing Amos' request was true.

"Is it early morning?" I asked. As I sat up, I would've sworn that I could feel every muscle in my body tender and pounding between constant use and complete stillness.

"Yes. Your mother is not yet awake, so try and be quiet. I've already mended the fire and grabbed some bread for you." Amos was making his bed as he spoke to me about his morning.

"You'll make a fantastic housewife someday, Amos," I joked while trying to convince myself being awake and alive was a good thing.

"Oh come on now!" Amos smacked me with one of his pillows while speaking through a gritted whisper. The impact of the pillow was enough to get me out of bed, dressed, and on the trail with Amos. He offered me a piece of bread he found in the kitchen. I ripped it apart and ate it thankfully.

"You know in File and Rank their bread is flat and dense. I remember when I was a boy and I'd go to the shows with my father, they'd have the most beautifully crafted loaves. Not necessarily many of them, but the few they had were works of art. After Thann decided to increase the work required in the mines for gold, I never saw such beautiful things again," I said, speaking of a memory that I'd almost forgotten. Once, it was a memory of beauty. Now, it only reminded me of my anger for Thann. It reminded me of how though he is absent in person he holds everything so tightly in his grasp that it feels as if he's everywhere. Amos, sort of just nodded. He was too sympathetic to make it lighthearted and not willing to say anything that poorly defined the action.

"So you really believe someone other than Haben is going to become king?" he asked after some time had passed. It was odd to me how we spoke of Haben as if we knew him. We really only knew for certain his name and relations and just imagined the rest.

"I don't know what I believe. I know what I hope. I want to believe there's hope. Strength has many able men. I'm sure many have passion and might enough to challenge Thann and Haben. We've already heard of a few." Hope was all I had in terms of change. Hope was all anyone had in terms of all of our unknowns. If we were right to have it or just making ourselves into fools couldn't be known for sure at this time.

"Perhaps. But you assume they will be good? That any who oppose Haben must be pure and noble? For all time, many have fought for the throne. Its power attracts many kinds of men. Even horrible ones versus terrible ones," Amos said. He also spoke from a perspective I'd never really thought of. He was right, I did assume that if Haben had an opposer, they'd be good. That their heart would be for the people. But Amos was right. Power attracted more cruel men than it did good ones.

"That is what the tournament is for," I answered while we crossed the bridge that had the trail to the Fordwin. That is exactly what the tournament is for. That is why the Founders arranged it in such a way. Let all of the prowling beasts come try to take the throne. That is why they are tested for more than just strength.

In the light, the town's preparation for the tournament was more visible. The store owners were priming their properties and the people seemed more lighthearted than the last time I had watched them. I could understand why. It felt almost exciting. All of it. The Sovereign Days, the festivities, the celebration.

"Will you be coming home tonight?" I asked Amos before our paths split.

"My father invited company over tonight and wants me to be there," he said in an unenthusiastic tone,

"Company? Your father invited company over? Who did he wish to share his company with? I thought he only cared for you and the chickens," I asked, shocked by such ordeals.

"The Dians. Apparently, my father and Mr. Dian have bonded over tomatoes and cucumbers. It'll be fine. I'll see you soon though. Assuming you'll be at the forge tomorrow?" Amos said, trying to be gracious about the whole ordeal.

"Of course. I hope your time is at least not entirely

dreadful."

"Right. Be safe, friend," he said, walking backwards in the direction he needed to go.

"And to you," I answered with a humble bow, "be steady."

I was becoming eager for the Sovereign Days to come. Everyone had whispered about it for years and now it's so close I could actually see it coming. Passing the Bolg, I saw some soldiers who were practically crawling through the doors. I now remembered that this whole time they had been climbing a mountain. I wondered how many were still climbing. I also wondered what the rest of them were thinking. Maybe wondering what time Captain Allester wakes up? Before the forge was the school house. You wouldn't be able to find it unless someone pointed it out. A single room structure that looked more like a home than anything. Not as many windows as I would've liked growing up. There would be plenty of flowers around it even when the season of spruce comes. Not all children went to the school house. It wasn't required yet. Those children did all of their education at home, or in all honesty, not at all. The ones who did attend, didn't get all of their education from the place either. The teacher lectures on a few subjects and the rest is your own parents. My teacher was Mr. Sabaar. He was of little help. Always running his mouth about the subject, the weather, and whatever else came into his head. My mother taught me most of what I know. How to write and work with numbers. Adalric actually taught me how to read. Mrs. Ivory came along later with some other mothers to teach us more thoroughly. By the time they arrived I was skipping many days to help my father. I had little love for my school years.

Now coming to the forge, it looked exactly as I'd left it. For that I was happy. Although, I found that I had grown a suspicion towards things being left as they were. I think I would have had more peace if I saw a hammer left out of place or the water barrel half emptied. Things left untouched meant things needed to be dealt with later. I'd seen a man's establishment burned for an unknown reason when they had never been touched before. I heard of a woman being thrown out of her home in Dagrun for who knows what when a lot of brigadiers counterattacked the soldiers. The king wasn't afraid of destruction, so why leave his enemy untouched? Apparently it increased greatly after his second victory. I wouldn't know much because I was so young. But I do know what he has always been- a snake.

I spent the rest of every hour slamming hammers and holding iron in fire. Making a standard sword was second nature to me. However, making the sword loads of three men as one man, was not. If I hadn't done it so many times, I would have made every mistake possible. I realized after several hours that I hadn't thought once since I'd begun my work. My body was now in control; therefore, my mind had no ground to reason. If my mind was in control, I would've stopped before now. Stopped at least to comprehend what I was really doing and why. Even though it was frigid outside, I worked in light layers. It was by the Greater alone that I hadn't gotten sick due to treating my body as if it were spruse in brumal.

My mind felt as though it had slowed to a crawl when my day was done. My feet had stopped their aching only because they'd become numb to no longer being a part of my body. Inside the forge, I found a seat at my father's table. I needed to find the tax papers to finish out the notes required. Tomorrow I would be done and the day after I would deliver the blades. I smiled at the thought. My body was in desperate need of a break. In desperate need of recovery.

"Here," I said to myself. I exhaled and read over the demand. In the peak hours of the next day, everything would be met and my father would return to completion. It seemed a miracle that I was able to finish it all, but I was diligent and worked the hours of three men. Placing the papers square on the desk, I saw the drawing for the dagger my father had asked me to make. I'd honestly forgotten about it in the work the tax presented. I looked more in depth at the dagger. The snake twisting unnaturally around the blade. It turned instead of curved and slumped where it should be gliding. Its head was most impressive, thin enough to not hinder the movement. The tongue went out not far ahead, smooth except the divide. At the end of the two-tipped tongue it curved up and back. A brutal design that would rip the flesh when the dagger was pulled away. When this happened, it would look as if the snake was drinking the opponent's blood. The color red would be on its mouth. A sturdy handle, wrapped in black silk. The snake and veins slithered from the head of the dagger to the bottom of the handle. I was intrigued by whom this prize blade would belong to. More curious, why my father wouldn't want me to know. Why would it matter if I knew or not? Unless it was a favor for a friend and the name was simply too dangerous for me to know. I returned the paper to the desk where it belonged.

It would have to be a task in the future. As for today, I would forget my body's pain knowing tomorrow it would be finished.

Thinking of having to walk back home hurt more than the reality of it. I would've stayed the night at the forge, but I feared my mother's loneliness. Anything to give her peace of mind nowadays I was willing to do.

"Norium!" Amaryllis smiled as I came through the door.

"Is he home?" Mother yelled from the kitchen.

"Yes! Let me take your layers," Amaryllis demanded, taking my coat from my hands. I walked towards the kitchen before she stopped me. "Not yet. Wash up and go to the dining room." I obeyed. I scrubbed my hands and rubbed water all over my face. Taking a rage to scrub my face and arms, I was able to see how much ash had clung to my skin. I peered into the kitchen to see both my mother and Amaryllis busy at work. I went into the dining room which was lit by candle lights and smelled of meat and fresh bread.

"Sit here," Mother ordered, pulling out my father's chair at the table.

"What is the occasion?" I laughed while sitting down. "I feel like a king being served in such a way." They had begun to bring in a meal for many more than three to the table.

"Then you will understand how I feel towards you at this time," she said, placing a bowl of hot rolls in front of me. I didn't stop smiling the rest of the night. I ate until I was filled more than anyone should be. We ate red meat with potatoes and beans. Rolls with butter and honey. Amaryllis made flavored tea with sugar cubes and cream. The pinnacle of completion was a chocolate cake topped with white cream made by my mother.

"Your favorite," she said with a wink. I sat back and laughed to myself.

"It has been too long since we've done this. I'd forgotten what celebration looked like," I smiled.

"I agree! We should celebrate more often. Today, for sacrifice in hard labor. Tomorrow, for Strength and her people. And, in time, perhaps redemption," Amaryllis eloquently said. "I'd celebrate anything if it meant cake." She said her own opinion on the matter. My mother grabbed her hand from across the table and smiled.

"I-" my mother began before being interrupted by a knock on the door.

Amaryllis said, "Maybe Amos."

"Or Kane." My mother stood with eagerness at the thought.

"I'll answer it," I said, walking past her. Amaryllis and Dara waited in the dining room to see who the uninvited guest was. How perfect if it were my father. Coming home to a feast for a king and cake to celebrate. Again the door was knocked. I didn't even bother to crack it to see who it was. I knew. "Captain Allester," I said. I could feel myself almost straighten my posture because of his undivided attention.

"Allester? What brings you here at this hour?" Mother asked, addressing the captain by name. He wore layers of black instead of his usual white. "Is it Kane?" My mother came closer to the door.

"No, Dara. Ease your conscience. May I come in for a

moment?" he asked while coming through the door with three other soldiers, all in fine clothing. They must have been from the Polished Ring. I closed it behind them and stood waiting for his explanation on why he and these soldiers were in our home. "Pardon my intrusion, I simply needed to deliver this to the head of the Durnin household. Urgent message from Lord Arres." He raised a brow and extended the letter to my mother. Arres, the son of Thann and father of Haben. Lord of Area Four. The weak one. She stared at him and looked as if she could cry. Before the captain had time to question her on the matter, I took the letter and opened it like it was mine from the beginning.

"Would you like some tea, Captain Allester?" Amaryllis asked, lightening the situation.

"No, thank you," he answered without even attempting a smile.

"Sit, Dara, I'll bring you some." Amaryllis broke my mother's tension and allowed her to think more clearly.

"Thank you, dearest," she said, finding a seat in my father's chair as Amaryllis had instructed her to do.

My mother turned to the captain, "How are your men, Allester?" The captain answered her but I had stopped listening. I was enthralled by the letter. Gold trim with crisp words perfectly written in heightened cursive. As I read my heart grew fainter and fainter.

"This is impossible," I mumbled beneath my breath.

"What is it son?" my mother asked, clutching herself.

"This cannot be done!" I yelled at Captain Allester and held the paper close to his face. I knew the other soldiers weren't his because none of them moved an inch closer to intervene. My mother stood trying to understand my sudden rage.

"Adinorium! What on this lands does it say?" she asked.

"Another tax. A new sword demand. It has to be finished before the Sovereign Days, not just by them. Requested by Lord Arres himself," I said, handing the paper to my mother to read.

"Such a high honor. So high it is punishable by disrespect to the priorities of the throne," Captain Allester said, already knowing the content of the letter.

"This is impossible, Captain! I cannot complete this by the time you desire it." I found my voice pleading for mercy in a way I hated doing. My body was already in great pain and although diligent, I had slowed down much because of my constant use of it.

"I'm sorry, Durnin. What the lord says I cannot contest. Unless, you have some better reason for your father's absence. Perhaps, then the lord would be willing to recant his desire." Allester was cunning, they all were. Of course, this wasn't really about lack and need. This was a ploy to make me say something. To make any of us say something. But what if there was nothing to say? Allester was clever but I was no fool myself.

"I have already told you of his dealings! Our last trade wasn't profitable, so he had to leave again. I don't know what more you want from me!" I yelled in anger. I had gained new blisters and calluses on my hand from the constant gripping and rubbing of slamming hammers and shaping iron. My mind had begun to fade due to lack of sleep and insufficient rest. I tried not to complain and think much of my pain, but the thought of it all going on nearly broke my determination. Allester came close to me, making his face only a few inches from my own. Amaryllis stood beside my mother and rubbed her arms trying to keep her calm.

"I think you're lying, Durnin. I think there is more, and you know it. Unfortunately, I don't pity you enough and, bluntly, I don't care enough to stand up for you. I can only suggest that you beg the Greater for a revived spirit and a miracle." I could feel the spit from his exaggerated words hitting my face. Fortunately, for his sake, my mother and Amaryllis were here. I shook my head quickly and proceeded to smile at the captain as if what he said had been a bad joke.

"Thank you for visiting, Captain Allester." I walked around him and the three soldiers, whom I had no fear of, and opened the door implying they needed to leave. Allester dropped his head and joined in my fake smile and passive hatred.

"Please bring whatever ones you've already completed to the Bolg as soon as you have a moment. And," he hesitated, "for any of you, I'm always ready to listen to a plea for mercy if you think of one," he finished, putting his hat back on his ugly head that could be seen through his thin hair.

"Of course." I slammed the door.

"Adinorium." My mother tried to comfort me yet all I could think about was how she knows what the captain is longing for. Even Amaryllis knows. And yet, they remained silent. They allowed my persecution for the sake of keeping secrets. They allow me to feel this and yet tell me nothing.

Brushing past Amaryllis, I locked myself in my room. I slouched onto the floor and buried my face into my hands. My feet felt like weights and I almost felt like crying in hopes that it would relieve something inside of me. I hated them. I burned with hatred for them. Because a crown is placed on his head and a brigade is placed in his control, the king and his men strive to destroy those who don't yield to them. Not strive, they do. Not even those who don't yield, those who simply breathe. My hope faded for a new king. Thann has us so tightly gripped that we might be ignorantly believing we have any power at all. I moved to lay in my bed, unchanged from the clothes of the day. Hatred wouldn't complete the swords, but plotting would help. I laid awake making a list in my head of everything I needed. I'd pack in the early morning and wouldn't come home until it was finished. I wouldn't give in to them, as I promised Allester, until my body breaks. I laid there thinking it quite funny how a single day can destroy so many more. Within only minutes, or a few words on a page, everything changes

Chapter 6
As Iron Bends to The Will of Fire

I did exactly as I told myself I'd do in the anger of my night. I left my home in the early morning, along with all of my needed things. I went to the forge walking past a town still asleep and a Bolg that laid silent. I kindled a fire and never let it rest from burning. My hand constantly gripped around the hammer's body. My back was being slowly burned like the iron over the fire to be molded into its hunched place. I slept for a few hours a night and with all other time, I labored. And my labor never faltered.

Amos came and I didn't speak or stop or rant. I only gave him the letter from Arres to explain. He told Phoebus who, in turn, kept my coal and wood sufficient. Even Phoebus' father, Berg, brought more iron to make sure I had what I needed. Adalric came and read to me one of his stories, even though I never commented or asked him to continue. He read to me his story about a star that fell from the sky. At first it was sad that it had fallen from its high place where the rest of the stars arrogantly stayed. But the star realized the world below, where it had fallen to, was covered in darkness. So, the star learned to dance and bring streams of light upon the faces of those below. Every star who fell afterwards, the first one taught to dance. After time, the place below was brighter than all the stars that stood separated and prideful above. And the star was happy.

My mother came every other day and would leave food for me to eat. Amaryllis came the opposite day from her and would stay until I did eat. Even Allester had the occasional visit. He'd ride his horse on the far side of the road and watch my fainting body. He'd set a guard to watch me from a distance as if I wouldn't have learned of his watching. My labored hours turned into labored days and the labored days to labored weeks. Yet no one could ask me to stop. The only thing they could do was give me their pity. The only one who could help was gone. All others had their own tax to complete, whether it was mining coal or making coins to pay the crown. Moreso, they had no skill in the craft of forgery. Everyday I pleaded with the supposed Greater for a fraction of a moment that I would look up to see my father coming to save me, but after that small moment, I faced reality. I knew I wouldn't. Every sword I made I imagined Thann trying to take it from me and him cutting his hand on the blade because of how perfectly sharp it was. I imagined Arres' disappointment when he received the letter telling him I completed everything as I was required to. I imagined my father asking my forgiveness for making this cursed thing my reality. But as iron bends to the will of fire. Thann will bend to mine.

Chapter 7
A Voice and A Black Being

"How much longer can you do this?" Amos asked. He sat across from me while eating dinner. I sat in my father's chair and he pulled up a stump on the other side of the desk. My mother had brought a brothy soup with chicken, carrots, peas, and other things I didn't care to think about. I sat in a complete hunch with my head hanging low. My body was dethawing by the fire even though I'd been hot and sweating all day. If anything, sitting in front of the fire gave the illusion that it was really freezing me because of my sudden stillness. There were only a few candles in addition to the fire. A somber mood for the graven night. I didn't reply to Amos. He and I have had many silent dinners over these past few weeks. If the nights weren't silent, Amos was the one speaking and I would say nothing. I was always listening though. "Adinorium, I'm serious." Amos' voice was growing louder. "Adalric, Phoebus, and I agree that this has gone on for much too long. We cannot watch you kill yourself over this! I can't just watch you be destroyed! Look at you! You look like an old man even in your youth. Your hands may remain black forever and your back permanently crippled. What is possibly so valuable that this is a fair exchange?" He was wearily yelling now, and a tear had fallen from his eye. I don't think he meant to be yelling at me though. It was more his own anger with the situation. Amos was dependent on being able to help, on being able to mend. Yet when I needed help most, he could do nothing. The way I was laboring would kill me if I kept on. I gave my body no rest and so it began to break down without redemption, because I never allowed it the needed moments to build back up again. I had no time for it to.

"You know exactly what is valuable enough for this exchange," I said. These were the first words I had spoken in days. I raised my head and straightened my back though it made me wince. My voice was weak and cracked trying to speak. Amos stared at my broken movements. He wasn't wrong in describing me. I felt as though I'd been brutally beaten with a stick, then left for my entire body to bruise, only to be beaten again. "That is the only possible thing it could be." For all my days and all my agony, I had one thing to dwell on, why? Amos dropped his head and didn't argue. "I think we've known for some time, haven't we? The timing, the secretiveness, the sacrifice, the shadows, the whispers." There was, in fact, only one thing that would be worth this exchange, and that would be a secret. "I realize it now." A secret that had been broken. That had been sought out and spoken. "The only thing that could really destroy Thann, was himself. Certainly, my father knows how Thann deceptively gained the throne and has tangible truth to convince justice without any question. That is how my work persists. Knowing it leads to Thann's destruction." Amos stood from the table to begin cleaning up our mess, seeming indifferent to the idea.

"You're wrong," he said bluntly. I cocked my head to the opposite side, listening to his bold statement. "Even that is not valuable enough for this exchange." I dropped my head again and smirked at his remark. "I mean, how close are you to being done?" Amos threw his hands in the air in anger. "You're not going to last at this rate! Every sword is the equivalent of a year off your life!"

"You're right. This is impossible." I stood from my seat and began to walk towards my makeshift bed. My feet were only weights that had to be dragged along. Amos stood watching my pathetic strength. "But if I don't die trying," I picked up the dagger that lay beside my bed, spinning it in my fingers, "then my father will die having committed a great wrong to our precious king and lords," I said. My gentle voice was conflicting with the intentions I had for the dagger in my hand. Into the letter from Arres that Amos had nailed to the wall at the beginning of all of this, my dagger flew across the room and found its place. I slowed my breathing and sat down on the side of my bed. I unlaced my boots and peeled them off my feet. I closed my eyes and rubbed my face with my blackened hands. "I'm willing to die trying," I finished and looked at Amos whose eyes were holding tears. I laid down and kept my eyes closed even though Amos had not yet left.

"You just might," he said after blowing out every candle and releasing the fire from its toil.

***

A snake slithered through a garden. It was quick, knowing where it wanted to go. Water poured from above heavy and strong, stinging the skin with every strike. It was raining. It never rained in Strength. I watched the snake prowled past a great headstone. Engraved were the names of all of our Founders:

Angus Draconian - Gifted Strength
Baron Jisme - Gifted Nobility
Heller Arrogs - Gifted Wisdom
Abaddon Brown - Not gifted

Heller Arrogs? The man gifted wisdom was an Arrogs? How? How did I not know? I found myself in the King's Gardens, at the very top of Strength.

"My king! The waters, they're rising!" I saw a servant of stature run out into the garden calling to me. "Come and see!" He called me to an outlook where I could now see a great land. A desert, a dune sea, a channel broad and far, a range of many mountains. Looking down I could see all of Strength. I could see the wall and how grand it really was. Except there was an opening. A great door that didn't exist before stood opened to the desert. Like the servant said the waters were rising. Although there was a door, the rain came down too quickly and too mightily. It began to fill the walls like a dry well. The people needed to flee into the desert or begin climbing the mountain. But there was no leader to show them such a way. I could not find the king anywhere, and when I went to ask the servant, he was gone. Again I saw the snake and now I followed it. Down the mountain and into the woods it went. I furthered my distance as I saw an establishment. Small with open walls and stone pillars holding a roof. A crowned being stood under it, protecting itself from the rain. The snake slithered and met the being who'd reached down to grab it. The snake settled coiled around his arm.

"Adinorium," a voice said to me, but it did not come from the crowned being. It came from behind me. It was instantly familiar, but I had no idea who it was. It was a sure voice. A man's voice. Somehow the rain didn't stifle it. I turned to see the figure of a being. His identity was hidden from me covered by a sheet of water caused by the rain. A cry stole my attention to the being under the covering. They had fallen to the ground and laid in complete stillness. I ran to see what had happened. The snake spiraled on the man's chest. This man I knew. He was in fact the king, Thann Arrogs. Dead. I wiped my eyes with my hands trying to better see. My body was ten pounds heavier, soaked with little hope of being dry for some time. I looked at Thann's cold body. His eyes had lost all feeling, it was as if it wasn't even him. After only a moment, a black being that seemed to be made of shadow came out of nothingness to stand over the dead king. I could hear the breathing of the shadow over the thunderous rain. It wasn't a strained breathing, more disappointed and even. It spun its neck as if it had only just realized that it actually had one. That wasn't true though. I wasn't sure how, but I knew he was very much sure of his existence.

"Auh. The fitting follower. One for another." It spoke comfortable and clean. I began to take steps back, realizing his intentions were towards me. "No, this one is mine," the one who had called me by name said. However, I still could not see him. The black being became terrified searching for the other one who the voice belonged to. It seemed he didn't see the body of the voice either. But his terror made me assume he knew who the voice belonged to. I could feel him look at me once more, even though it had no eyes to see. It growled in its breathing, lowered his head to the ground and fell to join the darkness. I then turned around in a circle searching for the one the black being feared, who knew my name, who said I was his; but I found nothing.

***

"Adinorium. Adinorium," a voice said. A faint, unfamiliar voice was attempting to pull me back to life. I shot up from my bed, sitting with my back straight and body tense. I was in the forge and dry and no other was there to call my name. I shut my eyes trying to decipher if this was truly my reality. I looked at my hands, they were still black and stained. I relaxed my body and felt no pain in my joints or aches in my bones. I stood with my bare feet on the ground and could feel the dirt floors but there was no agony in holding my body's weight now. *I could feel.* The trouble was I felt anew. I changed clothes while eating bread with the honey my mother had left for me. I walked out into the brumal's crisp air that filled my eyes with water. I smiled as I ran my hand along the brim of the forge's fire pit. I didn't know how; even more so I didn't know why. But I was revived. This task before me would be completed, even more so completely faultless. I didn't understand what had happened. It was like a dream, but something entirely greater. I remembered all of it, unlike normal dreams when you wake and forget. I didn't understand the being I had seen nor the other I had only heard. I felt greater fear now thinking of the black being. I'd never seen anything like him. He wasn't cold or warm, he felt almost hollow yet full of passion all together.

I now worked with greater speed than I had ever before. In my haste, however, never once did I sacrifice precision or dull tips. I moved swiftly and felt joy in my work. I didn't feel as if I was being driven by a desperate anger, rather, I felt as if I had a power to complete what was required. Knowing it to be impossible, I smiled as if unaffected by its impossibility.

"What happened to you?" Adalric smiled and furrowed his brow as he noticed my change in disposition when he arrived at the forge.

"I had a dream!" I announced and for the first time, I stopped my work to meet my friend. I embraced him with strength I wouldn't have had the day before and kissed his forehead.

"Uh huh," he said after awkwardly hugging me back and looking at me with madness. He held his book, papers, two mugs, and a parchment bag in his bundled up hands. His cheeks were red from the cold state of the weather. His questioning was well earned. Last he'd seen me, I was miserable and looked like death had told me my time was little.

"Adalric, believe me when I say, last night I had dinner with Amos and I got in bed a cripple who might not physically, emotionally, or mentally be able to get out of that very bed again; but, when I was sleeping, or maybe I was dead, either way, I had a dream. This dream was so clear, it was tangible. I could actually think and reason and feel. When I woke up, it was as if I'd been given a new body. I could feel the ground beneath my feet again!" I felt as puzzled as Adalric looked while explaining what had happened. Although I felt confused explaining it, I was doubtful of it. Adalric tilted his head and contemplated what I was saying.

"I'm not really sure what to make of this, Nori. It seems like a thing of the Old History. However, I have learned that when all else fails, celebrate the good of it!" Adalric said, surrendering to his confusion and going into the forge.

"Don't let me stop your merry work!" I grinned and followed his orders.

Adalric cheered, "I've brought you a celebration!" Out of the closed portion of the forge he brought two beverages that steamed when met with the cold.

"What is it?" I questioned while he handed me one of the mugs.

"Don't worry about it," he said, assuring me in the least assuring way. I raised a brow and looked into the cup filled with a deep brown liquid. He found a seat beside the fire and stopped for a dramatic moment of silence. "Here's to," he raised his cup before moving it about trying to think of what to celebrate specifically, "revived bodies!" I nodded to his toast and sipped the concoction blindly. It was sweet with cinnamon and other warm spices. It was, in fact, good for toasts and celebrations. "Mm. I am quite talented," he said and took another gulp of the drink.

"I will humbly second that. Although, it sort of tastes like one of my mother's candles."

"Oh hush!" he said, holding his mugs with two hands and breathing in delight.

"My apologies." I raised my glass to him and, this time, enjoyed the simple pleasure.

"I really don't understand. I really don't get it. You're anew." Adalric said, softly looking at me. "Why do you think you were given this?"

"I don't know. That I have wondered most." I replied grinning.

"You're going to finish this tax, aren't you?" I couldn't tell if Adalric was questioning in an encouraging way or in a way that questions if my sanity was still lost.

"Yes, it's going to be perfect." I said, examining the likes of a sword that was in my hand.

"I think it will be." Adalric gave me his confidence. "Then keep laboring my friend! I will be here to celebrate with you when you've reached perfection! Do remember what Allester's face looks like so you can explain it to me." Adalric smiled. "And I must going!" He stood in a hurry seeming to have just remembered something.

"A short visit," I said while throwing wood into the fire.

"I'm afraid so," he said. He fidgeted a bit with his hands. "I'm meeting with someone."

"Someone as in a woman?" I said surprised even though I wouldn't have been surprised at all.

"Yes, but no. She is a woman, but not like a woman I'd be going out with or something. She's an author, writes books and stuff." I rolled my eyes.

"I know what an author is, Adalric."

"Yes, well, she is going to be reading my poetry, because she's an author," he said, trailing off. He was clearly daunted by the whole idea.

"That's wonderful! I'm overjoyed for you! Don't be so intimidated. You're talented! If she's good for anything, she'll be able to see that." He inhaled and I could see his hand grip his journal more tightly. "Now stop wasting time here!" I pushed him away from me as if he'd done something wrong. He exhaled until his lungs were empty and nodded strongly. "I was afraid that I was going to have to get your affairs in order today. Things like what flowers you like and the wood type for the fire; but happily, you look far from death!" he said to me once more. "Be safe, friend." he grabbed my shoulders and meant the farewell entirely.

"And to you be steady," I said. I encouraged him to go all the faster. He took a few steps down the road then ran back to embrace me again.

"Thank the Greater you are well!" he said, speaking less to me and more to the Greater. When he pulled away to look at me, he had tears in his eyes. "You'll have to tell me more of this dream."

"Yes, I will."

***

Tonight, I smiled when I sat down to eat a meal. I found that I'd been doing that a lot today-smiling. I had set my father's desk properly for a meal so that my mother would be able to eat with me. I was glad to show her all that had happened to me.

"Son, what's wrong? You're usually still working at this point." She peered at the table with a second chair and candles. "I don't understand. You look as if you've been restored to your youth." She stood over me and held my face with her right hand. Not smiling but confused.

"I had a dream," I said as if dreams were a normal thing that restores someone's body. Setting down the basket she held in her left hand, she found her seat across from me. All she could do for the first few minutes was stare at me. Then she broke into a broad smile.

She said to herself, "The Greater has done this for you." I nodded, even though I had never said or even thought of it being the Greater. But I wasn't agreeing to please her. For some reason, I nodded as if I myself had the same thought and had found it to be true. From the moment he called my name. His voice alone made the black being tremble.

"It is hard to explain because it is so penetrating. Every part of me feels renewed," I said as she listened intently.

"You don't understand how much of a mercy this is to me. I have written to your father every night begging him to make haste. Pleading that by some miracle you would be able to be done with this. Oh, my son. All I have is thanks to give you. All I can ask is for your forgiveness. You have reason to hate me and your father. It is our doings that have made this your reality." She dropped her head in shame. I took her hand across the table and comforted her.

I said sweetly, "There will be a time for confessions of anger, but for now I am hungry and glad to be with my mother." She grinned and laughed softly. She proceeded to pull out of her basket whole, steamed potatoes, green beans, and sliced ham. I breathed through my nose and melted into my chair. For the first time since the beginning of this, food felt restoring and satisfying. I devoured all of mine, finishing almost before she'd finished serving herself.

"Please, eat more! I would be happy if you ate it all," she said, handing me the spoon for the beans. I obeyed her gladly.

"Have you heard anything from Father?" I asked. The night was soft and although there was joy in my miracle, the looming knowledge of my father's deals hadn't vanished. She sat down her utensils, wiped her mouth with a napkin, and adjusted herself in her seat.

"Yes, I have. He's been in the Polished Ring, Area One for the past three weeks. The preparation for the Sovereign Days are very extravagant there. He's had much business which has been very consuming. He hasn't said much more than that." I knew she was being honest. I nodded as if satisfied with the answer. "How much longer do you think this will take you?" she asked, changing the conversation.

"At this rate, I'll be done by the end of the week. I'm going to take them to Captain Allester as soon as I can before he and Lord Arres get ideas about being greedier," I said, scraping the last crumbs off my plate. I looked to my mother and although she had lived many years, none of them being easy, she was quite beautiful. She had the same hair color I did. Brown, sort of, but really it was black. I always found it was her eyes that remained bright and made her feel young and lively. Even in her stress and worry their crisp blue remained brilliant.

"That is remarkable. Your father is going to be bewildered!" She smiled and took my hand. She breathed slowly and intentionally. As if finding every breath to be precious. It was silent for a few minutes.

"Adinorium!" Amos rushed through the door.

"Amos, are you alright?" Mother said as she stood up. Amos had paused after bursting through the door. He looked terrified and pale though his cheeks were red from running in the cold night.

"Oh, thank the Greater," he said and rushed to embrace me, leaning his tired weight on me. He held on tighter than I believed he ever had. I sat down the dagger on the table and hugged him equally. "Adalric told me. I came as soon as he did. I had to see with my own eyes that you weren't dead on the floor holding a half-finished sword in your hand." He examined a very different person than he had left last night.

"A fair belief, but the sword would have been finished," I said.

"Don't ever almost die like that again!" he demanded, finally gathering himself.

"I will try my best." I smiled, sitting back down in my chair.

Amos said, "Hello, Mrs. Durnin!" He hugged my mother too.

"Hello, Amos." She grinned happily at his joy. "Would you like whatever my son did not devour?" It was only a single potato that I was still contemplating eating.

"That'd be lovely. I'm famished." He took her offer and put an end to my contemplation. "It's been insanity at the practice today. Three men all with deep sword wounds from duels all came in and bloodied up everything! Yooldee had to leave after being summoned about two others for the same injury. I swear there will be no one to fight for king if they all wound themselves before then." Amos ranted in a complete swing of emotions.

"I'll put on some tea." My mother was quick to find a remedy for my friend's rush of nerves.

"Wonderful idea, Mother." I was standing to assist Amos. "Here, Amos, sit down." I took his hand guiding him to my seat. "Are you sure you're okay?"

"No, Nori! I was anticipating that you were going to die today! I still don't understand what on this land has happened." He rested his head against the back of the chair and rubbed his eyes. I smirked at his statement and took the chair across from him. I wasn't making fun of his ignorance. I was just glad that I had the problem of explaining a miracle. My mother stood by the kettle she'd placed in the fire and was waiting along with Amos to hear more of this dream.

"After you'd left, I went to sleep. At least, I think I was asleep. But I had a dream. I haven't had a dream in a long time, but never have I had a dream like this before. It was alive. In my dream I was in the king's garden and I saw a snake. It was slithering away quickly when I was distracted by the call from a servant to the king. The servant was warning that waters were beginning to flood the kingdom. It was pouring rain, which I swear I could feel and, as the servant said, the water was rising. There was also a large door in the wall that was opened, but not big enough to stop the flooding. When I looked back at the snake, it was entering the woods. So, I followed it."

Amos added, "Naturally."

"The snake led to Thann who was under a structure of some sort. Anyways, a voice called my name, but I couldn't see them because of the rain. Thann yelled and I rushed over to find that the snake had killed him. It was then I learned that it was Thann," I paused thinking of the black being. I was still afraid of the thought of him now. Regardless of my fear I continued, but almost in a whisper. "A black being, it came from the shadows. It stood over him in disappointment. Then he looked to me. He had the most terrifying presence. He said I would be a fitting follower. One for another. I have no idea what he intended to do with me, but before he could, the same voice that called my name rebuked him. The black being fled. Then I woke up and my body was healed," I finished. I was rubbing my thumb against the palm of my hand. My mother stood behind Amos' chair awestruck by the story. We were all silent, no one knew exactly what to say about such a thing.

"I'll get it!" my mother said after the kettle had been squealing for a long moment.

"Do you think it was a prophecy?" Amos said quietly from across the table so my mother wouldn't hear.

"I don't know," I whispered in reply. "I hadn't thought of that." Was this a foreshadow of Thann's death? Of Strength's fate? Adalric was right, it sounded like Old History.

"Tea?" My mother was holding the kettle out to us. She seemed a bit out of sorts.

"Yes, please." I moved my cup towards her.

"Thank you," Amos said after his mug was filled.

"Quite the dream," my mother said in a forced calmness. It was as if she knew something I didn't, and it made her fear greatly.

"Indeed, it was." I joined in making the dream pettier than it was. I looked to Amos who shared my suspicion of my mother's sudden change in demeanor. "Amos, would you walk my mother home? It is dark and I don't like her being alone," I said probably too abruptly.

"Of course! I need to be getting home too," he said. "Who knows the afflictions that will need mending tomorrow."

"I am very well to walk by myself. Thank you for your willingness, Amos," she said, putting on her coat and not even bothering to take her basket. "I'll be back tomorrow," she said assuredly.

"I will be anticipating your coming back happily," I said. I disagreed with her confidence to walk home by herself. I was learning more that Allester and our lords find nothing and no one out of their reach. Despite my desires, she left right after, taking nothing of the things she'd brought.

"You're really renewed?" Amos asked, still struggling to believe it could be true.

"I am." I was still thinking of my mother.

"What do you think it means?"

"I have no idea. Did you know the Founder gifted

wisdom was an Arrogs?" I asked, remembering the headstone.

"Of course, Nori," he smiled. "We learned that in both the Old History and History in class." I nodded wondering what else I'd forgotten from those days.

Amos didn't stay much longer. We said very little actually. He now looked more tired than I did. Blood-stained spots of his clothes and his eyes dim. He agreed when I told him he needed to go home and sleep. He said something once more about his inability to understand all of it. I smiled and found delight in it. Although my body was healed, it was certainly still tired. However, I believe my eagerness to sleep was really a hope to be submerged in the story again. Taken away from this reality to another. I wanted to see him. In the least, hear him again. Whoever or whatever it was.

Chapter 8
The Tug of The Shift

The hammer's final blow met the blade. "Perfection" as my father would say lifting his work. That used to sound like arrogance to me. Now, I'd say it was less of arrogance and more of an obsession with the beauty in which he held. Yes, he formed the blade but the iron strong and bright is what wouldn't be matched or made by hand. The miracle Captain Allester told me to beg for had been given to me. Unfortunately, more dreams had not. Four days had passed since that night. Not only had my body been restored but the days seemed to be stretched out longer to compensate. Taking the final sword in hand, I examined it thoroughly. At some point I had stopped scrutinizing the blade and started to think of what had happened. It began years ago when my father spoke vaguely to my mother over dinner of some gathering. That ignited in me the desire to know what was hidden. To be a part of something more. To be a part of greater things. It was no longer about shows and swords, but secrets and shadows. As time progressed, the gatherings became more and more, yet the idea of them less. In the year of the Sovereign Days and Last

Days Feast, my father left instantly after a meeting or show in File and Rank to be gone for weeks. That left me, who simply burned for something more, with the front line of defense. Guarding a prize I did not know. Naturally, a tax was due and nearly completed before evil itself set a trap disguised as honor. By miracle or hallucination of no pain I had defended that line. Although I'd argue it was also overstepped. That is all this was. A line being placed and overtaken for a new line to be made pretending it was still the first. My mother had come and left dinner, but she never spoke of the dream or father or anything that required pondering.

"I don't understand," Phoebus said when he came to visit me.

"Thank the Greater we don't have to. But look at me! I am stronger than when I first began!" Phoebus nodded. He didn't settle with joy like Adalric, Amos, and I had. I had yet to speak to Amos about our common conclusion of what all of this was for after we'd been given time to think about it more completely. Adalric hadn't visited and I had begun to worry for him. Amos told me Adalric hadn't left his home since he met with the author. Whether he was eternally broken or deeply inspired no one knew.

Most of the day was already gone and the sky was becoming a deep orange. I had carefully wrapped all of the blades, preparing to take them to Allester tomorrow. I decided I would take whatever swords I could carry to the Bolg on my way home tonight, bringing the rest tomorrow. It wasn't necessarily the smartest idea knowing Allester could send his men to steal swords to sabotage me in the night, but at this point I decided to have a little faith and go on as planned. Besides, he had been keeping watch of me this whole time already. The door to the Bolg stood open as both drunk guards and clear minded ones still swept in and out just as busily as they did during the day. I walked in being met by the smell of sweat, soured bread, and fermented juice. A group of men stood swaying like worn-legged miners singing some song none of them knew well. I suppose this is what the end of the week brings to the Bolg. Allester sat at one of the long tables straight to the back, writing on a stack of papers unconcerned with the noises and actions around him. I was surprised to find him in the common place. Disregarding his business, I dropped the bundle of swords directly on his papers.

"And I'll bring the rest in the morning." I didn't smile but carried myself like a man hardened by life and unafraid of any other. Allester elegantly returned his pen to its ink and unraveled the covering of one of the swords. He examined the blade and laid it down before him. I was disappointed by the lack of shock and anger on his face. I wanted to see his forehead wrinkle when his brows lifted and his chapped lips bleed when split apart.

"I was told to find errors in the blades if you were, by miracle, to complete them all. I told them there was little hope there would be any, if you were to complete them all. They insisted and guaranteed me the opposite. Unfortunately for them, they will stand corrected. It's undeniable that the Greater blessed your hands. And when it comes to matters he involves himself in, I avoid invoking anger," Captain Allester said of the blade as if it were his own. His blue eyes were clear and sure of what he said. The way he spoke his words with bliss and power uneased me. "I will say, Durnin, you seem much better than the state I'd last seen you in. I began to worry about you. Considered ending all of this for you. For some reason my confidence remained." His confidence. I had no tolerance for his confidence. His slender hands clasped in front of him. His whole person was bored with life.

"Why were you to find error? This is honorable tax?" I questioned. I was disgusted by our lords and king. I should've left and ignored him, but I was angry, my father's son, and desired to engage in his little taunting.

"Why?" he retorted, almost laughing to himself. "We both know why. Whether completely or in idea we both know why. For all things we could neither know more than the other. But neither of us can deny that something's making the winds shift softly and is forcing them to do so. Shadows and whispers can always be seen and heard, Durnin." I lifted my chin in response to his provoking ideas. I agreed with him entirely and that made my heart fear. I felt the shift he spoke of. I feel it in my father's tone, in my mother's concern, in Magnar's choice of word. Those are all close to me though. But, when Captain Allester shares the shifting tug, this is a new addition to feeling the wind. Yes, I could feel, but now I can touch and hear.

"I'll be back in the morning," I said, beginning to see myself out as quickly as I can.

Captain Allester called after me, "Durnin!" I turned but spoke nothing. "Truly, your work is impressive." I nod, unable to give thanks. It still felt like a threat when he gifted me kindness.

Walking through the streets I didn't skip and sing as I thought I would. I walked with a nerve that made me look over my shoulder whenever I heard a sound and when I heard no sound at all. I was settled and happy about completing both the bondage tax and the honorable tax. As if I believed that would fix all of my problems. I held the line, and my battle was over. But Allester was quick to remind me that Thann and his lords play with life. To them the toil that killed my body was a signature on a piece of paper. A simple attempt to defeat their dragon. I wasn't even the one they were looking at or anticipating. As if they'd forgotten my name amidst the hunt. The anger I thought I had overcome returned to me. I wasn't even allowed to be satisfied for more than a day. Sure, I was given a miracle, but greater things still had everyone's heads turned. It would be no different had I died on the forge's dirt floor after all. I go through the square quickly. Even now there were more people in town than I was used to there being. I don't think I enjoyed the crowds. They made me feel like strangers were coming into my home, but the door was stuck open, and I couldn't stop them from entering. I had no desire to interact with any of them, so the ground was an easy place to rest my eyes. Soon these same streets would be filled with music and dancing, stories, and fire. I remembered it faintly in my memory. There was more joy then. A large banner had been hung on the front of some of the buildings in the square reading "The Chronicles of Strength". It seemed to be a play of sorts to celebrate the day of when we honored Strength. That made me wonder about my dream and how it seemed like something from the Old History. I knew of the Old History because of my parents, my mother mainly, but I'd forgotten the details of it. My father believed in the Old History, but he didn't speak much of it. He, along with my mother, spoke as if we still lived in that way. With the Greater and the prowling darkness and the Bountiful Lands and the prophecy.

"Please forgive me!" she said after she'd run into my body. Her nose hit my shoulder. I felt much worse for her. It seemed I was busy looking at the ground while she was busy looking up to the sky. I had just crossed the Fordwin when her whole person collided with mine.

"Please don't apologize. I should've been paying more attention." I attempted to take the blame.

She argued, "I equally could say the same."

"No, if anything we should actually all be looking to the heavens and everything else is the distraction," I said, sounding like Adalric. Although I did not know her name, I knew I'd remember her. She was handsome and in a way alluring. Not because of some elevated features or exuberance. She was a bit taller than average, sure, but not much. Her hair was a rich brown and laid in waves. I couldn't tell where she was from. I assumed Conservative being that she was here. You could tell she would have dimples if she smiled, although I hadn't made her yet. Her eyes were the same pale green as Amos' eyes. But where his were dim, hers were bright and had a certain fierce wonder I hadn't seen.

"A philosopher who looks at his feet," she said, looking up to me.

"I'm no philosopher. I'm a simple person, who goes about business like everyone else," I said in a tone more bitter than I meant. She raised her brow, clearly not believing me.

"I see. Well, again my apologies. Perhaps now we can both be of simple business and look ahead as we continue on our way." She smiled politely and sure enough she had faint dimples. I grinned and nodded my head in agreement. She brushed past my shoulder in obedience to our decision.

"I'm Adinorium," I added before she was too far gone.

"Adinorium," she paused as if she'd known the name before. "Pleasure to meet you." Her words didn't match her expression. It seemed more troublesome than a pleasure to meet me.

"And your name?" I asked under my breath knowing she was too far away to hear. Although it had been of no benefit to run into her, she had momentarily distracted my mind from its seething. I decided to take that opportunity and be glad for the finished labor. Even if it had no meaning to any other, I was relieved of the toil.

Seeing my home felt like finding a shaded place in the desert. I hadn't realized how much I missed it, not just the shelter it provides. I needed to speak to Amos about Allester's words. A childish part of me wanted to tell him about the girl I had run into. I don't know what I wanted to say. There was really nothing to tell. I wished there were wildflowers along the road for me to pick for my mother, but by this point the brumal season had stolen them all.

"Mother?" I questioned opening the door to find empty rooms. It wasn't the grand entrance I was hoping for, but the fire and smell of pine sufficed. I assumed my mother had gone to sleep. Which I was glad for. I took my time alone and bathed before changing into clothes that had been washed before being worn for a third and fourth time. I wasn't able to completely rid my hands of the black that had built upon them, but progress was made in mending them. Maybe Amos or my mother had some cure to remedy stained hands. I returned to the main room and found a seat in my father's chair. It still smelled of him, like deep in the woods, when every tree, plant, and flower is grappling for the most prominent perfume.

"Son!" my mother exclaimed. She was coming through the back door. My heart stammered seeing her. I wasn't sure what to make of it as she walked over to embrace me.

"Why do you smell like smoke from a fire?" I was concerned by the oddity of her being out at this time of night, coming through the back door meaning the woods, instead of through the front meaning she would have come from the road.

"It doesn't matter. Look at you! Cleaned up and refreshed. Is everything done?" she said, leading us back into the living room. I knew she had lied to me about the importance of smelling like fire and coming from the woods by her lonesome.

"All of the swords are complete. Tomorrow I'll have to take the rest of the blades to the Bolg," I said. I now sat on the larger sofa feeling I no longer had the freedom to sit in my father's chair.

"I really can't believe it." She smiled and for the first time in weeks I saw her relax herself. I shared her happiness, thankful that she knew of my toil.

"Neither can I," I assured her.

"Did Allester have anything to say?" she questioned remembering it was to him I had to answer. I briefly contemplated telling her of his threats and knowledge, but I decided I would tell a little lie of my own.

"Not really. He was a bit surprised, nothing more than that," I said smoothly as if it were the truth itself.

"I see. That's good." Now she forced a smile and returned to her state of nerves. "What am I doing! You must be famished!" Sitting up quickly, she began to rush to the kitchen.

"Mother! Calm yourself. I'm perfectly alright." I grabbed her hand to still her. She realized her nerves and worry. More so she realized I was perfectly aware of them.

"Can I at least get you some tea and bread?" she offered, holding her delicate hand to her head.

"Yes, that'd be good," I said as softly as I could. I was becoming more concerned for her. This constant peak of emotions and worry would not be able to be managed for so long before she fell from that peak. I got wood for the fire while she prepared something for me. I looked all around but saw no fire that was near or far from here. Where had she come from and why was there fire? Returning inside, she brought me brown bread and tea with hickory. "Thank you, Mother."

"Of course." She remained standing awkwardly before requesting to retire for the night.

I calmly affirmed her, "Please do! I will be here if you need me."

"Thank you. And I, if you need me," she said, speaking softly. She closed her door and left me again to the fire, my thoughts, and an overwhelming sense that nothing was as it should be. I wanted to visit Adalric and hear all that had happened to him. I needed to see Phoebus and see if they had managed to complete their taxes or if they would. I missed them all. I was eager to tell Amaryllis of my completion knowing she'd take joy in it with me. But really, I thought of the meaning of all I had done. What silent war was being waged? Whether it was Thann being king, or my father being his betrayer. Either would overwhelm one's being to complete drunkenness in thought.

Chapter 9
The High Captain - Garvish Saxon

I slept for half of the day. I knew because the sun rays were over top of my home and not striking through my window. I hated this abundance of sleep in many ways, but I had to force this exception on myself considering the lack of rest I'd had for the past weeks. I could hear Amaryllis in the kitchen talking to my mother. Instead of the whispers I'd become familiar with I heard laughter. She sounded happy. I grinned having no idea why she was in such a mood, but I was glad for it. "Good morning, girls," I said, leaning against the door frame leading to the kitchen.

"He lives! Your mother told me everything! I am amazed by such a thing! Forgive me for not coming to see you all the sooner." Amaryllis frowned. I put my arm over her shoulder like we were small children at play while we watched my mother prepare pastries with cherry centers.

"No need to apologize. I am glad you have kept watch of my mother."

"She is my mother, too. And I should be sorry. Thank you for your graciousness though."

"How'd you sleep, son?" Mother asked happily. It was evident that Amaryllis put her at ease.

"Very well. I am very grateful for it."

"Yes! Sleep is a lovely thing. But I prefer being awake. That is the only time we really have the chance to live," Amaryllis said, hugging my waist with one arm and holding my hand over her shoulder with the other.

"Why so happy?" I finally asked, looking down at her.

"Because you are well and the Sovereign Days are nearly here which means dancing, and too much food, lovely gowns, and happy girls!" she said using my hand to spin herself around.

"Oh, is that why?" I said as if that would never have been the answer. "I hadn't realized it was so close." I furrowed my brows not feeling the joy of celebration I had felt a month ago when thinking of the coming days. I stuck my finger in the cherry jam and licked it before my mother could hit my hand with her spoon.

"You know the first time I noticed Magnar was during the Sovereign Days," Amaryllis said with giddy excitement. I hadn't realized she enjoyed them so much. I suppose it isn't something we talked about often. And when we did speak of them, it was never celebration. It was always only weight and worry. Never really had a need to. I began to try and remember how that last one ended.

"What? You could have been but a literal baby," I asserted, confused by the way her mind worked and what she remembered. She was the same age as me, but her birthday was earlier in the year.

"Even then he stood out."

I scoffed, "Yes, because of how terribly annoying he was at five."

"Terribly handsome!" she protested. "You know he is good to the eyes."

"And terrible for the head!"

"Nori," my mother said not in complete annoyance but like a mother does when a child says something they really shouldn't.

"Leave me my romantics, Nori," Amaryllis said, following my lead with her finger finding its way into the cherry jam.

"Enough of you little thieves stealing my jam!" my mother said, shooing us away.

Amaryllis kept on, "Perhaps this year someone will stand out to you." It felt like she mocked me standing on the far side of the room.

"Oh please. Spare me your heart shaped perspective." I crossed my arms and leaned against the counter.

"Now, Nori, a woman is good for grounding a man. He needs emotional connection to remind him that he is, in fact, a living person. A woman is good for helping the man. Whether that is by raising children, keeping a home, or coming alongside him in whatever his venture. She is good for protecting the man, in more ways than you know. I could go on, rambling about all the other amazing things in having a woman: a loyalist, a lover, a greatest friend. But I suppose I will restrain myself. I don't want you to be too embarrassed when you have to confess to me that I was right." Amaryllis stood with her arms tucked behind her, as cushion for her back against the wall.

"Amaryllis-" I began my argument before my mother interjected.

"She isn't wrong. Having a wife wouldn't be a bad thing."

"The both of you can keep your giddy ideas and I will do my best to entertain the pair of you. Now, is there any way I could get one of these delectable pastries in my mouth before I finish making the impossible, possible." I announced, although I really was far from the praise of the claim I made. Without intervention, I would be far from this place.

"Oh lands! That is quite the task," Amaryllis said playfully.

"Only because I love you," my mother said, kissing my cheek and handing me one of the delicacies. I raised my brows quickly and happily ate away at the luxury. I spared no time in leaving with all hopes of taking this weight off my shoulders. I had to choose to take joy in what was accomplished and not in the deeper circumstances I found myself in.

Amaryllis walked with me to the forge wanting to get a few things for her and my mother. Everything had been untouched since the evening before. I was pleased, but, for some reason, I was not surprised. I felt as if I should've been because this was a golden opportunity to destroy that which I'd done. In other words, I wasn't used to things being as they should be.

"Do you miss him?" I asked Amaryllis while loading all the swords in a small wagon. It was an old one belonging to Amos' father. He had used it for gardening until he supplied himself a new one. My mother called it a kind gesture, I called it a play. He gifted it to us only a week after Amos' mother left them and Amos had stayed with us the prior weeks. I suppose it has proved to be useful and in that since I'm grateful.

"Yes."

"I suppose he is handsome," I said, suddenly feeling bad about my poor intentions. I had no need to create more division between them. I just couldn't understand why she married him. He was handsome. But that wouldn't have been enough for Amaryllis. His hair was a shade lighter than mine, but still a darker brown than most others. His chin was sharp and he had a faded beard that made him look strong but not as if he was going to push over a tree with his bare hands. He did have a faint scar on his forehead hidden by the few curls that hung just above his brows. That was done by my hands. The only physical display that he could be wounded. The sad thing is that it happened the one time I wasn't trying to hurt him. We were boys, climbing a tree. I was a limb above him. A weak branch broke under my foot and my heel rammed into his forehead. He didn't fall or cry or even whimper. But he was angry. Very angry.

She answered, "Yes, he very much is." She was holding her basket in front of her, prepared to go to the square.

"Your children will be beautiful I'm sure," I said, picking up the last handful of swords. She looked up towards the sky as if to see something unusual.

"Our children. Yes, they will be marvelous," she said, letting her eyes linger on the above. Looking to the heavens. A good thing to do. I interrupted whatever she was imagining by telling her I was headed to Bolg.

"And I am off to the school house. I have something for Deago."

"Tell her I said hello." I said. Deago was a gingerly lady who began teaching shortly after Mrs. Ivory left.

"Very good. I will see you when we meet again. Be safe, Norium," she said with a newfound tone of seriousness for the morning.

"And to you be steady," I said, assuring her that I would be wise. At least, that I'd attempt to be so.

***

The Bolg looked abnormally busy, but I needed to get my business done. I left the wagon outside and went to find Allester.

"Is Captain Allester here?" I asked a young soldier who seemed to be the closest to me with some brains. It always surprised me how little I interacted with all of the soldiers. I just never found the time nor the need. I also didn't really understand them. Our worlds were so entirely different.

He replied, "No, he left early this morning and should be returning soon." I nodded, thanked him, and went outside to wait. I sat against the wagon and threw stones I found sifting through the dirt. Unraveling a scarf that had been tied around a loop in my pants, I placed it over my face to block all the people around me. Today felt different. The sun was actually providing warmth to me. It didn't take long before I was awakened by a kick to my boot. I was hardly removed from my long days and sleep still summoned me. I pulled the scarf from my eyes and for a long moment could see nothing. Once my eyes adjusted to the light, I saw it was the captain standing over me as I'm sure he always feels like he's doing.

"Get up, Durnin," he said with an undertone of urgency. I obeyed and was quick to remark.

"Captain, I was just coming to bring you the rest of the tax."

"Hush. Stand straight and be alert." Like one of his own, I followed what he said.

"Pick up a bundle of these swords and go to place them inside. You never came to see me last night and you are just now delivering every one of the swords." Allester didn't even look at me while he spoke. His words didn't match anything he was presenting. Oddly, I believed I should do as he instructed. Picking up a bundle I followed his orders, joining the new swords with the ones I'd brought yesterday. Coming back out to my wagon I saw Allester was now accompanied by a Polished man. I knew he was Polished for two reasons, his attire and his air. Together disclosed the most inexcusable reality of someone who is Polished.

"Saxon, this is the son of Kane Durnin, Adinorium. Adinorium, this is Saxon, the high captain of Area Four. He is Lord Arres' highest ranked commander," Allester introduced the well-aged man. He seemed to be poorly kept and like he should be more handsome than he really was. He was proud, and his lack of smiles portrayed his constant distaste and superiority. He matched Allester in some of those characteristics, however the captain also seemed to have a difficult time being beneath this man.

"An honor, I'm sure." I nodded and stuck out my hand

for him to shake. He accepted my offer with an overly aggressive grip and no eye contact.

"Be more than assured," he growled.

"These are the swords?" Allester interrupted to ask. He undid the cloth I'd wrapped around one of them and lifted it to the sun. He examined it for himself then passed it to the high captain, Saxon.

"Yes sir. The order in full. They're all of fine iron and without error. I do hope Lord Arres approves and is pleased with the completion," I said, standing with strong posture and assurance. I didn't want to speak with all of their formalities, but it was a part of my cunning. Speak in their language and they'd better understand you. Saxon gripped the blade and examined it shortly.

"Any fault?" Captain Allester asked after Saxon returned the blade to him.

"Most impressive, Mr. Durnin. The dedication and determination you must possess to produce an abundance of such fine work, with so little time, done alone is most impressive. As I'm not mistaken you were alone?" High Captain Saxon questioned. Both men looked at me with squinted eyes from the sun. It seemed a common trait of these kinds of men to compliment sweet as a flower with questioning evil as a thorny stem.

"Yes, my father has gone to some shows accompanied by my brother," I said in all innocence, as it should be.

"I see. Do you know when he is to return? I have a small prize dagger to receive from him," High Captain Saxon questioned.

"I'm not sure. I've seen the dagger. It will be ready in a short time," I answered his request. I had to clench my jaw so it wouldn't drop. There was something significant in my father making this blade. The timing and questioning all screamed of something deeper. An interesting buyer my father was selling too. Why wouldn't Father want me to know of him? Aside from his close relation to Lord Arres there is nothing significant about it. I wonder when they had met.

"The swords are satisfactory," High Captain Saxon admittingly stated. He fixed his hat under his arm and began to take off his gloves. "Get your men to finish unloading the swords and return the wagon to Mr. Durnin's forge, Allester. I believe Mr. Durnin has earned the assistance and a drink. Please, Mr. Durnin, join me." Allester obeyed reluctantly. Not that the orders were harsh or difficult but that they were uttered by Saxon. I wanted to decline the offer and would feel much happier to finish my work and know the forge wasn't going to be torn to pieces or burned to the ground in the meantime. Seeing that wasn't going to be a suitable alternative, I joined the prestigious pair inside.

"Saxon? People of the dagger?" I asked the Polished man. He and I along with Captain Allester had been shown to a room on the second floor of the Bolg. It was a dark room with a fireplace and many beast skins. It had thick furniture and was lit by fire even though it was mid day. It seemed to have no use aside from a place to lounge. The second floor of the Bolg hadn't been like it was described to me. Coming up the stairs, I was met with a hallway. Four doors on the right, a window across from each of them, nothing more.

"Yes, you know your families?" he asked, pouring a mixture of blush liquid into a small glass.

"Not massively, just particularly. I've heard the name as a smith. Your family is the only line to work with gold?" I continued.

"Precisely. A beautiful history. My forefather was the first to arrive after our Founders. After everything was established, gold was found in the mountain. It had been decided that only the line of kings should be taught to work with gold, but Hildry Saxon, who was loved by the Founders, insisted it should be given to others. They brought the best smiths to construct a small blade to determine which family line would be given the honor of goldsmith and undoubtedly Hildry's was the finest. It has never left my family line," he said fondly of his history, as he should. Not every detail would be able to hold weight; but, nonetheless, they were interesting. I wondered why he'd be getting a dagger made by my father if his family could make one apparently far superior.

"Yes, riveting history," Allester complimented coldly. In a way, his words were correct, but his tone gave away the fact he couldn't care any less.

"Why aren't you a smith? Being a high captain is most impressive, but an interesting trade?" I questioned. Saxon raised a brow and cleaned the rim of his glass with his finger.

"I have four brothers, three above and one below, I found no need to perfect a trade when so many others were eager to. Arres has always been a good friend to me, and when the offer came around, I was most ready to take it. Although, I have no doubt I would have been a wonderful smith." He didn't even attempt to cover up his arrogance. The root of Allester's hatred was also revealed. No doubt the captain would have had a fighting chance to become the high captain, and yet this "friend" of Lord Arres was simply offered.

"Undoubtedly. We need to continue on with the orders Lord Arres sent for you. Durnin, unfortunately that means your leave." Allester hurried us along. I was thankful for the first time for the captain's bluntness and distaste for me. I stood ready to take my leave but High Captain Saxon spoke a little too quickly.

"Take his leave? By no means. Please, Durnin, stay. An opportunity to observe the intentionality and brilliance of our king and lords." Saxon slowed his speaking in emphasis to his words. An interesting arrangement as well. It felt like less of a compliment to King Thann and more of a threat by him.

"Garvish, let us use our own wits and brilliance and not allow our vanity and fear determine our ways," Captain Allester refuted. Saxon inhaled ragefully. I could hear him swallow from where I stood feet away and was trying my best to not show my nerves. This was a most unique opportunity. The witness of conflicting powers. I felt more than ever my need for my father. More than every night my feet stung of pain and my hands bled from use. I needed to tell him everything and understand more. I quickly weighed what was best to do next. Any other time I would have felt the confidence to stay and gather whatever information I could. I would feel the confidence to hold my character and leave no trace of a play of faces. This time I couldn't. I felt as if I stayed, I'd catch fire. I'd break and question and tell and only the Greater knows what else.

"With all due respect, this has already been such an incredible opportunity. I wouldn't want to hinder anything and believe me, I have already witnessed the brilliance of the king and lords," I said, snapping the cord of tension between the captain and high captain.

"Of course. Take your leave," Garvish demanded as politely as his kind could. I bowed a bit lower than normal and walked out carefully. I closed the door behind me and as soon as the doorknob had returned to normal, Allester began speaking.

"Why do you insist on being such a peacock! It's as if you want him to know!" Allester was one foot over the line of a controlled yell.

"Perhaps I do, Allester. He is young, he will break fast. Certainly he knows something," Garvish said more loosely than when I shared their presence.

"This one won't. I've tried to pick his mind, Arres tried to break his body, you've tried intimidation. Forget him. He will be of no help to you. You have other concerns like the union established in six and the split union." Allester's words sunk deep in my stomach. I stepped slowly backwards trying to reach the stairs without a board cracking giving away my presence.

"I have no concern for them," Saxon dismissed the thought. "Did you hear him descend the steps?" Saxon questioned having a small moment of revelation. My breath quickened while I heard Allester walk to the door. He pulled open the door in a cool, confident manner.

"You see, Garvish. Forget him," Allester remarked looking down the empty hall. I had found a place to hide outside of an open window. The door closed once more and I was quick to vanish from the Bolg and hoped never to return. Outside, my wagon was already gone. Hopefully it was being returned to the forge and not burned in the woods somewhere. My body was at a peak and my mind noticed everything. All felt like a potential threat, making me act accordingly. Doing my best to appear innocent, I made my way to the practice to find Amos. Soldiers were far more plentiful than I believed I'd ever seen in Chalmar. I'd imagine they were the personal men of Saxon. They all looked more intelligent and stronger than the other soldiers, but I wasn't sure if I was just imagining things.

"Nori, what's happened?" I was stopped by hands being latched onto my shoulders. Adalric had somehow evaded my sight, but I was most pleased to see him. "You seem afraid," he said, finding that to be some kind of an impossibility.

"I'm alright, Adalric. I need-" I started before he interrupted.

"I agree. Let's get you off the streets." He read my mind rightly, which I was thankful for.

I asked him, "Are there more men of the guard here than normal?" Adalric was now my gauge of reason.

"Yes, they came with a man named Saxon. He's the high captain of this area. Second only to Arres." It seemed Adalric had already heard of all this.

"Do you know why he's here?" I asked. Of course, I knew why he was here, but I wanted to hear what everyone else was saying.

"Some are saying it is common practice. Some say for Thann to know what faithfuls he has. However, most

Interesting was the opinion of a man who believed it's a bit more specific. He believed he's here to see you. I was actually on my way to find you when, oddly enough, I actually did." He pointed and we walked into the Hummer. "Here."

"Where are the others?" Mr. Doolby asked as soon as we stepped foot inside.

"Busy. Could we just get two spritz please?" Adalric requested. They conversed across half the room, but no one seemed to mind much. We sat in our corner, and I did my best to seem alright.

"Your spritz." Doolby sat them down at the table and paused as if with something to say.

"Thank you, Doolby." Adalric smiled politely trying to get him to move along.

He asked the pair of us, "That's it? Are you alright?"

"Perfectly!" Was the best I could manage. Doolby nodded, being summoned to another table. "What kind of man had such ideas?" I questioned. We spoke quietly and probably looked suspiciously serious, but I could do nothing more.

"I couldn't tell his relations. He didn't seem quite anything. Not kept quite enough to be Polished, quite too well off to be File and Rank, but a stranger to everyone making it next to impossible for him to be Conservative. I know I've never seen him before," Adalric explained.

"Who was he speaking to?" Surely something gives way to his knowledge.

Adalric went on, "Well, I don't know. Someone had mentioned Saxon and then they all started speaking of why they thought he was here. He didn't speak loudly, and no one acknowledged what he said. I may have been the only one who heard him."

"Did you acknowledge him?"

"No, I looked over at him but not fully. I left quickly because I had a stirring feeling he was right. After Allester, the whole sword shenanigans, and your father's absence, I know this High Captain Saxon wasn't coming to commemorate you. If he really *is* here for you." I sat back in my chair and felt my head spinning. Adalric hadn't touched his drink meaning he was nervous too.

"It's as if this man was intentionally warning you. Like he wanted you to come and intervene or something. Still, how would he know? Why would he know? Why would he want you to intervene?" Question after question flooded my mind. I didn't understand this. How did no one know him, or he knew to tell Adalric. Obviously, Saxon's own words were that this was all an attempt to break me. If I was right about my father's dealing, then this would make sense. Surely the reach of my enemy wouldn't stop at Allester.

"So, your father left someone to protect you from an unsuspicious distance," Adalric said after we both reasoned in our minds for a moment.

"I'd never considered that. But why would he go through you?" I followed.

"Unsuspicious distance. If he had gone to you directly, they'd be certain you knew something." Adalric had to explain to me.

"It is true. Saxon did come for me. But not to see me, to break me. At least, those were his words," I said leaning forwards resting my face against my clasped hands.

"So, you came from the Bolg?"

"Yes, from being in the pit of the snakes," I said, getting a distant look in my eyes. "Also, Saxon is having a blade made by my father. Naturally, that means I'll be making it. I have a suspicion that I need to go back to the forge and complete that as urgent business. I need to leave unconcerned and calm." I settled myself and finally felt like I could speak reason. I didn't give Adalric enough time to think through what I said.

"I think I'd just die if I were you, Nori. Too much of everything." Adalric relaxed back in his chair feeding off of my settled nerves. Then I remembered Adalric's meeting and his absences.

"I thought that you were still locked in your room, on fire, unknown if it was good or bad."

"Something like that." Adalric grinned and sat rocking his chair onto the back two legs. "I actually went out of town. I left a note to be delivered to Phoebus, but on returning home I realized he never received it."

"The meeting went well?" I asked. Glad to hear of someone other than myself. The Hummer was quiet at this time. It was mainly the older class of the town who still felt the need for someone else to make their tea.

"Yes, it went rather perfectly. She not only loved what I had but encouraged me that it could be even better. I'm going to be meeting with her again after the Sovereign Days to discuss publishing a book of poetry and such." Even though this was one of the craziest things Adalric has done, it tamed him. Perhaps it was the importance or the realness of it.

"Unfortunately for you, I can believe it! I'm very happy for you, brother. This is a good thing," I said, congratulating my friend. I loved Adalric for his poetry and his ability to romanticize life. It truly was a gift I did not possess. Hardly anyone possesses it really.

"I suppose it is." He smiled. "But you're the one who's defied death three times. Here's to you, friend!" He raised his glass to me.

"I've defied death for now anyways." I raised my glass and joined in the toast.

"I did need to tell you, Nori, that I was only okay to leave because I saw you were renewed or whatever had happened. I would never have left you in that terrible state."

"I believe you, Adalric. I'm glad you were able to go wherever you needed." I smiled.

"I will say, if I ever lose passion, I'll simply ask you to recount to me your woes. I would hardly have to dress them up to have something worth reading," he joked, making lighthearted my trouble. I needed him to do so. I felt as if I needed every possible thing to make me do so. If it weren't for Amaryllis' delight, Amos' loyalty, Phoebus' understanding, and Adalric's perspective I would have simply died just the same as he had suggested.

"I will surely do what I can," I said, and I meant it. To see him prevail was one of my life's greatest desires.

"So, what did Saxon have to say to you?" he asked. I'd almost forgotten that we hadn't spoken of that part. I said much to Adalric, but I usually ranted about my father's deals to Amos. I found that I hesitated for a moment before speaking.

"Nothing more than they usually have to say. Questioning my father's deals as if I'd know something." I sipped my spritz and did my best not to overreact thinking of Garvish and Allester's later conversation.

"Is he going to fight for king?"

"My father?" I was surprised by the question. Not because it was a bad one, I had just never thought of it. "I don't know." I confessed, "I don't know." I straightened my posture like it suddenly mattered. It shouldn't have struck me as it did. I had already determined my father's dealings.

"People would vote for your father. What else would threaten them so much?" Adalric said, resting his elbows on the table. I didn't answer. I didn't have to. He shared my gaze and, as if he'd read it from a book, he knew what I was thinking. "Oh, my lands," he whispered. "I don't think I'm able to believe that." I drank the rest of my spritz knowing in my mind it was true. I was on the other side. Incapable of believing it was anything else. Treason. Exposed and bloody. "Does your father know what you think?" Again, I hadn't thought of my father thinking that I knew. Last he knew, I was only suspicious and observing.

"If he does, he's in denial of it," I said truthfully. Adalric nodded.

"I'm sorry, Adinorium." He ran his fingers through his hair. "I don't know why you weren't destined to live a quiet life. Fall in love, raise a family, work hard, always going home at the end of the day. Clearly, that is not your path."

"Please, you don't have to apologize. You know I would have been driven half mad if that were my lot in life. The mundane wouldn't sit well with me." This was true. Adalric sat back, exhaled, and just smiled at me. "What!" I almost yelled after I felt stupid from his look.

"I just think you underestimate the wonder and adventure in the simple life. By simple I'm more referring to not almost dying weekly. But if you were to allow it, the mundane can possess the greatest things." I listened to his ideas. I don't know if I disagreed with it or just didn't understand it. Either seemed to be a real possibility.

"So says the poet," I said, now raising my glass to him. He smiled and joined me. We found many things to toast to within the hour.

"Might as well get together while we can before this Saxon or, even better, Allester takes your life," Adalric said, mocking the genuine reality.

"Here, three nights from this one?" I suggested. "That way Phoebus has plenty of time to plan to be here."

"I wholeheartedly agree! I'll tell Amos if you tell Phoebus."

"Very good!" He finished off his spritz, slamming his mug on the table like it was a chalice. "I am actually preparing something. Yes, so, that time will be good for me too."

"Oh really?" I asked, taking interest.

"Yes, but it is a secret still. Now you have a dagger that you need to go and chisel away at or however you whittle those blades into existence. Your life probably depends on it and you just don't know it yet." He smirked and I agreed.

"Put it on my tab, Doolby!" Adalric requested and we took our leave. He embraced me saying, "Keep your wits about you, aye Nori."

"Yes, and find your own sometime," I mocked, hugging him back.

"Be safe, friend." He bowed.

"And to you be steady," I answered. He was a good friend to me. Only a short while ago, I had been walking through town in danger of what I myself could have done. Adalric was the one who came to my aid and mended me. Not that I didn't have questions and wasn't still looking over my shoulder and avoiding looking directly at any of Saxon's men. But I felt stable again. I still questioned why they hadn't taken my father prisoner yet. What did they feel they needed to wait for? What knowledge did they think I possessed? Who was this stranger who clearly warned Adalric? When was my father going to return? When he did return, what would it be like? Waiting for the Sovereign Days felt like a match that had been lit and now I waited for it to burn out.

Chapter 10
Spoken and Unspoken

"Oh, thank the Greater!" I sighed, seeing the wagon had been returned to the forge in a single, untampered piece. I looked in all of the cracks and crevices to assure there was nothing left or stolen. Everything was as it should be. The crowd passing by was even at its normal pace. The day was cold, but not freezing. I had sufficient wood and iron for this specific dagger. Inside, at my father's desk, I plotted my actions. I wanted to bring this snake to life. Today, I would work on the dagger itself. Tomorrow, in steady detail, I'd craft the snake. It was intertwined in leaves as if hiding from an unsuspicious prey. If I was to be making a blade for a Saxon, then it was going to have to make his family's legacy look average. I forged the blade with anger and precision. I sculpted it with pride and perfection. It felt like my moment to show my own intentionality and brilliance to the king and his lords.

***

For the remainder of yesterday I worked on the dagger. Then, I took the long way home. That way leads through the meadow. I laid in its comfort and calmness until I was able to completely rid my mind of all thinking. Even in brumal the sun shines gold there. Home was how I'd left it. My mother and Amaryllis had spent the day straightening. Preparing for my father's return as he should be home before the Sovereign Days begins. Meaning, at any time one could look down the path and see a wagon pulled by two horses coming down the way. Along with our beloved Magnar, of course. I spoke nothing to my mother about Saxon and his threats. I found no need. This morning, I walked to the Fordwin alone. I was still eager to tell Amos of my visit with Allester and Saxon, but the time never presented itself for reasons I don't understand. I wasn't angry with the loneliness. I think I needed it more than I realized. Yes, I'd been alone for most of my time in the forge, but I was focused on the task at hand. I needed to listen to the stream and hear the sound of dead leaves cracking underfoot. I needed to simply be and not feel the strain of my world and all of its troubles. I'd been thinking about what Adalric said of a simple life. It was interesting because I never really thought of it as a bad thing. Afterall, that is the kind of life I want for Amos, Adalric, and Phoebus. Not because I don't think they could do anything more; I just think that's how they'd be happiest. Amos having his practice, Adalric sitting in some room with the windows open writing his poetry, Phoebus being able to remain in his routine. But I couldn't be satisfied. I'd always be wondering what greater things there could've been. Wondering what more there could be. I wanted to believe that I would learn to be satisfied with the mundane. With such a way of life as all generations have lived before me; but I think I know myself well enough to know I wouldn't be able to rest. If I couldn't find them, the greater moments, I'd always be searching. If I wasn't in them, I'd always be thinking of them.

Now I passed through town as a shadow. Unseen by anyone, being sure to be careful that I wasn't found out. I kind of liked feeling kindred to a secret. Like if they only knew, they'd all be staring at me. Allester stood outside of the Bolg yelling at some of his men for who knows what. I continued on, by grace, unhindered. Getting to the forge I felt a new familiarity with it. It had been more of my home in the past month then my own home had been. The smell of smoke and pine saturated its walls and its floor was dry dirt. Today, I fashioned the snake. Its curves and turns. It made me think of the snake coiled on Thann's chest that brought about his death. It was ironic but almost disappointing. His own kind brought him justice. Every being he'd wronged far from him.

I suppose my morning at the Fordwin and my daydreaming in the meadow were too sobering. I had no desire to finish the blade or even work towards its completion. At this moment I didn't even care that it belonged to Saxon or that my speed would impress him. I didn't care if his anger raged or his praises sung. I decided there was no need to hurry myself. I believed I had done that enough. I followed the same routine as I had yesterday. Going to the meadow and laying in the protection of the tall grass. I did this because of this untrue belief that if I wasn't seen, I was safe. I found the small head stone and saw the patch of flowers that had grown over the body of the man gifted wisdom, Heller Arrogs. I could hardly understand that his descendants were as they were. My enemies. I kicked stones down the dirt road all the way to my home. I looked above to see the clouds gray and circling. If I didn't know that it never rained here, then I would think it might. I had seen rain on this mountain, but it was only in a dream.

My house looked asleep. The fire was going but all of the curtains were drawn, and the windows closed. I began to hurry my pace, concerned by the oddity. Looking to the back, I saw my father's wagon. He had returned. It felt unreal. It had felt as if I was someone who'd been waiting to see the dead again. I was more than overjoyed, but I also felt cautious, reluctant even. The timing was almost insulting. I finished all of the work not but two days ago. Suddenly he'd returned? Him being home also meant all of Allester's threats would leave me. He's home, there's nothing to question. And if there was, they could ask him. The Sovereign Days would begin five moons from now. Was time acting as my friend or foe?

I opened the door slowly as if I was afraid to see what was behind it. The conversations didn't stutter, and I slipped through the door unnoticed. The wooden floor remained quiet as I took steps forward. They were conversing in the kitchen, meaning I could stay hidden by the wall. It was imprudent, being that they could appear at any moment finding me out. But I believed if I could overhear Captain Allester and High Captain Saxon, surely, I could remain unfound in my own home.

"How dangerous is it, Kane?" my mother asked my father. I heard concern in her voice, but more than anything, curiosity arose in me. How dangerous was what? She already knew what he was doing, I suppose the danger was now in what he'd do next. "Dara, you know the risk as much as I do. It's treason in every idea of the reality," my father said, his deep voice ringing in my ears. I hadn't heard it in so long.

"It wouldn't be treason, because you wouldn't be wronging a true king," Magnar rebuked. At the sound of his voice my body stiffened. I was angry that he was being trusted with these greater things. He was being trusted with the unknown while I was not. He would be trusted with a plan for treason. Knowing Magnar, the betrayal was probably his idea. But then again, no. At the root of it, it's far too noble a thing, bringing light to darkness, to summon Magnar's concern.

"Magnar." Amaryllis's kind self tried to temper him. Her kind heart had too been trusted with dangerous knowledge.

My father said calmly, "Steady yourself, Magnar. There will be a day when you can use your might for something greater." I never trusted Magnar, but my father did. That brought a measure of conviction to me, that if I was to ever really need Magnar, he would be there for me.

"Fidel brought the final proof of our concern, and we now have justice convinced." My father continued. Fidel? That was the first time I had heard his name. I could hear my mother breathing deeply. I wanted to go in and comfort her. Rebuke them for bringing such agony to her. I had to trust my father was remorseful enough by what he'd brought about.

"And when it's done?" my mother asked the only logical question.

"We will bury the snakes," Father said on the verge of coldness. I didn't like the sound of his voice like that. It felt rageful and dark. Like an impure motive even if it is a worthy cause. He then broke their moment of silence. "When will Adinorium be home?" It was as if they had all stopped and were weighing all the new realities that could come from this.

"I wouldn't know. He's now working on something else. I don't understand how he's still going," she paused. "It was too far, Kane. It was too much." She was my defender.

"I know, love." I imagined he had taken her hand and rubbed it gently. Trying to soothe her anger or anxiety, whichever she felt.

"You didn't have to see him though. See your son beaten and keep going for your sake. You didn't have to hear him rage and be justified. You didn't have to watch him gather his things and almost wish that he was choosing to run away!" I could hear Magnar's heavy steps starting to move towards the living room. Naturally, he'd be the first to curse my labor.

He scoffed, "It was the lightest burden of us all." Just before he appeared through the door frame, I opened and closed the front door loudly.

"Magnar." I do nothing more than acknowledge him. He looked me up and down but couldn't even muster the respect to reply. But I knew he had no suspicion of me.

"My son!" My father celebrated me. He came and embraced me at the door. I said nothing but rested in his safety. All of my anger and bitterness tempered. In some ways, I wanted it to stay so I'd recall all of my pains and agonies of both body and mind. However, I knew this was best. "How I've missed you." He was holding my shoulders and looking intentionally in my eyes. The house felt more somber now. The oddity of closed windows and low flames now felt more guarded and restful. He clarified. "I'm eager to hear everything."

"Amaryllis and I must be going," Magnar interjected. He had no use in hearing of my ventures. No time to listen to what his brother spent his days doing.

"So soon? You're welcome to stay for dinner," Mother encouraged. I didn't look at Magnar, but Amaryllis. She was looking at Magnar expectantly, but she did not dare speak a word knowing his answer fully.

"Not tonight. Thank you, Mother," he replied more graciously than I expected. "Father." he nodded, making his leave.

My father nodded, "Son."

Amaryllis was doing her best to smile. "Thank you for the invitation! I'm sure we will be back soon."

"I'm happy you're home," she said to my father who returned the compliment. Their leaving made the home surprisingly quiet. My mother brought tea to the living room. I sat on the sofa, legs on the ground and back straight. My mother sat on the far side of the sofa from me, her legs tucked up beside her. My father sat in his chair. The rightful king of it had returned.

"Before you tell me of all of your days, son, I do want you to know that I'm sorry. I wanted to come home more than anything. Every day I hoped would be the day we left. Only the Greater knows why it wasn't. But do know, son, I hated leaving you here. Leaving you to the beasts of Allester and Saxon." He looked intently at me, but my mind wasn't thinking of the kindness of an apology, it was thinking of what he said. I hadn't told him of Saxon. I didn't tell my mother of Saxon for her to relay to him. He knew. I had only a moment to decide if I should confront it or let it be.

"I wished the same. Thankfully, by whatever miracle, the beast laid quiet," I calmly said. I proceeded to recount all of my happenings to my father. Namely the finished tax, Allester giving us the new one, my work from there, then I told him my dream. Every detail, the snake, the gravestone, the rain, the servant, the rising waters, the open door, the absent king, the woods, my following, my name being called, the yell, the dead man, the coiled snake, the black being, the terror, and the revival it gave me. Frustratingly it was hard to keep anything to myself.

"It was raining?" he questioned. He had a similar response to my mother. It was curious, but I didn't exactly understand why. The thought of my father questioning the weather as he had with Saxon crossed my mind.

"Yes, pouring. The main reason I knew I had awoken was because I was dry. I could've sworn that I had actually become wet." I smiled at myself in the ridiculousness of it all.

"Who else have you told of this dream?" he asked next. I intentionally showed concern on my face, I wanted him to know that I was questioning his interrogation.

I answered plainly, "Amos, Adalric and Phoebus."

"I think it'd be wisest if it remained that way." Clearly, he was demanding more than requesting. All I could think of was, yet again, I would have to surrender and trust him.

"Very well." I was choosing obedience.

"Tell me about the High Captain Saxon," he requested,

skipping to the end of my accomplishment. Looking at my mother, she seemed unbothered by the question. At least, in the regards of my father's ungrounded knowledge. For her sake I decided I'd wait. Wait until it was my father and myself alone to ask how he knew. I spoke directly to my father in retelling the story. I wanted to see his every reaction, see the way his mouth shifted after different elements. Impressed by the idea, he asked, "They took you into their own chamber?"

"Yes. I asked about Saxon's family. He then happily told me of all their accomplishments and history. The captain hurried us along and insisted I leave. Saxon insisted I stay. He wanted me to witness the brilliance and intentionality of the king and his lords," I said slowly, reminding myself of the fear I felt being in their domain. "The captain rebuked him saying they should not act in vanity and fear. There stretched a line of tension so strong you could tangibly see it. I felt as though I could have burst into flames or broken into a million tiny pieces." I wanted my father to question why. Question my knowledge of anything. But he didn't. He simply continued to listen. "'Perhaps I do, Allester.'" I was telling of the moment I stayed to listen. At this point, my mother's face had become completely furrowed at the idea of what I had experienced. "'He is young, he will break by fear. Certainly he knows something,'" I said calmly and bitterly. I wanted the weight of my father's actions that afflicted me to sink in. It was wrong of me, but it felt reasonable seeing that he will tell me nothing yet sentence me to this fate. This fate of ignorance was mine while Amaryllis and Magnar knew. Seems all of Strength knows but me. My father sat forward in his chair as if he already knew how serious the threats against me were. He opened his mouth to speak, but I began before he could utter anything.

"Leaving, before they discovered me, I stumbled about through the town just trying to get away. Coincidentally, I ran into Adalric who was on his way to find me. He had overheard an unfamiliar man speaking to no one, suggesting Saxon was coming to speak to me. Adalric took me to the Hummer, helped me settle myself, and then told me about that man. Since then, thankfully nothing." I forgot how much anger I'd felt. Well, I remembered how much anger I had, I had just chosen to stop living in it.

"This all happened the day before last?" Father asked. My mother's anxiety was rising. I bowed my head, gathered myself. I was angry, but my mother was afraid.

"Yes. They did return the wagon to the forge in good shape," I added now trying to take away from the strain I'd created.

"I see. That was quite the visit." He sat with his back to his chair once more.

"That it was. It is done now. Like I said, I've had no other interactions. All is well it seems." I looked at my mother trying to assure her I was alright. She managed a non-convincing smile before anxiously looking back to my father. He now looked to fire to console him. But I was waiting. Waiting for him to grant me explanation. I knew all was not well, and I wanted him to tell me why. Tell me about Fidel. Tell me about the blade for Saxon. Tell me about the Sovereign Days. Tell me everything I do not know. But the minutes passed, and he had nothing to offer.

"I think I'm going to go for a walk in the woods." I stood trying to get any response after his insulting silence.

"Yes, fresh air is always good. I'll have something for us to eat by the time you return." My mother surprisingly joined in my movement. I suppose she was just eager to run away from the strain of it all. "Kane?"

"Yes, love." My father looked over to her inhaling.

"Would you help me?" she requested.

"Of course, dear. Where are you going, son?" He turned and asked after finding me on my feet. I opened my mouth, but it took a moment for anything to come out.

"A walk. I'm going for a walk in the woods. Fresh air," I answered.

"Good! That should be good," he awkwardly answered before his attention went back to the fire. Into the woods I went. My mind was blank like dreamless nights of sleep. It was so swarmed with emotions, ideas, and reminders of responsibility that instead of it solving anything it hid from everything. I wasn't used to my mind acting like this. The way my father was tonight. I wasn't expecting it to be like that. He wasn't joyful. He wasn't really relieved to be home. He was eager, even though I could tell he was trying so hard to hide it.

I don't think the fresh air did anything. I felt as if I was walking, but I was in a dream. Now I was waiting to wake up. Waiting to feel something. To think about something. Seeing it was no good I returned home. It was still quiet, but the table was set. My mother was now buttering bread and my father was pouring drinks. The door closed softly, following my slow appearance. I skipped the kitchen and found my way to the dining room table.

"Adinorium." My father returned from the kitchen accompanied by my mother and the freshly buttered bread. "I want to apologize. I never intended any of those things to happen to you. I never wanted you to have to endure any such trials. I'm sorry that I was not able to protect you as I thought I was. I was not able to save you." He was sincere. And this time I was able to receive his apology instead of questioning him. I sat in my chair looking up at him, as if I was a young boy again. The rushing winds that spun my mind settled. I saw the failure he felt in his eyes. I knew my father loved me. I now had to remind myself that that same love can make a man blind to realities that he deeply doesn't want to be true. I nodded quickly. I could feel myself starting to cry. I didn't want to cry. I didn't want to feel like I needed to cry. But I did. I needed to rest and that first meant the burden of tears had to prevail.

Chapter 11
Lions and Snakes

Haben Arrogs

I live with my grandfather. My father and mother are sufficient, but their home is not the palace, and their perspective is limited. I am to be king. This I know. All of my strivings and labor are to grant me satisfaction. I have found that my striving and labors are the only things that can. I know my grandfather is seen as a snake. I believe myself more to be a lion. Patience is better than pride, but the lion possesses both. The lion does not need the cunning nature of the snake. The snake lies and cheats, like my grandfather did in gaining the throne. Not only the second time like all presume, but the first time too. The first was even more brutal. Envy is poison and power. That is what the snake's power of deception earns him. It is the lion's bold pride that wins him everything. He doesn't have to steal anything from anyone because all give to him freely in fear. I will not have to do as my grandfather did. I will call upon my pride and they will boldly present me. I will judge with all wisdom and do so rightly. The noblemen were fools in thinking a test would satisfy their highest priority. For nobility can be learned, even if one does not believe in it. Strength. The battle to satisfy blood. Let any man face me. I already attested to my labors. My skill has been forged like a well-crafted blade. I do not rest in courage or will, but discipline and assurance. My grandfather fears he is to be found out, although he never shows it. I know because within the walls I can hear his anxious breath and his moments of pondering. He is a dead man who refuses to die.

"Haben, Grandfather wishes to have an audience with you." My sister Lila invaded my privacy as if she did not know of such a thing. I wished her gone from me. Dead even. She was malicious and full of folly. When I came to live with my grandfather, she followed suit. He adores Lila. I swear it must have been magic and charms she used on him. My grandfather is more foolish than he likes to believe himself to be. I lived on the west side of the palace. It is my own. I have my own servants and gardens, balconies, and library. It is connected to the rest of the palace by a stone bridge alone. It hangs over the mountain, mocking the fall below it. I walked between stone pillars and smooth rock underfoot to the main part of the palace. Details draped every inch of the walls, floors, and ceilings. It was more beautiful than I even imagined the Bountiful Lands had been. It was all temporary though. Simply time spent in one place over another.

"Ah, my grandson. Please join me." My grandfather had aged well. Riches provided him that to this point. He was impressive in stature. Even in his older age he still had an appearance of kingliness. But I had looked at his face so long that I only saw its withering away. He requested I join him in his walk to the Harlum Balcony. It stretched a great distance and from there you could see across the Dune of Dower, and if your imagination granted it to you, to the Straight of Mashel, the City of Lesginty, the mountains of Gash. I had spent much time studying the lands beyond our walls under my old tutor. For the sake of entertainment alone. Perhaps hidden desires as well. Not many books had been written on the subject. On the Old History. The subject I took interest in. The ones that were about Old History, however, could be found in our library. "Here the lords, my officials, and I will gather as we discuss the Sovereign Days and the travels we are to partake in. I want you to be among us. I also want you and your dear sister, Lila, to join in all travels. Allow the people to see your face. Behold your excellence. See who their new king will be and choose to fear him or take pride in him," he spoke in politics. He spoke little with his hands, keeping them stiff to himself. His body looked as if it longed to rest. In time it would. Very soon it would.

"Your grace, Master Ferrox, Master Avijna, Master Barnett and Master Quillonn have arrived," Abdur stated.

"These things I will do," I said, agreeing to my grandfather's request. I had no desire to see the people, only a desire for them to see me. As for fear and pride, a foolish thought. For I can not be denied either. I left with haste to greet my companions.

"They are waiting in your great room, your grace." Abdur walked with me. He was the head of my servants and my most trusted. If I was to keep anyone it'd arguably be him.

"Thank you, Abdur. Also, keep Lila away from us," I said to Abdur leaving him at the West Wings entrance.

"Yes sir." He bowed his head and began the great

process of protecting my borders from my sister and the traps she sets to ensnare my men. Brumal could be felt throughout my quarters. I commanded most of my windows to remain opened, because I liked seeing clearly at any given moment. I didn't speak while my servants dressed me in proper sparring attire. That is why my own had come: another opportunity for them to attempt to be greater than me with a sword, and another opportunity for me to display my superiority to them as they surrender under my sword. I looked at my reflection for only a moment while busy hands clothed me in many layers. It was always an odd thing to be within yourself then to see a reflection of your being. All of my servants were men as I wished to interact with women as little as possible. I hated the power they possessed over those weaker than me. I've seen their ability to turn men into fools.

"My union strong! You are all perfectly poised today." I exaggerated my blessing to them. They were all spread about in the great room. Barnett lounged comfortably across the coach, Quillon and Avijna laughed together over women and gossip, and Ferrox read a book which had been standing among the stack I'd gathered on my table.

"And you seem perfectly, well, whatever word would satisfy you today," Ferrox replied, closing his book and making his way to embrace me.

"You confess that you are a liar in compliments. Unfortunately, friend, I already knew such things." I smiled holding the back of his neck. "Tell me Barnett, what more has your father said about their small squabble." I sat in my own chair while the rest of my men found their places.

"He spoke his name. He also angrily ranted of his son." Barnett sat up, engaging in the story. Barnett Saxon is the son of Garvish Saxon. He is my father's high captain. Barnett and I were boys together. Much like Ferrox. However, Ferrox's family is low class Polished. Or at least they were until he and I became friends as boys. He and I shared a swordsmen class. I enjoyed his company and requested his visit so often that my grandfather gave them enough wealth to move up the mountain. He didn't like the idea of his grandson being so closely attached to a less fortunate family. Avijna and Quillon are more of my acquaintances. Avijna is son of Section Three, Lord Kiro. Quillon is the son of Section Two, High Captain Diyan.

"Go on," I insisted. There is believed to be a man who lives in the Conservative Ring of Section Four who can prove my grandfather's scheming to be true. At least, that is my suspicion. My own do not know of my grandfather's deception and believe him to be an unwanted rebel of sorts. Nothing more than a brigadier. It's been an ongoing watch for months. No one can say with certainty if he really knows anything or not. Although I have not asked my father nor grandfather about him; I know they do not kill him because they don't know the reach of his hand. They seek to snuff out the smallest flame of a possibility that they could be discovered for their treachery. I find that I agree with their waiting. The snake and lion both patiently prey in tall grass. Because if my grandfather is discovered, I, being an Arrogs, will be banned from ever even attempting to win the throne. Thus, I lie in wait with them.

"Kane Durnin. An iron smith. He has two sons. The older one is named Magnar. I do not know the name of the younger one. The father and older son were recently at a trade show in the Polished Ring. Suspiciously, they'd left for the Polished Ring immediately after returning from a show in File and Rank. That left the younger son to complete the bondage tax alone. Seeing that the lords needed more information, your father gave their forge a new tax, an honorable tax, doubling their normal demand. Knowing it was the youngest son alone who would have to complete the impossible, they offered grace if he could give them any better excuse for his father's absence." It amused me to watch the ignorant minds around me take interest in things of the people below us. They listened as if they lived in another world from us, not merely below.

"So now they have what they need and they can squander this little suspicion," I interjected. I sat holding the back of my chair with my arms and my legs stretched out. The others sat intrigued. Unfortunately they were only waiting for the boringly beautiful end where the weak become weaker and the one who can only whisper becomes silenced.

"No. He finished the entire demand, every sword without blemish," Barnett spoke with his hands emphasizing the story. I furrowed my brow and stood from my chair.

"Impossible. If I know anything about forging, which I do, then I would be the first to see through the lie of such things," I said confidently.

Ferrox joined in my refusal of the story saying, "I believe Haben is right, Barnett. The boy's body would have slowly broken down to an inevitable incompletion. Surely, there was help that was somehow hidden."

"That is why my father was so angry. There wasn't. They kept a constant watch of the forge. Apparently, the boy was on his way to their hoped fate, when one day he arose anew," Barnett pleaded the story's truth, but I found it to be nonviable.

"Impressive. He must have quite the ambition. At least now he possesses the story of his life. Those poor simples." I made fun of this boy. Knowing in my mind that if this were true it was most curious. People don't simply rise anew. It sounded like the beliefs of the Old History. I chose to make light of the story so the rest of them would treat it as less impressive than it was.

"Yes, my father even said that the Conservatives' celebrations are simple," Avijna mocked their simplicity. "They all join outside in the squares because no home is large enough to host them." I found no humor in them. None of them were even worth thinking of. Although, I knew we all had the same fate. Death. Bodies being given over to the sand to swallow whole. They went on mocking their way of life, not even being able to think any farther down of the people of File and Rank. From the top of the mountain, it seemed as if they didn't even exist. All they knew was the Conservatives were below them, making File and Rank soil that held only weeds.

"Let us redeem this time with a bit of practice shall we," I proposed, but also commanded. Greater than lowly iron smiths and their children, it was finally the time where we would be able to rise to the calling we'd been given. To hold the sword of power and claim Strength.

Chapter 12
The Weaker Man Carries

We want to believe that rest will always come to the weary but that isn't true. However, rest did come to me. It came from laying down that which was not mine to be carrying. At least, the elements that were not mine. It also meant acknowledging the parts that were. My father didn't tell me any of his secrets or expose any of his plots, but he did comfort me. He restored my faith in his judgment. Though in my heart I still rebelled against the greater things kept from me, I now felt as if it wasn't for my sake, but for the sake of Father and Mother. They needed me to surrender. For now, I would. Although I was no fool to my own self, knowing that if the opportunity presented itself for me to again raise my passions and desires, I would do so. The morning rang gently. The sun's rays felt softer than they had other mornings. For the first time in months, I laid awake in my bed. Telling the day and all of its struggles that they'd have to wait a little longer. My mother was still asleep when I finally decided to face the day. I was glad because that meant she felt secure enough to rest. It was odd to me how we fell into rest so easily. It was only yesterday my father had returned. He sat at the dining room table scribbling away on a piece of paper with six or seven others in front of him. He always sat in that same place when making his correspondence. There was a small drawer under the lip of the table that I knew he kept things in. I'd always wanted to take a glimpse inside of it, but also feared discovery too much. Father greeted me from his place.

"Good morning, Son," he said. I leaned against the door frame, which I found I was in the habit of doing and said to him the same. "I'm going to unload the wagon today and have a few things to do in town. I would love for you to join me."

"I'd be glad to." I smiled, truly pleased with the direction of the day. I made myself breakfast and made some for Mother too. She joined my father and me on our trip to town, needing to get a few things for the home and a new set of candles she'd be making. Chalmar was almost ready to have a celebration. Lanterns were beginning to be strung across the square from building to building. Wooden tables of every height and shape were finding their places. Wreaths of green were being gathered to be hung above. *The Chronicles of Strength*, the play telling of the Old History, was becoming more and more popular with the days. I was surprised at my excitement to see it in all of its beauty two nights from this one. My father was steady. He smiled and waved at passing friends and acquaintances whenever he saw them. My mother seemed happier as well. She even laughed on the occasion Father said something she found humorous. We left my mother in the middle of the square and my father and I rode on to the forge. Inevitably we passed the Bolg. Allester was mounting his horse and tilted his head in acknowledgement of seeing my father. My father stopped the horses, waiting for the captain to converse.

"Kane Durnin, it's been some time hasn't it," he said, slighting him.

"It sounds like you were trying to put my son in the grave," my father spoke coldly, completely ignoring Captain Allester's remark.

"Sure. Clear your conscience and blame me. But I never left, Kane," Allester said truthfully. His arguments in these situations were always reasonable. The way Father and Mother spoke to Captain Allester always surprised me. They spoke as if they were old friends who grew to hate each other.

"You had a say in it. Don't deny me that," Father called back. Captain Allester looked around and did his show when his actions didn't match what he was saying. I looked away from my father and Captain Allester feeling it to be a conversation I should not be around to hear.

"It was the only thing to do to satisfy them. Do not forget, Durnin, I owe you nothing. His pain was not my responsibility." My father inhaled and nodded. Captain Allester spoke of himself removed from Lord Arres and High Captain Saxon. And if my pain was not his responsibility, whose was it? "He did perfectly, you should know," he said finishing. He rode on before my father could say anything else.

"I had no doubt," my father said to me. I didn't smile at the compliment. In some ways, it didn't feel like a compliment. More like an equal threat to Captain Allester. We rode on. I asked no questions, and my father gave no explanations. "Look there," he said, pointing to the forge. "A well-used forge and an even better kept one. It will thrive under you for many, many years." He stepped down off the wagon.

"I'm definitely well acquainted," I said. The ground was hard and chilled, but the sun provided warmth in addition to its light. I unloaded the little they brought home while my father looked over his papers. "Looks like it was a successful show," I commented, bringing in the last box of small pieces.

"Yes, very much so. All of the Polished spare no expense for their Sovereign Days and all of its feastings and celebrations." My father explained the way they decorate whole homes with flowers and have silver place settings enough for a hundred people. How the women buy our iron chains, take them to jewelers and make necklaces worth more than a lifetime of living in File and Rank. I was intrigued, but too bitter to appreciate all of their theatrics. I hated how extravagant they were. How little they understood the harsh realities of living and boasted of such ignorance. "This is coming along beautifully." He had found Saxon's dagger. The blade and snake were made but separate. I hadn't even begun to work on the leaves the snake preyed in.

"I think it will be an impressive blade to whoever holds it." I smiled sitting on my father's table while he examined the blade made half in anger and half in sheer discipline.

"Yes, indeed it will be," he said in all confidence.

"How did you know about Saxon?" I asked. I hadn't really thought through what I was saying or asking. I knew if I thought too hard, I may have said nothing. Instead, I spoke whatever naturally came from my mouth. He breathed deeply and stood strong across from me.

"Yes, I realized after that I shouldn't have really had a good way of knowing that. To put it simply, a friend told me Saxon was going to come and examine the blades on behalf of Arres. Before I had even asked another friend to be prepared to steady you, that friend was already gone to do so. I told him of your friends and how they'd be the least suspicious option." He was more honest than I thought he'd be. He didn't even whisper as cautiously as I thought he would.

"The man who warned Adalric," I finished.

"Yes. Son, all of this is going to be over very soon. I know you wish to know and, I promise you, in time you will. But for the present moment, I can't tell you. Clearly, it is too dangerous. I don't want any more harm to come to you. I wish the opposite. For the Sovereign Days, I want you to be lighthearted. I hope you can celebrate and find joy in them. It is the least you deserve." My father was now in a place of making amends. I nodded because I had too much thinking to do to use words. I don't think he understood how the unknown taunted me. How the greater things called me. How my ignorance still brought torture. He hugged me firmly, in a way that made me question his promise that this would all be ending soon. Something challenged that idea in my mind. Something convinced me that this was never really going to end. Whatever this was or what it was going to be. "I love you, Son." I recited the words back to him. If I were certain enough to say anything now, it was that. I loved my father deeply. That love for him was the only thing keeping my sanity. The only thing keeping me from lashing out and demanding answers. "Now," he began, picking up a sword, "satisfy your old man with some practice."

He was grinning. Behind the forge there were woods. Walking a little ways into them there was an open patch of field. The one my father taught Magnar and I to duel on. I picked up one of the dulled swords to practice before my father rebuked me saying, "Come now, Nori. Use your own. I believe they handle things a bit differently." I laid down the old and chose a slender long blade. They were my favorite to forge, and I was very familiar with their weight and stride. My father seemed eager. The last time we dueled had been before we left for File and Rank. A close match, but he still out strode me. We circled round, both patient for our discernment on time to strike. He looked at my eyes, but I looked at his hands. He transitioned the sword to his opposite grip and began to walk backwards. Before he found a comfortable stride I struck quickly and swiftly. In a burst of strikes we both settled ourselves and began to circle once more.

"Have you heard of the duels that have begun?" I asked, now watching his feet. He took his liberty and charged heavily. I stepped back, keeping a firm blade defending all.

"Yes, I have. The Polished find pleasure in it. They make their duels into games with bids and brackets. Have you partaken in any?" he questioned, finally letting loose on his challenge. I smiled and laughed at the idea.

"Unfortunately, time has kept me from such games. Perhaps before the season is out, I'll make a legend of myself," I joked, taking my own turn as the aggressor.

"I wouldn't be surprised if you did," he complimented after I eased back. My father had one weakness when it came to dueling: he assumed he was always a step ahead of his competitor. He yelled while his flurry of swings faced me. When all settled, his two hands held strong on my blade over my head.

"Surrender boy!" he threatened.

"Why would I surrender to a dead man?" I asked. My father broke his lock with my eyes and looked down at my other hand which held a dagger ready to strike his heart. He grunted, lowering his sword in surrender. I smiled gladly at my victory. My father grinned against his own will.

He was sincere as he said, "You are a strong man, Adinorium. A much stronger man than I am."

"I owe whatever strength I have to you." I picked up the load of swords we had brought to practice with.

"No! No! The weaker man carries, demanding he grow stronger," Father said, correcting me. I had heard that saying throughout my life. Inevitably, that had always meant I was the one carrying as my father and Magnar were both stronger than I was. When my father and Magnar would go out, Magnar carried everything back until he was about sixteen. One day, I was stacking wood for my father and they came out again together. But my father had the load on his shoulders. Magnar is mighty. He was always faster, always stronger, and always struck in the right place. "As for the strength you now have, that is the Greater's doing." Ah yes, the Greater. I am told he is the one who gives me my strength. I don't understand what that even means. Not really. But I had been thinking of the Old History. I had been thinking of my dream. Even Allester speaks in certainty of him. Even if I lived in constant remembrance of him, like those around me do, I wouldn't know what he would be. What that would mean.

"Let's go get your mother," my father said after we'd settled all of our things. In town the King's Host was more abundant. They were circling the streets, going into every establishment, stopping everyone to speak to them. A woman's scream made my father and I stop as we watched a soldier pull a man from his horse and his woman clutching for him while a soldier held him back. The man yelled different things as the soldiers took him away. Amidst all of their yelling it was understood that the man didn't have papers to be in this section. Meaning, he'd be put into prison for some time then given greater taxes after he was returned to his home without his horse. "Soldier!" My father was now calling out to a man who was sitting on a horse going towards the Bolg. "What is all of this?" The soldier was an average man, blond hair, blue eyes, a bit short maybe.

"Light accustoms. Making sure everything is as it should be, no plotting or any of that nonsense before King Thann begins his procession." The man sounded like he owned a false pride. Thinking himself to be intimidating because he rides a horse and holds a sword.

"What kind of things are you looking out for?" my father questioned. Any good soldier would have seen this question as potentially threatening. A way to know what to hide and what they could get away with. Clearly my father had the same take on the soldier as I did.

"Anything really! Bad papers, things like that. Mainly hidden things. Hidden notes, hidden swords, hidden daggers, hidden axes, hidden hammers, hidden spears, hidden places, hidden people, suspicious people, suspicious places, suspicious-"

"Seems as if there's quite the concern. Is every area under this much, how'd you say it, accustoms?" my father said, interrupting the poor man who I believed would have continued for hours.

"Not as strenuous." He loosened his posture and looked over his shoulders. "You can't tell anyone, but we're suspecting something is going to happen here. No one has told us what, but there's a man who lives here whom King Thann has deemed a rebel. A potential scandal if you ask me." This poor soldier was selling his secrets for the small price of reaction.

"Really? Then you must be under a lot to do your job thoroughly," my father said with a false sympathy.

"Yes, it is. The utmost importance." He fell for it beautifully. I could hardly restrain myself from rolling my eyes.

"Did they even tell you the name of the man whom they've called a threat?" My father was cunning and slightly grinned realizing so bluntly that I got all of my eloquence in speaking from him.

"No, unfortunately only Captain Allester knows," the soldier said, straightening back out his posture feeling proud that he knew things we could not. Even if he really didn't know of anything of real substance. "Please, find me if you hear anything suspicious or find anything. I'll be able to take it from there."

"Of course, soldier." My father nodded. The soldier looked around once more than rode on in a dramatic fashion.

"I'm sure Allester loves him." My father smiled. I think I was supposed to say nothing about my father being an official rebel of the king. Even if not all the soldiers knew his name, they understood the thought of him.

"Dearest!" My mother waved, summoning us. I got out of the wagon and helped her up. I took the two baskets which were full to the brim of many things like wax, perfumes, and fruit and placed them in the back.

I called up to them, "I'm going to see Amos." I was forced to speak loudly over all the noises of the town.

"Very good!" My father encouraged me. I stepped back from the wagon to let them leave. I waved to my mother until they had disappeared down a wooded trail. I avoided the soldiers as much as possible. I avoided their directions looking for more people to interrogate. Finally getting to the practice, I opened the door to see a wounded man on the table, his mouth clinching a towel to distract from the pain. His wife sat in the corner crying while holding a young baby who was also crying from the chaos of the room. Dr. Yooldee held bloodied pliers while Amos held the man's leg down.

"Nori! Get the lady and baby!" Amos commanded, looking over his shoulder to see me. A bit flustered, I went over to the woman. Giving her my best, I asked to take the wailing baby. She reluctantly handed the infant to me and I grabbed her hand.

"Come with me," I said gently, leading her outside. I helped her sit on the doorstep of the practice and turned my attention to calming the baby down. "Stay here. I'll be right back." I made sure she was looking me in the eyes and waited until she shook her head to acknowledge me. I hurried to the Hummer, which was aggravatingly crowded.

"Whose baby is that?" Doolby asked, greeting me at the bar.

"Not mine. Can I get a cup of tea quickly?" I requested switching the baby who had stopped crying, to my opposite arm. I hadn't spent much time with babies but holding this one felt surprisingly natural to me. Doolby slapped his counter and hurried for my sake. "Thank you, Doolby!" I said with all sincerity as he was back to me quicker than any bartender serving tea usually was. I took a coin out of my pocket and placed it on the counter. "I'll be back tomorrow tonight. I'll bring the cup back then! Me and my own are coming for dinner!" Before Doolby had time to reply, I was out the front door. "Here. For the nerves." I handed the cup to the woman who had just stopped crying herself. I began to talk to the baby saying the silly little things we mutter to them.

"Do you have any children?" Her voice sounded tired but settled.

I replied more strongly than I meant to, "No, I don't." She was young, about the age of Amaryllis. Her child shared her red hair with subtle curls.

"You are," she began saying between sips of tea, "good with them." I awkwardly smiled, looking down at the child in my arms. I noticed her new skin and innocence. I wondered now who she'd grow into being.

"What happened to your husband?" I asked, feeling she was able to answer now.

"A duel. We didn't have enough money to pay for his

File and Rank sister to come to our home during the Sovereign Days. He hasn't seen her in years. A band of men started paid duels and offered him a match. He assured me he'd be fine. A man stabbed a dagger into his left leg. Ander had to forfeit. A group of the lads helped carry him here. The money that he won for entertainment will now be the doctor's wages." She inhaled and shook her head in a bit of anger.

I tried to console her, "I'm sorry. That is certainly a grim situation." I felt as if I was doing a poor job. Adalric would've been much better suited for the task.

"Mrs. Holds, the doctor will see you now." Amos stepped out of the door wiping his bloodied hands with a towel. She eagerly stood and handed Amos her cup of tea. Amos closed the door and sat on the doorstep himself. I sat beside him still holding the baby who'd found her own voice by cooing.

"So, this is why I haven't seen you for days," I said more than questioned. He nodded. He threw the stained towel to the ground finally surrendering to his hands not being fully cleaned. "I'm sorry for not helping you or visiting sooner," I added.

"Nori, you had no time, same as me. I was perfectly satisfied without your visit as long as it wasn't your bloodied body coming through this door." I knew Amos meant that full well.

I confessed, "I have so much I've wanted to say to you." We both watch the people passing. People I knew the names of but nothing more.

"I've wanted to hear everything. I will be able to soon. Yooldee sent a letter to a friend of his from Section Seven.

Another doctor. They studied together in Section Three. He should be arriving today and Yooldee is going to give me some time to recover." Amos was tired, yet he still held his familiar steadiness. "These duels have become deadly. As bids and prizes became involved the wounds became more severe."

"I'm sure," I said. We sat for a moment just watching the passerbyers. I needed Amos. I knew it full well. "My father is home." Amos looked sharply at me wanting to see the face I wore.

"And?" he asked.

"I will tell you later. But it isn't right. None of it is." The doctor and woman's nearing voices interrupted our conversation. Dr. Yooldee was giving orders to the woman who frantically nodded, committing everything to memory.

"Keep him off of it. Change the cloths daily. If anything worsens, don't hesitate to come and get me." The wounded man had his arm over his wife. She was his only support at the current time. She also held a wrapped sword around her. The wrapping had become red in different parts from what I assumed was the man's own blood. Amos and I had stood to clear a path for them, but looking down at the baby in my arms I knew this wasn't going to fare well for the woman.

"Uh, hold on to the wall dear." She helped her husband steady himself. "Thank you so very much!" I handed the baby back to her. It felt wrong returning her to her mother. I think the wrongness was really felt in having taken her at all. Holding her daughter in one arm she began to attempt to hold her husband with the other.

"I'll help you home," I said, walking over to the man for me to become his new support. The woman received the offering knowing it'd be impossible the other way.

"Thank you! I can't even begin!" On account of all the blood the man had lost, he seemed on the verge of fainting.

"The Hummer tomorrow?" I asked Amos before following the woman.

"Yes! Adalric told me," he said. I hadn't meant to leave him in greater concern, but this time seemed to be full of it.

"Bring the cup!" I yelled walking away. The woman led us the opposite way of the square. I didn't visit this part of Chalmar often. After we'd been walking for about twenty minutes, I was practically dragging the man. We turned to a narrow path that led deeper into the woods. I stopped and readjusted my grip. I wanted to ask how much further, but I knew I needed to refrain. The woman had already been through enough in the past day alone.

"Just through here!" she hollered, walking yards ahead of her husband and me. I could see the trail break open and did my best to hurry myself. A home was beyond the tree lined hallway of the woods. It was small. A slanted roof was over the house and provided an open wall covering on both sides. The woman went through the front door leaving it open for me to enter. Inside the whole home was contained in a single room. A fireplace and chair were by the front window. A bed not much bigger than mine was in the back corner with a crib at the end. A small place for preparing meals was on the opposite wall across from the bed, along with a small table with three chairs. I helped the man to the single chair and assisted in extending his leg. The woman had put the baby in the crib and left with a bucket to draw water. I also went outside and found a log that'd been cut from a tree that fell on the edge of the land. I took one of the pieces inside and propped the man's leg onto it.

"Are you a doctor like your friend?" The man mumbled after moaning from his leg's movement.

"No, I am a smith." I looked over to see the baby had fallen asleep in her crib. I took one of the covers from the bed and laid it over her. The woman returned and lugged the bucket onto the counter. She scooped out a cup of water and helped her husband drink.

"If you are a smith then surely you know how to hold a blade?" he asked me. The woman sat back on her knees and looked disgruntledly at her husband.

"You can assume that." I was unsure what he desired from me. Wildflowers had been put in a jar on the table. It was beautiful to see the small details the woman gave to the traditionally non-impressive home to help it grow.

"My sword." He pointed to the wrapped sword in the corner. "Is it pure iron?" I walked over to the table and undid the wrapping. It was a handsome sword, impressively detailed in the handle specifically. I picked up the blade and turned it in my hand feeling the grip. I moved it around, spinning it to feel how its weight balanced. It was light. A softer metal. Then I looked at the blade from many angles to observe if it was flawless or layered.

"This is an impressive blade. Where did you get it?" I asked, walking to stand in between the fireplace and the man.

"I got it from a friend. He stayed with us for many days.

He gave it to me as his thanks." The man had gained more strength from sitting still along with the water his wife continued to give him.

"It is not pure iron. It is pure silver." I laid the blade on the table. "It is a sure thing to know your guest is very thankful," I added.

"Fidel is a gracious man," he said, grumbling in a way of pleasure.

"Fidel?" I looked back to the man whose eyes were closed.

"Ander? Ander?" The woman stood to her feet to try and shake him.

"Shhh! He is sleeping. See his chest still rises and falls. That is good for him." I calmed her, allowing her to find peace. She sat on the end of her bed and closed her eyes. Her home was finally quiet, and her family was in the protection of its walls. "Be safe." I bow my head to take my leave now that they were all well.

"I don't even know your name," she began while wiping moisture from her brow, "yet you have gifted me and my family much kindness." She found no vitality to stand. Her twisted hair was steadily becoming less that way.

"My name does not matter. I'm glad to do such things. I hope for a quick recovery."

"Thank you. And be steady." She smiled gently and allowed me to take my leave. The man named Fidel had been here for days, yet it was him who brought the final proof to my father. How could both be true? Fidel must have been the one to warn Adalric of Saxon. Perhaps he's Conservative from Area

One. I didn't understand his movements. Clearly, he was no longer staying with the Holds. Where was he now? I decided I'd go to the forge and craft more of the dagger. My hand in my father's silent affairs.

Chapter 13
The Gifted

The paper felt fragile in my hardened hands. I was in awe of the water. Even though the picture stood still I could perfectly see it going in and coming out. The ground was like the sand in the dunes, yet it looked softer as if it'd be good for bare feet. I think there was a breeze. A warm one from the sea. One that would fill your lungs to satisfaction and perhaps smell of something I don't know. As for the cliffs, I think they were taller than the picture portrayed. I think I'd have to lay down on my back in order to see the land that must seem flat and stable above. But what might it all look like now? I studied the painting gifted to me weeks ago and made by one with Eyes of a Gazer. Old History things. Things only few believed. But this place. I longed for it. Deep in my gut I wanted to be there. To be on the shoreline, to see the infinite seas I could escape to for a moment but could not stay.

The night before I had stayed awake thinking of my dream. The thought started when I felt how tired my hands were from my work on the dagger. Then I began to relax my body, feeling the muscles unclench to rest. Because of that, I remembered the feeling of that morning. My hands didn't hurt. They weren't sore or tired or in rebellion against holding things. They gladly took up my hammer. They gladly labored for me. I had little left to do for the dagger. But little left leaves more to do still. I laid the painting on top of the dresser in my room. I'd kept it there since I brought it home from showing Amos. I wanted to show Adalric next. I think I'd show it to Phoebus too for him to grow in appreciation of beautiful things. Mother and Father had gone for a walk together in the backwoods of our home. I wasn't used to being in my home alone. I didn't despise it as I thought I should have. I believed that showed how the sort of walls that make up a home and things that adorn them, can be a kind of company on their own. I carried the concern I had told Amos about yesterday. It seemed an unshakable burden. Surely in time it'd roll off my back, but within it, that seems an impossible thing.

"I'm going through Chalmar to get to the forge. I was wondering if you need anything while I am there?" I asked Mother after her and Father had returned from their walk. My father was still outside tending to the horses.

"Actually, yes. I have a book you can take to the bookstore. Let me find it," Mother said, hurrying into her room to retrieve the book. "Here it is! Just give it to whomever's at the counter. They were kind enough to let me borrow it for a short time. I got it so I could begin making new scents for my candles. I wanted something ready for cordial." The windy season. I nodded to her answer. "Wonderful knowledge one can learn from books without having to figure it out on their own." She smiled. Neither Magnar nor I read much when we were kids.

Something that now felt daunting to me in trying to begin.

"Yes, it seems so," I answered. "Can you tell Father when he returns inside?"

She answered kindly, "Of course!"

"Oh! And I'm going to the Hummer tonight with Amos and the others."

"Good. I'm glad you are." I decided to walk, leaving the horses to my father. As I began to enter Chalmar I didn't know what to think. She'd nearly readied herself for the celebration that begins tomorrow night. A celebration that wouldn't allow any to sleep for weeks. It was unfamiliar for me to search for the sign that'd been newly done above the bookstore. Freshly painted in green letters, the sign read *Borrow and Buy Books by Berti*. I shook my head not wanting to go inside. I always felt dumb going into places full of books. I was a terrible mirror of my own self-inflicted foolishness. The keepers of the store had tied a little bell onto a string that made noise when the door was opened. I understood why it was needed at the sight of the girl behind the counter, whose face was fully vanished behind a book. She was Ellis Ivory. Her mother, Berti, schooled a group of the children in literature including Amos, Adalric, and myself. Amos always had a fancy for her. I suppose she was fine. I'd never spoken to her. I'd never really wanted to. Her eyes didn't even look up from her reading when I entered. Unwise. What if I had the desire to rob from her? I could've for all I knew!

"Hello. Looking for anything in particular, out of the ordinary, or plain boring?" she asked while her fingers gently flipped to the next page.

"I'm not sure what it would be considered," I answered, taking a step closer to the counter before tripping over a tower of books stacked on the floor. It wasn't enough to make me fall, but I did knock over the mound and two others trying to find a place to stand. Only the sound of the fallen books made her put down her own and hurry to set them up again.

"Oh," she licked her thumb, "the covering got a scuff." She was now scrubbing the book's velvet cover.

"My apologies. I wasn't looking for mounds of books on the floor," I said half sorry and half thinking it was their own fault for leaving piles of books all over.

"And you hardly know what you're looking for! Seems you better begin to gain your bearings, Durnin." I looked over at her while correctly arranging the last pile to crumble over. I was surprised she had taken note of who I was.

"Little Ivory?" I corrected myself. "Ellis!" In the days that I spoke about her everyone called her Little Ivory. It was because her mother was the teacher, and we all called her Mrs. Ivory. It seemed entirely wrong now. Almost like I was saying it as a term of endearment, which I was far from. She took a couple of the books she deemed in need of attention over to her counter and again seemed to be completely ignorant to my being there. "Here. I'm returning this for my mother," I said, extending the book in my hand to her. Of course, she was too focused on other things to take it. So I laid it on the counter myself. But seeing the book on the counter and all the others around me I thought for a second longer of what my mother had said. How books have a terrible amount of knowledge that's all gathered up already, so you don't have to discover everything on your own wits and account. "I'm looking for books on Old History," I blurted out awkwardly. It wasn't because of her, but I suddenly felt like a thief who was trying to be crafty in his thievery. She looked up at me confused by my outburst of a statement.

"Finally taking interest? Let's see." She paused to think. "It only took you seven years longer than the rest of us." I furrowed my brow not understanding her dislike of me. We were never friends, but not enemies either. My guess was it had something to do with the books she spread about and began to mend.

"Do you have any?" I asked, giving no rebuke to her insult, and wanting to leave quickly if they didn't.

"Look. Why didn't you just read them when your father had them all?" she asked.

"My father?" I questioned before realizing I shouldn't be questioning that. "He hogged them the whole time," I lied. Well, not entirely. I suppose he had hogged them, but it was more of locked them away with his secret things. I didn't like the way she looked at me now. She was suspicious. But it was the kind of suspicion that would lead to answers. She wasn't quick to answer me or really believe me. She had finally stopped to look at me to make her judgment. She'd grown up. Obviously. We all had. But she looked different now. Not so much like Little Ivory anymore. It was an unwelcome representation of time that I did not need now. So, I decided to pretend I had no idea who the woman was in front of me and continue on with my business. My business also seemed to have been my father's business.

"All the way in the back, top shelf, right side," she said, going back to her mending. "And Adinorium."

"Yes?"

"I'm glad you're taking interest in it. Now is better than later. Better than never really," Ellis said, seeming to have convicted herself. "If you have any questions, I'll help if I can." I nod my head.

"Thank you, Ellis." I was glad to find her now more as she used to be. Kind. Things like that. I exhaled in my victory once I was hidden by books. I began to walk down the rows of shelves crammed and found there was no way that there was an order to them. "What am I doing?" I thought out loud to myself. There also wasn't a way for the shelves to go on as they did. I found the back wall impossibly far for the outward appearance of the building. To the right side, top shelf, seven or eight books close together. I looked over my shoulder once more before reaching up for the first. I flipped through the pages but didn't think it was what I was looking for. I didn't know what it was that I was really looking for though. The next and the one after were no different. Then I reached a dim purple one. I took more time to look over its cover. *The Gifted*. What of these Gifted? I thought of my painting. Did the old woman's husband really have gifted eyes or was he just a creative man with an imaginative head? I knew by how the spine groaned a bit when I opened it that this was the book I wanted. The first page read:

When the Greater had gathered all he wanted to Strength, the wall was scaled shut not to be opened again until the prophecy was fulfilled. The first generation, aside from the Founders and the great immortal, were natural beings. Ones whose hands did nothing more than what hands had first been made for and eyes not odd colors that see undiscovered things. Those began to come in the second generation. It was discovered that there were five kinds of gifts given. The gifts could only be had if one was born with them. They could not be learned.

I frowned at this line. I was thinking of the journal from Fox Tramp that I'd hoped would be able to teach Amos the art of one of these gifts. If they really were real.

These beings would be called Irregulars or The Gifted. The first gift was called Eyes of a Gazer. It was the ability to see the Bountiful Lands as they once were and what they shall be restored to. This gift was given to remind the people of Strength of the land they had once known and would know again. These beings are typically easy to identify because of the color of their eyes. Bright purples, oranges, and yellows. Or the natural colors of blue and green, only more magnificent.

I tried to remember the color the old woman said her husband's eyes had been. It was one of the natural ones. I think green. I wondered if the painting she'd given to me was of how the Bountiful Lands were or how they will be. That really was the only gift I'd come to read about, but it had my attention and so I continued on:

The second gift was called Draconian Blood. The one who

possessed this gift possessed strength beyond the natural man. Gained by gift, not by effort. No natural man could obtain the strength these ones could. It is also true that those with Draconian Blood are harder to kill and wound. Thicker skin protects them, richer blood flows through their veins, and their hearts are twice as strong. This makes them live longer than the natural man, but in no way are they eternal. This gift was given to remind the people of Strength of a greater strength than their own. A greater strength than their walls, mountains, or even their most gifted. These beings are typically easy to identify because of their physical excellence. A head taller than the natural man and muscles firm. This gift has only been possessed by men.

The third was called Hands of Plenty. The ability to heal the physical body. Wounds, illness, poison, broken bones, trifle hearts. It has been proclaimed that one with Hands of Plenty has been able to raise one from the dead, but never by witness has this been done. This gift is a reminder to the people of Strength that there is one who rules the body and being. That there is one who will bring healing to them. These beings are impossible to know until their older age. When all others' skin begins to sag and pale, those gifted with the Hands of Plenty will still have firm skin that won't begin to sag and pale until they are much older. They are not immortal but will only die from age. No illness or trifle heart will take them.

I thought of Fox. I wondered what he had healed. What had he done with his hands? What could he do? Why did he spit on his gift and refrain from healing? I was nearly certain if these things were true that he had Hands of Plenty. Why did he find pain and death to be better than life?

The fourth was called Depth of Sound. This is the most unknown gift in terms of their potential. It is the ability to hear the voice of another while not being with them. The Irregular one has to have seen the face and heard the voice of the one they listen too. But when they have done both, they can choose to hear the voice of that one no matter how far from them. This gift is to remind the people of Strength that there is one who hears them even if they are not seen. These beings have no specific thing that sets them apart. Their gift is invisible unless confessed to another. This adds to their ability. However, this gift has only been found among women.

The final gift was called Second Sight. These are the prophets. The ones who see what is yet to come. The Irregular gifted with Second Sight is given one vision in their life from the Greater himself. They cannot die until what they have seen and spoken of comes to pass. This is to remind the people of Strength that there is one who knows what is to come and will bring it about as he desires. These beings are known by their eyes that are wholly white with a pupil of gray. They are also known by how long they can live, as they become immortal until their prophecy comes to pass.

I had only heard of one gifted with Second Sight. I remembered him quickly. The one silenced and locked away. At least, that was the rumor in my youth. What did they say? What did they see? Have they died in their secret place? Or do they live on, unable to rest for many more years?

These are the gifts of the Irregulars.

I closed the book after the first few pages, afraid to read on. I didn't understand. Why haven't I seen any of these gifts in people I know? What happened to them? How was I supposed to believe in the Old History if I did not find proof now? The one who still lives with Second Sight could be stupid gossip. Fox could be a liar. Where were the Draconians? Where were the colorful eyes and the ears who hear from afar? I pause. I'd been gifted a painting created by a gifted one. It almost seemed harder to believe someone could create such a wonder from his own head. He must have had eyes that could see the Bountiful Lands. My breath was shaky when I inhaled. The Old History is either true in its entirety or not at all. And what of the Great Immortal they speak of? The one to guard our walls? Where is he? Does he spend his eternity outside of Strength? Prowling around the walls waiting for the prophecy to be fulfilled? And what of the Greater? If he is the one who hears, why hasn't he listened to me? Or had he. I returned the book to its place and looked down at my hands. What had I seen in my dream? How was I restored? I was overwhelmed by it all. I had my fill of this knowledge for the moment and decided I was very ready to get to the forge. "Thank you, Ellis," I said before rushing to leave.

"Wait, Adinorium!" she called, standing from her seat to stop me. I held my breath feeling like I'd been caught in my scheming. I turned to face her. She extended her hand for me to take a worn brown book with no title or name or author. "Here. Take this one."

"Why?" I did not understand why she suddenly felt the need to give me something.

"I don't know." She was shaking the book a bit for me to take.

"Well what is it about?"

"I don't know. I can't read it." She was nervous. Not curious like I would've been. She extended once more for me to take. So I did. It wasn't small enough for me to fit it in my pocket, so I'd have to carry it.

"Thank you," I said. I thanked the Greater when the peaked sun and sounds of business met me outside the store door. I felt an odd sense of fear in me. Not the same burden of fear I felt towards my father's deals or being threatened by the crown. This was a kind of fear found in smallness or maybe ignorance. As if the world around me was not really as my eyes had learned to see it. I inhaled, shook my head, and headed to the forge.

Chapter 14
Knowing All and Nothing

The dagger still wasn't finished, but the day was breaking and I had somewhere to be. I hadn't been able to redeem my mind since visiting the bookstore. Not that I was thinking of all of those things. I just couldn't think of my work at hand. I cleaned myself up and began walking towards town. A faded memory came to my mind of only a few weeks ago making this same walk towards town alone after I had completed the first tax. That walk had been more painful. But even then, we celebrated. I agreed with my father when he said he wanted to be that lighthearted again. I needed to be glad again. I looked up to the heavens, as we all should be, and inhaled deeply. For tonight, I would be lighthearted. Off a rugged trail came a horseman who began to follow behind me. I knew he followed me because he wasn't from here. I could tell by the way his horse had been prepared for travel. He also followed at too perfect of a distance behind and he tried to remain as quiet as his horse would allow. I paid him no mind as if he were not even there at all. I knew how to deal with these kinds of things. I had been brought up in a home of privacy and swords and a head that never remains looking in one direction. I suppose being in the midst of those very realities was the next inevitable thing. The town was slowing down, leaving most everyone to close shop and return home. I looked across the way at the book shop and wondered about the book Ellis had given me. I had left it at the forge. I was too disheveled to read it today, to even glimpse inside. My own waited for me outside the Hummer. I was glad to find them in high spirits. Except Phoebus. I embraced him first, but it was weak. I had seen him least the past few weeks. I missed him, but it was difficult for me having him angry now. The Hummer was now in her true glory. I looked over my shoulder to see the rider once more before following the others inside. Every table was filled with miners, soldiers, girls, and all the town drunks. I looked at every guest to see if there were any that took a keen interest in us, but every party seemed to be satisfied with themselves. We found our table empty and waiting for us. We were like lords and the Hummer was our domain.

"Dear, she's a beauty!" Adalric smiled from across the table.

Phoebus corrected the apparent glory of the compliment, "You think all of them are."

"And is that a bad thing?" Adalric asked. I smiled naturally, which felt good.

"How was the day, men?" I asked. I didn't mean to look around as I did, but my head was busy thinking of many things. I supposed Amos noticed because he kicked my leg under the table making me look at him. He then cocked his head a little as if asking why I was acting as I was. I widened my eyes and cocked my head back at him. Then I eased into the evening with my dearest friends.

"Dark, cold, dirty and ehh long," Phoebus said, starting us off.

Adalric clapped back, "I can tell!" He scruffed up Phoebus' hair to see black coal fall from it. Phoebus batted away his hand and brushed himself off.

"I heard about your days, Nori. Well, I suppose I've heard about your past few weeks really. Adalric has been filling me in." Phoebus shifted to the more serious mood I was trying to avoid. He spoke bitterly. Maybe he was just tired or upset. I hadn't told him much of my experiences. I didn't know what was wrong.

"I have so much to tell all of you." I grinned. "I can't wait to show you all the blade! Now she is worth a little longer of a linger," I replied, choosing to assume Phoebus' bitterness was from a long day and trying to pull us from the engulfing pit of problems. I spoke highly of the blade even though I'd struggled with it so much. It was very good already and when I was finished, I was sure it'd be perfect.

"Right. I have a feeling Adinorium would take a block of iron over a woman any day." Adalric rolled his eyes. Naturally, he switched the subject back to girls.

"I've already got three of you to deal with! I couldn't keep up with another!" I jokingly argued back.

"Don't play stupid, Nori. You know it's different. Need I clarify, I mean a girl." I loved picking on Adalric about his obsessions. He was dramatic and always reacted as you'd want.

"So they tell me," I ended.

"My lords are here! The place was starting to feel dull

without you! Anything new?" Doolby championed us like we were long lost survivors. It's partly because he's a politician and partly because we do entertain him.

"It has been sometime since we've been here. Long enough for the normal to feel new again. So, I'll take my normal. Thanks, Doolby!" I played into his dramatic nature. Amos, Phoebus, and Adalric do the same. I tried to take delight in being with my brothers. They provided good things for me. I didn't feel as alone nor as unseen in my unknowns and searching. But my head was hard pressed to keep easy things at the forefront of my mind. "Have you seen anyone strange or has anything odd happened recently?"

"Not in particular. There have been more guests due to the tournament steadily approaching, but nothing more. Why?" I glanced at Amos and decided I had to lie to Doolby.

"No reason. Just wondering if you had any good stories or suspicious activity we could ponder for fun," I said, slightly pushing his arm as if to make him feel like he was taking it all too seriously. Doolby was all smiles.

"Oh! Of course! My studious corner of academics. I don't have anything to whet your appetites, but give me a few minutes and my food will do just that!" We joked around and I kept my convincing act. I saw a memory of how my life had been at one time. I have never had to act like this. My past was innocent. No, not innocence. Freedom. Yes, freedom. An ignorant freedom, sure. But it was still how I lived, how I thought, how I breathed even. I looked around the table and saw my brothers. I've known for a while now that times are changing. Everyone did. The Sovereign Days always change everything. Even if the same man becomes king again. I think of the dagger I'm crafting for Saxon. The snake hiding in the weeds, tongue fixed on having blood. I think the blade described Thann's rule and reign perfectly. Better suited for him if I were to propose such an idea.

"I heard of a split union being established," Adalric said.

"Yes, I'd heard the same," I said thinking of my time with Allester and Saxon. "Another was established in Section Six as well."

Amos asked, "What's a split union?"

"It just means that not all of the men are from the same section. I think this one has some men from seven, six, and two," Adalric said.

"Two? That's surprising. I'd think all Polished were for Haben," I said.

"So, tell me, Adinorium," Phoebus said, leaning forwards on the table, completely disrupting our conversation of unions, "how's your father?" He was kind in asking, but it felt like he held a small dagger, and he kept poking me with it.

"He's better. Good even. I'm very glad he's home. We all are." I felt like I was being interrogated by Allester or Saxon by the way Phoebus sat forward on his elbows and hadn't the thought to smile.

"Of course. The rest of us are very pleased he's home also. It seems he brought with him the entire host too." Phoebus forced a humored sigh, but the rest of us didn't share in it.

"Are you angry with me, Phoebus?" I asked, unable to act ignorantly towards him.

"Why would I be?" he asked, but it felt rhetorical.

"Your tone of bitterness. Your laughter of mockery. Your cold disposition. Please tell me how I have wronged you. I cannot bear this season with friends who are resentful towards me in addition to the resentment of the throne," I said sincerely while possessing a bit of annoyance of my own. Even Adalric was put on edge by Phoebus' person.

"You can't bear it?" His eyes glossed with tears. For the first time in our entire friendship I feared him. I feared his intentions.

Adalric demanded, "Phoebus, what on this land is wrong with you?"

"Don't ask what is wrong with me. *He's* the snake." Phoebus was pointing at me. "He's the one who is going to get us all killed. He's the one who is going to destroy Strength. And he's the only one who will be able to bear it in the end!" He was looking at Amos and Adalric, pleading with them. As he continued speaking, his words started fading in my ears. I could now hear my heart beating above all the other noise. I could hear strained breathing. It sounded as if someone stood directly behind me. No, not behind me. Beside me. Behind Phoebus I saw the black being from my dream. Now I could see his hand thin with fingers twice as long as any mans, calmly grip Phoebus' shoulder. He wasn't looking at Phoebus or Amos or Adalric, his gaze fell upon me. I thought of how he fled from the voice. It wasn't because of some blow or wound. Rather, he fled from the words of that voice. I feared him, but his hand upon the one whom I loved brought a far greater fear.

"I'm sorry, Phoebus," I whispered. The black being's hooded head leaned to one side. I then realized the table had gone quiet. "I'm sorry for all of it. I'm sorry for the strain my father's absence put on you and your father. I'm sorry I never came to visit you and tell you of everything. I'm sorry my father brought with him this watchful eye. I'm sorry being my friend puts you in a more vulnerable place. I'm sorry, Phoebus. Truly." Tears began to fill my own eyes. I was purely afraid. I hated seeing Phoebus at the hands of the shadow-like being. I hated that the unknown had torn Phoebus and me so far. I was battling with everything in me, doing everything asked of me yet I still lost. In the silence, the being's hand started clinging stronger to Phoebus' shoulder. He was claiming his prize. At least I thought that's what was happening until I saw his fingers slowly release him. His head shifted from me to the other side of the room. I didn't understand why, but looking at me once more, he turned away and vanished into the shadows themselves. Then, Phoebus' demeanor softened. He spoke in his own voice again. He reached and took my hand.

"No. Forgive me. I have spoken selfishly. Forgive me for adding to your load when I should be the very person helping to lighten it." The black being had no hold on him now. But he was real. I knew I must have looked petrified. I was. This was no dream, but he knew me. How? I had only dreamed of him. I looked at Phoebus terrified by what I'd caused.

"Adinorium?" Amos questioned as I had been made speechless. Looking at Amos, I swallowed hard. It couldn't have been what I thought. I exhaled and looked back to Phoebus.

"Forever, friend." I gripped his hand tighter.

"Now please, tell me of your burden so I may share in it," he requested. I nodded slowly gathering myself. It must have been my own imagination. I was tired and weary. It was an illusion. Yes, that is what it was. I looked to Amos, then started with my father's meeting months ago and led him, along with Adalric, through all of the previous week's events. I ended with the horseman.

"So someone followed you here? You could be attacked or stolen or something when you leave? Adalric asked, seeming to understand the threat more than I did.

I answered loosely, "Well, I suppose that could be the case." However, I didn't tell them of the shadowed being I'd just seen. I didn't tell Phoebus how it had held him. As for the horseman himself. I'd nearly forgotten about him until I recited all that had happened. Where was he now? Waiting outside to kill me like Adalric suggested?

"So they were to find flaws in your tax?" Phoebus asked, astonished by the gravity of my days.

"Yes." I now had to fight my eyes from lingering across the room. I was thinking again of the black being. Something made him leave. Even if he was just like the dream I'd seen.

"And Adalric met the man, who was your father's friend, who brought the final proof, who was also staying with the man and his wife who were at the practice?" Amos said, doing his best to understand all the facets.

"Yes, Fidel is his name. I don't know if he is still here or not," I said. Doolby brought us a feast that we all shared in between questions and explanations. I didn't eat though. I had no hunger.

"Adalric," said Phoebus, picking up a piece of meat. "Have you seen him again?"

"No, I haven't," he replied. He had just finished eating an entire bowl of roasted sweetcorn himself. A loud clash was heard, stealing all of our attention to a drunk man who had just proposed to a woman. "I hope he doesn't regret that tomorrow," Adalric laughed.

"Is that the horseman?" Phoebus asked from beside me. My heart sank but I didn't look over instantly. I waited until the room burst in with laughter and glanced at where Phoebus had nodded his head towards. A cloaked man with eyes covered slowly followed the wall line. My glance stayed with him. Amos kicked my leg under the table again.

"Nori, you're giving yourself away!" Amos said sharply.

"I know him," I mumbled, unable to look away. I stood and began to weave my way through the chairs and glad company. The man noticed I was following him. He walked faster and only looked ahead. He disappeared into the back hallway. I followed suit. Passing through the curtain door, I found the man was very near to me now. In fact, he had waited for me on the other side to hold my mouth shut with his hand. He motioned for silence with a finger over his mouth.

"Come with me," he said.

"Adinorium!" Amos yelled as he came through the curtain. I covered his mouth the same as my own had been moments ago, I communicated with my eyes the seriousness of my sudden aggression.

"Are the others coming?" I asked.

"No, I told them to stay." Amos' eyes were set on the man.

"Come on then," I whispered. We followed the man down the hall and up a narrow flight of stairs. We were making our way to the second floor when our leader stopped. He felt the wall with his hand and with the gentlest push, the wall gave way to a door.

"Follow," he said and led on. All other thoughts disappeared from my mind as I realized I was once again living a story I'd soon have to explain.

"We're in the Bored Daisy," Amos said, recognizing the paint color or something like that. I nodded and followed the cloaked being to a door on the left of the hallway. The man knocked, but not like he was visiting a friend. More like he was trying to discover if the room was occupied. With no response on the other side, he grabbed the handle which seemed to turn blue upon his touch and the door opened. On the inside, the room was normal, just like any other in the inn. A bed, chair, and vanity were the basic contents of the room. Some furnishings, of course, a poor resemblance of a home. He closed the door softly behind Amos and me.

"I apologize for the theatrics. It isn't my ideal way of doing things you must know." He went about the room grabbing the wax of the candles to catch them on fire. I searched for a box of matches but couldn't find them.

"I'm sorry, who exactly are you?" Amos interjected. The man smiled, taking off his hood.

"I apologize again. I am Shervan. A pleasure to meet you, Amos." He bowed his head respectively to Amos.

"Shervan. You're Shervan?" Amos furrowed brows turned to raised ones.

"I am he."

"Yes, a joy for you both to finally meet, but why under these circumstances?" I asked, feeling as if I could hardly take any more on this night. The curtains were already drawn in the room and Shervan found only three candles sufficient for our meeting. I still couldn't see his face as well as I would've liked to, but I found no need to complain.

"My business is brief and must be treated as nothing. You, Adinorium, are currently crafting a blade. A dagger to kill and kill intentionally. Don't finish the blade, put it in a box and bury it, melt it down to nothing if you must." Shervan's eyes never left mine. My stomach turned and I remembered the hatred I had forged the blade with. I remember my father not disclosing its soon to be possessor. I remembered thinking it was a beautiful blade but cruel and cold.

"You came all this way to tell me this?" I felt a new stream of questions and unease starting to flood my mind.

"You must understand, Adinorium. You do your dealings in the world of men. There is a deeper battle happening then your eyes can see and ears can hear. Deeper than the shadows. Deeper than the speaking in the tongues of the wind. You would live in terror if you only saw a glimpse of the enemies who are far more deadly than daggers. There are inner workings in that world, and they affect this one. You must not finish the dagger. I've seen its prophesied future and your own. I was never supposed to tell you any of this, but felt I had to," Shervan said. I was struggling to piece his words together.

Ideas beyond me. Was that the being I had seen? Was he no illusion? Had I seen him really? Had I felt his breath?

"You must have Second Sight? I have so many questions, Shervan. Please, put my mind at ease and help me understand." I didn't understand why I spoke of the Old History things like they were true, but I did with conviction. He sighed giving me my answer without using a word. "You can't. Can you? It is a matter greater than me. And, as always, if Adinorium knew all would be lost!" I said in a fear masked with passion and anger.

"Adinorium," Shervan began, putting his strong hand on my shoulder. "I don't know why the Greater intended it this way. I can't tell you matters of men, but I can tell you that hope has been awakened. I've lived a long time, and eyes that possess hope are of the greatest sights to be seen. Your eyes- your eyes have hope. You will find the way." I wasn't satisfied with his answer. I wanted someone to trust me enough to tell me those answers. I don't understand how even the supposed Greater demands I do not know. "I must take my leave. Amos, be loving to your friend. He will need you to be." He left quickly. Amos hurried after him to the hall, but he was gone. I sat down on the end of the bed and gripped a fist full of sheets and covers, holding them as if to suffocate them. Amos said nothing. He just stood and watched me.

"It's getting bigger and bigger. Everyone keeps pulling me in further and further, yet the curtain is still closed, and I can only hear muttered voices from behind it." My curiosity had run its course and delivered me to rage. Amos tried to speak reason to me, but my ears were deaf.

"I know this is maddening to you, but you must listen. If anything has been revealed, it's that it is bigger than you and me. We must play our parts in confidence that everyone else will play theirs," he said.

"Yes, play our parts. Given commands and lines to perfect but not knowing if you are speaking to a man or an animal. Amos, the Sovereign Days begin tomorrow. We've been close enough to see the fire. Now we are coming to a place where we won't be trying to understand the fire and its purpose because we will be getting burned by it instead. Everyone is asking me to be lighthearted because I know nothing and therefore, I should be glad. Yet they do not understand that getting beaten with a mask over your eyes for reasons you do not understand is far more brutal. Let the unknown haunt me until I find her, but then I will only be forced to become a mute, silent, as if I know nothing. If the Greater intended for me to know nothing, then why did he allow me to find everything? Please, tell me again how I am not to know. Tell me again how it is not my battle. I will reveal to you all that has been hidden and I will show you my scars from the battle." Amos found nothing to say. What was he to say? He found himself in the same war, just as Phoebus said. What was the difference? Why did I crave it so much more? How was it that I was able to find it? Why would a dagger matter? "I'm going on a walk. Tell the others I'll meet them at the festival tomorrow. You can tell them whatever you please."

"Nori, I'm not letting you go off alone." Amos grabbed my hand to stop me.

"No! I am not going to sit still and be held to the

ground like this! It is cruel! All of it." I jerked my hand from his grasp. Shaking my head, I left him alone in the room. Down the halls of the Bored Daisy, I went. I wanted to escape its walls.

***

My walk led me back to the forge as my walks normally do. Inside, I lit candles enough to see what was before my eyes. I sat in the chair behind the table and stared at the almost completed dagger. Finding a box in one of the old cabinets, I placed the blade inside to soon bury it. Staring at the blade in the box, I couldn't convince myself to cover it. This was how I was going to prove to the king that I was superior in skill to even that of the Saxon line. It was me forging something my father couldn't. I thought of Shervan's warning. Never had I heard of him forsaking the wall to relay a message. Yet he came to me and pleaded with me begging I not make the blade. As far as I could see, this was the first bit of power I possessed in all of this. I should listen to Shervan and bury the blade in good faith of a friend's warning. But what if I didn't? What would happen then? How could something as insignificant as me making a blade alter what is to come? Surely it isn't because it's a blade. If Saxon didn't have this one, he'd simply get another. It is such a lovely blade. Perfect even. I must finish it, then I'll bury it.

***

"The Opposer is raising himself. He is looming. He is hungry for Strength." My eyes opened without command. The voice was alive in my head. Belonging to a stranger, the voice was pure and sure. I had finally had the ability to rest yet my body wouldn't allow it. At least my mind would not allow it. I sat on the side of my bed and held my face in my hands. At some point, my father had come to the forge and gathered me. On the way home, he had muttered something of his concern that I had been taken. I was so exhausted I had no ability to hear him. I felt like I had been drowned by sleep. It was still a few hours before sunrise, but I saw no use in letting the whispers taunt me until then. I escaped through my window to the forest. I knew it completely. I knew the way the trees stood beside each other and their roots tangled. I knew where the sun would make her entrance and where the moon would replace her when the sky grew dark. I walked as if on sacred ground to find the Polished wall. With help from a tree, I climbed and laid on top of the thick rock. Shervan's words were heavy on my mind. All of them. He spoke of men and things more. Terrors and evil. Such things are what the wall was created to keep us far from whether by man or Greater. He spoke as if they had seeped in. As if our world was already saturated in that very evil. I thought of the black being I'd seen. What about him? What of all of it? I looked up at the clouds swirling around the mountain's top. They were reflecting the moonlight and stars over my head. For a moment, and only a moment, without thought or will, I knew the Greater was real. As if I understood a fraction of who he was. As if the clouds were of his hands and this mountain was his doing. And my dream was no dream at all. But as quickly as the moment came, it left me. My mind shallowed. Again, I saw only a sky and thought no further. A mountain that had simply always been. Numb to anything more, I stared mindlessly into the eyes of the night.

Chapter 15
Celebration

All of my life I've lived believing that when the time comes, when it all depends on me, I'd do right. Yet as I stood, holding the completed dagger in my hand, my mind sang a different song. I rode to the forge early this morning before my father and mother had put weight on their legs, before the Bolg was bustling, even before Chalmar knew of festivities and busy souls. The morning was easier to dwell in than the night. I felt the black being was further from me, even if he was all in my head. I found a wooden box and stuffed parchment in it to cushion the prize blade. Allowing my eyes to rest upon the dagger once more, I laid it in its tomb. I nailed the lid, assuring it a dead man's fate, or a living one's at that. Behind the forge I walked into the woods where we practiced our duels. In the middle of the circle, I began to dig. Forcing the shovel into the heart of the mountain. I gained a new respect for Phoebus and the men of his trade. The brumal chilled ground was not forgiving. It resembled warm iron that a smith would foolishly try and force to bend. I dug deeper than required, but still I felt as if I should have continued to dig more. I shoved the box in its grave and covered it swiftly. Perhaps after all of this was over, I would come back and dig it up. Keep its beauty as my own. If this was ever over. Ridding my hands of the dirt, I mounted my horse. His name was The Horse. His brother was named The Other Horse. My mother asked my father for weeks what their names should be and my father kept replying, "The Horse and The Other Horse." It took a few more weeks before my mother referred to them that way. It has proven to be most convenient, however odd it may be. I did enjoy riding, but it was always restricted. I'd imagined before what it would be like to ride without limits. Run and not grow weary or longing for what was left behind. Over the dunes effortless enough to run across the waters.

***

"Where did you gallivant off too?" Mother asked. She and my father sat together in the living room. They allowed the morning to be somber and slow, being that this night would be anything but that.

"The forge," I replied, leaning against the mantle for the fire to bring life back to my legs.

"Finishing up that dagger, are you?" Father asked.

"Something in that realm," I replied, thinking of every nail I used to demand its inexistence. My mother handed me a cup of tea.

"Magnar and Amaryllis are going to meet us here before we leave for the celebration tonight. Do you know if any of your friends are going to meet us too?" she asked.

"I don't believe so. We all planned on meeting there," I answered, sipping the steaming tea slowly. I wanted to ask my father about Saxon being the one the dagger was for. Why was Garvish Saxon, one in the Saxon line of goldsmiths, getting a dagger made by him? Or what about all the books he'd gotten from the Ivory's store? I wanted to ask him what he is searching for? Or what he was searching for? I wasn't sure if he'd already found what he needed to find. Instead I just asked, "Are you excited for the Sovereign Days?" He exhaled and seemed to be taking a moment to think. I was thinking of what Adalric had said. Was he threatening the kingship? I had thought his desire alone was to condemn the Arrogs. But if his desire was not only to condemn the Arrogs, then it'd be the throne itself he was condemning. As it is, there will always be a king, even if one is overthrown.

"I am not excited, no. I am more eager for it than I've ever been. Eager, anxious. I have no idea what this year will be like," he said, not really talking to me or my mother. It sounded more like a conversation that was going on in his head which he didn't realize he was saying aloud.

"Yes, I think it will be different," I said neither smiling nor frowning. A gut feeling more than anything. The shifting of the winds as Captain Allester said it.

"I have some pies to bake. Care to help, Norium?" my mother asked, standing after a quiet moment.

"Of course." I stood to go with her. "You'll have to tell me your predictions, Father, at some time." I turned and walked away, leaving the door open. Leaving the conversation incomplete. It was an odd thing to be needing answers, knowing who has them, and being with them daily yet never getting those answers.

***

The sun had sunk low into the earth, allowing the moon to become brighter. Amaryllis and Magnar came as my mother had said they would. Amaryllis' excitement infected the rest of us while we rode to town with the horses and our wagon. My mother and I had made four pies to contribute to the celebration and Amaryllis made three more. Tonight she wore a light pink dress that laid loosely on her shoulders. She spent her time pointing out to Magnar all of the small beauties the night held. Magnar, who wore his best, seemed to actually be enjoying her. It took one whose joy did not falter to make him smile for a moment. A task I could not do.

"Nori!" Amos waved to me once we stopped in the town. I nearly tackled him getting out of the wagon. He had already found Adalric and Phoebus who were happy and seemed to have thought no more about our troubles. Their joy along with Amaryllis' happiness helped me step away from all my woes, if only in part. I chose to be glad. Adalric jumped up on the back of the wagon while the rest of us stayed congregated around it.

Magnar scoffed, "Let me show you how gentlemen do it." He jumped down while Amaryllis stood up, he took her hand and bowed his head, then pulled Amaryllis so she'd fall into his arms holding her like a husband holding his new wife down the aisle.

"Simple enough!" Adalric exclaimed and threw himself into Phoebus' arms. It wasn't as graceful but we all got a good laugh. The town looked more glorious than I had given it the ability to even reach. Lights made the darkness look like a towering ceiling. The many long tables made it look as if a massive family had come back together after many new generations to feast. My own and I helped my mother with all of the pies by taking them to a table piled with many more delicacies. The two tables to the right of the one full of sweets were both brimming with meats and greens and potatoes and plenty of bread. Simply looking at them all overflowing made me both full and hungry at the same time. It seemed no expense had been spared. I wondered what wealthy donor was really behind it all. My people were not well off enough to celebrate like this. Adalric had already picked a table for us on the top half of the square that had a lovely view of the entirety of the event. The square had buildings on three sides of it. The floor that the buildings sat flush on, had a fair sized path of its own. Two steps down, and one would be on the solid dirt ground that made up the roads and those sorts of things. There were so many native people from Chalmar that the King's Host seemed less domineering. I nodded to Allester who sat on his high horse watching everyone intently. I saw Father and Mother shaking hands with Amaryllis's parents and joining them at their table. Out of all the chaos, a loud voice boomed over the crowd's chorus of voices.

"Good night to you all!" Fitin Klaw took the middle of the square to begin his speech. His father was the wealthiest in Chalmar, giving him more power for some silly reason. Perhaps these luxuries were provided by his pocket. I had avoided Fitin for most of my life. He was always clever in speech and was trying to commit treason. It never worked because his father just pleaded that he was a foolish boy. That was a true statement, but he is not a young boy anymore. Everyone fell silent and listened to his opening remarks that he made on behalf of his father. "Welcome to the beginning of the new beginning. The celebration to bring many more celebrations. We have all been eagerly awaiting these days for many different reasons and many the same. For some to rejoin with family. For others, a bit of joy was needed. For the ones who wouldn't dare whisper it, a chance. And this chance was gifted to us! A gift from that of our Founders. A gift born in wisdom, nobility, and strength for the common good. A chance to put a new head under the crown. So let us celebrate the years we have had but let us not forget the name of such a time as this. I welcome you all into the Sovereign Days!" He began a chant and all joined in his rally. I clapped reluctantly and looked at my brothers to see their hesitancy.

"Fitin is playing with a fire he hasn't learned burns wildly," I said. I glanced around at the eyes of all there. I didn't see hope like Shervan said he could see in mine. I couldn't find it at all. Fitin wasn't wrong in his speech. If it was anyone else saying it, I may have stood on the tables to cheer. It seemed there were only a few outspoken rebels like Fitin or the Ebony Winds. I didn't think I wanted to join them as they were. Seeing everyone clap and cheer felt wrong to me. It felt more like they were all in a state of drunkenness. Cheering ignorantly just as Fitin speaks.

"Now, now! To make our celebration grand, we always want everyone to join. This is a time when we rest from our labors and look strangers in the eyes until they become friends. Tonight, the celebration has begun. Tomorrow, we honor

Strength. On the third day, King Thann begins his tour and, by the eighth day, he will be here. We will celebrate well until the day all of the many unions present themselves. And then the fun really begins," Fitin said smugly. "Please, embrace such a time!" He closed and walked out of the square to his father's table. The members of that table were all standing up applauding. Music began to play and the feasting commenced. It didn't take long for every plate to be filled to overflowing. The strangers Fitin had talked about slowly became a little more like friends although they also became a bit more strange. I chose not to take any care of Fitin's words. Instead, I'd join in the jubilee as it was.

"I can't imagine this lasting for days," Phoebus said, looking down at his plate.

"It's going to be grand!" Adalric encouraged. "I'm going to get more pie!" Adalric stood to leave. I saw Amaryllis approaching our table.

"Amaryllis!" We all cheered for her like a queen. She sat beside me and leaned in for all of us to hear.

"Wait! I'm coming!" Adalric rushed back with four pieces of pie on his plate. Whether they were all for him or one for each of us, we couldn't tell.

"I've come to point out suitors for you all." Amaryllis grinned. "Fitin forgot to mention this is also the chance of a lifetime to meet more than mere friends."

I protested, "We don't want to hear it, Amaryllis!"

"Oh, hush now, Nori! For each of you, I will point someone out and you can't refuse me," she ordered. I smirked at her persistence. Amos awkwardly smiled, while Phoebus looked terrified. Adalric listened intently to every word she spoke.

"Adalric, over there, the girl in the yellow dress. That's Zaila Crooshion. She comes from old money and is very lively. She's a bit younger than you and her parents are waiting, with little patience, to marry her off," she said, insulting one of them, I wasn't sure which though. We waited to hear what else she had to say before realizing what she wanted. She wanted him to approach her. We all turned to look at him.

"Here goes the only one of us with a fighting chance," he said jokingly, but none of us disagreed. We watched him go over to the curly haired girl and ask her to dance. You could practically hear her horse laugh from where we sat. The sound of it was more obnoxious than it was lively.

"Unfortunate," I said aloud.

"Amos, for you I have selected a lovely girl named Neri. She has an adventurous spirit. I've seen you tame that sort of spirit well. She fills her cravings in books though. That is why you can always find her in the Ivory's bookstore. Over there." She pointed out a blonde headed girl who sat with a few others at a table, including Ellis. She seemed far tamer and less like a headache.

"She seems tolerable," Amos said, looking back at me as I shrugged in agreement.

"What about Ellis?" I suggested.

"Little Ivory?" Phoebus said, trying to find the face of one he used to know.

Amaryllis added, "Not so little."

"No, I'll do as Amaryllis said. Neri is perfectly alright

and I suppose a single dance won't hurt." I wanted to grin at his flustered firmness. I pushed him while he walked on. His approach was far more awkward than Adalric's but it seemed gentlemanly. She accepted and seemed equally as awkward as him. I didn't know if that was a good thing or a terrible one.

"I can't believe you got him to do that." I was impressed.

"I am gifted, what can I say!" She grinned before turning her attention to Phoebus. "Phoebus, for you I have chosen a very peaceful girl. Her name is Shanti Briggs. She and her mother came here from File and Rank when she was about eleven and her mother remarried. She was tutored at home and doesn't come into public often. She is kind and one of the most gracious people I know. We bake together sometimes." Amaryllis spoke most fondly of this girl. "Over there." She nodded her head to a quiet girl who was standing with her mother. This girl was short with brown hair and had an easy smile.

"Thank you, Amaryllis but I can't do that. I'm far too unprepared and silly when it comes to such things," he said.

"Be brave, Phoebus. I believe you'll be fine." I gave him my gentle assurance. Though he stood too quickly and walked over too pointedly, eventually she took his hand, and he led her to dance. The music carried the night. I was glad to see everyone so happy.

"And finally, for you," Amaryllis said with far too much complacency.

"No. No! Not for me," I said. I sat with my back against the table looking out at my friends and their partners. I had no desire to join them.

"I have none." She turned around to join me.

"What?" I was surprised. I smiled and entirely agreed with her. "Well, my apologies for being too difficult a suitor." I was satisfied with myself. I probably should've been ashamed.

"Too complicated actually," she said, correcting me. I cocked my head not knowing what she meant. "But you must tell me. Have you ever met someone? Even ran into a stranger, who caught your attention?" Unfortunately, my face and body gave away my answer. "Oh my lands. You have!" she squealed. It was my own foolishness in reacting. "Tell me, Nori!"

"Amaryllis. I didn't say anything." I tried my best to seem like she was being silly.

"My brother, you didn't have to," she said in all confidence. I lowered my head and exhaled in a playful annoyance.

"Only once," I said. She smiled and settled in for the story. "I was walking home from the forge and accidentally ran into this girl. She was coming from our trail looking up at the sky, while I was staring at my feet. We had a brief exchange, and both went our own ways. There's your story." I made it as boring as possible. And yet that didn't matter. Amaryllis began her interrogation.

"Did you get her name?"

"No."

"How not! Did you tell her your name?"

"Yes."

Amaryllis gasped, "So you really liked her?" She was giddy like a young girl.

"What?" I was confused how she was drawing her conclusions.

"Was she pretty?"

"Beautiful," I corrected her. My thought was that I'd never see her again and Amaryllis was taking such joy in it, so there was no real harm in being honest. And if I really wanted to, I could start making everything up. Amos and Adalric returned to the table both seeming fully satisfied not to dance for the rest of the Sovereign Days. "Thank you, Amaryllis, but I think I'll be sitting out the next dance and all the others after that," Adalric said, slumping against the table, looking over at Zaila Crooshion while she pointed in our direction giggling with her friends.

"Sorry, Adalric. Zaila may have been a bit of a desperate suggestion," Amaryllis admitted. "So did Adinorium tell you all about-"

"Amaryllis!" I hollered to interrupt but my fate had already been decided.

"What! Nori! You didn't tell me about her!" Amos shouted while Adalric's jaw practically hit the table.

"You are all making this far bigger than it really is! I met her once, haven't seen her since, and will never see her again!" I tried to calm the entire table before others noticed.

"So, you've looked for her!" Amaryllis grinned while Amos and Adalric practically hugged each other in excitement. Adalric looked to the heavens feeling as if all of his efforts were finally coming to fruition.

"I never thought I'd see the day!" he exclaimed.

"It is nothing! You are all being ridiculous!" I said,

looking over my shoulder to see if anyone's noticed our absurdity yet. Unfortunately, Magnar was the one to notice and felt the need to march over.

"What is all of this for?" he asked. I looked at Amaryllis and tried to convey that I would never forgive her if she told him.

"We were just happy watching Phoebus. He's on his second dance with the same girl," she said convincingly. I had never seen Amaryllis lie. Magnar looked over at the dancing to find Phoebus.

"It seemed as if you had all heard the greatest news of your life," he added. I looked at Amos and rolled my eyes at their silly excitement.

"Come, husband. Now you must dance with me," Amaryllis said. Thankfully Magnar obliged her.

"Was she pretty?" Adalric asked as soon as Magnar was too far to hear.

"Oh hush!" I said, throwing a roll at him.

***

The rest of the night was far better than that of our silly conversations. Phoebus eventually came back to us. We watched the happy crowd and together devoured nearly three pies. The celebration went on until the tables were cleaned of food and everyone had a somber, full demeanor. My father and mother had left hours ago, but I stayed with Amos, Adalric, and Phoebus.

"Hey Durnin!" Fitin walked over to our table, a bit clumsy from one too many drinks. Adalric had decided to lay on the table to watch the stars while the rest of us reminisced about old times.

"Fitin," I said, changing everything to a tone of seriousness.

"How'd you like my little speech?" He put his arm over my shoulder before I promptly removed it.

"It seemed like you put a lot of thought into it. Made your family happy," I said as graciously as I could.

"Yes, of course. That was all a given though. What did you think about what I said?" He persisted further. "It was meant for you." He smiled and seemed for a moment sober. I didn't understand if he meant it as a threat or a compliment. And why would it be for me?

"Hey Fitin?" Adalric interrupted. "Has your mother found out about your little shenanigans?" Fitin's face turned to anger.

"Is that a threat, Elm?" he said, putting his hand on his blade.

"Oh good! He's more perceptive when he's drunk." Adalric sat on the side of the table unyielding. Fitin began pulling out his sword.

"Why you folly filled little-" he began. I pulled out my own dagger and stood in between the two of them.

"Forget it, Fitin," I said, offering him peace.

"You think you and your little dagger frighten me?" He snickered at the idea.

"It should. Tuck your tail between your legs and go back to your father, Kraw," Captain Allester said, walking over to our table with all confidence. I thought he had left when my father did. I hadn't seen him return. Fitin sneered at the captain but did as he said.

"Thank you, Captain Allester," I said, nodding to him. It was the first time I'd ever uttered such ridiculous words to him; however, I felt I owed him more than I realized. He looked at me and my own.

"You all should return to your homes. Don't want any more problems, now do we?" he said in a way that suggested he would make problems if we didn't leave as he suggested.

"Certainly."

"That was the oddest thing I've ever witnessed in my life." Adalric said after the captain was gone and we stood from the benches at our table.

"Indeed it was," Amos said with a bit of suspicion in his tone.

"What? I was thankful to him for cleaning that up quickly," I said, defending myself.

"I found it rather refreshing," Phoebus said.

"Thank you, Phoebus." I raised my mug to him.

"I meant the part about going home," he said smartly.

"Oh lands." I fussed and splashed the last bit of spritz in my mug onto him. They all laughed and together we prepared to leave. "Do you want to come to my home tonight?" I asked Amos. His father was prone to drunkenness when drunkenness was offered. And even when it wasn't.

"I should make sure my father made it home," he said responsibly.

"That's probably the good thing to do. I'll walk with you," I said.

"Tomorrow night?" Phoebus asked the lot of us.

"If not sooner," I said eager for their distraction.

"My home. Meet there tomorrow." Adalric offered.

"Should we be nervous?" Phoebus asked.

"Phoebus, my dear friend, would there be anything I could do to make you feel nervous?" he asked before answering himself. "Perhaps. But don't be nervous. Be eager. Tomorrow morning!"

"Tomorrow morning." I bowed my head. "Be safe, friends."

"And to you be steady." The rest of them said to me. Amos and I walked in the moonlight to his home and made sure his father was there. We found him on the kitchen floor appearing to be dead. Together we did our best to move him to the bed, but that could not be managed. A pallet of blankets and pillows on the living room floor had to suffice. Amos decided he'd stay at my home. We agreed we could go to the Fordwin in the morning before going to the Elm's home. Amos got a few things for himself and locked the doors once we left.

"I meant to ask; did you destroy the dagger?" Amos asked before we fell asleep safely in my home. Magnar and Amaryllis had stayed the night as well leaving Amos and me in the living room. He slept on the sofa and I on the floor. I'd forgotten Amos was with me when Shervan came. I hadn't forgotten he was literally there. I'd forgotten that he heard everything I did and had thoughts too.

"Yes. Well, I buried it."

"Good," he paused. "I can understand what you mean about Shervan now. There's something about him that is unnatural, but in a good way I think. Just mysterious."

"Yeah."

"About the other night."

"I'm tired, Amos," I said more rudely than I should have.

"I know. I wasn't going to say anything about Shervan. About what Phoebus said. I don't blame you for any of it. I know it's all out of your hands. I know you don't desire it to be like this." In the darkness, my eyes filled with tears. My throat was too sore to answer him. I didn't think Phoebus had meant it either. It was the black being. But I was struck with Amos' care for me. He didn't carry all of the same worries I did. His concern was for me. "It will all be over one day," he said before sleep. If my body wasn't so tired, I knew I would've laid awake for hours contemplating when Father was going to take his next step and all of the worries Amos hadn't taken up. But sleep found me quickly. I surrendered to her pull with reluctant gladness.

Chapter 16
The Chronicles of Strength

"Go on. Knock already," Amos said, insisting that Phoebus be the one to engage in such a terror.

"No, you do it." He turned and gave the command to me. I returned the task to Phoebus.

"His mother likes you best."

"No, she likes Amos the best." We argued standing at the door of the Elm's home. It was one of the few two story homes in Chalmar. It sat in a circle lot with many windows and a modest landscape accompanied it.

"Fine." I surrendered, even though I was never once accused of being the favorite. After knocking on one of the two front doors, a housemaid opened it instantly as if she'd been waiting just on the other side. "Hi! I'm Adinorium Durnin. This is Amos Hawthorn and Phoebus Alder. We're here to visit Adalric." She bowed her head not speaking a word and opened both doors for us to enter.

"This way," she said with a commanding tone. Her face drooped with wrinkles and they weren't the smiling kind. We didn't come to Adalric's home often. I only remember being here maybe a handful of times in the past fifteen years of our friendship. She turned and went deeper inside the home. I looked to Phoebus and Amos for help on if I should follow her. They shrugged their shoulders leaving the task for me again. Seeing as she left the door open, I followed her which ended up being the desired thing for us to do. "He's in his room there. Tea will be served in a half an hour in the reading room."

"Thank you, kindly," Phoebus said to the maid now that all was known. She took her leave with a slight nod leaving us outside of Adalric's room. He lived so differently than the rest of us with servants and maids and lawns and assigned tea times. "I'll knock."

"Oh, will you!" I complained. But I found myself shutting my mouth quickly remembering the black being's hold on him. How I'd caused his anger.

"Adalric, we're here to meet you as you requested," Phoebus said in an overly polished way to mock him. Phoebus' father, Berg, had allowed Phoebus the day to himself while he gathered his papers to make sure they were all in order.

"Maybe he climbed out his window and ran off in a dramatic fashion," I joked. After a moment longer, he swung open the door appearing to be out of breath.

"Come in!" He was patting his head with a cloth. "Thank you, Chambers," he said to a middle-aged man who held things for sparing. The man nodded his head and left the massive room. Adalric only had two sisters and they never appeared in our society as their mother was desperately fighting for them to marry Polished.

"Were you just dueling?" I asked. I was confused. I had

never seen him duel before now.

"Yes. I picked it up about a year ago. Chambers used to be in the King's Host. He's now an instructor for them, but has private sessions with me weekly," he said while getting himself a beverage and sitting in the chair by the fire on the far wall of his personal room.

"Why didn't you tell me you were doing that? We could've practiced together or something. I could've taught you. Swordsmanship is a massive part of my life."

"I just didn't think much of it. I didn't mean to offend," he apologized seeing how much I cared.

"No need to apologize. I'm just a bit surprised, that's all." I was more offended then I admitted but I believed he really meant no offense by it. No need to take one up. I didn't want Adalric to be the next one under the black being's hand.

"Why did you request we come to your humble living quarters?" Phoebus asked. Phoebus and Adalric were closer to each other than I was to either of them. It was no different than Amos and me. However, Phoebus always had struggled with his state of living being a far cry from Adalric's. He told me more about that than Adalric. It clearly made him uncomfortable being here, but I was glad he was trying hard to appear comfortable.

"Right!" Adalric stood clapping his hands, remembering why it was that we were there. "Please, find a seat," he insisted. Phoebus and Amos sat in the two chairs, and I stood behind Amos. Adalric went into a closet of sorts and came back with a rolled-up banner. He opened it wide and allowed us to interpret for ourselves the meaning.

Amos read the words out loud, "The Chronicles of Strength." It was a painted display of the show that would attempt to hold this generation of Strength's attention tonight. It looked very similar to the one I'd been seeing in town.

"It's for the celebration of Strength tonight, correct?" I asked, trying to decipher what he wanted us to gather.

"Yes, a reading of sorts of the Old History, accompanied by a theatrical reenactment. The performance is taking place in Serqumance. At the Lustrous Branch! I'm in the performance!" he said with all smiles.

"Adalric, that's amazing!" Amos congratulated him first. I held open my arms in pleasure before clapping in celebration. Amos and he hugged while Phoebus patted him on the chest.

"Now the poet conquers the stage," Phoebus said.

"You truly amaze me," I said, clutching his face between my hands.

"I've wanted to tell you all more than anything! The day the author came to read my poetry, she introduced me to the director of the show. We conversed over afternoon tea, and he asked if I'd want to join the performance. I went to Serqumance with him that day. That's where I'd gone off to," he said, explaining like a child explains the new thing he's found.

"Congratulations, my friend!" I gave him an added expression of joy.

"And I wanted to tell you all that you're invited! I already got tickets for you. I desperately want each of you to come," Adalric spoke hesitantly but in a tone of complete eagerness.

"We will arrive early so we can sit as close as possible to the stage." Phoebus' discomfort had faded in excitement for his friend.

"I'm nervous, giddy even. Keeping it to myself in some ways made it feel like a dream. Like it wasn't really going to happen. Seeing all of your faces and hearing your words has entirely eliminated that reality. I'm so pleased that you are all excited!" he finished, embracing me again.

"And proud and impressed and curious," Amos said, adding to the list of things we all felt for our friend.

"What does all of this mean for your day?" Phoebus asked after we'd all settled down. Adalric rolled the banner back up and laid down on the floor looking to the ceiling. Amos and Phoebus remained in their chairs, but I sat down on the floor beside Adalric.

"I have an early rehearsal I will leave for soon. I suppose you all can just gallivant around with all of this unfamiliar freedom until this evening. It doesn't take long to get to Section Five from here." Adalric rolled his thumbs one over the other. "What festivities do they have today?" he asked, changing his gaze from the ceiling to us.

Amos answered, "I believe Fitin is doing a reading, obviously feasting, too much dancing, new tradesmen, and other things in that capacity."

"Actually, Phoebus, I wanted to ask, would you mind staying with me until rehearsals? I have a few things I need to go over before then," Adalric asked, sitting up. Phoebus sat forwards in his seat and nodded, agreeing to the task.

"Amos and I will meet you at the Hummer once you're

done," I said, turning to Phoebus. "We'll tell our families and ride there together, making it early enough for a good viewing place."

"I'll meet you there then," Phoebus said. For an hour or so more, Adalric told us more of this happening and how eager he was for its coming. We said our goodbyes while Amos and I had our last jab at Adalric's nerves. We left by the old servant lady leading us out. We'd missed tea time and something told me she was offended by such actions.

"What do you think is next for him to do?" Amos asked that which had been lurking in my mind since my father uttered such things. We sat across from each other on the fallen tree. It was on the edge of the meadow where we'd decided to escape from the crowds and festivities for just a moment. It'd been too long since I'd been with my friend alone and time enough to talk.

"I suppose to expose him," I answered. I rubbed a leaf inbetween my thumb and fingers until it dyed them a pale green.

"When do you think he will?"

"I presume the day the unions present themselves. Makes the most sense. Expose him, end Haben's chances, the unions are then selected, the tournament begins, and a new king is soon crowned," I said.

"You think that is what he wants? Simply for another king to be established?" Amos asked a question like Adalric had. I shook my head, having a difficult time finding words.

"I don't know. I don't know what his heart wants," I answered him without truly answering anything. The Fordwin, the meadow, the woods behind my home, little pieces untampered by us, they were the places that revived me. Made my world feel bigger than a single mountain I was never allowed to leave. Tonight, I'd be told why this had become our fate. Why there is a wall. Why we begged for it. What we were running from. What we won't be able to outrun. Why there is a king. Why there is such a way to establish him. I thought about telling Amos about the black being that had become alive from my dreams. Or at least the illusion of him. But I didn't know how to or what he'd then think of me. We'd never spoken much of the Old History versus the New History. I suppose we didn't know what to be true because we'd been taught both. I had taken time to read them in the old study books I had in my room. The New History, or History, as I essentially can put it, teaches that a group of men had gone out into the desert to find a new home that they could establish as far from the evil of the world as they could. How they saw Strength and journeyed here across the Dunes of Dower. How more came to them and together they built a wall. How they named the mountain Strength because by their strength they built themselves a strong hold. How the wall was sealed so none could leave. And if one did the land would be so poisoned, they'd die. No prophecies. No gifted beings. Simply a mountain that had always been and the people that built upon it. The Sovereign Days had the same beginning. But the Founders were just men with different perspectives, not ones gifted with different things. They used language as if it were magic. Myth were in the threads of the mountain and their rise from nothing. There was such a place as the Bountiful Lands. We were told that before the wall was closed it was discovered that it had been burned with fire. That's why it gained the name Pravity. There was no Greater and no great being of evil that opposed him. Strength would stand forever. No end could come to her. But the Old History. The one my mother spoke of and my father believed. It was filled with depth and darkness and greatness and wonders hard to believe. It had never become more to me than a story. A legend. I hadn't worried much about where we'd come from and what that meant. But I knew the story I had been told. I had never begun to imagine what it could mean.

***

Talk of *The Chronicles of Strength* had flooded the mouths of all in Chalmar. Few were able to afford tickets to the performance, meaning they'd have to settle for feasting together again and Fitin reading the history through his skewed eyes. Once Phoebus was finished at Adalric's, he met us at the Hummer. From there, Phoebus, Amos, and I left around midday after we'd told our families and cleaned up our attire.

"For you." Amos gave Phoebus a black dress coat to be appropriately dressed being that he had no clothes for such events. We now found ourselves in Section Five or Conservative Ring, Area One. This area was under Lord Adonis. We did many trades in Area One and Area Three because they bordered Area Four. I'd been to both areas enough to know my way around. I'd never been to Area Two though. It was furthest away and we had no family to visit so I never had reason nor time enough to go there. The Lustrous Branch was the grandest theater in the entire Conservative Ring. I'd never been to a single show, being that it was never in my parent's interest, and it was quite expensive. Adalric had gone to many shows and always came back marveled by them. Every time he'd do his best to reenact them for us. We left our horses in a community stall outside of the town square. The town in full was called Serqumance P. Forare; where the name originated from and why it was so long, I did not know. Thankfully, everyone referred to the place as Serqumance alone.

"I suppose this is it," I said as I walked up the stone steps to the front of the Lustrous Branch. It had the appearance of a palace disguised as a home. A massive banner with the words *The Chronicles of Strength* was hanging between two pillars. Behind the words on the banner was a desert scape with a single guarded mountain. I wondered if that's what we looked like to the outside world looking upon us. The theater was the focal point of the square. They were celebrating Strength much like Chalmar was now. It felt odd being a part of the high crowd able to enter the prominent place. Phoebus handed over our tickets and we entered with ease, though I had noticed many soldiers outside the doors carefully watching for unwelcome guests. Inside were four staircases leading to the second and third balconies. Everything seemed to be wooden with the exception of the silver adornments, chandeliers, and lanterns. I imagined the Polished Ring had to look similar in grandeur. Straight ahead, I saw a row of open doors to the main floor.

"The Ebony Winds are said to be making an appearance," Phoebus whispered to me once we had entered the large foyer.

"How do you know that?" I asked, always surprised when anyone, aside from Adalric, knew about such things.

"I overheard two soldiers." That made more sense. I wish they would. I wanted to see these brigadiers that I'd heard of so many times but never seen.

"Look there." Amos pointed to a group who arrived in hooded carriages with servants and laughter. "Polished," he said, nodding towards the symbols on the back of their necks. Every person in Strength on the day they turn nine are engraved with a marking symbolizing the section they were born in. One to three horizontal lines for their ring: Polished being one, File and Rank being three, and Conservative being two. Accompanied by one to four shorter vertical lines for area.

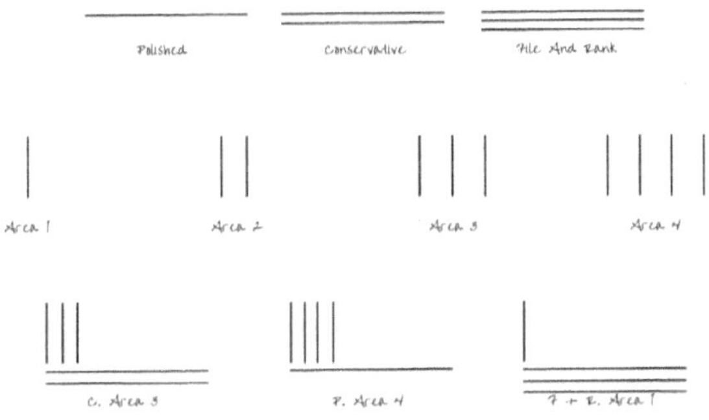

Amos, Adalric, Phoebus, and I all have four short vertical lines that are placed over two horizontal lines being from the Conservative Ring in Area Four. These marking matters when it comes to privilege in traveling through the sections and all other confining things.

"Every last one of them," I said. They went around all of the people and were led in by the Lustrous Branch's host herself.

"Bless me. It's the king's grandson," a crooked Conservative man blurted out. He had stopped in front of us watching the lot of them being led upstairs.

"Which one is he?" I asked, looking up with the man.

"That one there." Having to account for his bent finger, I found the one he was attempting to point at. I stared at him alone. Of course it was him. He could be no other. I could feel my breathing slow looking upon the one I had only known about in idea. He didn't smile and laugh like all the others. He would only smirk or grin occasionally. He was different from those with him. He hardly spoke and when he did, it was to the same man who seemed closest to his stature. He didn't look angry, but serious and sure. His hair was a warm blond that glinted from the fire and jewels. His posture was strong but he was perfectly comfortable.

"He's impressive," Amos whispered. I could feel anger rise in me. He was not yet my enemy, but I felt convinced he certainly would be.

"Come, Nori." Phoebus grabbed my arm to move me along with the crowd. Seeing him was different then exchanging words with Allester or shaking Saxon's hand. It was like meeting someone and having conviction you would soon know them well. Like finally seeing the long-awaited fire that you had only known by smoke and smell. We found seats in the middle of the ground floor. The stage was elevated, but we could see it clearly enough. I looked up to find Haben Arrogs and his own taking their seats in the right hall floor reserved for the wealthy and important. Perhaps his attendance was the real reason for all of the soldiers. I was surprised to find him at a performance of the Old History. I would have thought all the Arrogs believed the History. Then again, if his ancestor was one of the four founders that might lead to belief. It appeared he was with his soon to be union. Four men and whatever women they had found acceptable. Three of them were all smiles. I wondered who each of them was. Moreover, I wondered who their fathers were. The one Haben had spoken to seemed between both. He smiled more than Haben and even laughed a few times, but he carried his seriousness.

"Greetings all from near," a short man, with a scar above his brow, bellowed from the center stage, extending his hand to us, "and far." He was now offering his welcome to that of the king's grandson. I exhaled and chose to watch the stage instead of Haben and his union."The Lustrous Branch is most pleased to entertain you tonight." Without warning, a curtain fell in front of the man. Women gasped. I could hear the sound of jewelry being clutched. "However, we wish to do more than that." The man's voice carried as if he was still before your eyes. The curtains flew open, and my chest sunk into my chair. The stage was black and hollow. There was a chill that rolled like a morning wind from the emptiness. "Darkness. The heart beats in fear because of it." A single being appeared on stage. Barely visible by the gloom of the black. "This is why they ran." The back of the stage was set to fire. It was a picture of the Bountiful Lands being burned from below. "The Gut was opened and a fire conjured by the darkness was let loose. How? The Opposer." By the fire's light, we could now see that this being was surrounded by a physical darkness. Many hands at different heights held a sheet of black cloth. Its hands moved slowly making it look as if it was alive. It was explained that this being surrounded by darkness was Acklina. She was the one who'd been deceived by the Opposer. The one who took hold of his opened hand. The narrator continued, "By one he began his rule. By many he displays it. The shadows made alive. The soul made void." Many more beings appeared on stage. They, however, weren't surrounded by the darkness like Acklina. They had black streaming from their mouths. They did not take the hand of the Opposer, he did not offer it. Instead, he consumed them. The multitude of beings representing those plagued by the darkness. They didn't dance or speak boldly. They just stood, in a way that made you believe their souls were no more and their mind not their own. "Across the seas." The fire fell revealing a painted ocean. The plagued beings and Acklina left, and the helm of a ship was pushed onto the stage. Many swung from ropes and appeared to be searching desperately. Among them, Adalric joined their fleet. "Til the dunes were found." A new pale curtain dropped in front of it all, leaving only the shadows to be seen. The storyteller told the way of the sea and the dunes. The vastness of this world we did not know. We watched the ship disappear and the dune sea rise. Four people crawled and trudged until on their knees they'd all fallen. "The few who still lived believed it would've been better to die by the heat of the sun than to have their soul touched by the darkness. And this belief was almost their reality." Overtaking the dunes and the beings, a light shined so brightly that it almost burned my eyes through the curtains. "The one the Opposer himself fears, appeared before them. He was greater in every way. Pure light and goodness shown from him."

The light was tamed and again we could see the four men before him. "This greater being graced them with shade, saving their bodies from the land. He proceeded to give them each something more to wield against the evil they feared." The four men stood, and the light was now above them as the sun in the sky. "To the first he gave wisdom." The man bowed, not even lifting his head. "To the second he gave nobility." The man dropped to his knees but rose with his hands lifted to the light. "To the third he gave strength." The man crumpled his body, before holding his arms strong showing his might. "The last man spoke in haste. He challenged this savior, commanding an answer as to why he'd let the darkness come at all." The pale curtain rose to reveal the fourth man, Adalric, and the "Greater"' draped in white, standing as tall as two men. The light shone so brightly behind that you could not discover his face. Adalric's chin lifted, he stood shameless before this being. "The Greater showed the man how the light shone brighter in the darkness. How strong bones seemed mightier having known frailty. How he was the Greater, not like this lowly man." Performers had run on stage and acted all of the things in a display of the Greater's words. This left the last man on his knees, ashamed to look at the one called Greater. "The man was given no gift, because of his foolish actions." The stage was cleared and a third curtain opened revealing a replica of Strength. "In the desert, the Greater raised a mountain before the men. It was more glorious than all other things on the land. The Greater told them the beauty would be fleeting, because the other three did not admonish their brother, he would give them this land to establish and flourish, but in time it would fall to the very darkness they feared most." The four men celebrated the mountain, embracing and weeping with one another. "Because the men looked to the mountain as being more glorious than the Greater himself, he cursed them. Being confined to the walls alone was their new fate." A faint whisper came from behind. A black curtain dropped, and everything was pure shadow. I felt a warm breath on the back of my neck. I looked at Amos and Phoebus but the darkness was too thick to see them. But I knew this wasn't part of the act. It was him. *He* was here. Not as an illusion, as a living being of darkness. One walked gracefully on the stage holding a flame that became the only thing anyone could behold. "But the Greater had chosen his remnant. He made another vow to the men that day. From them, he would raise one to defeat the Opposer, by the strength of his own hand." The curtains opened back to the flames of the Gut. The being walked into the flames, and they ceased their burning. The storyteller kept speaking, but all I could hear were his sighs and questioning groanings. How would he have told this story? I closed my eyes, unable to watch on.

"Look!" A voice called out to me. It wasn't the storyteller or the Greater. I didn't know who it was, but I knew they were calling to me. In my searching my eyes returned to the stage.

"Time has continued, and it will go on until the day the snake is slain, the waters rise, and the unfaithful is found." The curtain was closed again, a shadow more ferocious than life was conjured. There stood a man with a crown upon his head. In his left hand, he held a sword, his right was lifted high with a snake slithering around it. Two more men joined the display.

On both sides, they bowed before the crowned being, but one of them held a dagger behind their back. Slowly, we watched a consuming shadow rise from their feet until it had devoured all that could be seen. The crowd erupted in cheering, but I found no strength to join them. They found the display beautiful and mysterious. I found it to be a terrifying reality. I needed to leave this place. I rose and felt invisible weaving through the people to make my escape. Unseen except by him. Where had he gone? I could not feel him anymore. He's looming over me. What had I just discovered? The theater air felt as if it was slowly being drawn out until all would be dead because of its lack. Fumbling through the doors, I saw only one other. Haben Arrogs. He looked at me and I at him. He from his high perch and me from the common man's place. We paused in the space and for the moment, fully saw the other.

"Quite a show," he said descending the stairs.

"Quite the reality," I replied with brazenness. We were slow but not hesitant in approaching one another. I could see in his solid green eyes, he had seen what I had seen. This was no mere legend; it was the destiny of us all. It was our creation. Somehow, I was completely certain. I think he was too.

"Nori!" Amos called, coming from the doors behind me. His walking faltered seeing Haben. Haben ran his hand through his hair and straightened his posture. "Why'd you go?" I looked from Amos to Haben feeling we would've given the same answer.

"Haben," a second man's voice came from the balcony. He was the one who spoke often with Haben earlier. He came to stand beside the King's grandson, assuming the power that gave him. He looked at an uneasy Haben and turned his attention to me. "Ferrox Wren." He extended his hand, but I did not take it.

"Haben! Haben, what's wrong?" A dramatic girl ran down the steps. She shared the color of Haben's hair and his warm ivory skin. Ferrox's attention and extended hand turned to her. Not giving Haben's true state any care, the girl grabbed his face trying to make him look at her.

"Stop, Lila." He aggressively removed her hands from him. "Come Ferrox, it is time to leave," he said.

"But the rest!" Lila complained. Haben had already looked at me once more and departed as if it was the last time we'd meet. The girl gathered her pouting self and trotted back up the stairs having no acknowledgement of us.

"Adinorium, what in the Greater's name was that?" Amos said, grabbing both of my shoulders to assure my full attention and his seriousness. I paused gathering myself while the sound of more applauding from the crowd could be heard. I had too many things in my head. Too many for even myself to know. I'd seen the Opposer. I'd heard the Greater, the only one he fears. And if they were real, it all was. The gifts, the immortal, the prophecy, the darkness, the end.

I confided in Amos, "An understanding."

Chapter 17
Dishonor

Haben Arrogs

The king has begun his parade. The beginning of his last moments of glory and control as king. For thirty-six years these people have been his. It's about time their knees bend to me instead. I, along with my sister, Ferrox, Father, the other section lords, Grandfather, and a few other unneeded persons, greeted our first crowd in Section Twelve. The people are brittle. Should I say, the women are brittle. There were no men present except for the ones who may die if left standing for much longer and weren't capable of work. Black dirt covered most of their hands and their faces were soaked with grime. Filthy, dusty creatures.

"There are so few. Where are the others?" my father asked Saxon, the father of Barnett. His voice got confused with the pin of squealing pigs beside one of the stables in the town. Being a friend of my father, Saxon was chosen to be a leading figure for the Sovereign Days. I disapproved but found no need to fight against it.

"Most of them are still laboring. They did not have the

ability to both complete their taxes and celebrate," said Saxon.

My grandfather said, "That is a tragedy." I lowered my eyes knowing that what he meant as a tragedy and what the people would find to be a tragedy were far different things. "What taxes do they have?"

"All sorts, Father. They should finish them within the month," Lord Arres said for his own section.

"That certainly won't do. No time for celebration. They will finish them in half that time. Make sure it is done. If not, their next tax will be doubled," Grandfather said. "Actually, no. They've spat in my face because they haven't come to me. Double their tax, if they do not finish the demand before the Test of the Common Man is completed, then punish them."

"Punish them how?" Saxon asked.

"I don't care. Burn their homes. Tie them to a tree and beat them. Sell their women as slaves. I want them to suffer for this dishonor." He then filled his chest with air and stood upon the wooden elevation that'd been built for visits and proclamation. "People of Gydon." My grandfather began a speech that was not a proclamation of good tidings but the damnation of these people. "Your inability to celebrate is a tragedy to me." I saw Saxon speaking to a soldier who would soon be inflicting the undetermined "punishment" to come. "I want all to celebrate. I demand all to celebrate." How fragile we are. How is this our foundation? The kingdom of Strength is not a kingdom of many but a home of one. Strength is simply the king's home. It is his. All is his. These people are free-slaves. They believe they can move and live and be. But that is an illusion. The King's Host is not to protect these people. They are the outstretched arms of the king. Why do they obey? Because they can not run away. They need the stability of the king. They need to be slaves, because they'd die if free. It is not a complex thing. A fragile thing. Mysteriously kept. "Welcome to the Sovereign Days. Welcome to the celebration of my grandson, Haben Arrogs." My grandfather had little to say. At least, about these things. "Give the order," he said, brushing shoulders with Saxon on his way to his carriage. He left with my father and Lila, a full command of soldiers, and a coiling hate. Ferrox and I rode horses in between them and the strand of carriages holding the other lords. Leaving the town, the sound of hopelessness and anger arose from the guts of Gydon's women. They understood what it meant. Our venture was demanding. We would be traveling to the next section everyday allowing Grandfather to give his speech before moving on to the next. I found it to be a pointless endeavor. Seeing the scum of File and Rank gained me nothing.

"Are you ever going to speak of what happened last night?" Ferrox asked once we were far spaced in country land. I smirked looking around at the fields and the grandeur of the mountain. I smiled because it was nothing trying to be made into something. After leaving the Lustrous Branch, I spoke little that night and had said nothing of him. The final scene I'd witnessed had been burned into the back of my eyes. The king stood tall in complete ignorance of both the snake and the traitor close to him. If neither of them killed him the waters would. Strength would flood until all perished.

"What do you wish to know?" I asked Ferrox who did not understand me as much as he believed he did.

"Who was he?" he said, speaking of him, the one who saw what I had seen and in the same way I had seen it. It had been as if the Greater had given us the same understanding, in the same way, at the same moment.

"I don't know."

"I don't believe you. You both seemed like you knew the other well. Tell me at what time you met him?" He persisted towards a lie.

"I speak the truth. I do not know him. But you are right that it felt as if I did." I was honest, even if not completely. I never lied. I found no need to, unlike Grandfather did as if it kept him breathing. Then again, it probably did.

"And what do you make of that?" Ferrox was too arrogant to see the clemency I gave him. If he did, he would believe it to be a gift not a potential curse. I looked ahead at the land that seemed barren. A closer resemblance of the desert around it and not the exuberance above it. As for what he asked, the familiarity of him I did not take lightly. The likeliness of us meeting again was slim to none, yet I was entirely certain we would. How or under what circumstances, I did not know. For the time being, I would choose not to dwell on the matter. After all, if it is certain then pondering and searching would be meaningless.

"I think there is nothing to be made of it."

Chapter 18
A Promised Drink

We waited for Adalric outside to congratulate him on such a performance. The second half was displaying the Founders and how they established the Sovereign Days and the Last Days Feast. I couldn't remember much about it. My mind was so far from that place. I do know I felt timid. Small is probably a better word. I promised Amos I'd tell him what had happened if we could finish the play. I just needed more time to think. Not really in a way to prevent one from drowning. Rather, a good curiosity. I couldn't tell if I was excited or terrified. He is real, the Greater. But that means the black being, the Opposer, is real too. And I'd seen him. The town of Serqumance would entertain us for the rest of the night. A jamboree pulled us all into her clutches. Adalric needed to allow all of his nerves and excitement to be unleashed. In a similar way, for different reasons, I needed the same as him. Amos was the least taken of us all. He was anxious to hear my interpretation of what happened. He wouldn't get his explanation tonight. On the dark paths back to Chalmar, we rode by moonlight and in ignorance of the danger around us. Phoebus swore he saw someone in the woods. Adalric joked that it was a brigadier. Amos didn't find it funny. Neither did Phoebus. In short, we were all relieved when our bodies were resting in our own beds, safe in our own homes.

***

I was certain the stone stayed cool while the sand absorbed the sun. I studied the glimpse of the Bountiful Lands which I held in my hands. I saw it differently now. It is now reality. A true thing. I frowned, thinking of it all being burned. I wondered what was in Acklina's head when it was all over. Did she regret what she'd done? I exhaled and felt a pain in my own heart. I thought of the snake blade: perfected, it lays in the ground. I needed to visit Shervan. No, I didn't. He already said he would tell me nothing. But what of the Greater? The Opposer had to be the evil he spoke of. I gently laid the painting back to rest. In its stead, I picked up the book from Ellis. I decided I'd take it to the Polished wall and wouldn't open it until I got there. If it proved to be nothing, I would still be happy because I was in the forest. Maybe it had something to do with all of this.

"Nori! Just the person I needed." My mother smiled when I came into the kitchen. I was trying to find something to fill my stomach.

"Why's that?" I asked. I'd become skeptical of people needing me.

"Your father and I spoke last night and decided we're going to travel to Treften to visit my sister for one night. Would you like to come?" I had been surprised that we hadn't visited or planned any visits with our extended family, nor had we ever invited any of them over to our home. This surprised me too being that it was understood as normal for family to visit together during the Sovereign Days. In my mind, it just further proved my suspicions of my father's knowledge and his potential doings.

"One night?" I didn't want to go if the visit was going to be long. "Yes, leaving tomorrow morning and coming back the evening of the following day."

"I don't see why not." I was mostly wondering if my father had planned another meeting and if he had, could I get close enough to listen.

"Wonderful! Amaryllis and Magnar are coming along too." She only now informed me. I wanted to say that was reason enough not to go. But I'd already agreed and my curiosity outweighed my annoyance. I took an apple from the kitchen and made my way into the woods behind our home. I found a tree to sit up against and stretched my legs out in the grass. I looked down with pessimistic eyes at the book.

"What is your meaning?" I asked the book as if it could respond. I unfolded the walls meant to protect what was inside: *I tell the story of another. One who does not walk under the same sun we do. One who learned to understand what we still have not.* But then nothing. Every page after was empty. I closed the book aggressively. I was angry with it. I found no reason for it to be given to me. Ellis must have been joking when she said she didn't know its purpose. Amusing herself by making me look foolish in my intrigue. But as I had told myself, I wouldn't be angry. I went back into the house, found a closed drawer in my room where the book would sit without my ever giving it another thought. It seemed a good time to find Amos and tell him of Haben and the Opposer I had seen.

The mornings and afternoons of Chalmar remained the same as they'd always been. When the sun began its descent, the stores began to close early, and soon the night would be busier than the day. I was nervous to go into the practice again. The last time I was there, I had first found myself holding a baby then a bloodied man. Thankfully, this time the practice was quiet. Yooldee was prescribing medicine to an older woman while another doctor, I assume Yooldee's school friend who Amos had told me about, wiped his hands clean with a stained cloth.

"Mr. Durnin. Hello there," Yooldee said, greeting me.

"Hello Yooldee. Is Amos here?"

"Amos!" the other man called to a room behind a curtain door.

"Yes?" Amos questioned. He appeared in the doorway with tweezers and plants filling his hands. The doctor nodded in my direction. "Nori! Yooldee–" Amos started before Yooldee cut him off.

"We're fine for now. You've done more than enough, Amos. Unless you'd like to come back and finish your study, I think you can be done for the day."

"Thank you, Doctor." Amos smiled. "One moment," he said to me before disappearing behind the curtain. I waited for him outside. I always found an unwanted awkwardness when I waited inside the practice.

"I'm going with them to Treften to visit my mother's sister," I said, now sitting beside Amos. We were undecided between the Hummer and the Fordwin. We found the thought of the quiet of the Fordwin to be superior to that of the chatter in the Hummer, so to the Fordwin we went.

"Your Aunt Kaya?" he asked.

"And my cousin Carlens and his wife," I added. I had brought Amos with me to their wedding last year. He understood their unmatched stupidity. Not my aunt. Only my cousin and his wife.

"What really happened last night?" Amos changed the subject completely. "You left in chaos. You know the Old History. I didn't understand why it struck you in such a way." He wasted no time in his questioning.

"I think I feel as if it should be a hard thing to explain," I said, rubbing my hands together for warmth. "But it really isn't." I didn't look at Amos when I spoke. I looked out, through the trees, boulders, and places where one could see the mountain rock exposed. "I believed it."

"What? The Old History?"

"Yes." I nodded. He made a sound of contemplation and then looked out as I did. "What do you believe?"

"I think I always believed in the Old History," Amos began. "But I hadn't ever really thought of what it could mean. Everything just seems so normal. I can't imagine the wonders they claim to exist actually existing. But I think it is true. The Founders could have built a wall, but I don't think life is that simple. Perhaps I could imagine Strength's beginning being of man. But what of man's beginning? What of existence at all. In glimpses, I see wonder. I think of your being renewed at the forge. I wondered if that was him. The Greater, I mean," he finished. I inhaled deeply, making my lungs hold the pure air for a moment. I knew Amos was right. Allester believed it was. My mother probably did too. I thought again to tell Amos of the black being from my dream, that I now knew as the Opposer, who had manifested himself in my own world. But I felt I couldn't. I wasn't sure how to explain it. I didn't think I wanted to explain it.

***

"Kaya will be so happy to see all of you!" I hadn't seen my mother this joyful in months. It wasn't the joy that comes from relief. It was a joy that came from peace. Before Amos and I parted at the Fordwin, I told him how it felt like I'd known Haben before that moment when we met outside the theater. How I thought he was having the same revelation I was. Amos didn't have much to say about that. He thought mostly in his head. When I got home from Treften, I imagined he'd have more to say. My father and Magnar sat on the front bench of the wagon. Mother, Amaryllis, and I all sat in the back. I decided to believe Magnar sat beside my father because he was larger than me, not more valued.

"I'm excited to see her again, too," Amaryllis said, squinting her eyes in the sun. My uncle had died from some kind of illness a little over eight years ago. My mother tried to convince my aunt to move to Chalmar, but Kaya was set on staying. Carlens wanted to move. He's Magnar's age. Up to the day of Magnar and Amaryllis' wedding, Carlens had tried to convince Amaryllis to marry him instead of Magnar. Somehow, I think that would have been a worse fate. He ended up marrying a girl named Cenie last year. I'd never met someone so perfectly stupid. After meeting her, even Amos had to admit she was full of folly. While Magnar wasn't a good husband, he was protective over what was his. Between Magnar and myself, I had no fear for Amaryllis when it came to Carlens. Lands! Left to Magnar alone, I wouldn't fear for her. I felt the wagon slowing. I heard a familiar voice yell to my father.

"Where to now, Kane?" I had only just now seen Allester. I scrunched my posture to be lower in the wagon. When the captain looked at me, his face of suspicion seemed to ease. Of course it did. He knew they wouldn't be taking me somewhere really important.

"Treften. Going to visit Dara's sister, Kaya," my father replied, having stopped the wagon to speak to him. Captain Allester raised his head and began to look around.

"Not everyone's eyes are blind, Kane." My father looked into the distance as the captain had done.

"I know." My father acknowledged the warning.

"Dara. Adinorium." Captain Allester nodded to my mother and me. My stomach fell a little when he said my name. After he'd passed, I looked over to Amaryllis. She had lowered her chin as if she was guilty. Allester was threatening my father's decision to leave Chalmar at all. I knew they were watching. How closely? What were they waiting for? What did they think my father knew? Everyone was surprisingly quiet for the rest of the trip. Nothing serious was ever mentioned. I wanted to ask them about the Old History. I wanted to tell them how I knew it was true. But it seemed not to be the time. We passed through the open gates between the lines of Section Eight and Section Seven. Father nodded his head to the soldier leaning against the gate with little care of us. We all did well at seeming not to feel threatened by him. Without him even asking for our business, we passed through. I grinned at how little he understood about who he had just let slip away.

Treften was larger than Chalmar. More people lived in town. Homes could be found above the stores and things. My Aunt Kaya's home was one of those. She lived above the tailor shop. She was a seamstress for the business. It was uncomfortably small, containing two bedrooms the size of a large pantry and a living room and kitchen that shared the rest of the space. The thing I did like about it was that the ones of us who didn't fit into the walls of the home could sleep on the roof. It was half sloped, half flat. On the flat side, strong blankets had been hung up by ropes for one to be able to lay inside all bundled up. The place had a clear view of the heavens with all of her glories. We arrived in Treften before dinner, before the square was filled with their own kind of celebration. I enjoyed seeing how all of the towns and people celebrated together. Chalmar was modest, friendly and everyone felt familiar. Serqumance was far livelier and more extravagant. Extravagant for Conservatives at least. I imagined Treften to be the rowdiest of all the Conservative towns. They had become known for their spiked drinks after having discovered some kind of plant that makes one silly. Amos explained it to me, Adalric, and Phoebus after we saw a man stumble into the Hummer and ask if he could get a goat and refused to leave without it. The plant is called a Gumpah Pearl. A hard berry that used to be used for medicine. Now it is used for escapism and celebration.

"Dara! Oh my dearest sister! I've been long awaiting you!" Aunt Kaya had run out from the tailor shop to embrace my mother as soon as her feet had found the ground. My mother smiled and welcomed Aunt Kaya's embrace.

"Kaya! It is good to be with you!"

"Come inside! Everything will begin soon." I helped Amaryllis down and carried in the few cloth bags we had. My aunt was so thrilled to be with my mother that she seemed not to even notice the rest of us. I wasn't angry about that. I was glad someone was fully seeing my mother and rejoicing over her. A narrow set of stairs was found inside behind a curtain door that led upstairs. Aunt Kaya had arranged an assortment of nuts, fruits, bread, and cheese for us.

"I thought we could stay in for the night. Treften hasn't been celebrating very well. Everyone has become behind on taxes and the folks have been commiserating together rather than celebrating," she said, holding her hands together close to her chest. She resembled my mother, but I'd thought they looked more like cousins than sisters. My mother is the younger sister. Even though it was only a few years difference, it now looked like many years. Grief from the death of her husband had taken a terribly heavy toll on Aunt Kaya's wellbeing.

"Seems a good idea," said Father.

"Very good! I am so thankful you all came. I can hardly believe how long it has been. I mean look at little Nori. He is now a man. Magnar and Amaryllis are in their most beautiful years." My aunt hadn't stopped smiling or softly grinning since we'd arrived. Now she looked like she could burst into tears.

"Speaking of growing up, will Carlens and Cenie be

joining us?" Mother had to ask. I would be lying if I said I was hoping Aunt Kaya would say "no".

"Yes! They should be here now actually." She furrowed her brow. "Well, they will be here soon enough. Please, make yourself comfortable! Eat until satisfied. I want to serve all of you well!" We honored her request. I found it to be a satisfying time. We all seemed okay. Good even. I took time to look around at all of those with me. I loved them all. Even Magnar I had a reluctant care for. Mother and Aunt Kaya had gone on about how quickly time was passing and how they measured its passing by their children.

"Actually, I have some news. Carlens and Cenie are going to have a baby!" she said with excitement but also a bit of nerves.

"Oh Kaya! That's wonderful!" my mother said sweetly, putting her hand over top of her sister's hand.

"Yes, I am asking the Greater that it'd be a good thing." I wondered if that is how many chose to speak to the Greater. What good did it do? Did he really listen? I don't understand how he could.

"I'm sure it will be," my mother said, comforting her.

"Don't be," Magnar mumbled sitting beside me. He was becoming restless with the simplicity of the evening. Thankfully my aunt didn't hear him, but the sound made her turn her head to Magnar and Amaryllis.

"What about the pair of you? Will I have to begin to understand Magnar as a father?" They'd been married for three years, and I hadn't really thought about Magnar being a father. I had thought of Amaryllis being a mother, but never thought about that making my brother a father. I looked to find my own father grinning.

"Yes! Please tell me I will have to watch Magnar's heart melt over a little child," Father asked.

"Perhaps. One day," Magnar said, answering for the both of them. Amaryllis smiled but didn't nod. My mother looked down at her lap and I knew she had wanted to hear something different.

"I'm late! I'm drunk! And I'm very happy!" I heard a voice shout from the narrow stairway. Kaya stood and the smile she had worn vanished entirely. Carlens stumbled up the stairs with the help of a sober Cenie under his arm. I now better understood Aunt Kaya's remarks about Carlens being a father. "Oh my lands. Aunty Dara. Good heavens, you look wonderful," he said, leaning forward as if his head was too heavy for his neck. Carlens wasn't very handsome. He even made me look good. His hair was long, nappy, and in need of a washing. His beard was no different. His teeth were stained and lips chapped to bleeding. Mother opened her mouth to speak but before she could say a word, Carlens had noticed Amaryllis.

"Amaryllis, my first love–"

Magnar interrupted, "Don't forget you're drunk, Carlens. I won't treat you any milder for it." Magnar stepped in between him and the hands that were reaching for Amaryllis' own.

"Carlens," my father said, putting out his hand for him to shake. He stared at his hand for a prolonged moment before taking it as offered.

"Carlens! Why on this lands are you being like this?"

Aunt Kaya said. I could tell she was trying to conceal her desire to yell at him instead of whisper as she had done. She pulled him to the side. My mother did her best to make conversation with Cenie who seemed a bit shy but really just unaware of everything else happening.

Magnar leaned over and whispered to my father, "I don't like him here."

"Then let's get him out of here." My father agreed not liking him being around my mother nor Amaryllis. He was clearly upsetting my aunt. "Kaya. I think my sons and I are going to go into town for a bit. Carlens, why don't you join us." My father wasn't asking him.

"You all don't have to leave, Kane," Aunt Kaya said. She was wishing the enjoyable evening would return.

"We're fine." I had been right in assuming our visit was going far too well. I brought my own dagger and sword with me into Treften. It wasn't that I planned on making war with anyone, but I wouldn't have felt comfortable without them.

"Are you sure it is wise, Kane?" my mother asked in a whisper while we were all putting on our coats. Everyone remained quiet while we quickly prepared ourselves to leave. The only reason Carlens stayed speechless was because his mouth stayed constantly filled with food.

"I'll be fine, Dara. Enjoy your sister's company." He kissed her forehead. Carlens began to protest about coming with us, but my father patted him on the back and promised him a drink.

"Bruder! A drink! Heavy," my cousin said while his voice lowered with his desire. We walked through the square which was made light by massive piles of burning wood instead of the lanterns I was accustomed to. The tavern had both of its doors open to the people in the square and let the celebration flood inside. I noticed the people were drinking burning liquid instead of spritz. The man called Bruder seemed to be the only sober one in the whole establishment.

"Back already, Carlens. I don't think another drink could make you any more ignorant," Bruder said. I liked this man. He was heavy set and had a great auburn beard. He was so large that he could only take a few extra steps behind the bar. He wasn't fat necessarily, just massive.

"Bruder, he is under my watch. I promised him a drink," Father said in defense of Carlens who squinted his eyes trying to understand what the man behind the bar had said. He nodded and poured him a pint.

"Very well, sir."

"I'll take one too," Magnar said. He was standing on the other side of Carlens. It was hard to hear anything much, but occasionally a loud bang would come from the square. I wasn't sure what made the sound, but the people always reacted strongly when it happened. The smell made my nose flare, and I knew my face looked stern and unfriendly.

"Did you say something about the Ebony Winds?" Magnar asked the men at the bar beside us.
"Yeah, a duel in Dagrun left a soldier dead and they think it was them," he said. Dagrun was in File and Rank.

"Fifth one since the king's tour started," the other man chimed in. My father said nothing, only turned his back to the bar.

"If only we heard about as many unions as we did duels. Then we might actually have something." They continued their discussion between deep gulps. After Magnar and Carlens got their drinks, we stepped deeper into the tavern. A door was open to a back alley where people could ride if they wished to avoid the main square. Another large fire could be seen and the sound of swords heard. I led us through the door where we found duels taking place. Men with hair wet from sweat danced back and forth with each other. A thick crowd circled around them. The sound of coins filling bags and hands being fisted into the air mixed with the now faint echo of the larger celebration on the other side of the building made one feel as if they'd found a hidden place full of unclaimed goods.

A man approached us saying excitedly, "You look like able men. A tournament is beginning, care to join. There's a heavy prize for the winner." The man who spoke put his arm over Carlens while speaking to the rest of us. His clothes looked Polished but seemed to be worn ragged. I wonder if he got the old things from the Polished or if he killed the one who previously owned them. I expected my father to speak for the lot of us. Saying something like, "No, we don't gamble with life for heavy prizes."

"Sons?" he asked us instead. I can't imagine how shocked I must have looked.

"I'd love to join," Carlens said, pointing his drunk finger towards the sky.

"Not you, Carlens." My father broke the sad news to him. He didn't take it as an insult. More like a misunderstanding.

"What's a bit of fun, aye?" Magnar said with a prideful smirk. I exhaled and lowered my head and knew I shouldn't agree. Dueling was illegal. Who knew what ramifications could come from this. But Magnar agreed. I wasn't going to let him have yet another thing to hold over me.

"Why not," I said as if I hadn't just listed off a thousand reasons in my head explaining to myself exactly why not.

"Perfect!" The crafty man moved his arms from Carlens' shoulders to Magnar's and mine. We promptly removed them. "Very glad you decided to join. This will be very fun." I looked only ahead of me. The problem with all of this was that I agreed with him. I felt eager and suddenly angry enough to overcome any opponent. Maybe it was because my father was watching. Maybe it was for my own sake. Magnar handed his wooden mug to a man on the side and told him to wager on him. The grungy man raised his mug back to him and took a deep gulp. The duels didn't take place in a straight line as they traditionally did. The two would fight around the bonfire. The current duel was ended by the surrender of one man under the blade of the other. The crowd made of men cheered. They were satisfied with the battle. "It is finally time for the promised event of the night. The reason all of you undoubtedly are here," guileful man said. I looked around at all of them and thought of the terrible odds of us being here at this very time. I was waiting for a soldier to come and call a whole brigade to arrest us. I kind of liked the nerves. "The tournament of sword and dagger. A handsome prize for the handsome victor. Unfortunately, most of you are terribly ugly and will ruin that idea," he said, insulting the entire lot. The crowd laughed. I looked over at a smiling Magnar. Surely, he was thinking he was the embodiment of such an idea. I hadn't crossed swords with Magnar in nearly two years. I wanted him. I wanted to show him how strong I'd become. "The contenders are ready, the fire is hot, and the prize is waiting." The first names were called to include Magnar's name. He'd brought his own sword and didn't even take time to steady himself. His opponent was a man a few inches taller than him. I wondered if he was Draconian because of his height and appearance of strength. However, after Magnar took off his coat, threw it to my father, and brought him to his knees within four strikes, I knew him actually being Draconian was very far from reality.

"I surrender! I surrender!" It was odd to see such a large man weeping, but his leg had just been deeply wounded by my brother's blade. And the tip of a sword to your throat should make any man nervous. Magnar was now cleaning his bloodied blade with a piece of cloth he tore from Carlens' shirt. I breathed heavily while three more duels happened. All of them childish and without skill or proper understanding of how to use a sword. Unfortunately, each man appeared better than they were because the other was equally as bad.

"Daveed Murk and Adinorium Durnin." I rolled my shoulders and stepped out of the crowd into the makeshift arena. The man I faced was a strong man. The one who had ended his last duel with the other man underneath his threatening blade. I had already taken off my coat and given it to my father who didn't wish me the best or pat me on the back before I went out. He taunted me, "You don't look frightening like your brother." I smirked and nodded my head playfully.

Before the man could join in his humorous comment, I aggressively began my attack. His hair was coarse and had small braids scattered throughout. Some of those braids were falling into his eyes as he defended my attacks. He did his best to keep up with me, but I was too strong and efficient. I had his blade pinned and asked if he would like to surrender. Instead, he hollered and tried to push back. Again, I pinned him and he scurried away to continue the battle.

"Stupid boy," Magnar shouted from the crowd. It drove me to act in anger as if Daveed Murk was my brother. But he wasn't Magnar. Nor was he prepared for my wrath. I yelled while lashing out with my blade strike after strike. I sliced his right arm, then the inside of his leg. He kept his sword up to fight me, refusing to go down. Finally, I came down over him with my blade. He could barely hold my strength. Just as my father had missed, my opponent had failed to notice my dagger that had stayed tucked in the shadows. With one strong arm I controlled his blade, and with the other I held my dagger against the side of his neck.

"Surrender," I said with dominance. Behind me, the tavern went quiet, listening carefully to his forced submission. "Surrender," I said once more. His eyes hardened before he spit in my face. I paused for a moment gathering my anger. He managed to make a crowd of grown men hold their breath in fear. I tilted my dagger, looked him in the eyes and pulled my dagger aggressively upwards. He dropped his sword and cried out in pain holding the place his right ear used to be. I walked out of the circle confidently while wiping his spit off my face. The man got up and stumbled out of the arena. The crowd began to cheer only after the next duel was called. I was thinking of my mother and Amos's reasoning, "You're forever altering this man's life for no good reason!" I thought of Phoebus's disapproving face. I think even Adalric wouldn't know what to do with me. But in my pride I stood unmoved by pity and justified. Magnar dominated in the rest of his duels, the same as he handled his first opponent. The older men fought most aggressively against me. My victory over Daveed Murk didn't scare them away; it made them want to defeat me all the more. I fought men called Epthan Grosco and Prier Briggs. By the end of each duel, I had made them both say the word they didn't believe they could before the match had begun.

"Isn't this an event? The final battle. The sons of Durnin!"

"Adinorium, you don't have to prove anything to these men," my father said, grabbing the back of my arm before I went out as Magnar already had. I managed to scrunch my face and smile at the same time.

"You think I will lose?" I asked him. It was the first thing my father had said to me since the tournament began. He inhaled and let my arm go. I walked into the arena and told my nerves to quiet.

"Fight!" Magnar was patient this time. All the other times, he made the first move and he did so seamlessly. Now he waited. He was letting me make the first strike. I gripped my wide blade more tightly then stepped towards him swinging broadly. He defended but didn't counter-attack. We resettled circling around the fire.

"Come on!" The men were getting restless wanting more thrill and blood. Magnar wasn't feeling pity for me, he was making his display of power over me. I swung again, he defended, we reset ourselves. I slowed my breathing, set my gaze on his steady brown eyes then launched forwards. This time I didn't stammer or slow. I kept my persistent pressure until he had to fight back. And he did. The moment he became the aggressor, I could do nothing but defend. There was no time or space for me to advance or make a swing of my aggression. I pulled out my dagger after he'd made my sword fly out of my hands. He exhaled and, for the first time, let his eyes fall away from mine.

"Surrender, brother," he said as if this was his having mercy on me. But now I was like all the others before me. I had forgotten how to say the word. My tongue would be numb if I even tried to form it. "Surrender!" he yelled and came forward strongly. Stepping backwards, I tripped over my own sword. Without thinking my hand reached over and grabbed a branch from the fire. It was like a torch or sword of fire that I held against him. He stopped his forward march towards me. The fire didn't stop him. He struck the branch until it broke and kept pushing me around the fire. He didn't want me to surrender anymore. He wanted me to burn. With an angered grunt, he picked up a fire dipped limb of his own. But he didn't use his like a sword, he thrusted the entire burning branch at me. I dropped my own branch made sword while my father ripped my shirt off me. I hadn't been burnt too badly. I was only a little uncomfortable. I was confused by the small effect the fire had on my skin. I thought it would've burned me more than it did.

"Enough! This duel is finished," my father demanded. My breathing quivered and my body was burning all over. My father aggressively grabbed my shoulder, forced me to my feet, and led me out of the crowd. I heard the men celebrate for Magnar. I looked back to see the skinny man raising up his arm. They got their handsome victor and he got his handsome reward. I covered myself with my coat.

"Are you alright?" Father asked once we were inside. He brought me to the bar where Carlens was trying to convince Bruder he wasn't drunk.

"I'm fine."

"Magnar is strong," Father began.

I quickly added, "I'm strong too."

"I know, Son. I know." I leaned against the bar, trying to appear less tired than I was. I sniffed and pulled my coat a little tighter around me. I'd lost. I wanted so desperately to prove that I was greater than Magnar. I wanted to prove that I was the strong man my father actually needed. The dominant man my father could give greater things to, but I lost. I was proven weak. I never discovered what Magnar's prize was. He never said and I never asked. I kept my long coat on until I could put on another shirt. None of us said anything to my mother or Amaryllis about the dueling tournament. And we had no fear of Carlens saying anything. He babbled about how Murk's ear being cut off was my doing and how his shirt was torn because Magnar needed some cloth. But everyone only took him as a drunk. My father and I slept on the roof. Magnar joined us after he'd become good and satisfied with drink, making Amaryllis perfectly worried. I was so cold to him, that I couldn't even be moved towards grace for Amaryllis' nerves. They were foolishness to me. We left Treften the next morning.

***

I was glad to get home . I was undecided about telling my own about my duels. I stayed awake for a long time looking at the stars over my head. I thought of her for a moment but pushed away the thought as soon as I realized I'd been thinking it. I had far better things to think of than strangers I'd run into. I thought of the snake blade and how my father still didn't know of its burial. I thought of how it was now mere days until King Thann would come to Chalmar. Days until Haben came. I wondered what my father was thinking of. He seemed to be ignorant of any need to worry. Playing faces. I thought of Captain Allester's warning. I thought of a place beyond our walls. But then I slept. Without dream. Without struggle.

Chapter 19
The Call

The king's tour began seven days ago. In those seven days he paraded himself around making heartless speeches and all other pointless things. With him was Haben. His heir. I wondered what Haben thought of when he looked at the people. I imagined he looked more at the wall. Maybe he saw rising waters. Maybe his limitations. Chalmar celebrated every night with dancing, food, and for the past three days, trading. Adalric had gained much favor with the townspeople. Even his mother and sisters came to join the festivities for a night. They came just to gloat about their relation to someone who had performed in *The Chronicles of Strength*. I wondered if they had even been at the performance. My father had been merry like a man with a clear conscience. I didn't understand it. His stability calmed my own heart. Allester had even begun to look to others when my father was present. Phoebus had become quite taken with Miss Shanti, making it difficult to hold his attention for even a short conversation. I thought it was good for Phoebus to be finding joy. He and his family had finished their taxes. But they had to ask for more time, which the Bergs had never had to do. They still worked throughout the day in the mines gaining more coal for the next tax to come. I knew Phoebus had to be exhausted, but he still merrily went about with her. I was glad his father had given him this time to still celebrate. Chalmar's celebration had gone only to being in the nights. Everyone taking on the same philosophy as Phoebus. You must strive to get ahead so as to not fall behind so that you can hope to survive at all. Adalric told me the people used to never labor during the Sovereign Days. Their taxes were easier and allowed them to finish sooner to celebrate in such a way. Allester had already taken away three men during the celebration because they hadn't completed their taxes and had never got an allowance for more time. I wondered how much more severe their punishments would be because they were found out while celebrating. Amos was becoming more and more uneasy about everything going on. My father, his doings, me, what I might do, Shervan, Haben, Thann. All of the things that if I thought about for too long, I would also become disquieted about myself. I think the reality of their preeminence in my life began to numb in my mind being that everything seemed so normal. My father was perfectly fine and the King's Host never laid a hand on him. I didn't understand that. But I did know my mother was happy. At least, she was mostly happy; especially when accompanied by my father. I think visiting her sister had brought her much needed joy. I hadn't spoken much to Amaryllis even though we'd been together for the past few days. She wasn't smiling as much as she normally did. I could think of plenty of reasons for her lack of cheeriness, mostly revolving around Magnar, but I wasn't entirely sure. On the sixth day, I went with my father to help Amaryllis's father at his carpenter shop. I didn't make anything. I just moved around wood and delivered a few things for him to be able to complete his taxes during his extra time of allowance. Amaryllis had no siblings, so her father was forced to labor alone. My father suggested he hire another, but Capri, Amaryllis's father, was stubborn against the idea of needing a helper. For now, he was fortunate to have us. Seeing that the King's Host had been vigilant about taxes being complete, if one was lucky, his friends would take pity enough to help him. I'd asked Phoebus if he wanted any help before their taxes had been completed and they had to request an allowance, but he was stubborn like his father and was quick to deny me. I couldn't help but think of how the next tax would be given under the new king. The thought gave me neither peace nor terror. Tonight, we'd be partaking in our own festivities. It was a night when all would share a meal around their own tables with their families. I insisted on having Amos. I would've invited Adalric and Phoebus too except they had families. At least, tolerable families. But Amos declined the invite being the honorable child he was. Magnar and Amaryllis would be coming, meaning it'd be a most delightful evening.

***

"Amaryllis, dear, may you pass me that?" my father requested a bowl full of corn that had been drowning in warm butter all afternoon. She obliged him gracefully, leaving the table silent again. The entirety of the day had been quiet. It seemed everyone needed a moment to rest from all of their interactions. To me, it felt more as if everyone was holding their breath. Tomorrow Thann will come. Tomorrow we'd all painfully look up to the one we've called king for too long.

"Adinorium, I've been meaning to ask if you'd completed the dagger yet? I am finally at the time in which I need it," Father asked. Magnar distastefully ate his meat like an animal, making it hard for the rest of us to eat peacefully. I'd been waiting for my father to ask. Why now? Maybe Saxon is traveling with them, and it will be the most convenient time. Or maybe even the agreed upon time.

"I did," I said. I thought of Shervan's demand. How I hadn't confessed to my father that he had come to me. That I had buried the blade over a week ago letting it melt into the ground.

"Perfect! I'm eager to see its finished display."

"Aren't we all? Eager to see if he crafted a snake or a curved line," Magnar scoffed. I lowered my head because of my father's eagerness. I didn't speak because of my brother's knowledge of the blade. I wasn't surprised that he knew. Just disappointed. I thought this could be the thing between my father and me. A secret I knew and not all others did. Our secrets could only be called that because of me. Had I not existed at all, it'd all just be knowledge.

Mother was disappointed in his obvious slight saying, "Magnar."

"Adinorium is a very accomplished smith, Son. I have all the faith in his abilities. Even more so than my own." My father defended me.

"But I buried it," I added. I had to ignore Magnar's existence, which wasn't very hard to do, to speak honestly to my father.

"You buried it? Why would you do that?" My father's tone seemed angrier than I had imagined it would. I anticipated confusion more than wrath.

"Because" I shifted in my seat. "I was told to." Everyone had stopped eating because of the new tension that replaced the silence.

"Who would have told you such a foolish thing?" My father leaned back in his chair, making my own spine stand straighter. I looked to my mother who had no defense for me then to Amaryllis who looked at me with empathy.

"Shervan. The day after you returned, he visited me." I was speaking to my mother more than my father. I was afraid to look into his dark eyes and watch him rub his hand over his beard, probably feeling the raised scars underneath.

"He speaks lies," Magnar taunted me. I turned my head sharply to him.

"Magnar!" This time Amaryllis refuted his cruelty.

"Magnar, be silent," Father commanded. I hadn't heard my father rebuke my brother like this in years. He lowered his head as if that'd help him think. "Shervan, the immortal, left the wall and came to you? What did he say?" His interest had peaked. Mine had too. Shervan wasn't immortal. He was a man. What did he mean?

"He told me not to finish the blade. Melt it to nothing if I had too." I was disappointed in my own confession. I spoke slowly. I felt wrong sharing. As if I was supposed to keep this to myself. I thought back to all of my feelings towards the blade. How this was my moment to join the story in a glorious way.

Magnar ridiculed me yet again, "You were given one

responsibility. Why could you not fulfill that?"

"Do not speak to me of failed responsibility!" I roared back at him. As if back at the forge again, my body became heavy. The weight of death coming over me. My bloodied feet and blackened hands played again in my mind. I didn't mean to lash out. Unfortunately, I wasn't in the habit of apologizing to my brother.

"You are nothing but a boy who's convincing himself he's slain dragons. Show me their bones," he said, making a fool of me.

"What are you, Magnar? Tell me, what makes you so high and mighty?" I gritted my teeth and spoke with all feelings of vengeance. Perhaps I was just angry because I agreed with him.

"Nori! Kane, do not let this go on!" my mother demanded. I looked at the table in front of me. I wasn't ready for this moment yet. Every feeling I had since my father began to speak in the shadows was welling up in my throat. Of course, I should feel the same tension as Amos and hold on to it. Nothing was as it should be. It was just quiet. Not sleeping, prowling. I shook my head angrily. I hated the power my father had given Magnar over me. My father's leaving me and not forsaking all to save me. Would he have let me die? My mother said she wrote to him and told him everything. And now, I bury the dagger and I am punished. What haven't I done for them? What more could I have given?

"Let them speak. Go on, my sons. Let the others hear what you have to say," Father said. His tone was stern. Apparently, he wished to hear no more of Shervan and dealings of daggers, but I did. And what of immortals? My mother pinched her lips together looking down at her hands in her lap. Now I looked at Magnar who looked too comfortable for his disrespect.

"Go on then, brother, make yourself plain." Magnar began.

"What am I to make plain?" I asked as if ignorant. They all knew I was very much aware. But I wanted him to say it.

"Clearly you find me lacking," he began, before I interrupted.

"Good."

"You think you're such a wit. So impressive to behold." Magnar said with a mocking grin.

"Thank you for making yourself plain." I said, now mocking him.

"You're unbelievable. If your thoughts were swarming with things as heavy as mine, then you would have hung yourself from a tree years ago. So go on, dear brother. Do tell why you think you're more than the boy I've claimed you to be," Magnar said, turning all the attention on to me as if I was the unreasonable one.

"I don't. I don't think I'm a man, if a man is what you are. But if being a man means possessing the responsibility and heaviness of thought, then I've been a man for most of my life. But I am not a man. Or at least not the man you claim to be, because I have something you cannot possess," I said with passion and authority. My father was right in assuming this discussion was bound to happen. It was inevitable. I was bound to break in anger. In truth, I have no regrets about it being against Magnar.

"And what is that?" he spit. His smile had turned into a look of disgust for my words.

"A heart," I said plainly. At that he slammed his fist against the table, then went on to laugh hysterically.

"Stupid, brother! If you believe you are a man because you wrestle with unknowns, then you have little understanding of living in dark realities!" Magnar's words burned me. If we were alone, I know words wouldn't be my response. Only fists and blood would suffice. I knew he was stronger than I was. I knew he had set me on fire three nights ago, but he could not overcome me like this.

"Don't insult me in that way. You are only proving my point all the more. You have no ability to even understand me," I replied. I knew of dark realities. I'd seen the Opposer!

"I have no need to understand you. It would be lessening what I already know. You say I have no heart, but I have more heart than most," he said. I almost laughed at his ignorance. I sat back in my chair, throwing the kerchief I had on the table.

"And how would you know, Magnar? What heart do you possess? One for your wife, I think not. You treat her as an object, a fine jewel to adorn you. Our mother? No, you disrespect her as if you're greater than she. As if she didn't give you life! Our father? Perhaps, but you are not a man like our father, nor are you capable. So go on, Magnar! Tell me of how I crumble in your idea of a man, and I will rejoice, because I am different from you. Speak to me as lesser than you and I will smile knowing you think of me like our mother. Treat me as someone you have to use, and I will think of myself as kind like Amaryllis. Push me aside and I will be glad knowing I'm gone from your memories like every other soul you've encountered!" I ranted until my eyes were threatened by tears. I never looked away from Magnar's obnoxious being. Yet all he did was eat a bit of food, completely numb to my words.

"You're a fool, brother. And from the way it sounds, you're destined to be one forever," he said, talking through his full mouth. I nodded to his remark, exhaled, and stood from the table.

Calmly I said, "Thank you for dinner. I'm sorry I had to bury your blade, Father." I had to leave through the back door before I leapt across the table with my dagger aimed at my brother's throat. As I passed the kitchen window, I noticed it was open. Curiosity charged me to stay and listen.

"You see," All was quiet in the moment before, "he can't even bear a conflict."

"He's your brother, Magnar. You should feel saddened as well," Amaryllis interjected.

Magnar retorted, "There is no time to feel saddened as he does. He felt a small flame and cried out in pain. Being a man is being able to hold yourself together in the fire, even when you are getting burned." His tone of anger had a way of instilling fear in my chest. I was angry that it was I who had to leave, but he never would. I didn't want to listen anymore, so I left the kitchen window and allowed the woods to choose my path. I had no desire to be somewhere familiar. Everything felt as if it was collapsing onto me. My father was dancing with fire, and I buried a blade. The lies were like a snake slowly coiling around my neck. That is why I hated these unknowns. Because now they were not unknown, yet I had to live as if they were. I knew my father had the power to condemn Thann. I knew he was going to. Everyone was lying to me, and I was playing faces to everyone else. My interaction with Haben, and all that was said between us without words, haunted me. My dream and the prophecy. What was I supposed to make of it all? I had nothing. I did not know the Greater, yet I felt as if he spoke to me. Shervan speaks of evils I cannot see when even now I see their silent hands taking blows at hearts. And still, here I was, in the woods with only the moon above me. I looked as far up the mountain as I could. Upon the top of this mount was the root of all of my distress. I closed my eyes and wished to do nothing more than disappear or forget or be forgotten.

"You must dwell on these things," his voice spoke to me. Opening my eyes, I spun around looking to find grounding. As I had longed for, I was nowhere I knew. I stood on untrodden ground. I was still among trees, but this forest did not know me. In a way, however, they acted as if they did. Perhaps it was only I who did not know them. I looked for the voice, for the one I now understand to be the Greater, but could not find him.

"Why! Why does it matter? Why do they fall on me all together? Why do they live in my head and refuse to leave or be numbed?" I cried out in desperation. I still did not know what to make of him, yet I spoke with certainty. As if I believed more than I could reason.

"The days are evil. You must live with understanding. You must ready yourself." He was gentle. I didn't feel I knew that way of speaking well. He spoke of things no one else dared whisper to me. Of the reality of it all. My father had given me ignorance. All others protected it.

"Why am I to be ready?" I asked, feeling like the insignificant being I was. I realized I had stopped my desperate searching and let my head fall down with my vulnerable heart.

"Because I have commanded you to be," he answered, sounding close. He always sounded close whenever he spoke.

"But why me? I am not allowed to know of such things that need to be readied for. I have been told to let down my guard." I felt heavy, as if the burdens I had in thought were now physically upon me.

"I have told you. I have shown you. I have given your body strength and your mind understanding. I've given you enough of both. You don't need to understand everything. Not yet. I am the Greater, you are the man. As I have said it, so it will be done. Now ready yourself, Adinorium." I looked up to the heavens and found nothing more to say. I had no need to argue. No thing that was left unresolved. I felt too small too. Yet in my smallness, I was seen. He was the Greater and it was him I knew I must yield.

"I will be ready," I said, stable and sure. What he really meant, I still did not know. I didn't understand him: his workings and his ways. Call it a shift in the wind or whatever you please, but I knew he would remain silent. However, more than other times, I again felt him to be close. As if the night's darkness had now been broken by the sun, I now knew where I was. No more than fifty steps from my home. I still had anger for Magnar and fear toward my father, because of the blade. Although now I did not regret how I dealt with both things. I wouldn't say I felt sure or relieved or even at peace. But I knew I would. Just the certain hope of knowing I'd one day attain them in full, gave my heart pieces of them now. But I also felt troubled. He said the days were evil. Something was coming. I'd have to be ready. I didn't know what he wanted me to prepare. A strong arm? A steady mind? An army? A peace offering? I didn't know what I could give to him. It felt like my hands were empty.

Chapter 20
A False Belief

Magnar and Amaryllis were gone when I came back home. I felt as if I had been gone forever yet in the same breath it felt as though it'd only been a moment. I didn't know how long they stayed or what the conversation consisted of when I left, but I found that I didn't care much. Closing the back door behind me, I found my parents sitting in front of the fire. They seemed calm. I believe they were able to act peacefully after the dinner's festivities. I took time to look at them honestly. When looking at my father I had to think that he, Kane Durnin, had the power to end Thann Arrogs and all of the living Arrogs after him. What a power to possess. But even he felt small after hearing the Greater. I wanted to go to sleep. I found that speaking to the Greater allowed my heart to rest even though it had been given a greater burden to worry about. However, after everything that had happened, I knew that wasn't an option. I sat down beside my mother as I always did and waited for our breathing to fall in unity.

"Magnar is blinded to his own failings," Father began. "To correct a bit of flawed thinking though, he does have a heart. I don't think he is sure what to make of it and therefore, he does his best to lord over it." I nodded, but felt the need to say nothing. Less in agreement and more the lack of freedom to speak. "As for you. You are more of a man than I believe even myself to be. I think you are far greater than you know." I felt cautious towards his words. I wanted to believe them, but I didn't know what was true. It seemed odd for him to say these things after he was angry with me. "I'm sure the decisions you have had to make have been difficult," he said. My mother had been silently knitting a blanket. She went slowly, having to think about each motion. After a short time in the conversation, she realized that her mind was too occupied to continue on with the task so she surrendered altogether.

He now asked, "Why didn't you tell me about Shervan?"

"I don't know if I have a satisfactory answer. I was not prepared for him. Not prepared for the dagger to mean anything, then suddenly it did. I knew you'd disapprove, so I buried it after I had completed it. Knowing your disappointment and quite possibly your anger was somehow the better thing." I had no need to speak in lies. I was done with playing the ignorant part when I wasn't. But when the thought came to my mind to tell him of seeing the Opposer and speaking with the Greater, I quieted it away.

"I see." He nodded slowly and rested back in his chair. "I respect your choice. I'm sure it was most wise to take Shervan's advice." I felt my lungs release half the air they'd been holding onto. "Odd for him to come to you like that."

"I very much was." I smiled.

"Where did you bury the blade?" he asked in pure curiosity. I believed that it was just for the sake of knowing. I trusted that my father would honor my decision and the counsel of Shervan.

"At the forge," I answered.

"A curious command," he said. I nodded but found my eyes heavy with the sleep I'd been thinking about. I had been of little productivity all week, but I still struggled to rest. "I really should go visit him."

"I think he'd like that. He is so far from everyone where he is." I agreed.

"A place I'd like to be most days." My father said more to himself.

"You look tired, son." My mother said to me, but she was looking at my father.

"Yes." I stood to find my bed. "I love you both." I promised them. I felt I needed to. Tomorrow Thann was coming to entertain us all with his wisdom and I would begin to figure out how I was supposed to ready myself.

"Adinorium." My father stopped me. "Your brother does love you. If you ever truly need him, I believe he will stand by your side." I nodded, even though I wasn't sure I agreed with him.

"Rest well, Son." My mother smiled, bidding me goodnight. My room was quiet and cold. Empty. Laying in my bed, I exhaled the weight of the day. Everyone was so easy in surrendering their struggles. I was not. No food or drink, dancing or celebrating, company or aloneness could rescue me from the bondage of these days. I closed my eyes thinking of only the Greater. Not the snake blade of Amos, Adalric, and Phoebus or Thann's arrival tomorrow. I thought of what had happened, what it meant then I was able to sleep.

Chapter 21
He Resembled Me

The reality of living and what that really meant weighed heavier on me today. That was because I actually chose to live in it. Mother said my father had gone out early, being called away before the sun even rose. Who called him and what for, I didn't know. Today, the king will come to Chalmar. Thann Arrogs, his lords, and Haben. I had many things on my mind, the strongest being the king. Being that I would see his face today, hear his voice, listen to his thoughts. I had a solemn posture. There was no joy in a thing that I found no reason to celebrate as it so was. However, I did have a newfound ambition. I had been given a command. A command that welcomed me into the greater things I'd pleaded for. I always thought that would come from my father, but he never gave them to me. It had to be the coldest morning of the season even though the bite of the chill had gone away, she had returned and made herself well known. I took The Horse to town and found Amos at the practice. He was busy catering to the people with injuries of all different sorts. He said he'd meet me in the square before the king's speech that would be taking place at sundown. I told him that I wanted to speak to him sooner. I knew I had to tell him of the Opposer and how I'd spoken to the Greater. I decided I'd go back to the bookstore and read whatever I could about the Greater for the day. I thought I could try and find Adalric and ask him my questions too. I figured he'd have a better understanding now, being that he was in the Chronicles of Strength. I needed to understand what kind of being he was.

"Amaryllis!" I called her from across the square. The rush of production and people made all the other days of a busy Chalmar seem slow. Everyone was scattered going from here to there. Thann was coming, and they acted accordingly. Riding over, I dismounted The Horse and found her appearance frightening. "You look pale. Are you alright?" She tucked her face down and seemed too desperate to hide what she was feeling. "Come on." I helped her onto The Horse, abandoned my going to the bookstore, and took her to the forge. It was closer than home and I knew I'd be able to start a fire for her quickly. "Where's Magnar?" I asked after giving her whatever additional layers I could find including my own.

"He left with your father last night," she said. She was trembling as she spoke.

"Last night? I thought he left this morning," I asked. Why did they have to leave so urgently? Why did my mother lie to me about it? I warmed my own hands by the fire now, but I remained concerned because of Amaryllis's appearance.

"After you left, they knew they needed to find the dagger. Your father came and gathered Magnar later and they haven't returned. I was on my way to the forge when I felt something. I don't know how to explain it. A sharpness. A pain." She looked nowhere but the fire. I put my lips to her forehead to feel her temperature. She felt fine but looked as if she'd been left outside all night.

"I'm going to go get Amos." I made her look at me and nod knowing she understood what I said. But before I could leave the forge, I saw three shovels with fresh dirt on their mouths. Her words finally made themselves clear to me. I looked over to her with my new understanding.

"No," I whispered. Running into the woods, my eyes filled with tears from the cold. They'd found it. My father unearthed what I had laid in the grave. A dread came over me. I didn't know when they had found it, but everything was too perfect. Finding the blade, both he and Magnar being gone, the king coming tonight. The blade wasn't for Saxon. It couldn't have been. I ran back to the forge. Amaryllis was standing looking at the road. "Amaryllis!" I went to go demand she sit, but my eyes saw what hers were set on. An entire band of the soldiers riding towards town on horses. All armed and in full dress. "Stay here," I whispered to her. Mounting my horse, I rode without stammer to where they went. They passed the Bolg and I knew they rode for the heart of the town. Charging on, I dismounted and left my horse unaccompanied. A large crowd had formed in the lower part of the square. All of their business ceased, and their feet became frozen to the ground. The sky wasn't glad. It looked like it could have burst into tears. No, like it could send down lightning to strike us. It wasn't disheartened, but angry.

"What is happening?" I asked a man who stood in front of me.

"King Thann has come!" He exclaimed, pointing to the head of the square. A group of king's soldiers stood with swords in hand. Allester was their lead. Without thinking, I moved closer to figure out what was taking place. No one seemed to really know, and they all assumed it was the king's tour coming early. But the day was too cold, and my heart was too heavy for it to be such a thing. "Allester! Captain Allester!" I began yelling. If anyone was to have answers for me, it'd be him. I continued getting closer and calling the captain, but it seemed pointless. Until he finally looked in my direction and I waved until his gaze met mine. At the sight of me, his eyes softened. They weren't cruel like they normally were. I would almost call them remorseful. Why? A band of horsemen rode to the front of the stage, followed by a completely closed wagon. Saxon led them to their place above the crowd and they dismounted. I looked towards Saxon only to realize he led the king and his men. Why were they already here? I stopped at my place seeing the king. He needed no platform to stand above the rest of us. He appeared taller than all others, but then I noticed this was only because of the crown upon his head. His face looked younger than he could actually be. He had a certain ferociousness in his gaze. Though, if you looked for long enough, I think you'd find his gaze was not truly ferocious but afraid. They were the same mild green as Haben's. But his hair was dark, and his complexion was all different. I didn't understand why he didn't fight for king again. From here he looked youthful enough to. Arres had a fainter resemblance. His hair a weaker brown and his eyes dull. He didn't try to hide his posture of fear. It wasn't a fear of the people though. I think he hardly noticed them in regard to himself. It was a fear of his father and if Haben was as I'd known him, a fear towards his son. I frowned when I saw the girl, Haben called Lila, come from a covered wagon. She wore a grin that no one wore when genuinely happy. I had no care for her. Actually, I found that I detested her. All the while I was looking for him. For Haben. I found him by first finding Ferrox. Ferrox, who had previously extended his hand to me, rode beside him. It was very clear he was Haben's favored. He seemed to share Haben's seriousness and lack of joy all together. I inhaled as if preparing my body to battle when my eyes settled on Haben. He remained stoic. Never even looking down at the people. For he was above them all. It would be a shaming of his own self if he did such a detestable thing. I wanted him to look at me. I wanted him to see that I was here. I exhaled my pent up nerves when the other lords who also rode with them came before Haben to bow their heads to him. They were: Adonis Winick, Thelonius Brim, Kiro Kant. I nearly laughed to myself seeing them bow their heads to Haben and not him bowing his head to them. I was impressed by Haben. He had managed to make the crown fear him and treat him like he held power before he held any. But my desire to laugh ceased when remembering the look of the captain's eyes. I changed my focus to the crowd looking for Amos, Adalric, Phoebus, my father, even Magnar, anyone I knew. My heart was heavy with physical pain as I only found half-familiar faces or total strangers.

"My people," Thann's voice said loudly. The confusion now stood still, captivated by the mighty voice. Thann had spread his arms open like a father welcoming his children. I clenched my jaw in rage, giving my all to hold back my tongue. I hated him calling me one of his own. I tilted my head noticing the gold jewelry that hung from his ears and neck. His teeth looked whiter because his mouth was surrounded by a beard. His hands adorned with rings molded around stones. "I am pleased for you all to join me, my family, and your lords before the appointed time," He lowered his hands and began scanning the crowd with an intimacy I hated. Having the sheer audacity to look these people in their eyes, as if he was ignorant to what he has done. No, he was perfectly aware of what his hands had accomplished, and that was the greater evil. "There is a certain urgency and unease to things coming before their appointed time." I felt as if I could hear my heart beating in my head. He spoke in a mystery that I could only imagine had a cruel conclusion. But that wasn't the only reason my heart began to pound. He was here. Not the Greater, the Opposer. His black being came from the forest line. His hands were clasped behind his back. He looked upon Thann with dominance. I now remembered the last time I'd seen Thann. It was in a dream, and he was dead. "I had wished to meet this day with jubilee. Chalmar and the people of this section are most beautiful, as my forefather believed." He spoke of the founder who had been gifted wisdom and whose body was buried in the meadow. "And yet, we meet before our appointed time, with a spirit of disappointment." I imagined the man who had been gifted wisdom would have been disappointed too. Not with the day but that this was his blood. He nodded his head to Saxon who called upon some of his men. From the back of the crowd came a tree being held by six men. It had been stripped of its branches and bark. It appeared as if it had been carved until smooth to the touch. Two shorter trees followed. In the center, the tallest one was placed and to both sides the shorter trees. It was a traditional execution display. The body and head would be tied to the middle and the arms hung over the smaller two.

I was watching this ordeal only passively. I was truly looking through them and at the Opposer who stood proudly behind it. I knew no others could see him, because if they could they'd be screaming out in terror. "This time was supposed to be a display to my people that I am a king who sees them. I see their struggles and their triumphs. This was supposed to be a joyous thing. But some among you have decided I must display this in a different way. I am a king of justice and seeing all, means seeing even the shadows that wish to devour us." How dare he speak of justice. How can he speak of seeing shadows when he stands in front of the Opposer, unaware of him. "Treason is a weighty thing. A powerful thing and the strongest form of betrayal, and I must grievously punish it." Thann walked over to Arres who held a closed box. I began again to slowly move closer to the platform feeling drawn towards it. Arres opened it and handed his father the dagger inside. It was the most beautiful dagger I'd ever seen. Taller than most, on its blade rested a snake mixed with vines and leaves. At the end, the tongue of the snake extended and sat up like thorns. Pure iron. Without flaw or blemish. And evidently, it even had the power to be raised from the dead. A cold feeling came upon me as the whole world erupted. Not the crowds, just mine. My world erupted yet remained silent. A man, who had been beaten so severely his face seemed unrecognizable, was dragged in front of all the people to the higher ground beingwrest bound to a soldier's horse. They strung him up on the tree just as I thought they would. But I knew the man. Even with his face covered in blood, bruised, and beaten. His face resembled mine, but his heart didn't. For his heart was not mine, because it was greater. My father hung from his hands and his head laid low. I shoved my way through the people with all force and brutality needed. I didn't look at the Opposer again. My eyes were on my father. Thann took his hand and shoved my father's head against the post with a fist full of hair. He placed the dagger on his neck and first pressed down, drawing blood. I cried out, but none cared for me. He pulled the dagger across quickly, letting his own blood drown him. I thrusted myself past the soldiers and held my father. I put my hand over his throat as if I could stop the quick stream of blood. I used my body to hold his weight up, but it was pointless. A couple of desperate attempts for air, then he hung dead. I sobbed while muttering things one says, as if there was hope, though you know there's none. I didn't know what was happening around me. The people weren't silent, but their voices were not of rebellion. Only confusion and fear. No more soldiers were needed to hold them back. No one moved or raised a single hand against the act. Thann and his lords were quick to relieve themselves of these people who were lesser than them. I didn't care about Thann's satisfaction or looking Haben in the eyes for him to see who's father he'd killed. Was this what the Opposer had come to witness? Was this the work of his hand? I slowly lowered our bodies to where his ropes would help hold him. My eyes blurred making me for this time blind. I cried out in all the pain and rage I possessed. What had he just taken from me? I wasn't even thinking. Nothing made sense. My mind was seemingly as dead and empty as my father's. Magnar came behind me and had to tear my body away from his. Where he had come from, I didn't know. Some of the local men took down my father's frame, covered him, put him in a wagon and took him somewhere I could not follow. His blood had fallen on the ground. Scaring this place forever. My breathing picked up while my mind honed in on the new reality of living. Reality. How was I supposed to live in this reality! Magnar left me as soon as Amos and Adalric had come. I still sobbed in pain and fought against not following him.

As in a blink of an eye, I was in a wagon on the way to my home. Amos and Adalric sat on both sides of me. Magnar and Amaryllis sat in the front. I wondered if she was watching. If she'd seen what I had. Across my shoulders sat a blanket for warmth, but I found no comfort in it. I looked down at my frozen hands to see them covered in my father's dry blood. I was shaking from the cold, but also terror. I now sat dull and senseless. What had just happened? When we arrived home, my mother's wailing could be heard from outside. Someone had rushed ahead to tell her, or maybe she already knew. Magnar opened the door, and I slowly made my way inside. Mother was crumpled on the floor while Captain Allester stood by the fire. I saw his remorse. I understood why his eyes softened the way they had. He had known what was going to happen.

I could only mutter, "Mother." Seeing me, she motioned for me to embrace her. It was a fierce hug but her bones felt weak. I hugged her back with my head resting on her shoulder. We were on the floor together for minutes before she let go and took Magnar in her arms. My eyes were becoming dry from the amount I had cried, and they went from blind to burning. Adalric went to the back to get some more firewood and we had all found our own places to settle. Amaryllis and my mother sat side by side on the sofa. The sound of soft groans and sniffs came from them. I sat on the ground in front of my mother. As near as I could be. Amos sat against the wall across from me. I knew he mourned for my father's death, but I was sure he was more sorrowful for me and frightened by what I would do with the new burdens placed upon me. I looked up to Magnar who stared into the fire, not breaking his gaze. Where had he gone? When was he separated from my father? How did he not save him? Allester had left promptly at our arrival. I suppose he saw the look in my eye that told him I had the passion and ability to kill him if I felt it so necessary. I inhaled a quiver and exhaled through my mouth. I had never felt so afraid in my own home. Never so exposed.

"How did it happen?" my mother asked, being the first to speak into the silence. Night had nearly come. Phoebus arrived a short time before. When he came through the door he dropped to his knees beside me and pulled me into his arms. He was still blackened from the mines. You could see that he had been in a panicked cry by the streaks of pale outlined by a deeper black on his face. He stayed seated beside me since then. I closed my eyes tightly now, seeing the scene in my head. I clenched my teeth and tried to swallow my tears down my raw throat.

"I don't know. I went to the forge where I found Amaryllis," Magnar replied, finally engaging. He sat down in my father's armchair too carelessly for me not to cringe. How dare he take it without caution! How dare he take it so quickly! Did its master not just die? Did our father not just die! We sat silent for a moment longer. I could hear my mother slowly crumbling the cloth in her hand that she'd filled with tears and sobs.

"This morning I felt the tension of the day. Not just in the cold, but in my chest." My voice cracked as I spoke. I didn't look at any of them as I began. I didn't want to. I couldn't bear to. "It was bound to come. The day of tears, when all is revealed." My neck snapped down remembering his beaten body. His inability to even speak. "I went to Amos, then found Amaryllis. She was unwell, so I took her to the forge to care for her being that it was closer than home. She told me that Father and Magnar had gone out to find the dagger. The dagger that I should've burned!" I said in sorrow. I think of Shervan's warning, but with it, I inevitably have to think of my pride. It was my blade that got my father his audience. It was my blade that made his time come sooner than it was appointed. "Amaryllis and I saw a full band of the King's Host riding strong. I followed them knowing it wasn't going to end at the

Bolg but in blood. The entirety of Chalmar seemed to have gathered. Then I saw the king in all of his power and glory." I didn't speak of the Opposer I'd also seen. He made Thann look weak, in his black robes old and dull. He didn't need to speak, he could simply be. "He spoke of urgency and time. He spoke of seeing all and how we should take joy in that. He deemed this day as one of disappointment. He said treason was the strongest form of betrayal. That he had to punish it grievously." I gritted my teeth and mocked our ruler. I mocked his speech, his power, and his existence. "Then they dragged him from their hidden place. His skin was red from blood and blisters. His face almost black from the amount of times it'd been hit. They'd stripped his feet. I could see the slashes which I imagined covered the rest of his body. His chest was bare and shallow knife cuts dressed him. They bound him to the tree. Thann, with all care, placed the dagger against his throat ever so gently. Only enough for him to feel its sting and destruction before it would end him. Then he was dead." I was speaking of a memory that would be forever with me, though it had taken place a short time before this one. I shouldn't have spoken so explicitly in front of my mother. I had no control of my lips and my heart spoke for me. No one could break the silence in a cry. My mother put her hand on my shoulder, but now I could not bear comfort. I left through the back door. I needed to clean my hands of his blood. My eyes again glazed over as the tears began streaming. I started a fire under the wash bin, and began pumping the faucet for water. Steam began rolling out from the bucket as the cold air claimed any warmth it could. I got down on my knees and viciously scrubbed my hands trying to rid them of my father's blood. My breath quickened, as I played the scene back in my head over and over again. It wouldn't leave me! I cried out in desperation. My hands kept the faintest hue from his blood. I took the dagger that was tied to my side and I saw it with a new power. I felt a new desire for its purpose. I wanted to kill him. I wanted to shove it into Thann's chest. But not just Thann. I would start with Haben. Then go to Arres. Then his lords. I would want all of them to happen slowly. Give him enough hope that he could save them, when in all reality he couldn't. He would die last. Knowing what all loss was like. Knowing that it was him who brought it upon those he loved. I don't know if I even wished to kill him. I almost wanted more to lock him in a cage and give him just enough to make his eyes open in the morning. Let him live out his misery instead of relieving him from it. My thoughts should horrify me, but they don't. I should be ashamed I could even manage to conjure them, but I'm not. I was commanded to ready myself, but this was far from what I thought could happen. If I had destroyed the blade, my father couldn't have gone. He wouldn't have had the time to make another and it wouldn't have been good enough to give to Thann himself. It was my blade that ran across his throat and spilled his blood. It was my hand that brought his destruction. That blade was the first part of the greater things I had been entrusted with. And with it, I killed my father.

Chapter 22
Son Of Wisdom

Haben Arrogs

"His son. What is his name?" I questioned. I leaned against the mantle staring into the heart of the fire. I recognized its burning.

"Durnin's son?" my father asked, stirring his liquor with his finger.

"Yes. The younger one." I left the mantle and sat in the chair across from him. A shot of the burning liquid was given to me and I drank it quickly.

"He is called Adon- Ada- I don't know. Something strange. Adinorium! Yes, his name is Adinorium." My father clinched his teeth, embracing the burn and his easing mind. Yes, I recognized the fire's passion and burning. I had seen it before in his eyes. Whatever rage and sorrow he felt, I had never felt so strongly. I'd never felt like the fire.

"A shame he had to so closely witness his father's death. He even forged the blade himself." My father leaned his head against the chair and closed his eyes, satisfied with his day. I found no such ease in my bones. He was the one to rise anew.

The one whose body was revived. The one they couldn't beat the truths he knew out of him. The one who'd seen the reality I had seen. The one who matched my gaze. The one who understood what I understood. The one who's father we'd just silenced. I left to find my grandfather. He was in his own room looking out of the window. I was surprised that he even took the time to watch these people. It didn't seem in his nature. However, I think he feared them more than he realized he did. We were now in Treften. We left Chalmar after the execution. I didn't like this place. Not the town. Not this room. It was somber. Yellow walls and white trim. The bed had been made the monument of it. Paintings of places and more windows than the other rooms covered the four walls but it was lacking. All it did was anger me. Reminding me of where I wasn't.

"Where is the snake blade?" I interrupted his stare.

"Haben, I'm glad to see you. I wanted to talk to you about the execution. It was a needed thing. Kane Durnin had the ability to destroy us all," he said, reasoning with me. I almost mocked how much power he held. How fragile our throne was. How close a single man was to destroying the king.

"And what of the others who whispered in the shadows with him? You simply assume they will not speak?" I questioned his confidence. He smiled at me.

"Kane Durnin was their mouth," he explained while pulling a box from a dresser drawer. "I have cut out their tongue."

"And what of his son, Adinorium?" I spoke his name with a seriousness no one else seemed to feel. I couldn't stop thinking of him rising anew. I had seen his fire, but it was burning him, breaking his soul. Yet he had endured pain. Completing a perfect tax without blemish. How strong would he become if he endured this? My grandfather opened the box to reveal the dagger. It had been cleaned and rid of Kane's blood.

"I cut out his heart." He looked between my eyes and I could almost swear he had. "Here. Keep it. A gift." He handed me the prize dagger and made his way back to his window. Only that I now held the blade in my own hands, could I see the skill it took. From the black silk handle down to the two tipped tongue. I rolled it in my hand and established a familiarity with its grip. I would keep it as my fire. Remembering the heart it possessed.

Chapter 23
A Trade of Blades and Death

The thing about death that I admire, is it always does exactly what it says. It warns saying, "I will take from you," and from you, it takes.

We rode in front of the wagon that held my father's body. I wondered what it looked like now. I hardly understand that the last I saw of my father was him at all. Not only was I given the burden of never seeing him again, but I was also given the burden of last seeing his body as beaten and destroyed. That made the last time I saw him as he really was, being when he told me Magnar would stand with me if needed. I focused on the clouds rolling by. I was thinking back to the Greater's command to me. My father's death was tied to his words. The Greater had called me into something I thought was a creek, not a chasm. I remained lost in thought about the Greater, his doings, and my father as the wagon continued to travel over the bumpy road. The wagon was pulled by Heber and Nadim, friends of my father. I didn't know them well, but apparently, they knew him in that way. It was the second day since his death. I wondered if Haben saw me at the execution. I imagined not. Surely, I was dead in his mind. My brothers never left me. Amaryllis and Magnar had been staying at our home. If it hadn't been a comfort to my mother, I would have wanted them to leave. It was natural for me to want Magnar gone, but it was foreign for me to want Amaryllis to be absent with him. We now rode to File and Rank, the last place I went to a show with my father. We were taking his body to the wall for Shervan to burn it. I would have to face him. Surely he'd know the blame was mine. Surely his warning would be on his tongue as the flames grew. Leaving our home, we would go through Chalmar. Traditionally, all would stand outside their homes or dwellings, holding candles to light our path. But no one held the small lights this time. No one bowed their heads to mourn. They stopped, starred, and thanked the Greater it wasn't their body lying in the wagon. He'd been accused of being a rebel. Accused of treason. He was not allowed to be mourned. In the early morning, the sky was an ugly gray as if it was sharing in our sorrow. The clouds circled the mountain and seemed to frown on how we had come to understand the meaning of strength. Down the mountain, past a bowing, tearful Mando, we went slowly and peacefully. Riding past the Crow House, I pulled the horse's reins back. I didn't say anything, didn't think much either, a distant memory of a different time. When I'd just met a fox and my father met the shadows to plot his rebellion. When I had to give my father the reins. I looked down at them in my hands now. I gripped them firmly, raised my head needing more air, and rode on. We were all different people then. All a bit more confused and uncertain of what was to come. There were many things it could've been. But surely none of us thought it'd come to this. And if we had thought it, surely we didn't understand it. Through the small town I caught a glimpse of Fox Tramp glaring through his window. I wondered if he started grinning when we passed. Thann had so beautifully proven his philosophy of life for him. The rest of the day was spent in a silent remembrance that made the mind lifeless. We were all trying to understand something only time could teach. We had to go further down the wall to meet Shervan. There he stood readied, meaning he already knew. Who had told him? He doesn't usually know the dead until they are brought to him. Maybe he had known I would fail and also knew that meant my father's death. The burial place was already prepared. A circle of ground that had been uprooted to dirt, a thin layer of dried grass was laid down in an oval, six dried branches laid a foot apart and parallel to each other and a single thicker branch laid across all of them. The dried grass, wood, and cloth would all be sufficient enough to ensure the body was entirely burned. I dismounted my horse and helped my mother, who had ridden behind me the whole way, to the ground. Shervan bowed to my mother and gave his condolences. He bowed to Nadim, Heber, Amaryllis, and Magnar all giving them his sorrow. I stood closest to the wagon looking down at my feet. I hoped he would go past me and take the body without a word. Instead, he embraced me. Holding the back of my head firm. My body went stiff, but after a moment, I broke in his arms.

"He was always going to die. I was warning you for your sake, not his." He looked at my eyes, but my face winced, still unable to look into his person of certainty. He released me and moved to the wagon. Nadim and Heber lifted my father's soul emptied frame onto the place Shervan had prepared for him.

"His dagger," Shervan asked Magnar who'd carried it. Magnar took it from his side and placed it into Shervan's hands. Going to the wall, he used it to carve the name of my father into the stone. It would dull the blade and steal its entire tip. It was an honor for a blade to save one's name. It was tradition that if the lost had a dagger that one should be used. If they did not have one, a fine one should be purchased in its stead. Standing so close to the wall, I felt as if my father was the one freed from this prison, as if we were the ones still captured inside. Fox's philosophy. Shervan handed the dueled blade to my mother.

"Now his name is sealed by these walls." Shervan bowed his head to us. "His body can rest now." Birds fled from the fields with the sound of fire gasping for air. This was really the last time I saw my father's body, even though it was now hidden in cloth and rope. My mother hugged me, sobbing on my shoulder. Everyone else wore grim, tear stained faces. Amid their tears and sorrow, however, I saw only fire in their eyes. I knew there was only fire in mine.

I helped my mother onto the horse after we'd watched for a long moment. The others had already ridden ahead to find the tavern we'd be sleeping in tonight. The fire would burn late into the morning. I wanted to stay until it went out, but Shervan always sent the ones who remained away, so their memory would be of a burning fire and not cold ashes.

"Adinorium," Shervan said to me before I left with my mother. He stood at the wall where he had carved my father's name. He was close to my height but more slender. His hands, however, were large. You'd never guess they belonged to the rest of his frame. "Your father made his own choices. It was not you that killed him."

"But it was my blade," I said, unable to be speechless now.

"Yes, it was. And those are the consequences you'll have to bear. But you did not kill him." I finally looked him in the eyes. "Thann did," he said without fear of the brutality in which he said his name. "This will now either be your fire, or the fire used to burn you to your own death. I beg you to take hold of it. I beg you to make this fire yours." What he was asking me to do, I didn't really understand. I was to ready myself and I did not. I was supposed to ready myself to come alongside my father and I didn't have time. Why would fire be needed? Thann already burned everything to ash. And fire is no good if all is ash.

"Be safe, friend," I said, embracing him before leaving. All other times I felt certain I would see Shervan again, but this time I didn't share that same confidence. I said goodbye like it was a final parting.

"And to you, don't let the fire die." He sent my mother and I off to find our place. I looked over my shoulder to see Shervan looking at us, but instead my eyes found the fire that raged behind him. Its flames were very much alive. But I knew, by the morning it would be no more. His fire would not even attempt to help the sun. How was I supposed to keep something alive that is going to die?

***

"My condolences." I was sitting at the bar in the tavern. It was more of a handrail than a bar really. We stayed in a tavern called

Tham Cep. In the town called Noph. The tavern was the only thing in the town and the only tavern within a half day's journey. It was late. My mother and Amaryllis had already retired to their rooms, and I wondered if the fire that had been ignited to take my father's body was still burning. Fox Tramp had come and stood beside me, shuffling his hat around in his hands. I was surprised he'd come here. We were a decent way from his shop. "Your father. He was young. I'm sure whatever happened was a tragedy." I wasn't drunk with alcohol when Fox spoke to me, but my mind was clouded.

"Whatever happened?" Magnar was drunk when he opened his mouth and stood from the table he shared with Nabim and Heber. "He was executed by Thann!" I got up quickly standing in between Magnar and Tramp. I was surprised I had the heart to. I would've thought my heaviness would have kept me from even trying to build a wall of defense.

"He said he didn't know, Magnar," I said calmly, but it was more from tiredness than being truly calm. Magnar retorted,

"Then he should be enlightened! He was executed by the king and his lords for treason! Treason!" Magnar was now yelling to nothingness in anger. He stumbled about before falling against a table. I was glad no others were here to see him like this.

"I spoke ignorantly then. That is more than a tragedy," Tramp said, turning to Magnar.

"Thank you, Tramp." I nod to him. I wanted him to leave so Magnar's rage could be no more but an internal steeping.

"Was it true?" Fox questioned once I had turned my back to him and Magnar went in search of another glass.

"The only one who could've told you has been silenced," I replied feeling a bit of anger arise in me now. It was a fair question, but clearly the answer had just killed my father. Heber and Nabim sat quietly but put off a tension that Fox Tramp was either ignoring or curiosity called him to exploit it.

"So it's true then. Someone found a way to expose the king," Tramp's voice grumbled. "And the King slit his throat to keep him quiet." He found a seat at the bar beside me. I didn't look at him, feeling fear by his words. I looked straight ahead through a small hole in the window behind the bar. I wanted to run out into the land I saw. Open fields with broad trees on hills sounded calming. I'd build a tent and sleep under the stars every night. "So," he began in a whisper, "are you going to fight for king?" I looked at him sharply. My vision of the tent on the hill vanished. I felt as though Thann was going to burst in here and kill me for only listening to the treasonous question. "You look stunned, boy. From my eyes looking in, that's the *only* thing to do." I would've laughed if I wasn't so frightened by the thought. I looked over my shoulder to see if the others had heard. Magnar was staring at us, but he was still seated which assured me he hadn't.

"That can't be done. Not by me. No one would follow and rightfully so. I wouldn't know what to do. That is a world I do not understand." I frantically pleaded for such an idea to be seen as pure foolishness. Instead, he inhaled and exhaled slowly. While he breathed, I held my breath like he'd stolen it from me. He leaned in even closer than he had been; so close his eyes couldn't meet mine equally and he hardly had to whisper for his voice to fill my ears.

He proposed dangerously. Accused viciously. "How do you kill a snake?" I didn't have to pause, but I did. He was a cunning man. A sly fox. Showing me that I could not deny what I already knew.

"You cut off its head," I whisper, less to him and more to myself.

***

"Adinorium." Amos was the first to greet me when arriving home. He offered to stay at our home to keep the fire hot and prepare the place for us when we returned. Magnar and Amaryllis parted ways with us in Chalmar and went to their own home. Nabim and Heber would stay a few days longer to make sure the King's Host wouldn't be coming around. They weren't comfortable leaving my mother without defense, even though I was confident in my own abilities. I think it was more so my mother wouldn't be lonely. Nabim's wife, Nila, would come after her mother came to keep their three daughters who were still young. My mother also wrote to my Aunt, Kaya. If she would come to visit; I didn't know. I wanted to intervene and send them all away, but my mother allowed them to come and stay; so I said nothing. In the times of quiet, I thought back to my conversation with Fox Tramp. He had left after a few more drinks. He didn't say anything else. Just patted my back and asked for a round. I chose not to think of what he said. I feared death would be inevitable for me if I even allowed the thought to linger. Besides, the strongest men fight in the tournaments. They are the ones who truly believe they can overpower both the king who reigns and the others trying to reach his throne. I hadn't been strong in days. I was living in mourning. Everyday I would lay awake without the ability to get up, much less pick up a sword. It was the eleventh day of the Sovereign Days. Thann would be far from me now. In the Polished Ring someplace. Maybe Nocrah. In eight days, Haben would stand strong and present his union while I would be crouched at my knees before my father's grave. In the days to follow, many would come and give their condolences to my family. Most would bring meals and share their fond memories. I never did much more than smile when they would laugh at the tales of my father which they were reminiscing. I found that if anything was true of my father, it was that he was the best of men. His death was a sacrifice. A sacrifice for every person who came through our doors and many more who didn't. He loved them enough to fight against the evil for them. But now he is dead. It felt like the hope of one strong enough to continue on died too.

Chapter 24
The Burden

"Dara," an unfamiliar voice said, offending the silence in our
home. The stranger entered without warning in the late hours
of the day. Outside, the moon reigned and inside the fire was
our sun. He was the youngest person I'd seen come to visit
alone. My mother seemed to know him well, although I'd never
seen his face. He was unkempt in clothes and appearance. Yet,
he was a strong man, armed with a sword and from what I
could see, three daggers. Heber left on the thirteenth day, once
Nila arrived. It was only the fourteenth day now. Nadim and
Nila shared my mother's room, she had mine, and I slept in the
living room. Only Mother and I were awake when this stranger
came.

"I wanted to come sooner." He sounded sure of himself
when speaking to my mother. Although he was the youngest
one to visit, he was still years older than me. A few years older
than Magnar maybe. His sureness of voice carried to his
posture. I was confused as to where he was from but wouldn't
be able to discover it because his dark hair covered the markings
on the back of his neck.

"I am grateful for your sacrifice. I'm sure you have been all the way around the mountain by this time," my mother said. By what time? Why would she know when he had begun? I stood behind both of them staring cold at the stranger. I felt like I should've known him. He was too familiar to my mother.

"Something of that." He smiled. "I'm sorry." He took my mother's hands giving his remorse.

"He knew it would come to this. We all did," she replied graciously, but it was a lie. I didn't know it could come to this. I didn't know anything. I was thrown into the fire without knowing one had even been ignited. My mother had an unusual empathy for him. Why? He knew. That is why there is grace. No other did my mother comfort by saying my father's death was a possibility. His attention now shifted to me. "Adinorium?" He was more intimidating when his sole heed fell upon you.

"Yes, this is our second son," my mother answered and stepped back for the stranger to observe me.

"He resembles you more in features, but his manner is of his father," he said without a grin or a smile. He was beholding something new, but at the same time, familiar. "I have long awaited our meeting, and long been afraid of it." I furrowed my brow not understanding him. Why want something you fear?

"Who are you?" I asked bluntly, exposing my ignorance. I had not long-awaited meeting him, nor had I long feared it.

"My name is Fidel Deep," he answered, unveiling my eyes. "I have been your father's closest companion since the beginning of all of this." Of course. That is why I felt to have known him. He was the one Adalric saw and described to me, the guest in the family's home, the one to bring the final proof, the one who would have to flee around the mountain to conceal his own knowledge and action. "I have come to mourn with you, but I have also come with a request in urgency," he said with an edge of Polished tongue: ultimately just trying to attain what they desire. But something in his tone or demeanor made me think he wasn't purely that way. What now confused me was that he wasn't speaking to my mother. He looked and spoke to me directly.

"What possible request could you have for me?" I said. I could hear a mourning man who wished to simply mourn in my own voice.

"Dara, may I have a word with him alone?" My mother smiled close lipped, grabbed my hand, squeezed it sweetly, and shut herself in my room. I knew the walls were thin and if she wished to listen, she could, but the emptiness she left uneased me. Fidel walked over to the fireplace, focusing on his breathing. I believe he was piecing together whatever he had to request. Standing by the fire, I could analyze his face more. His skin was tan and used to the sun, much like the people in File and Rank. His eyes were dark, but in the fire, you could see that they were a rich brown and not a pitless black. He had a beard cut close to his face, it seemed to be the only tamed thing of his person. I now understood Adalric's difficulty in understanding where he was from. I was also wondering where he'd been, why he was here, and one couldn't guess where he would go. "Your father did many things dressed in the shadows of our world. He said you'd understand them as greater things?" He looked at me for an answer to his understanding.

"Yes," I replied. For the first time since my father's death, I felt as if I had just begun to remember. I remembered a curiosity. I remembered how I burned to know of these greater things. It had felt as if they had been murdered with him, but the way Fidel spoke challenged something entirely different. I felt a flicker of life inside of me. Not Thann's death as I had wished. Something I was now cautious to feel. Something I feared to feel. "Adinorium," he paused, looking into the eyes of a boy who'd just lost his father. "Kane requested you take up his sword and fight for king," he said, explaining nothing more. I clenched my teeth so my jaw would not fall while trying to understand the entirety of his words. Something I could not understand so quickly.

"Take up his sword? Fight for king? Was that his heart? Ultimately to gain the throne?" I didn't believe he was speaking of my father. He was a mighty man, but he did not desire the throne.

"No! He never intended to fight for king. His desire was to tear Thann and his blood line from the throne. To prove the Sovereign Days are corrupted. However, we knew it was ambitious. Somehow the knowledge of our possessing secrets was exposed. By whom, we do not know. It was only a matter of time before Thann sought us out. So, your father decided to seek him out first by way of a dagger. The plan was to condemn Thann in front of all the people during the ceremony of the Chosen union. That way the people would be witnesses and we could begin a new kingship. But knowing if we did not act quickly they would silence us forever; your father went to

Thann at the section line, accompanied by witnesses of the Children of Nobility, high captains, and other people of prominence, to confront him. As we are both aware, instead, your father was murdered, and the people mourned quietly in fear. We agreed that if one of us were to die in a public way, and the people not ready themselves to fight back, that they weren't ready for something more. As it was proven, the people are too afraid to challenge for a new kind of kingship. They've been so deeply ingrained with the way things are, that they can't see what could be. Because of this, we'd have to meet them where they are. Meaning, our only way of change would be to fight for king." He was persuasive. Speaking with sureness of things most men would hardly dare mumble. He spoke of things I had only wondered. Within days of my father's death, another told me everything that had been forbidden to me. Not only did he tell me, he asked me to take hold of them as my own.

I interjected, "But why me? I wasn't a part of any of that! Why would you ask me to be the head of your union and potentially your king?" I questioned like I was trying to dissuade him. Convincing him it was folly to even think of such a thing. I knew I was equally trying to convince myself of the same thing. Telling myself this burden wasn't mine to take up.

"I didn't, your father did. He chose you. He believed you possessed something that the rest of us did not. I couldn't tell you what exactly," Fidel said bluntly. His reasons stung me, but I was far from offended by them. If anything, I appreciated his open hostility. He must have trusted my father's judgment wholly to follow through with his choosing me. Being so quick to make himself clear that it wasn't his own doing.

"Why listen to him? He's dead. You could have been the head and I would never have known the difference," I asked. I wanted to understand him. Fidel dropped his head. I suppose he was getting tired of me already.

"Because I believed Kane Durnin when he said he would bring change to this dark seized mountain. I believed him when he said he'd lead me well. I believed him when he said that snakes lived among us. I believed him when he told me to flee like a desperate man. I believed him when he said he'd be willing to die for this. I believed him when he told me this is only a moment, a glimpse of eternity. The only possible thing I could do when he said he wanted you to be the head, was believe him," he continued in a tone with enough conviction to bring tears to my eyes. The way he spoke of my father made me question if I, myself, had ever trusted him as Fidel had. "I'll tell you like your father told me: if you choose this, it is your choice alone. I can't carry you, but I can take your hand and stand at your side. Only the Greater knows what will come from this. Only the Greater has the power to do anything with it. It does not matter how sharp your sword." He stayed by the warmth of the fire. I sat down slowly into my father's chair. I needed to feel as close to him as I could at this moment. I needed to understand why he'd ask this of me. He said he never wanted his burden to be mine. He said he'd do whatever was in his power to keep it from me. Yet now it seems his dying wish was that I'd carry his burden even further while knowing I'd be running towards the very thing that killed him.

"And what of Magnar? Surely he does not agree with such things," I asked, remembering my brother.

"He didn't. I have not spoken with him since your father made us swear we'd establish it in this way," Fidel answered my questions kindly, although I felt as if he wished I had known already. I nodded and stared into the fire. Clasping my fingers together, I remembered my father's blood clinging to them. There had been blood dripped around every knuckle and soaked into every crease. I remember how effortlessly Thann killed him. How none opposed the king. How within a moment. my father was gone. As if all of these years were leading him to a moment beyond what he reached. How his greater things were ripped from his hands. Now it seems they've been placed in mine. "If you are to do this, you must ready yourself. It will be of greater brutality than you've known," Fidel stated. He gathered himself to leave, but my eyes stayed to the fire. I'd have to ready myself? I'd have to ready myself. The Greater's words screamed in my head. I thought he was preparing me for my father's death. However, Fidel made me think my father's death was readying me to fight for king. But I can't. How am I supposed to fight for something I cannot reach? How was I supposed to risk my life for something I cannot attain? I am not wise, for I should've burned the blade. I am not strong, for the desires of my pride should've been squelched out. I am not noble, for I should've heeded a friend's warning. I am not above the common man; they would never look at me as capable of anything more. Fidel concluded by saying, "The ceremony to present the unions is in five days. Tomorrow, the king and his tour will conclude after presenting themselves to Section One. I will be staying at the Bored Daisy, until I go to Area Two to the town of Redelah, where the unions are to be presented. Being that it's on the other side of the mountain, it will be a long day's journey. I offer you myself if you'll have me as part of your union. I will not lead my own, nor will your brother, this we have sworn," he said, finishing his last words before leaving in the night. I didn't have an answer for him. My head wanted me to stand firmly and say, "no." I, of all men, had no place in the tournament. I had no right to be king. But my heart. My heart would not let my tongue loosen and spill such words. Shervan said that my father was going to die. My dagger had just been a guilt offering to Thann. It was Thann who killed him. It was Fidel who quoted my father in saying choices were their makers' responsibilities. It was the Greater who commanded me to prepare myself. My heart was at battle between what I was commanded to do and who I was. How could I entrust such a powerful fate to myself? The room remained quiet for only a moment after Fidel's departure.

"He made his request?" My mother came and sat across from me. It seemed she was listening. At least listening enough to hear the front door close. I shook my head, looking over to her. She wasn't anxious like I'd seen her when my father left or when Allester came. I think it was the lies that brought her such anxiety. The constant fear of being discovered.

"You knew what he was going to present to me?" I asked.

"Yes," she smiled and nodded graciously. "I've been waiting for him to come. It was the only hope I had for these trudged days."

"Hope?" I questioned why this would bring her hope.

"Because, Son, it was the only thing reminding me that

your father did not die in vain," she said without caring whether I would accept Fidel's proposal or not. She seemed to have faith that I did already or, at least, would.

"Magnar can. Ask your friend to ask him. Then it will not be for nothing," I spoke in desperation. I needed this burden to not be mine. But my mother smiled and lowered her chin.

"It could not be your brother. He shares your father's passion, but he is too hardened. He'd be too blinded to be wise and too coarse to be noble. Even though he'd have the strength to rule mightily, that is not enough." She was disheartened by her son, my brother. I nodded in a somber agreement. "I see that this is very sudden. I can even understand any fear you have. Of course, you have a choice. If you wish not to, you do not have to. I will still love you as much as before because you are my son. But I have all the faith that you can walk this path. Not to say there will not be pain, because there already has been. If anyone had the heart of your father for good, it is you. Your heart has been the only whisper of comfort the Greater offered me. That is why I speak with such certainty. I know your heart will not let this evil be." I didn't answer her, exhale, nor nod. I waited until she kissed my head goodnight and went away to sleep. She spoke of my heart. I wasn't in the practice of going where the heart leads. My mother was far from that too. I've been told the heart is often evil, jealous, and vengeful. Often leading us away from what is true. But my mother was calling to the part of my heart that desired what was good. The only part that would be able to burn hot enough to convince the head to push on, even when the original flame faded. I looked down at my hands. I realized I had been doing this often. By my hands, I completed a perfect tax, cheered glasses together with my friends, and dueled with my father. By my hands, I had crafted a dagger in rebellion that assisted in my father's death, held my father's blood, cursed in darkness the name of our king. I did desire to avenge my father. I did desire to eradicate evil from my homeland. I desperately desired the greatest things. In the deepest part of me, I knew I desired to be king, and that terrified me.

Chapter 25
I'd Follow

I felt like a stranger among everyone. Even my mother felt like an unfamiliar person to me. Sleep was not gifted to me as I grappled the entirety of the night with my own motives. Today, I plan to meet Amos at the Fordwin. I am conflicted about what to tell him. I know he'll say it's simply my emotions and I should not act upon them. But I needed his voice of reason to tell me what I already know. I needed my friend to tell me that this is not my sword to take up.

Brumal had kept her chill, begrudgingly allowing the sun's warmth. I found no coats needed, only longer sleeves and some things to layer. I would watch the leaves falling and imagine what it would be like if they were rain. Amos had not yet arrived, so the rocks and the stream greeted me instead. Like old friends who had missed my company, they sang songs of life to me. Taking off my boots I stood in ankle high water. It was freezing, but I needed the sparking feeling to remind me I was alive like the forest's song.

"Your feet are going to fall off if you keep them in that cold." Amos made himself known. I couldn't grin at his words, too burdened with the nerves of what I was to ask him. We laid in the sun's comfort for a while. No words were needed. This was good for I needed to feel. I needed to feel the piercing water and cordial sun that were both gracious in their gentle call to the living.

"We are very far from where we were when this season began," I said with remembrance in my voice. I was forcing us to remember what has been.

"Very much so," he replied tenderly. I needed to express my thoughts.

"I saw it coming for weeks, for months. In my bones I may have known it even longer. I thought of it, studied its meaning, begged for its answers, agonized over their secrets. Yet now that I know, all I can do is remember. Remember the agony and the pondering. Remember that this is what we're all doing. But why do we strive to remember when we've already lived its meaning?" Amos allowed me to speak of my passion without anger or annoyance. The trees also sat still to listen.

Amos answered me in my own language. "I suppose because remembering is the only thing that gives living, life. It is the only thing that can ready us for the next greater thing." I looked over to him and felt as if he had read my mind and discovered my anxieties. If what he said was true, then all of this living I've done was simply preparation for what was now being asked of me. But how could that be? I laid my hands on my stomach and searched for the sun through the tree branches.

"Amos," I was afraid yet sure as I began. "If I were to tell you I was fighting for king, what would you say to me?" His breathing paused, knowing full well what I was really saying.

He sniffed and put one of his hands behind his head.

"First, I'd stop. I'd allow the seriousness of what those four words meant magnify in my mind. I would wish to scream in fear and beg you not too. But I would not. I would embrace you, make sure you were listening to me, and I'd say, "You've been fighting for something greater for a long time. Of course, I fear for you. Of course, I wish it didn't have to be this way, but I think you and I have also known deep within us that it always would turn out like this. Lastly, I'd pack my things, say my goodbyes, and I'd follow you," Amos said, friend of friends. My breath was filled with all fear. I sat up and looked at my hands. They had already done so much, what more could they do.

"Last time I was entrusted with something more, I forged the dagger that killed my father," I said. Amos stood and offered his hand to pull me up.

"Now those hands have a wisdom that otherwise they might not have had such a conviction about before." Amos was the wise one between the two of us. Far more insightful than my mind could reason. I didn't feel as much like the stranger I had been feeling I was this morning when speaking to him.

"I'm terrified," I said. Amos nodded and looked out to the land. By his side, I looked out at the peace I had taken for granted for too long.

"I suppose you'll have to be brave then." He smiled. "When does it begin?" We realized time was suddenly against us.

"It already began long ago. We will leave in four days from this one."

"Very well." He nodded his head looking down at the

water. I inhaled as we watched the mountain living in the forest and stream. We started walking although neither of us said where we were going. Maybe we would go sit silently in the Hummer and pretend like the mountain wasn't on fire. No, now I'd need to tell Adalric and Phoebus. My brothers. My union. The people would still be celebrating tonight although there were some among them who grieved. Fidel was right in saying they were not ready. I now knew what I had to do, but I hadn't found the heart yet to do it. Or maybe I've always had the heart and now I must figure out how to do what I must.

"Magnar!" I called to my brother. He was riding across the bridge to town when Amos and I came from the Fordwin. He dismounted his horse and aggressively came at me as if the reason he was on his horse and going to town was to find me.

"Did Fidel come to you?" he growled, coming all the faster. I had begun walking backwards to get away from him. I felt fear thinking of the last duel we had, and how if he so desired, no, if my father hadn't intervened, I would be a dead man now. "Did Fidel Deep speak a word to you!" I finally stopped moving backwards.

I answered him with fear and anger, "Yes, he did." Magnar got as close as he could to my face, and I knew he contemplated running his sword through me.

"Forget anything he said," he commanded, calming himself. He went back to his horse. He was finished with the conversation, but I was not done.

"And why is that, Magnar? Because a boy could not be king?" He ignored my words. "Don't walk away from me, Brother! Answer me!" I yelled. He stopped in his way, breathing smoothly. "Why, Magnar? It will make no difference to you. If I die, you can rejoice. If I am put to shame, you can laugh at me!" I opened my mouth to keep on with my ranting, but I was not able to do so.

Magnar screamed, "I told you to strip Fidel's words from your memory!" The last thing I saw was his fist swinging in my direction faster than I could move.

***

"You could have saved me," my father said. He stood in the oval place prepared for his dead body. His name could still be seen where Shervan carved it into the wall. Shervan wasn't here. The world around me was numb, lax even. An air of emptiness lapsed all of it. Nothing was vivid but browns and grays.

"I couldn't! I didn't know where you went! Who you were going to see! I couldn't have overtaken the King's Host!" I pleaded, falling to my knees. I did not see his face red and swollen, but his feet were uncovered like they had been and I could see the slashes on them.

He said again, "You could have saved me." Now he came close to me.

"No! No! I couldn't!" I said. I had been telling myself it was I who killed him, yet when he agreed I pleaded the opposite. He stood over me and began stroking my head. I couldn't even bear to look up at him. He was dead after all. I squeezed my hands around my face. I hated this. The dead not really dying. Staying vivid in my mind to condemn me. "This isn't true! You're dead!" My shouts were muffled through my hands.

"You could have saved me, Adinorium," said my father.

His voice was very weak. He moved away from me and looked at the wall. I looked up to him terrified of everything; like a dark room you know isn't empty. "Hand me your blade." He took the hand he used to stroke my hair and lowered it to be beside my face. My breathing halted at the command. He was dead, yet I feared he would use my blade to kill himself again. It was almost tempting to give it to him. I couldn't live with dreams like this, if this were to be the first of more. They're too alive. Curiosity questioned if he died in my dreams would he stay dead. I could not be tormented like this for long.

"I don't have a blade," I said. But would I rather be tormented or watch him die again?

"Yes, you do," he said. I slid my hand over my side to feel the blade ready at my disposal. I stood to my feet, and he took a few steps away from me. "He's already dead," I repeated to myself while I pulled the iron blade into the light. While the world was drained of color, the black ribbon around the handle gleamed in its brilliance. My blade had become his. It had become Thann's. Or was it still mine? I held the snake blade now. The blade that had caused his death once before.

"No," I muttered. The dagger would forever be in my mind. I knew I'd forever live with the desire to burn it down into nothing. Perhaps I only had one chance in my life to do that.

"Give it to me," he said firmly. His back was facing his grave. The winds began to grow, and it felt like Strength had become angry. The clouds went around the mountain peak, and the grass hissed.

"I can't do that," I replied, not taking my eyes off the

dagger; the snake hidden in the weeds.

He persisted, "I'll help you." He launched himself to grab the handle with his strong hand. I held on all the fiercer. "Son, let go." His deep voice shook my soul.

"No, I can't! I can't let you take it!" I shouted. I was grappling with my father for the blade and the wind. Wet brushed my lips, tears of fear and sorrow. I was a child again. Having to surrender to authority. So, I surrendered to him. I had grown up too quickly. Ignorantly eager to stand on my own two feet. Taught myself how to be strong against Magnar. How to stand alone after my father left for his shadowy places. But now, I'm helpless once again. It's not just in this dream. It's death. It's life. My own broken stability being paraded around. It was put on to display. It's a feeling of nakedness. But this dream only taunts my reality. I couldn't save my father. I slowly released the blade and my white knuckles, which had been drained of blood, began to regain color. Surrendering cut me deeper than the dagger could have. My father stood proudly not even looking at the sharp iron rod. He inhaled. Exhaled. Placed the dagger to his own heart. All the breath was stolen from my lungs. The perfect blade fell to the ground. The place prepared for death was filled. I stumbled away from him, not towards him as I had done before. I clinched a fist full of my hair feeling that the wind had ceased. I felt as if I could suffocate in the stillness. I shouted to the sky, groaning in the deep parts of me. Then I saw a dark being on top of the wall. It was the Opposer. I knew his name with certainty now. He was the one I'd seen before. He held strings that hung down the walls and were placed on my father's person. I had only just now seen the fragile things that had guided his motion. I felt no fear, only anger. A reflection caught my eye on the ground. Feet away from me laid the snake blade. I stared at it before choosing to take hold of it. Once I did, I called out to the Opposer to face me. "You killed him! You mastered the hand of the one who stole his life! Face me! Face my wrath!" Instead of him turning to face me, he only grinned. He came before me without a body to hold him. Only a hooded head and a black smile.

"You and I are not in the same realm. You are of flesh. I am spirit alone. Therefore, I can't take the pleasure of destroying you, the Greater's possession. But I like your wrath. It looks like mine. I can offer you something better than death. I can give you vengeance. I can give you anyone you desire. Even the king. If you want his throat, you can have it. As I said, I can't harm the physical. It was his hand that killed your father. Not mine." He was honest and I listened. I knew every word of his had to be carefully crafted. He had to think of what to say and how to say it. No- no, that wasn't right. Every word flowed with ease. He spoke as purely himself.

"What is it you want?" I asked the Opposer knowing he was a being who did not give freely. He smiled and laughed quietly to himself. His black train had tamed as his presence stayed.

"You know me well, son of Durnin." I felt fear for the first time when he said my name. "I only want you. I can make you king. I can help you avenge your father. With my strength, you will rule as the greatest being alive. None will ever overthrow you. Even Haben would have to bow." Why Haben over Thann? Wasn't Thann the one who I was needing to get revenge on? He spoke with such sincerity. But I had seen the way the Bountiful Lands turned to fire. I knew he was called the Opposer for a reason. I knew if he was calling to these desires in my heart, then something in the desires or the way I would attain them would not be good. I remembered seeing Thann holding the blade I'd forged. I remembered knowing it was my rebellion that allowed him to hold it in his hands. I did not know much of the Opposer, nor of the Greater, but I did know that one desired death and destruction and the other gave life in the desert.

"You desire me. Why?" I was cold to his trickery. I remembered the hatred he made Phoebus feel towards me. I remembered the remorse he did not have when Thann had died in my dreams. He did not answer me. Instead, a curl of anger went over his face. "You will not answer me, so I will tell you why you desire me. You desire me because you fear me. You fear me because I am not yours. You try to drag me into your pit of destruction, take me to where I am to go with the lie that only you can get me there. I do not need your strength. My revenge is against you and those who've fallen prey to you. Therefore, my revenge would be against myself if I was to give myself over to you." My heart began to burn quietly. I looked down at my father whose empty body laid limply in the place made for him. I looked again at the snake blade in my hand. He called me then, the Greater. He told me to ready myself. He told me these days were evil. I now stand facing the essence of evil, and he has extended his hand to me. "I will fight for king. I will avenge my father. I will obtain greater things. All of these, I will do without you. And though I cannot harm the physical body that you do not possess, I will make your soul burn with agony," I said, pledging this to him. I looked at my hands that had been stained with my father's blood. They were not stained with his blood because I killed him. They were stained because I drew near after Thann had killed him. I couldn't save him. He was not mine to save. But I could avenge him.

"You think I fear you?" The Opposer turned his wrath upon me. "Your strength would've left you dead on the dirt of the ground, merely because of a name on a letter. Men could destroy your strength without me. But you have chosen me as your enemy, and I have a gift in destruction. You can strive to whatever end you desire, but I will make you bleed with every step forward." Like a mist that vanishes at noon day, he was no more. I held my head sturdy although inside, my heart pounded and my knees began to feel weak. Even though he only possessed a sly tongue, whatever he spoke of in evil and wrath, I knew would be true. I now slowly approached my father. I moved his body to be in line with the oval of dried grass and his hands to be one on top of the other laying on his chest. With two black stones beside the place, I made sparks that caught fire when mixed with the dry grass and air. I stepped back and watched the flames take him again. I turned from him and looked up to the head of the mountain. I had made my pledge. I was going to fulfill it.

Chapter 26
Both Were Sorry

I had never endured such a severe throbbing as I did when I woke up from the dream. My mother had been tending to me all morning. Dr. Yooldee said I'd been cold for the past two days. I don't know if that means I was dead, unconscious, or sleeping without being able to wake up. I was glad it was the morning when I finally did. That left the rest of today and tomorrow before I'd have to go to Redelah.

"I feel well," I lied to Yooldee, who told me if I felt any pain I'd have to stay lying down.

"Very well, Durnin. I do advise you to do things mildly for the next several days. Be easy on the celebrating. You had us all very worried." He began to gather all his things into his black bag to leave. I nodded listening to his words, with no intention of really listening at all. He bowed to my mother and insisted she call on him if anything was needed. As soon as the door shut behind him, I stood, making my way to my room.

"Adinorium!" my mother said to me as I fell into my door frame. I corrected my action and assured her that I was fine. I picked up the picture of the Bountiful Lands that had been given to me and looked upon it for a moment. I was thankful for the small glimpse given to me.

"I need Amos, Adalric, and Phoebus. And also your friend," I said. I came back from my room dressed in new clothes and readied with my revived spirit.

"Did Magnar knock the sense out of you? Did you not hear Yooldee?" My mother was in a bit of a rage, but I had to persist.

"Maybe. But I don't think so. I have to gather them, Mother. Believe me. It is for the most urgent matter," I said to her directly, holding her two arms. She dropped her head understanding what I meant.

"I will ride and tell them of your need. I'll tell them to meet here tonight." My mother had pulled away from me and began to put on her coat. Before I could rebuttal at all, she had slammed the door behind herself. I was more relieved to settle myself than I had hoped to be. I imagine Magnar carried me here after the strike and Amos ran to get Yooldee. However it happened, I had no appreciation for it. Why Magnar reacted so strongly, only the Greater knows. I found something to drink then sat down, grateful not to be holding my body's weight. I was slow in thinking about him. Timid in thought as if he could read them. As if he was here now. I remembered something while I sat with closed eyes trying to endure my throbbing head and suspicion of the Opposer's presence. I opened the skinny drawer that rested below my father's place at the table. I had always known it was there but didn't have the guts to open it knowing it would cost me my guts, but now I had little to fear. I needed to know of anything more I could when it came to my father's deals and correspondence. Inside of the drawer, papers filled it to the brim. I pulled as many out as I could by hand and continued until the drawer was empty. My father's handwriting filled every page. They were letters to my mother. No other name or person. A very scattered journal with no dates leaving a knotted timeline.

> *Dear Dara,*
>
> *Today Magnar discovered me hiding letters in the boxes we sell at our shows. It was to inform Fidel that Saxon was on the move again. If it weren't for Allester, he would've already found us out. I didn't wish Magnar to know, but he is too spiteful to know just enough to get us all killed. I had to make him believe I was going to tell him all along, or he would be spiteful anyways. Adinorium knows too. Not everything, but enough to know something is at work. He calls them greater things. I can only pray they are things that belong to the Greater, although I don't think that's what he means. You must promise me you won't tell him. Knowing him, he'd join the cause and be the first martyr if he knew what we were fighting for. We're getting closer. I know we are. Only a year longer until this will all be over. Greater, it better be over.*

Another letter read:

Dear Dara,
The shadow is getting thicker. I now see him daily. It

used to be only when I would do bold things. Things that were in opposition to him, but now he walks beside me down the streets, he rides his crimson horse behind me, he smiles and blood spills from the gaps in his teeth. I think I will be gone soon. I fear it'll be only pain for all I love until I am. This also means our time is coming. Or else he would not show himself as he does. No other does he taunt as he taunts me.

Dear Dara,
Fidel is confident that he is close. We are so close, Dara.

Dear Dara,
Did he tell you anything more about his dream? That same night, I saw the Opposer. He cursed my name and told me he was departing from me, that I'd no longer have to see his sneer again. I fear he went to find Adinorium. This means he will watch him. Observe him. He may decide that he wants him. That he wants him to fall.

I stared blankly across the table. I held the fragments of my father's mind in my hands. What more did he say? What more did he think? He saw the Opposer just as I do. He even knew him well. How long did he live with his ridicule? How long did he have to endure his slithering tongue? I read over the letters again. Fidel was right to be confident. He found what he was looking for. I wondered what the proof was that could expose Thann? I exhaled in confusion thinking that my mother had told my father of my dream even though he asked and listened to it again like it was the first time he'd heard it. It seemed my curiosity was well placed in my mother's odd reaction to my telling her that night at the forge. But what my father said last made my heart beat slowly, not one of exhilarating fear, but instead one of quietness. As if I was holding my breath in fear of making a sound. He said he'd want me. Did he even understand what that would mean? I forced my mind to the next thing. Something that I'd find encouragement in. I found it in that he confessed never wishing to tell Magnar. I never knew why he would be allowed to know and not I. That was a desperate form of business, but an unavoidable one. I wanted to read all of them. I wanted to understand my father. The way Fidel spoke of him. The things he wrote in these letters. If he would've told me, I could've understood. I could've told him I knew the Opposer too. I could've told him I knew his pain and temptation. But he's dead now. These letters are only new to me. They are the thoughts of a man who no longer lives.

> *Dear Dara,*
>
> *I told Fidel to flee to the far side of the mountain. The people, they aren't ready. I'm going to confront Thann, and he will kill me. I'm afraid our battle needs a martyr and I'm the one who must go. Thann will know he is in jeopardy. He will react strongly. I've already told Fidel and Magnar that I*

want Adinorium to fight for king. They will be ready to assist him however needed. He won't understand, but in time, he will. He will fight. He has more fire than the Gut can possess. Be gentle with him. I know he is not gentle with himself. Allester will come to you after it is finished. He will be sure you are protected from Thann, Arres, Saxon, and any others who seek you out. Oh, my dear, Dara. I only wish I had more time to spend with you. Love my sons for me. Kiss their foreheads and tell them I loved them more abundantly than the stars in the sky. I leave now to find the dagger Adinorium buried. Now I will act as the fool and dig it up.

This was the newest letter placed in the drawer. It would also be the last one. How little I really know. My heart sank hearing Nabim and his wife approaching the front door. I had to hide the papers back into the drawer quickly, but I made sure I did it with care. I folded and slipped his final letter into my pocket. I would need to read that one again. And again. And again. And again. Until I could recite it to myself at night.

"Norium! I'm pleased to see you are awake and active. Your brother does have quite a nasty blow. I've seen it in its glory once or twice myself. Never felt it though. I can't say that I'm jealous," Nabim said, his wide mouth grinning. He was certainly in a chipper mood. I had done my best to make my appearance look like one of innocence. No guilt or hidden drawers or letters in my pocket. "We passed Dara on the trail.

Seemed to be in a mad rush." He kept talking while going into my mother's room. "We asked if you had- well- gone, and she called back "no" which I thought was too simple for the question asked." He reappeared with their bags in his hands, and it appeared as if they would be leaving today. I would be lying if I said I wasn't thankful. They were kind people, but I wanted the solitude of my home restored. "But as for Magnar, strong man. Wouldn't want to be on the opposite side of him."

"Yes, I wouldn't recommend the experience." I smiled. Red-headed Nila came out of my mother's room after him with some of her own things. She went straight to the kitchen for food of any sort.

"Most unfortunate indeed," she shouted from the kitchen. I met him at the door as we waited for Nila.

Nabim asked, "We hate to leave in this hurry. But now that Fidel has arrived we need to move on."

"I see. Yes, I suppose it wise." I felt as though all could do was agree.

"We will find Dara in town then, before we leave to say our goodbyes," he assured me. They were from this area, but they lived closer to the line of Section Seven than Chalmar.

"Good! She will be glad for that." I said. Nila came from the kitchen with an apple in her mouth and winked once she stood beside her husband. Seeing them together, I realized how strikingly different their appearances were. Nila is slender and pale. Nadim had broad features from his nose to his shoulders to his gut. I could hardly imagine what their three daughters would look like. Nadim then added, "We do love you, Adinorium. I don't know you as well as I'd like, and the idea of love is probably silly to you coming from me. But it is true. If you ever need anything from me, please do not hesitate to ask," Nadim said with sincerity. I nodded, receiving his words. It was kind of him to love me because of my father.

"Thank you. And thank you for tending to my mother and honoring my father," I said before they departed in peace. I decided I'd begin gathering everything I'd need for the journey ahead of me. Going into my parent's room, I took my father's dagger which my mother had wrapped and placed in the drawer beside her bed. I thought I would be able to resharpen the tip and use this dagger to my own defense and aggression. My heart leapt in fear when the front door had been aggressively slammed into.

"What on this lands, Nori!" Amos hollered. I'd locked the door after Nadim and Nila had left. Amos wasn't used to that practice. He didn't complain that he'd hurt himself, but for the rest of the evening I saw him grabbing at his arm. I asked Amos how he arrived so quickly. There wasn't enough time for Yoldee to get back to the practice. "As soon as your mother came I left. I didn't bother to ask Yoldee. No one was currently dying." I told Amos what had happened. How my mother was going to get the others. He was steady. Ready for it even. When my mother returned home, we helped her prepare a meal for dinner. Adalric and Phoebus would be arriving at sundown to share what we had prepared before I made my request. Except Fidel. I told my mother to ask him to come in the night. Phoebus and Adalric would not be so prepared as Amos. But I was confident in them. My mother told me that both had come when I was "cold," as we referred to it. Since my father's death they've stayed quiet. Adalric not leaving his home and Phoebus staying in the mines. I wondered if my mother had warned them to do so or if it was their own families not allowing it. Amaryllis has been ill since returning home. That's what Amos and my mother told me. I hoped Magnar was allowing her to rest now. I don't think he'd ever hurt her like he had me. He'd never hurt me like that before. My father wasn't here now to intervene and save me from him.

***

Sundown came with all her terror too quickly for me. Adalric and Phoebus came together, and I hugged them like I could lose them any day now. I knew in all reality I could. I missed them. All of them. Phoebus sat to my left and Amos on my right. My mother took food to Amaryllis and decided she'd stay the night with her while I had my union over for dinner. We spoke little of all the happenings during the Sovereign Days. We ate meat, bread, and greens. They honored me well, in allowing us a chance to mourn for my father's death. But I didn't want to dwell on it long. I couldn't let my mind slip to that place just yet. At one point my hand drifted to my pocket feeling my father's letter. I needed to remember why I had gathered my friends here at all. Thankfully, they were equally gracious in allowing the night to not be gloomy. We were happy to be together, and as my father would have said, that is reason to celebrate.

"Magnar finally followed through with his threats!" Adalric smiled. I had a fading brown knot still visible on the side of my head. Thankfully my hair hid it well and Doctor Yooldee said it would go down quickly even though there could still be some sensitivity there. We all laughed at the joke it was. Magnar hated me and the only way to not be terrified or constantly angry at him was to make fun of him. Make fun of how serious he made everything.

"I would've got him good, but-" I started to tease before Amos jumped in.

"But instead, you let him carry you home!" they laughed at Amos's smart mouth and I dismissed such an illogical happening.

"What now, Nori?" Phoebus asked after we'd settled ourselves.

"What?" I asked. Adalric and Amos continued to enjoy the night's good humor, but Phoebus made me forget all of that and remember the greater thing.

He clarified his question, "Are you going to take over the forge?" Amos had stopped eating and lowered his chin. I shifted nervously in my seat. I knew this was the best moment I'd get.

"Oh my lands! Forgive me, Nori. I spoke far too brazenly," Phoebus said, apologizing thinking my shift in demeanor had to do with my dead father.

"No! It's not that, Phoebus. It's about what I'm doing next actually," I said as strongly and yet gently as I could. Adalric had caught on to the shift and put down his utensils. I could hear everyone's breathing and the slightest movements could be felt by all.

"What *are* you doing next?" Adalric asked the next obvious thing. I looked at Amos who looked at me with steadiness and nerves. I grappled with whether I should explain or just begin speaking bluntly. I decided it didn't matter either way, for I knew as soon as I opened my mouth, I wouldn't really have a say on what came out.

"My father was murdered for treason. An attempt to end the king," I began looking from Phoebus to Adalric. "And he was rightly accused. He, along with his closest company, discovered proof that Thann dishonestly gained the throne. My father was going to expose him, forever disqualifying Thann or anyone tied to his bloodline to compete in the Sovereign Days. He was killed before he could do that. One of his closest, a man named Fidel, came to me with my father's wishes. He wanted me to fight for king." The words felt natural when I spoke them. They should've felt like a foreign language that I didn't even know how to speak. "The people aren't ready for radical change, but they need a leader who has time to grow them. They need a defender," I said, continuing to explain my reasons, but I paused knowing I needed to make myself plain. Everyone knew why we needed a new king. "I'm going to fight for king, and I want you all to fight with me," I proposed as elegantly as such a request could be made. Adalric sat back exhaling, letting his body conform to the chair.

"You want to fight for king? And you want me, Adalric, Amos, and only the Greater knows who else to stand with you to oppose arguably the most ruthless opponent ever?" Phoebus was afraid and whenever he was afraid, he got angry.

"I know it sounds ridiculous, but someone must fight, Phoebus. These people are afraid," I began before he interrupted.

"As they should be! Thann doesn't want justice, he

wants power. Your dead father is proof of that," he said shamelessly. All I could do was try not to take his cruelty to heart. "You're trying to fight an impossible battle. He has the ability to kill anyone and no one would turn an eye."

"I don't believe that," I said calmly.

"What?" he scoffed, leaning closer in to hear me. "I did. I turned my whole head and couldn't stop staring. There are good people, Phoebus. Good people who will rally with us," I urged him. I remembered the Opposer standing over his shoulder the last time Phoebus snapped on me. I didn't see him this time, that could only make me believe this was truly him and that hurt me.

"Cheer you on to your death? No, Nori! I will not be paraded in front of a blind people to a cruel death. And you shouldn't either." He offered me a friend's warning. It was the least he could do.

"It's more than that, Phoebus!" I now raised my voice, pleading with whatever part of him could hear me.

"No!" He slammed down his cup. "I will not follow you to my death because you think you can avenge the mountain!" I was angry with him. He was acting cowardly and was being cruel because of it. But I was also angry because he didn't understand the direness of this. He didn't understand the Opposer. But when my mind thought to tell them of the deeper enemy, my mouth refused to speak the words.

"Is that what you think this is? A quest for blood?" I asked, speaking with my hands. I felt a chill go down my spine. Another stronghold of my stability was breaking. Being exposed as muscles beneath the skin after a deep cut. My stability in others was still deep. Only this time, it was the people I had chosen, not my family that was given.

"Stop fooling yourself, Adinorium. This isn't just about justice, peace, or freedom. It's about vengeance. Just because your father died, doesn't mean you have an excuse to go gallivant around in the name of all things. I will not join in that delusion!" This was it. A moment I didn't see coming. A union breaking. A brotherhood dying. As much as I wished I was the person who was mature enough to stay silent and move on, I couldn't. I never could. Adalric stared into his lap contemplating everything in his mind. Amos was becoming restless in the confrontation, waiting for a physical display of our words.

"Delusion? Phoebus! Look around you! Injustice is your foundation yet you're willing to stand on it. I expected better of you. We're living in a vicious cycle! It may be Thann now, but if someone doesn't fight, it's going to be Haben next! You're surrendering like a coward. Afraid that if you strike the snake, he'll bite your heel!" I spoke without hesitation. My words felt rehearsed. As if I'd been prepared to say them all along. "But do what you must, Phoebus. Stand on your broken foundation. But you can't just stand on it, you'll have to fight on it! Selling your life to the king! That's what you're doing. You're struggling to complete the bondage taxes now. In time, you will be forced to join the King's Host and when he asks you to tie an innocent man to a post knowing he's going to slit his throat, make sure you do it proudly. Because if you're going to live in fear, at least sell your act to the snake or he'll bite you anyway," I said and as soon as I finished, I almost regretted my words. But in my heart, I didn't. I wanted them to sting. I wanted him to hurt like he'd hurt me.

"Nori," Amos said, grabbing the back of my arm. He was afraid Phoebus and I may begin fighting. But Phoebus just stared cold into my eyes. We'd harmed each other enough.

"Right. If I don't join you then I'm a snake. And this is how you're trying to convince men to follow you? Shame, Nori. And here I imagined if, by the edge of your blade, you became king, you'd be a good one. I suppose we were both wrong about each other." Now, I didn't know whether I should cry, fight, or scream. This was a different kind of pain. I've felt death. I've felt my own bloodline spit in my face. I've felt my body betray me. But never this. Phoebus thanked me for the meal and stood showing himself to the door. I rose from my own chair and helped him put on his coat. I looked my friend in the eyes and embraced him. Without hesitation, he embraced all the closer.

"I'm sorry," I said. I know he doesn't understand the extent of what I meant.

"Me too," he said. Opening the door for himself and nodding one last time, he'd ride on in the night. I watched him until the cold was too much for my thin clothes and the darkness swallowed him. I closed the door behind a most dear friend. Perhaps a dear friend gone for good. I mourned as if I'd lost him to death. In some ways, I think that death would've been more forgiving.

I leaned my head against the door and allowed myself to feel the pain of loss. Perhaps this was the first bit of blood the Opposer was making me pay. I already hated him so deeply. He can destroy my body, but why steal my friends? Why take my brother from my side? Why make me weigh my choices with a broken scale? Adalric came and faced me.

"You can leave. I won't blame you. I won't be angry with you. I understand this is a ferocious battle and a great sacrifice," I said honestly. I was asking for the ultimate commitment. Phoebus wasn't wrong in how strongly he spoke of the danger. If anything, he didn't speak strongly enough. Adalric lifted my head with his hand. His crisp voice brought comfort to me as he assured me saying, "I'm going to fight with you. We all are fighting ferocious battles. We're in the business of trying to choose the right ones." He planted his hand firmly on my shoulder. If Adalric had said no, I may have surrendered all hope. He is the poet. He is the one who can find hope in anything. If he deemed it impossible, then it is impossible. Amos joined us and together we stood strong and grieving. We'd lost our brother. We'd lost our friend. Phoebus may have rejected me, but he was also choosing to reject them. To reject the stronghold we had formed.

Chapter 27
The Union

"Fidel Deep. He's the man who warned me of Saxon?" Adalric asked. We all sat in the living room waiting for Fidel to arrive. We cleaned up the table quietly and found we weren't hungry for the pie my mother had left for us.

"Yes. Apparently, he was the one to find the final proof they needed to condemn Thann," I said. I sat in my father's chair as if it had always been my own. I'd grown to adore the chair in the last few days. I loved how the blue covered cushion was worn down to my father's body. It conformed to his tired legs giving way as he allowed the wooden limbs to hold him up. My hand felt over the small knicks on the right side from his mindless hand tapped the chair's arm with his dagger while his thoughts wandered. And its smell. Being so close to the fire, you could smell ash like he smelled coming home from the forge. But not of smoke from coal, more burning wood. Pine. It had been made worthy to be his throne. Adalric laid across the sofa and Amos sat on the floor against it while keeping his feet close to the fire. We were all so young. Sometimes that surprised me. We had so much living left to be done. Funny to think of life as anything more than the routine it had been up to this point. Yet in days soon to come, I know I will already be looking back on these times astonished that I couldn't imagine anything more.

"I think my mother will despise me," Adalric said, thinking allowed. "All she wants is for Esma and Shanasha to marry Polished so she can go and live in their high towers. I could make her the enemy of those people. I could ruin her ability to have what she desires." I wasn't going to disagree. He was being honest, and his honesty was true. She would probably hate him. I could hardly understand my parents choosing to hate me. A grace I'd been afforded. "I rather like the thought of being their enemy. Having to stand in their courts and know they detest me." He looked to the underbelly of our roof and imagined their beaming eyes. He always loved their society, loved the way they lived. I suppose he was finding joy in them giving him attention and he found that the attention brought about by hate felt powerful in its own way.

"Unless they love you. Welcome us with open arms like we were one of their own. Think of the celebration that would follow if we were victorious." Amos showed the opposite perspective. I loved to hear them imagine together. They saw the world so differently, yet shared awe and wonder.

"Yes, they'll probably have white tulips and kites, flying lanterns and candles to light our way to the palace." Adalric furthered the fantasy.

Adalric sat up straight and Amos stood on guard when the knock came to the door. He knocked like a man with business. Fidel had arrived. I looked at both of them and did my best to assure them of him. I stood, crossed the floor to the door, and pulled it open.

"Magnar?" I was confused to find my brother on the other side.

"Where is he?" Magnar demanded pushing his way inside. I closed the door to keep out the unwanted winds.

"Who, Magnar?"

"Try to be less ignorant, brother. Where is Fidel?" I assumed my mother had something to do with him finding out, but I wasn't entirely sure. Magnar was storming impatiently about the room.

"He isn't here," I stated the truth. Now Fidel's knock came. It was not welcomed. At least, not at this moment. I sighed knowing his fate and the rest of ours was going to be far more difficult now. Magnar looked at me with disappointment, but also a pride in having known. Brushing past my shoulder, he opened the door to a hooded man. He was shorter than Magnar, but not by much. And in a more rugged way, just as handsome.

"Do come in," Magnar said obnoxiously, showing him the way with his arm. Fidel unveiled himself and received the invitation. Once inside, Fidel nodded at me. "I told you not to come." Magnar instantly began his threats.

"Didn't you just offer I come in?" Fidel mocked my brother. "Insisted even?" Magnar was brimming with hatred towards Fidel. I was intrigued by Fidel's wit and willingness. The confidence he possessed in his dealings.

"I told you if I saw you here again, I'd kill you," Magnar said. He was coming closer to Fidel's face.

"Yes, I remember. Unfortunately for you, Magnar, your

mother invited me here. I would never turn down invitations from Dara Durnin." Fidel played with him as if Magnar's threats were that of a child. Magnar pulled his blade but Fidel was ready with his own.

"Enough, you violent beast! I need him," I growled at Magnar standing in between his blade and the stranger's. Why was I willing to stand in between them? I wasn't convinced it was because I needed him alone. I spoke to Magnar whose brown eyes were hardened. If he so wished, he could kill me now. Run his blade through me and finally end his life's greatest burden. Instead, Fidel put his sword away respectfully in hopes his opponent would, in return, do the same. I exhaled in relief when Magnar's sword was returned to his side. "Thank you, Brother," I said sincerely. Magnar held his look of contempt and sat down in my father's chair as if this was still his home.

"Adalric Elm, a pleasure to meet you properly." Adalric was the first to speak after the confrontation. He extended his hand to Fidel who understood his words and gave a similar introduction.

"Amos Hawthorn," Amos said, introducing himself.

"You're a doctor of some sorts?" Fidel asked. Amos grinned at the question. I believe he took it as a compliment to be called a doctor.

Amos's curiosity got the better of him. "That is what my efforts have been going towards. How did you know?" he asked.

"I've been at the Bored Daisy for some time. I often see you rushing out of the practice to help bloody men and assume you must belong there because they never kicked you out."

Fidel smiled.

"Fair observation," Amos said. I knew Amos was trying not to think about how odd of a thing it was for one to be watched from a window.

"Where is Phoebus?" Magnar asked from his chair. It was almost meaningful to me that he knew me enough to know when one of my friends was absent. I'm sure my mother had probably told him who was coming and he now noticed one was missing.

"He left," I answered solemnly. I found myself thinking back to the reason he left.

Magnard continued to demand, "You said you needed him. Get on with it." I was not taking orders from him, but I too wished to continue the night's events. I had my answer for Fidel, and I needed to tell him.

"I'm going to fight for king." After lots of thought, I discovered I could not have said no to this request. Now, I was saying yes with ease.

"Kane would be happy." Fidel nodded. "Men of your union?" he asked, looking at Amos and Adalric.

"Yes, they are my dearest and most trusted friends. The best of men." I was pleased to tell him. Magnar joined the conversation by pointing out the smallness of our union.

"And yet there are only four of you," Magnar said. He stood to the fire's side and made himself strong. He was right. We will be leaving for Redelah tomorrow. I didn't have nor did I possess time enough to find another to ask. I paused, knowing what had to be done, knowing what my father would have done.

"That is why I need you to join me," I admitted boldly. I feared speaking these words. I could feel Amos and Adalric's tension from beside me, but my eyes stayed with Magnar. I'd been weighing my options. This union needs strength. All of Haben's men have been preparing for this for the entirety of their lives. We were already a man less with Amos because of his inability to battle, and I can't sacrifice Amos.

"I told you not to pursue it. Few times in our lives, Brother, have I asked you so strongly to refrain from something. Why do you persist?" Magnar asked with more sadness than anger in his tone. I was not expecting him to respond in such a way. It was more gentle than I've known him to be.

"Because I must. I need to. I cannot give my life to the mundane knowing the mundane here would only be suffering in disguise. Knowing our accuser. Knowing our father is dead for something that became nothing. I don't think you could give your life to that either." I was honest with him, but not wholly. The death of my father was not the only reason. There was also an opposer. One who brought me to this. But if Magnar had a heart as he so claimed, then the death of our father would be the only way I, his hatred, could convince him to join *my* union.

"But why you?" He crossed his arms and turned his back from the fire. "Let some other challenge Haben. Let some other stand. For once in your life could you bow down to another?" he said with all his attention on me. It was one of the first times I'd felt him to really be looking at me. Maybe he possessed some kind of heart after all. I struggled to imagine it, but I thought of how there was something similar between us.

He was as passionate as I am. Our hatred for one another was because our passions often conflicted, not because either of us did not possess it.

"No one else *is* challenging," Fidel interrupted, looking at Magnar. "Alana has been following all who were building unions. After Kane's execution, they all surrendered. If this mass surrender was a result of his death alone or for some other reason, we don't know. But none other will stand. All others have bowed before Haben."

"When were you going to tell me that?" I asked Fidel. I had remembered the unions that I had heard of being established. It seems they were defeated before the tournament even began. I felt anger towards Fidel for withholding such things from me. But I couldn't forget that Fidel was seasoned. I was just joining this world when he's been living in it for a long time. This felt sudden to me but to him, it has been a battle of patience.

"You had to make the decision without compulsion from others," Fidel said, trying to keep our peace.

"Without compulsion?" Magnar defended me. "You tell a son his dead father's last request was for him to carry this task forward, and then you tell me he is not to be moved by compulsion." Perhaps Magnar's hatred for me lessened when there was one he hated more. I had never imagined there could be one he hated more.

"Magnar, you know your father requested it to be done in such a way. Don't question him," Fidel said without fear towards my brother. He was one who approached Magnar's strength as his equal.

Magnar replied with the same confidence, "Then don't tempt my brother to his grave." Magnar and I shared this as well: refusing someone else the last word.

"Will you fight with me?" I asked him with a revised hope of my trust in him. He glared at an unmoved Fidel before looking back at me.

"It seems neither of us have much of a choice," Magnar coldly responded. He grabbed his coat and began to make his leave. "I'll ride on with you tomorrow. The way ahead will not be kind." He slammed the door without care of its hinges. I breathed strongly knowing this battle had just become all the greater.

"Have you lost all reason?" Amos asked as soon as Magnar was gone. He seemed to be seething.

"Your father told me you hate your brother. Magnar has also expressed his distaste for you. I understand your friend's concerns about having him join as one of your closest friends," Fidel said.

"My father assured me that he believed if I ever was to need Magnar, then my brother would rise to strength," I replied, defending my choice as well as I could. I didn't tell them that my father told me that on the last day we spoke. It was like he knew I was going to need Magnar in my union, and he was giving me assurance.

"And you believe that to be true?" Fidel said. I looked directly into his eyes and spoke with the same amount of confidence he spoke to Magnar with earlier.

"You believed him enough to pledge your allegiance to his son, whom you did not know, in the strongest bond possible, that of a union. What words we choose to believe cannot be based on our preference for the situation they're said about." I was surprised I was able to speak so sternly to him. But that which I said, I was fully convinced of. Fidel would say nothing more on the matter. I feared more than any of them the idea of being tied to my brother. No other understood his strength and brutality more than I did. "Trust me, I hated one of my first decisions being a compromise." I now spoke to Amos who I knew would be the least forgiving about this. "But I knew this was going to be a battle of compromise. My task is to discern the least deadly of them."

He nodded. "I know." He was choosing to surrender this battle. He knew that I, more than any other, hated Magnar and was well aware of his many failings.

"Stay the night if you please," I said to the group. "Tomorrow, tell your families goodbye. We will ride for Redelah in the morning."

"I will ride ahead of you to the Twelve Taverns. I want to make sure that it will be a safe place," Fidel said. He bowed his head before taking his leave. "Magnar will know of the place."

I replied, "Very well. We will arrive at the earliest time we can."

"Do you really trust him?" Adalric asked once the three of us were alone again. I was happy for it to just be us once more.

"I cannot deny his love for my father. He could've made his own union or presented it in such a way for me to join and he be king, but he didn't. I cannot fault that. I will be on my guard, but I have faith in him," I answered, perhaps ignorantly. Adalric went home to sleep in his own bed. That way he wouldn't miss morning tea which would be the best time for him to tell his family. He decided he'd meet us at the section line. Amos agreed to stay at my home. I was glad about this. We could continue to discuss any lingering thoughts.

"Doctor Yooldee said that the journal was someone's attempt at trying to teach the art of healing. Not as a doctor with medicine, but in a more divine way," Amos said.

"Can it be learned?" I was pleased by his discovery. There was no light in the room, and we exchanged voices as blind men. It seemed Fox had given me a good bargain. I, however, was more thankful to have gained him as a friend.

"Yooldee thinks not, but I've started to try. I don't understand his language. It feels like I'm having to learn to read again," he said.

"I think you will learn. And I think you'll be remarkable," I said more than confidently.

"Everything is going to change, isn't it?" he asked. I had finally closed my eyes to sleep but they opened to answer this question.

"Nothing will ever be quite the same. Though, I think everything might always be changing," I answered. It never would be and it wasn't now. My home would forever be altered. The people would never know me as I am now. It could be years before I speak to Phoebus again. Even the way Adalric, Amos, and I know each other will change. I can only hope the meadow will be more peaceful in time. I can only hope I will find something greater at the end of this.

Chapter 28
Assurance

Haben Arrogs

"They've been eradicated. No other will stand against you. You will be king," my father said, informing me with pride. They had tracked down all who formed a union and had paid them off or scared them away. It is the seventeenth day, and I am staying in Redelah, in the mansion of Ceneric. It is only short time before my union is presented before the people, unchallenged.

"And you thought he would gather a union!" Ferrox drunkenly teased me. He laid across the arms of a chair with a drink in one hand and an empty glass in the other.

"Who?" my father questioned. I knew this was something that was of no concern to him.

"Clearly, I was wrong, Father. Pay it no mind," I asserted. He nodded in what I know was submission not belief. My father feared me. He knew in a short time I would be over him. I've been greater than him for many years. He would always submit over being persecuted. Much like the rest of Strength. He left Ferrox, Barnett, and me in my room. Avijna will be joining us soon from a meeting with a potential amalgamate. I don't care much about them. I will protect one in the battle. I will only be sure Ferrox remains. All the others can shift as they please.

"You don't wish your father to know of your fear?" Ferrox mocked me as a fool mocks a cliff that he stands feet away from.

"You're drunk, Ferrox. Seal your tongue for your own sake," I said, warning him patiently. I warned few so gently as I warned him.

"But you know his name so well. It'd be so easy to let it slip out. So easy to recall his, how did you say it, fire? Yes, his burning, blistering, beautiful fire. Seems it was squelched. Have no fear, dear friend, none oppose you." His tongue began to mumble before he passed into his intoxicated mind. He taunted me, but I took nothing from it. Barnett took his full glass of rum and drank it gratefully. He put both of the glasses on the table and crossed Ferrox's arms over his chest.

"You do not really fear him, Haben. Do you?" Barnett asked boldly. I looked at the fire and watched the way it burned with power. In my hands, I held the snake blade. I hadn't allowed it to leave my side. None of them knew it was first his. I smiled before answering my friend.

"Of course not." A satisfied Barnett left the room to find his own bed. I stared at Ferrox for a moment. I hated him when he was drunk. I inhaled deeply, thinking of the days ahead. I had no desire to stand before these people. The ones who love me have subtle and depraved minds. I've begun to hate it. Only in faint ways. Coarse joking, excessive drinking.

They only annoy me, which is pardonable. I now laid in a foreign bed. I felt as though I was able to rest like all the others. He wasn't going to challenge. I lied to Barnett when I said I didn't fear him. And I never lie. All other men I could destroy, but him, he made me question. Doubt is a powerful force. It has the ability to destroy a being's person with nothing more than a single thought. But now, I rested because assurance was mine again.

Chapter 29
The Twelve Taverns

The Greater was kind in blessing me with sleep. I found I was missing his voice. The Opposer seemed to always be lurking and whispering instead. The shadows now made me think of him, and there were shadows everywhere. The Greater seemed to only come in my desperate moments. I want to be with him when I am of a sound mind and good spirits. His hand was harder to see. I wondered if this is what he meant when he told me to ready myself. Amos had left this morning to go home to his father. I saddled my horse and now stood in my home knowing the moment after this one, I'd be leaving it unsure of when I'd return. I took the time to look out of every window to remember what the view was like. I ran my hand along every wall and held every door frame before entering the next room. In my own room, I made the beds and made sure everything was neat. The painting of the Bountiful Lands I left to the protection of those walls. Last, I went to my father's chair. I ran my hand against its arm to feel its life that showed itself in small cuts and ridges. I looked down at my hands. I remembered his blood. Now I know his blood was a sacrifice. In some ways, that made it easier, knowing he was prepared to die. But in my heart, it made it all the harder, knowing he was prepared to die. Where does a man find himself when he is prepared for death?

I left my home running. I couldn't go slowly, or I wouldn't be able to go at all. I rode The Horse because he was my father's. I would leave The Other Horse for my mother if she were to need him. Magnar's home was far into the woods. You could get to it from another path out of Chalmar or a series of smaller paths found before the Fordwin. It was the first home of Amaryllis's parents, before they built another home closer to town. It was a simple house, made well by her father. Magnar was splitting firewood to leave for his wife. I never came to their home unless forced. Not that Amaryllis wasn't a good homemaker. I just hated being in a place where Magnar was the head. I dismounted The Horse and looked to Magnar for acknowledgement. He continued his work as if I were not there. I stared at him for a moment, questioning my decision. I had to stop though. I would either question my decision the whole time or embrace it as the reality it was. Instead of calling out to Magnar, I went to the door. I knocked and smiled when I heard Amaryllis call out to me.

"Coming!" As soon as she opened the door, she slowed her hurry. She looked me in the eyes and gave me the gentlest smile. Her hair was down, and its radiance showed. However, her eyes looked dim, and she carried her body like it was tired. I'd forgotten she wasn't well. "Come inside," she insisted. I gave my thanks and entered their home. I paused for a moment to admire how similar it was to my own home: a small living room with a fireplace, a sofa under the window, and an armchair turned slightly towards the fire. It was different from the last time I came because it looked more like my home now than it had previously. It was as if Magnar had missed his old dwelling. To the left of the home was another room that held the kitchen and a small table for two people. To the right, the only bedroom.

She apologized, "You'll have to forgive me, I haven't been feeling well."

"You are the last of us who needs to apologize. I should've brought you something," I insisted and felt guilty for not being more concerned for her. She nodded while tears began to fill her eyes. To my shame, I hadn't thought of Amaryllis's pain. I hadn't thought of how I was taking her husband from her. "I'm sorry. If there were any other way-" I began and came closer to comfort her. Instead, she embraced me.

"I am not sorrowful," she interrupted. "I champion you. I champion the both of you. I am just afraid. Not that I do not wish him to go. But this mountain is not how it once was." She stepped back to be able to look me in the eyes. "You better fight as if death is waiting at the end of this tournament." There was a fierceness in her eyes. A determination to look at the strong and choose not to fear because you are weak.

"To the Opposer's shame, we will live all the bolder than our enemy," I promised her. She was the first one I used the language of a deeper battle. Naturally, Amaryllis would be the gracious one to remind me of the greater things. I hated leaving, but she reminded me that I had to look ahead. I couldn't dwell on what I left behind. As I told Phoebus, it would be burned whether I was within the walls or not.

"Son," said a voice behind me. It was my mother's sweet voice that had reached my ears. She had come from the bedroom with pink cheeks and a calm smile. Her hair was down this morning. It had grown long, making her wear it pulled away from her face most often. I noticed the grayness of it today. I saw how my mother's youth had begun to be old days.

"Are you mournful, Mother?" I asked, hugging her.

"No, Son, I am glad." She smiled, rubbing the back of my head.

"Because we go to fight?" I asked her.

She grinned happily and replied, "Because I have been given a son whom the Greater has blessed." I thought of the letter my father wrote. I thought of the Opposer and how he spoke to him. I thought of the Greater and his mighty voice.

"Does he speak to you?" I questioned in a tone that suggested this was a secret matter. She sat down in Magnar's chair and I sat across from her. Amaryllis kept flowers in beautiful vases all around her home: on the tables and shelves, and on the window seals and the counters. She'd taken delicate time to make it beautiful.

"He does. Not often. His words are so powerful that they ring in my head like thousands of words uttered every day." She had heard him. I understood the way she described his voice. It felt strange to me now that she spoke more constantly of him. HOw much more had she said of him when my ears were not listening? "Magnar joins you?" she asked, sounding more curious as to why he was joining rather than if he was joining.

"Yes, Phoebus rejected the offer. He will stay behind." My throat burned when I spoke of his rejection. "Fidel, Magnar, Adalric, and Amos are my union. We ride for Redelah today to present our union tomorrow. No other unions stand," I said to both of them. Amaryllis loosened her lips, understanding that meant all Haben's attention would be on us.

"Then all in opposition to Haben Arrogs will stand with you." My mother was sure of it.

"Yes, and we will fight as if it is the end for even those who do not stand," I said, looking at Amaryllis. Magnar came inside and looked around the room. He went over to Amaryllis and put his forehead against hers.

"Don't be afraid. Everything will be as it should be." His words were odd to me, but I paid them no mind because of the affection he gave to Amaryllis. He then disappeared into his room.

"I will see both of you soon." I stood to say goodbye to them. "Until then, take care of each other. Be safe until I come home." I embraced my mother then Amaryllis. Magnar came back into the room with a sack in his hand. He was used to traveling. Knowing both what he needed and how to say goodbye.

"Get Yooldee even if you're only wondering if you need him," Magnar demanded. "I love you." He kissed her forehead and made sure to look her in the eyes before he left. I was amazed by him. All other times, he would have left without even saying goodbye, and now he kisses her and professes his love? For her sake, I was happy and for my journey, I found a questioning assurance. Perhaps our tragedy had changed Magnar. Reminded him of all that can be taken. Amaryllis walked outside with Magnar and I stayed a moment longer with Mother. All was quiet as I looked her in the eyes.

"I miss him," I said in a near whisper.

"I know." She kissed my forehead and assured me that was alright.

"Be safe," I said after mounting my horse. Magnar rode beside me. My mother and Amaryllis now stood in the doorway.

"And to you be steady," my mother said, I knew she meant every word.

"Where do we ride next?" Magnar asked.

"To Amos. Fidel rode ahead to prepare a place for us at the Twelve Taverns. Adalric will meet us at the section line," I said, informing him while we rode on. We waved to Mother and Amaryllis. Same as had been with my home, I couldn't look back once I'd given my final wave.

"Did he seem in pain?" Magnar asked as we rode over the bridge to town. The leaves covered the path, making the horses' steps all the louder.

"Father?" I asked to clarify.

"Yes. When Thann killed him." I looked at him, but he didn't dare look at me.

"You saw his body. I'd imagine he was almost numb to it. Relieved by its ending. But, yes, he was in great pain. I've thought many times what he must have been thinking of when he felt the blade on his throat. If he could feel the first drop of blood fall. He was dead within a moment. I wonder if it felt fast, or if the final things he saw were slow?" I answered his question with the thoughts I had been considering myself.

"The blade. Do they still have it?" I didn't even think of Magnar pondering these things. I wondered if he would've ever asked these questions if we weren't here together.

"I'd imagine they still do. They certainly didn't give it back to me. I wish I would have thrown it in the fire before you went to find it." My voice was in anger. Not entirely at my brother, although I hope he considers what he did to me in helping my father find the blade. I was angrier at myself, and, in many ways, towards Thann.

"I wish for something in the same way. I was the one who discovered it. After I'd unearthed it, I opened the box and held it in my hands. Father was farther into the woods searching. Fidel along with him. It was the most beautiful blade I'd ever held. There was something mesmerizing about it. Something that made me stare. But it felt cold, cruel even. I struggled to imagine that you had made it. At that moment, I had almost felt as if I should've buried it back. Tell Father I wasn't able to find it. Dig ten more holes around it for him to see its resting ground as no different. But instead, I gave it to him," he said with a sorrow he had never possessed before now. Not even when speaking of our father's death. My heart grieved a little more hearing my brother explain the dagger. I had forged something that even he found to be cold. As we entered town, none paid any mind to us, preparing their own selves to make the trek to Redelah. To this day, all had been taxes and work until the night. Most all in Chalmar had completed their bondage tax. However, we were still a people who didn't understand rest. All now were eager to take this time to gather for the next tax, hoping the strain won't be so fierce when the next demand is given. I struggled to find pity for them because they still feasted as if they weren't dancing over the blood of my father. The ones who could afford to leave their business and travel, did so to witness the beginning of the Sovereign Days. Meaning, not many were riding on horses to travel. Passing the Bolg, I saw Allester inside through the open door.

"Give me a moment," I said to Magnar, dismounting The Horse and handing him my reins. I walked inside boldly, completely disregarding the soldiers he was talking to. "May I have a word, Captain Allester?" I asked although I was trying to make it feel more like a demand.

"Very well," he said. He left his men with the next man in command and showed me to the lounge upstairs. I had been fearful the last time I stood in this room with him. Now, I was far from fear. It looked the same as it did when Saxon was here, except there was a broken mirror in the corner, the fire was blackened by too many logs being shoved into it, and pictures that were hanging on the wall were now on the floor or carelessly leaned up against the walls. Whether this destruction was Saxon or Allester's doing, I didn't know or care much. He closed the door behind us. As soon as he turned around, I struck him on the jaw. It made him turn completely around again. I could only imagine the pool of blood gathering in his mouth. I shook out my hand once and walked over to the bookshelf that was covered with bottles of things to ease Allester's head at night. I grabbed a glass and handed it to him to let the blood drain into. He didn't fight me back. It would have been pointless for him to try. I was the bigger man. I had the stronger hand. More than that, I had reason.

"You knew he was going to die," I said, starting my rebuke. He spit out one of his bottom, front teeth that I had managed to rid him of. He straightened his posture like he always did.

"He was always going to die." Why did everyone keep saying that to me! Obviously, we're all going to die! He was not always going to die because of this!

"Why didn't you tell me?" I started yelling at the dreaded captain. "I would have put myself in front of the dagger. I would have taken his place if I had known." The way he looked up to me, the way his eyes had no remorse.

"Because you would've put yourself in front of that dagger," he stated with assurance. I stood staring at the captain. The man who watched me almost destroy myself to prevent the very thing that happened. "I already told you once, Durnin. And I'm usually not gracious enough to say it a second time: I don't mess with things the Greater has his hands in." I felt my chest soften. The captain confused me. I wanted to hate him. I felt as though I was supposed to hate him. But I didn't. I only found admiration for him. He was cruel and hateful, domineering and vain, but he possessed something I could not understand. He obeyed my father while not completely submitting to him. He spoke freely to Saxon without running a sword through him. He feared the Greater as he was, the greatest being in all things. I walked confidently towards the captain. He spit another wad of blood into the glass cup that had been filled with ruby liquid.

"Thank you," I said, and embraced him like a man. He stood stone solid, unfamiliar with the action. I left the room promptly. I paid no attention to the other soldiers on my way out.

"Finish your business?" Magnar asked, having become a little impatient about the inconvenience.

"For now," I replied as I grabbed the reins from his hands and mounted my horse. I know Magnar looked at my red knuckles, but he didn't say anything.

***

"Durnin! The treachery that you bring to my family! To my son! You knew he would come with you! You are ripping away every good thing from him!" Aris Hawthorn burst from his door with all outrage as soon as he could see Magnar and I riding up the path to their home. I ignored his rage and his screaming chickens, doing nothing while waiting for Amos. "Your brother, too!" He continued to yell. "Oh the Greater! Just what was needed! This was Kane's doing! Kane's deluded ideas." Amos's father never held my favor. I had to treat him as if he were nothing in order to not argue back with him.

"Amos!" I called out for him to hurry. I couldn't stand much more of Aris Hawthorn's mouth. Every word slithered.

"No. I hate you boy! With all rage one can muster!" Aris shouted like an angry child, batting away a chicken that flew towards his face. I stood without care of his insults.

"Father! Refrain yourself. I am choosing this." Amos hurried out the door, hearing his father's insults rising. Amos carried with him a pack and a sword I doubt he had ever used before now.

"For him! You are choosing him." Hawthorn looked up to his only son's eyes. The one he'd severed loyalty with yet lived by it. Amos was the first to feel the tear of disapproval. The first to hear the slander from one who loved him. If I didn't detest his father so much, I would have felt greater pity.

"I am choosing him. But I'm not doing this for him alone. This is for anyone, Father, who has been wronged by the beast we've called king. In that way, I am doing this equally for you. It is the good thing," Amos said his convictions. It appeared that he and his father had already had a similar discussion to the one Aris presented to Magnar and me. Amos mounted The Horse behind me. Aris was doing his best to hold onto his son. Amos made his final decision and turned from his father who stood sobbing on the other side of his shabby fence. "Come on then." He had enough courage and assurance to speak. I did as he commanded and went on. Riding past the meadow, I wanted to promise Amos it was all going to be fine, but I couldn't do that. That was a luxury none of us could be afforded. Who really could? Even in the mundane of our lives, one never knows if the king will demand a new tax that would threaten everything, including your life. Adalric had another horse waiting for Amos at the line of Section Eight and Section Five. There were no locked gates between the sections in a ring. *The Laws Upon the Mountain* were more lenient towards travel between sections within a ring, knowing they always had the authority to check markings on necks and inquire of their business. During this time, there were soldiers at the open gates. Being that travel was expected during the Sovereign Days. I'd seen them the last time I came to Serqumance and when we had gone to Treften. It was easy to find Adalric because he waved excitedly when we were in a visible distance. A slow trickle of travelers went through the gates as we met our friend.

"My dear friend." I dismounted and hugged Adalric tightly then held the back of his neck so I could see his face. Somehow he made me feel excited.

"My boy! If we venture to our deaths let's at least make them fitting to the lot we are." Adalric winked, jubilant about it all. He, more than any other, made me smile. He turned to Magnar and said, "Magnar," merely acknowledging him.

"Adalric. Did your mother sing in happiness at your leaving?" Magnar asked mockingly. Magnar and Adalric were always spiteful with one another. It always felt as if they were stooping lower and lower, the longer they were together.

"She began crying, unsure if she was proud or sorrowful. I'd ask about Amaryllis, but even if she is not relieved the rest of us are for her sake," Adalric replied. I ignored the pair of them and instead helped Amos tie his pack to the horse Adalric had brought for him.

"We have a long way to go. There's no need for our cold comments. After all, we are now all tied into a brotherhood," I interjected before Magnar was able to respond.

"Lovely, now I'll be able to better understand the hardship poor Nori was born into." Adalric said.

"Adalric." I said giving him a look like a mother. Magnar looked coldly ahead not caring that he was acting like a child. We rode swiftly stopping for nothing, passing many slower travelers. We had no trouble passing through the gates. I wondered if that was because no other unions were believed to be established. As we rode through Serquamance, I was reminded of the agony I was feeling. I hadn't even presented my union. I had realized that I had to keep the fire directly in front of my eyes. I had to look at this world as if it was burning. I had to remember the greater things. From the corner of my eye, I could see Adalric riding up behind me.

"The horses need water," he said. The sun was setting, and the day of unfamiliar riding had become taxing on us and the horses.

"At the next crossing we will give them rest and water. I don't want to ride too deep into the night," I replied. Within a few moments we came upon a small bridge that went over a shallow creek. We all dismounted and allowed our horses to satisfy themselves with water. Slowly encroaching Area Two, my unfamiliarity with it was becoming more apparent. I noticed differences after having been still for a moment. The sun hit differently, and things seemed to grow in a different direction. The water even seemed to flow faster than in Area Four.

"Here." Amos handed me a small loaf of bread that he'd torn in pieces for he, Adalric, and I to share. We all unspokenly assumed Magnar would want and bring his own things. I thanked him and together we sat on the bank watching Magnar and Adalric tend to the horses before eating anything.

"Does he make you afraid?" Amos asked me. I looked over to him with his wheat brown hair and emotional eyes. He always looked so gentle to me. Even when angry, he seemed to be sadder and more afraid than vengeful.

"Who?" I unfortunately had to ask. Did he speak of

Haben, Thann, Magnar, Fidel? There were many whom I could fear.

"Your brother," he said. I watched Magnar stroke the mane of his horse.

"I haven't decided. At times he does. At other times, I don't even think much of him. Do I fear him constantly? No. There are only two that I fear. My fear for them is still miniscule to what it should be I think," I answered, hinting at the deeper beings I had encountered. He looked up to the heavens. I imagined he was trying to understand the beauty of a sunset sky.

He questioned me further, "The Greater and the Opposer?" He had remembered our last conversation about them.

"Yes."

"They have become real to you?"

"They have." Even more so than he knew. He did not question how they became real to me, but I know, in time, I would share how real they were. Why they were real. And what I was going to do with that reality. I helped him up and together we took our horses reins from the others to have a chance to eat. "How much longer until Redelah?" I asked my brother. He saddled his horse before responding.

"Only a bit further to the place we're going. The stars will be in the sky within the hour, so we should ride quickly. Area Two becomes violent in the cover of the night. The Ebony Winds who hide their identity and prey on every passing person seem to do most of their living in Area Two. Keeping their ugly identity a secret until they're killed and left behind," Magnar splt.

"Brigadors? Here? Lovely!" Adalric said sarcastically.

Amos asked, "Why do you think the King's Host hasn't eradicated them yet?"

"It seems they are simply superior in skill," Magnar said intelligently. He was well informed about these people. I didn't know he'd taken such an interest in them.

"Then we will ride swiftly and carefully. Magnar will lead the front. I will ride in the back." I ordered. We rode quickly through the most used paths with keen eyes towards the woods. I was curious as to who the Ebony Winds followed. Crossing the Area Two line, I knew we were close to shelter; yet there remained a greater urgency. It was funny to me that had Magnar never said anything, I'd have no fear of the trees and the tall grass. But now, every swaying from the wind felt like a threat. I suppose I really should've been wary of them this whole time.

"Amos! You need to calm down or your horse will throw you. He is still unfamiliar with you." I rode beside Amos after he'd jerked his head and accidentally jerked the reins of his horse, Virg, along with him.

"The tavern is only a mile more!" Magnar hollered from the head of the pack.

"Hold the reins looser. If you are startled, it won't force your horse's head to follow your own," I said, explaining gently to Amos. Adalric and Magnar stayed close together until we reached the single tavern. Amos was under my watch. Fidel was waiting for us outside, spinning a copper dagger in his hand. He continued to confuse me of his origins by his many displays of different metals.

"Put that dagger away," Magnar quickly rectified Fidel. "You're bringing unwanted attention to us."

"You can leave your horses in the stable. There are two rooms kept for us." Fidel ignored Magnar and informed us of what to do next. We obeyed carefully and by Magnar's concern moved quickly. I wondered where Fidel had gotten the money to keep two rooms for us. He didn't seem wealthy. The place certainly didn't look expensive though.

"Why is it called The Twelve Taverns if there's only one?" Adalric asked the obvious question as we entered the tavern.

"Twelve rooms, simple," a crooked old lady serving drinks behind the bar had answered Adalric. A "simple" was the offensive name used by Polished towards the Conservatives, as they see us as simple minded and unable to be anything more.

"At least I wasn't the simple one who looked at a single building and was stupid enough to say there were twelve of them," Adalric protested under his breath. The tavern's main room was small and contained only a few tables and chairs, two fireplaces on the far wall, a single armchair in between the two fireplaces, a chandelier made of bones, a narrow bar that could fit no more than one working person, and a floor so unkept you'd assume it was merely a dirt floor.

Fidel said quietly, "Our rooms are up those stairs. I went to the grounds where the presentation will be tomorrow and all seems in order. Thann, Haben nor any other knows we are coming." He stood close to me.

"You're cautious. Why?" I asked him. This wasn't

business to be sharing with all, but his eyes never connected with mine. His stare wandered about the room looking at every person for however long he felt needed. "We sleep in the lowest cost place in Redelah. This is where those Conservative by birth but economic status of File and Rank, and the folks of File and Rank come. These men have been here since I arrived. They travel together but both never leave at the same time. Thieves and crooked men could be here, underground soldiers of Thann or Haben. However, this was still the best way to avoid attention," Fidel explained in a whisper to me. I saw the men he spoke of when we first came in. One being a broad man and the other a sly one. They sat on opposite sides of the room. They appeared to be manly men with scarred arms from what I only assumed was dueling. "You will share a room with me. Amos, Adalric, and Magnar will share the other." Fidel said, speaking to everyone.

"I'll share a room with Amos and Adalric," I disagreed.

"It's fine, Nori," Amos interjected. Adalric put his arm over my shoulders and said mockingly, "You have found a real hidden gem here, Fidel. Truly, I'm impressed!"

"Thank you, Elm. Perhaps one day you will be able to find such places," Fidel said smartly. He allowed me to leave, looking over his shoulder once more before going up the steps. "For you three," he said, patting one of the doors on the hall. "And ours," he said, opening the door to a room a few down from theirs. Fidel closed the window and kept only two candles burning. They reminded me of my mother. She had made candles and gave them away as gifts during the Sovereign Days. The ones she gave them too couldn't have afforded them otherwise. The second floor of the tavern felt more precarious than the first. We kept the small flames close to the middle of the room in fear that if they came even remotely close to the walls it'd catch them on fire.

"You never told me why you entered this whole world anyways," I said while Fidel sat on his bed and untied his boots before taking them off.

"In time." I wished to persist, but he quickly drifted into his own rest. I was not so quick. I blew out the candles and could see the light from stars coming through small holes in the roof. The sound of heavy footsteps could be heard walking past the door every so often. I wondered if Amos and Adalric feared sharing a room with Magnar or if their fear for him had been diminished. I needed to sleep. My body felt as if it had been beaten while riding on the back of a horse through the mountain all day. Tomorrow was going to be a terrifying display of what has only been spoken about in theory. I would see Thann again. I'd see the look on his face when he saw my own. When he heard my name. Durnin, back to taunt him again. I would see Haben and he would see me. I wondered if he'd think to himself, "I knew we'd meet again. I knew we'd meet like this.

Chapter 30
The One Who Opposed

The morning was misty. Nothing could be seen from the
window. When riding into Redelah, beings appeared drifting in
and out of the fog. It was quiet, aside from wind on loose
shudders and horses slowly walking.

"This way." Fidel nodded his head in the direction of an
open field with a massive cliff wall behind its area. The mist
lifted the closer we came. Now I could see the place was filled
with people from seemingly every ring, area, and section. At
least, that is what I'd been told. No one even whispered among
themselves. They all looked graven, ill almost. There weren't as
many as I thought there would be, but why come? If they all
already knew who was going to be chosen and become king.
Nonetheless, it was a greater assembly than I'd ever seen. A
platform had been constructed at the base of the cliff. Seven
bowls filled with fire were the first lights of the morning. A few
of the people sat on horses. Most stood looking out to the
podium. In the middle of the open place was a second, smaller
platform with a throne for Thann and one for each of his lords.
A full band of soldiers rode on horses surrounding Thann's

little higher ground. More of them made a wall between the people and the stage where Haben and his union stood, unopposed. A cold wind blew and turned my head to the narrow tree line that met one side of the field and there I saw the shadow of the Opposer listening happily to the silent crowd as Haben and his union dominated the place.

"My people!" Thann began his speech. I could see the air everyone breathed leaving their bodies. Brumal was cold, but this chill was greater. It must have been from the Opposer. His essence grew into a figure as his slender shadow legs strode to stand behind Haben. Now his eyes could be seen. His face was oddly contorted. Nothing really human like aside from eyes, a skull, and a mouth. He was grinning. Just the corners of his lips twisting upwards. I knew he smiled at me. He was flaunting the power he possessed. Mocking me as he stood behind my enemy, stood behind the flesh I would wage a war against.

"When you give your speech, do not be forgiving. The people will have laid their eyes on you. If they see Thann react in fear, you will give them hope," Fidel whispered to me. I turned to meet his eyes. I was not prepared to give a speech. He knew that fully well. Why he hadn't told me of the speech sooner was an answer I would soon know.

"Haben Arrogs!" Thann's words finally sunk into my mind. Whatever he had said before I had stopped listening to with locked attention on the Opposer, Fidel, and the thought of speaking. But his name. His name made me look to him. I knew our fates would intertwine. In the dark part of me, I hoped it would be this way. Haben didn't wave or smile. This was no parade or show for the entertainment of the people.

This was a display of power. He looked through the crowd not really locking eyes with anyone. Except me. Once his stare found mine, neither of us had the audacity to look away. My breathing slowed and I only saw my opponent. "His lords are Ferrox Wren, Avijna Kant, Barnett Saxon, and Quillon Prisper. Does any other union present themselves? Is there any other who will challenge him this day?" Thann called out to a crowd who had nothing more to do than watch. On my high horse I slowly began to ride towards Haben. The Opposer was completely pleased for me to come forward. He welcomed it.

"I," I said from the back of the crowd. "I challenge!" I said again with even greater confidence. The people parted for my union. We marched to Thann. "I present my union today before the people of Strength. I challenge the union of Haben Arrogs today," I said as I stood before him. I looked into his eyes without dread of his reach. I could swear his breathing quivered. I could see his jaw clench as he nodded for me to find my place on the stage. Before the crowd, Haben stood at the front of the raised place with his men to his left. I stood strong beside him with my men to my right. No one knew me. No one knew my name. No one knew my story. But they would. They would do more than know. I would make them remember.

"Haben Arrogs was first to present himself, meaning he is first to speak," Garvish Saxon, the host of these days, said. Haben looked at me with what I could discern as hatred, although I'd almost call it fear.

"Strength is ours. She is ours to hold and form as we so wish. I will not plead to you, but you will plead to me. I am the greatest one to lead you on. Let this be made known to you: I will be your king. You can decide if you will be my enemy. I can swear on your father's life, you do not wish to be," he said while looking out at his people. But after, he looked at me. He turned his entire body to prove he had no alarm in standing before me. To prove he did not fear to stand against me. I had to speak. No, I wanted to speak. And so I did.

"When did the king become a slave master? When did your towns become the dwelling place of his heavy hand? When did your life become his? When did you begin to bow down because your knees were broken and not because you honored the one who stood before you? When did you look your king in the eyes and realize you never knew him?" I stepped in front of Haben. I did not have to prove that I could stand beside him or against him. Rather, I had to prove I could stand despite him. The people remained silent before me. Whether listening to me or condemning me, I did not know. I searched for their eyes. For any who would choose to hold mine. "I will humbly plead with you. I will stand before each of you like my own and extend my hand for you to take." Now I looked to meet Haben. I wanted him to see that my stare was cowardly in meeting his. Hearing my own breathing slow, I looked at the people once more. I stood in front of them with a union, prepared to fight for king. What would my father be thinking now? I had started by talking to the people, but it ended with me speaking directly to Thann. I knew he wanted to dismiss me, but he couldn't. The crowd did not cheer for me. They did not rally around my name. In a way, I didn't want them to. I wanted them to hear me. To see me. I wanted them to feel how I burned. "Days ago, a man by the name of Kane Durnin was killed by Thann Arrogs because of a truth Durnin knew. A truth that would make a snake bite. I needed to tell you all these things: I don't know you all by name. I have not grown in the same place as you. My family has shared meals around a different table. I have walked in meadows you do not know. I have laughed with friends you have not met. But I have bled under the same king you have. I have had my living taken by our king. I have been robbed of many things by our king. I have nearly died under our king. I will not let him kill my brothers. I will not let him kill these people. I will not plead with him for life, rather he will plead with me for his." I looked at the weary faces and saw that this battle was bigger than my vengeance. I didn't speak now from vengeance. There was something else rising in me.

"I am Adinorium, the Son of Durnin."

I suppose a second (arguably third) round of Dedications is in order.

First, to my sister, Karleigh, because when asked who I should dedicate this book to she said, "Me. Obviously."

Second, to my sister, Mariah, who motivated me by writing multiple "books" while I wrote just the one.

Third, to my brother, Ryan. Thank you for listening to me read every so often even after naming Adinorium, "Andignoringhim".

Fourth, to my brother, Payton. Thanks for being my brother.

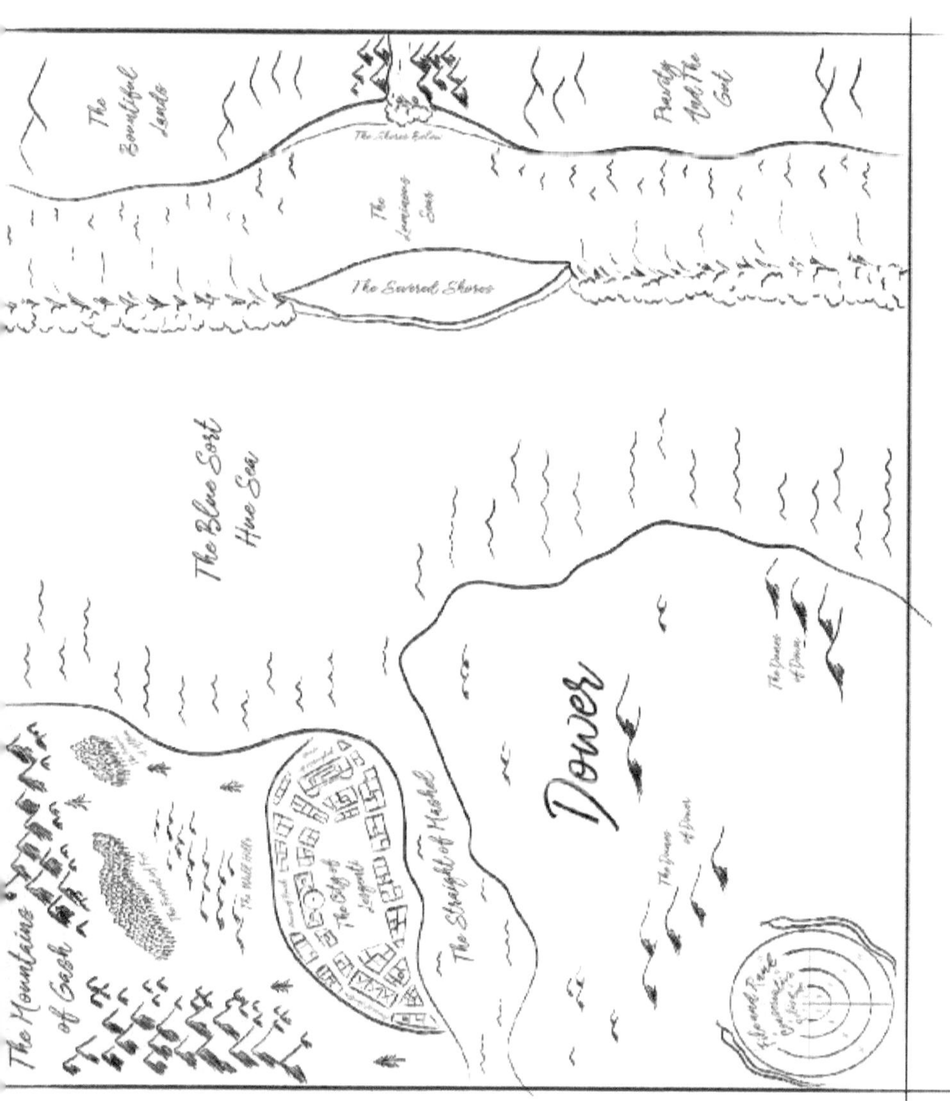

-A shallow overview of the land of Orina-

9 7 9 8 9 8 9 6 1 1 0 1 0